GUILTY CREAT...

Sue Welf... ...t
Desserts, ...
erotic nov...
perfectly p...
East Anglia ...
Sunday nove... ...winner of the
Wyrd Short S... ...the same year. She is also a
scriptwriter and her comedy 'Write Back Home' was
part of the 1999 Channel 4 Sitcom Festival. *Guilty
Creatures* is her fifth mainstream novel.

By the same author

A FEW LITTLE LIES
JUST DESSERTS
OFF THE RECORD
MOVING ON UP

SUE WELFARE

Guilty Creatures

HarperCollins*Publishers*

HarperCollins*Publishers*
77–85 Fulham Palace Road,
Hammersmith, London w6 8jb

www.fireandwater.com

A Paperback Original 2001
1 3 5 7 9 8 6 4 2

A catalogue record for this book
is available from the British Library

ISBN 0 00 710657 2

Typeset in Sabon by Palimpsest Book Production Limited,
Polmont, Stirlingshire

Printed and bound in Great Britain by
Omnia Books Limited, Glasgow

This book is dedicated, with love,
to my friend, Steve Gregory, who helped me
discover the joy of new beginnings and taught me
that not everything is my fault

'I have heard
That guilty creatures sitting at a play
Have by the very cunning of the scene
Been struck so to the soul that presently
They have proclaim'd their malefactions;'

Hamlet, Act II, scene ii
by William Shakespeare

Chapter 1

Mim Pilgrim had often wondered about the nature and extent of her window cleaner's tattoo. She had seen it once a week for the last two, or was it three years, come rain, come snow, an intriguing blue swirl that peeked provocatively above the collar of his shirt. Mim reddened; she certainly knew all about it now. It was a Chinese dragon that curled, scaly, breathing fire over his broad chest, writhing down over his flat belly, its tail finally snaking around his left thigh, clinging to him much as she was now.

Above her the window cleaner strained forward, once, twice, while making a noise somewhere deep in the back of his throat, shuddered violently and then without warning rolled over onto his back, breathing hard, and dragged pillows into a scrum under his shoulders. He looked as if he might be chewing gum. Like a magician he produced a cigarette from somewhere, lit it and handed it to her.

Mim had never made a habit of smoking but then again, up until today, she had never made a habit of committing adultery either.

'That felt so good. You okay?' he asked, voice thickened by exertion.

Mim nodded, not quite trusting herself to speak and took a long drag. The cigarette made her feel dizzy. The taste of burning was almost overwhelming. Alongside her he settled a glass ashtray amongst the rook's nest of hair on his chest and very gently took the cigarette back.

She shivered. As he moved, the dragon's tail brushed

against her thigh. She could almost feel its scales bruising her flesh and knew that she wanted more. Wriggling up onto her hands and knees, she straddled the window cleaner's slim dragon hips. Features softened amongst a rolling boil of cigarette smoke, he grinned up at her and slipped his hand down into the shadows between her thighs, the brush of his fingertips making her gasp.

'God, you're beautiful,' he murmured, as if he could scarcely believe his luck.

Mim blushed furiously and almost at once felt the dragon stir. It seemed that it was right what she'd heard about younger men. Wriggling closer, she hid her face in his hair, nibbling at his shoulders and neck, and then slithered off and rolled shamelessly onto her back amongst the tangle of bedclothes. The dragon boy needed no further invitation. He crept towards her, eyes still dark with desire, forked tongue already flickering over his Cupid's bow lips.

While he went downstairs to get a drink, Mim slid the TV remote control from under the pillow and flicked through the channels. There were adverts, cookery, some girl dressed in primary colours on a children's programme counting to ten with monkeys on sticks, a heated discussion on PMT. Back and forth she trawled. She could hear the window cleaner downstairs whistling *Evita* while making tea for the two of them.

Back and forth. The adverts faded into jaunty TV titles, and as they did, a familiar face peered out from the bright blue sofa of a morning chat show.

Mim turned the sound up a fraction.

On the screen a bright-eyed young woman in a loud suit waved in welcome towards a good-looking man beside her on the sofa. His face had a certain lived-in quality. He was

2

wearing a faded denim shirt, cream chinos; he looked safe, liberal. His hair was slightly too long.

'And this morning,' said the presenter, 'our resident expert, Fisher Pilgrim, is here on the couch with us, talking about the importance of family life. Fisher, how are you today . . . ?'

Mim fingered the mute button, silencing her husband's inane pop psychology at around the same time the window cleaner reappeared bearing a tray. He was naked and looked like some strange satyr, long hair tumbling down over broad, suntanned shoulders, an earring nestling amongst the dark glittering curls. Mim's mouth filled with saliva. He was beautiful and dangerous, like a feral cat.

The last thing she saw, as the boy got back into bed, was Fisher mouthing his lines like a guppy gasping for breath, a benign smile fixed on his open boyish face, his new bridge work looking unnaturally white under the studio lights.

'And we're away in three, two and one —' said the floor manager.

'Well done everyone. Great show. That went really well,' said Angela over the mike from the control box, giving Fisher the thumbs up. He grinned, off-camera now, and slipped the earpiece out. 'Nice response on the phone-in too, Fisher. Good man. Good work.'

He beamed and ran his fingers through his endearingly floppy fringe before shrugging modestly. On the couch, the programme's regular, small blonde host grimaced and eased off her high heels.

'Christ, they're killing me,' she said to no one in particular and wriggled her plump pale damp toes. When the cameras weren't rolling she assumed an oddly vacuous expression as if only truly alive when talking to someone on the phone lines with a cat on hormone therapy, or sampling the resident cook's dish of the day. She had a peculiar habit of talking full front, surreptitiously looking for a light on the camera, not quite meeting the eyes of the person she was speaking to.

By contrast, her male mid-morning co-host was on the phone before the credits had faded. When the cameras stopped his bonhomie vanished; trademark casual cardigan cast aside, he would seize his mobile and talk what sounded like gibberish to his unseen broker. His usually homely, reassuring face took on the demeanour of a basking shark.

'Two hundred at two eighteen,' he snapped into the little black box. 'And don't try and fucking fry me, George, you conniving little bastard, I'm on your case.'

Fisher, still a little unsure of himself, sat quietly and waited for one of the crew to come over and disentangle him from the microphone pinned to his lapel.

Angela, the programme's producer, teetered across the studio on her impossibly high heels, cradling the clipboard that shared her life. Dyed, curly blonde hair piled on top of her head helped add to her height, and the pallor of her creamy white skin helped accentuate her enormous brown eyes. She was smiling, Angela was always smiling; it did not necessarily mean that she was happy.

'Good man,' she said flatly to no one in particular and beckoned to Fisher. 'Are you free for lunch today?'

Fisher grinned, flattered. 'Er, yes. Yes, I am actually.'

Angela ticked something on her board. 'Great. One-fifteen, then. Constantine's. Meet you there. I've got a proposition.' She turned away and then quickly back, beading him with her dark Mediterranean eyes and pointed her pen at the centre of his chest. 'And wear that shirt. I really like that shirt.'

Fisher was surprised to feel himself blush.

During his mercurial rise to Eelpie TV's latest pop counsellor Fisher Pilgrim had changed his name from Frank to

4

Fisher, and taken to adopting a very slight transatlantic twang; although nothing too marked obviously, just the odd flattening and distortion of a few vowels here and there. He thought it made him sound more cosmopolitan, more worldly; Angela had already suggested that he might like to use the sunbeds in the gym downstairs to work up a little tan.

Lunch went extremely well.

Angela chose and ordered the wine, but Fisher was okay about that, he didn't need the secret boys'-club handshake with the sommelier to confirm that he was a real man. He would have ordered something a little less meaty, but then who was quibbling; after all the company was paying.

Angela smiled as their waiter cleared away the first course. 'You know, Fisher, I've been thinking a lot about you recently. How would you feel about hosting a regular programme?'

Fisher stared at her, finally a little plot in God's very own acre.

'We both know that you'd be great with a studio audience. You're a natural.'

Fisher murmured something non-committal so Angela repeated it more emphatically lest his mumbling implied lack of faith.

'You *would* be good with a studio audience, Fisher. I'd really like to talk product and possible time slots with Sven at our next meeting. We'll organise Andy and Nicole to come up with something really sexy for a pilot. I just need to know how you feel about the idea.'

Fisher nodded. 'Fine, absolutely fine,' he said, hoping it sounded as if he knew what they were talking about. 'Product, eh?'

'That's right,' said Angela, enthusiastically waving the sweet trolley closer. 'We're talking big here; think a cross between Kilroy Silk and Claire Rayner, and that other guy on Channel 4, what's his name?'

Fisher nodded again as Angela encouraged the small Italian waiter to increase the size of her portion of gâteau. She waved the cake slice wider and wider until Fisher wondered whether it might not be easier just to give her a spoon and fork and let her leave what she couldn't consume. Finally satisfied, she asked for Greek yoghurt instead of the proffered double cream. Fisher chose homemade savoury biscuits and Stilton, which seemed a very cosmopolitan and grown-up thing to do.

'Let me talk to Sven about it,' said Angela, through a moist mouthful of chocolate sponge. 'What have you got scheduled for next week? Are you fairly flexible?'

Fisher hesitated. His private practice in Denham Market, deep in rural Norfolk, was still relatively small although it had been on the up since he had started appearing on TV. There was his regular broadcast for Radio Washland first thing on a Monday morning, he had a hospital appointment on Tuesday for an X-ray on his bad knee, and then on Thursday his weekly seven-minute TV slot for Angela, but he managed to rally round and pout suggestively, implying he hadn't got a free moment.

Angela pulled a face and with a spare hand tapped up the diary page on her palm-top personal organiser. She had far too many things to remember to trust her life purely to memory alone.

'I'm in with Sven first thing. I'll pitch the broad concept to him, call you after lunch and if he bites, come up with some sort of tighter package with the team. See which way it rolls. I'll call you.'

Fisher nodded. He had scored top marks in his hypnotherapy class for listening positively and having a good expression and interested eyes. That had been on the one-day seminar in Norwich; the rest of his counselling course had been done by correspondence in twenty-five weekly parts.

His climb up the ladder to mid-morning magazine TV had been quite odd really. Fate, karma. Some might even call it destiny. He paused and buttered another savoury biscuit. They tasted like damp corrugated cardboard.

After losing his job on the sales team at Rushton Electronics in Cambridge, Fisher had taken a counselling course advertised in a Sunday colour supplement. It had always been something that interested him. With his redundancy money he'd paid for three months rent on a small consulting room in Lime Avenue, in an attractive Victorian villa by the park in Denham, and cheerily hung out his newly engraved shingle.

One of his first clients had been a producer from Radio Washland, who'd shown up looking for the chiropractor who'd rented the rooms before him. Six appointments and an awful lot of whining later, the man had suggested Fisher's positive listening might do very well on the radio.

Of course, they couldn't see his eyes, but not long after that someone on a holiday from Eelpie Productions heard his phone-in programme, liked his tone of voice and told Angela all about him.

Across the table at Constantine's, Angela was cramming a final gout of yoghurt, sponge and cherries into her exquisitely painted mouth.

'I see studio audience, intercut with film segments of victims and sufferers, PMS, ME, MS, SADS, and then something light to end with. Animals rescued out of drains, that sort of thing,' Angela was talking to herself. 'Programme within a programme at first possibly, fifteen minutes may be all we can swing initially. You know the kind of thing I mean – Or we could go for the brass ring, thirty minutes, forty minutes once a week, twice maybe. Could you keep it up for thirty minutes, Fisher?'

Before Fisher had time to answer, Angela had waved the waiter back and ordered coffee. And mints or course, extra mints, as she was still a little peckish. 'Thirty minutes should be no problem, no problem at all,' she concluded. Pausing to suck in air, she had jabbed in Fisher's direction with her dessert fork. 'You know, I really like that shirt.'

Fisher was very tempted to take it off and give it to her.

After Angela had settled the bill and headed off to another of her round of endless meetings, Fisher took a cab back to the studios.

Fisher had wondered when he'd first gone up to the TV studios whether his country roots would show, peeping through to reveal him as a bottle blond – but it seemed the reverse was true. The head of the production company, in fact the whole production team, seemed to equate his country life with some kind of fresh air honesty, an instinctive earthy, universal back-to-the-sod living.

The executive producer, Sven Hunter, had beamed at him and shook Fisher's hand firmly.

'Hi, went on the Cam once in a punt,' he said enthusiastically by way of a greeting. 'Fell in. Apparently everyone does. Took my girls down to Hunstanton when they were little, too. Great place, great place.'

Fisher had nodded. Hunstanton was hardly Lourdes but its uncomplicated old-world charm seemed to have stayed with Sven Hunter, like a touchstone, a souvenir of altogether simpler, less complicated days. Fisher had read in the gossip columns that Sven Hunter's elder daughter was now married to the lead singer in a band called the Possum's Arse and the younger one was in some sort of rehab in Florida.

'Lovely place,' Fisher had said lamely, as his potential employer pumped his hand more vigorously.

8

Sven frowned. 'Where?'

'Hunstanton,' Fisher suggested.

'Oh yes, we had a beach hut, sand and everything.' He indicated Fisher should sit. And that basically had been it, ten minutes, a cafe latte and Fisher had walked away clutching a bright shiny new career.

And now there was a chance he might have his own programme. Fisher eased his ageing Volvo out of the staff car park and smiled. 'A little plot on God's own acre,' he said quietly. God being Sven Hunter, a middle-aged, middle-England, right of centre fascist with bad breath, a bad temper and a trendy haircut.

Fisher smiled as he headed out of Hammersmith towards the M25. He glanced in his rear-view mirror. Couple of hours and he would be home with Mim. Wait until he told her the news. His own programme, bloody hell, he could barely keep the grin off his face.

Harriet Pilgrim, Mim and Fisher's daughter, noticed Reuben Harnwell's van in their drive as soon as she got off the school bus. Nearly half-past four and it was tucked up alongside the old greenhouse. Odd, as it was a Thursday. She hefted her rucksack up onto her shoulder and tramped up the overgrown front path, threw open the door and kicked her school shoes onto the pile under the hall stand.

Reuben sat in the big square kitchen at the table, drinking tea. Harriet prised open the biscuit tin before speaking.

'So, what are you up to then?' she asked. 'I thought you always did the windows on Monday mornings?' It was fixed in her mind as a beacon of the week beginning; a new school day heralded by the noisy arrival of Reuben's elderly Escort.

He wriggled uncomfortably under her guiless blue eyes.

'Rain,' he said, breaking their gaze and peering into the top of his mug.

She screwed up her face. 'We had games on Monday, it didn't rain.'

Reuben Harnwell's colour deepened to an unflattering beetroot. 'It's going to rain,' he said hastily. 'Said so on the telly. Next Monday. On the long-range forecast.'

Harriet pulled out the chair opposite him. 'Rain next Monday, really?'

Reuben didn't look up. 'That's right,' he said flatly. Between the exuberant waves of his long dark hair she could see his ears; they were almost as red as his face. She leant forward and taking his cigarette out of the ashtray helped herself to a long drag.

'Does my mum know you're smoking in the house – where is she anyway?'

'I dunno, do I?' Reuben spluttered. 'I was just finishing my tea.'

'What you need to master, Reuben,' said Harriet, sliding the mug of tea out from between his long grubby fingers, 'is insouciance.'

He looked up with a puzzled expression on his face. 'Do what?'

Harriet grinned. 'It's French for extremely cool. I heard it in English today.' She sipped his tea while absorbing the fact that he was peering down the front of her school blouse. Catching his eye she was delighted when he blushed again.

Behind him in the kitchen doorway, her mother, Mim Pilgrim, appeared, carrying a small bouquet of wind-blown roses.

'Hello, Harriet. I didn't hear the bus,' she said warmly. 'How did your day go?'

Her mother was wearing her favourite long grey silk shirt over a pair of navy and white spotted leggings.

They made her legs look impossibly long and slim. Her dark hair was caught up into a loose topknot, tendrils threaded through with wisps of silver escaping to soften her handsome face. A face, Harriet recognised, which would one day be her own, bequeathed by a generous portion of her mother's genes. She was suddenly extremely grateful that her mother looked so very handsome.

'Is Dad coming home tonight?' she asked, taking another pull of Reuben's tea.

Mim coloured. 'I think so, but I'm really not sure – he hasn't rung,' she began. 'He said he might have to stay on in town for a meeting.'

At the table Reuben was getting somewhat awkwardly to his feet. 'If you don't mind, Mrs Pilgrim, I'd really better get going.'

'Oh, all right,' said Mim, laying the roses on the draining board. 'See you Monday as usual. I'll settle up with you then.'

Harriet lifted an eyebrow. 'It's going to rain on Monday.'

Reuben glared at her.

Mim pulled a face. 'Really? In that case –' She appeared to be looking around for her purse, but was cut short by Harriet.

'Are you going to town, Reuben?'

The window cleaner shifted uneasily from foot to foot. 'Might be, why do you want to know?'

Harriet glanced at her mother. 'Mum said she was going to take Babe to the vet today. Maybe you could drop him in on your way by.'

Mim stared at her in astonishment.

'Babe,' Harriet repeated it as if her mother might be deaf as well as mute. 'You said he's got to go in and be done.' She mimed a scissor snip.

On cue, a large ginger tom cat oozed his way in non-chalantly through the cat flap.

Mim was flustered. 'Harriet, love, I couldn't possibly ask Reuben to do something like that. I was going to take the cat in first thing tomorrow morning.'

But Harriet was ahead of her.

'He could give me a lift. I'll take Babe in and then catch the bus back at seven. Get chips for my tea.'

Game, set, match, without Harriet so much as moving a muscle.

Mim pulled a face. 'Well, if he doesn't mind.' She turned to a somewhat bemused Reuben. 'Do you mind, Reuben?'

As her mother spoke, Harriet scooped Babe up into her arms and into the cat basket in a single seamless movement. Sometimes she felt as if everyone else was moving in slow motion. She really wanted to go to Goldes, the new burger bar near the bus station, her best friend Kate Hall would be there and Hannah Clark and maybe Gareth Walsh and . . . She paused long enough to tuck away any possible enthusiasm that might register on her face, afraid she might give the game away.

'Can you wait a minute or two, Reuben? I've just got to go and get changed.'

Before he had time to reply, Harriet was halfway up the stairs, her expression, so like her mother's, now triumphant.

'Can you get fish and chips for Liam while you're in town and then I won't need to cook tonight?' Mim's voice followed her up onto the landing.

Harriet paused mid-stride. 'Do I have to?'

The image of walking round with a bag of chips for her brother under one arm did not appeal at all, and it most certainly wouldn't help her with an air of insouciance.

'I really can't see that it's a big problem, Harriet,'

said her mother in one of those reasonable but firm adult voices.

Harriet made a whiny noise in her throat, the one guaranteed to annoy, and then barked, 'Oh, all right, I'll get them,' knowing full well that she wouldn't and would afterwards swear blind the chip shop had been closed when she got there.

Ten minutes later Harriet was sitting in Reuben Harnwell's van, which smelt of old damp rags and chemicals, with Babe on her lap in a cat basket and a dab of her mother's new perfume behind each ear. Easy.

At Denham High School Liam Pilgrim, Fisher and Mim's son, was playing tennis. He was at full stretch, returning the first serve on the frame of his racket. It ricocheted messily off his partner, Fiona Coffey's, back and rolled out amongst the grass clippings on the side of the court. She swung round indignantly and glared at him.

'Forty, fifteen, set point,' called Peter Feldman from the far end of the tennis court. Peter's partner giggled, changed sides, then crouched down, ready for Peter's next serve.

'Jesus,' Fiona hissed as she passed Liam on her way to the back of the court. 'What the hell is wrong with you today?'

Liam shrugged. He could hardly tell her that every time she bent down he had this unrepeatable fantasy about what lay above the little sliver of frilly knicker-leg he could see peeping out from under her tennis skirt. It hadn't worried him that much last summer but this year it was the most divine torture.

On the other side of the net Peter's partner crouched lower, turning her racquet in her long fingers, sprung and coiled, up ready on the balls of her feet. She winked at him. Liam reddened, feeling an unwanted stirring in his tennis shorts. With measured casualness he pulled his tennis shirt down to cover the bulge and hunkered down, glancing over his shoulder to ensure Fiona was ready for Peter's serve. She glared at him and then turned her attention back to Peter, who was winding up for another corker. An instant later the ball exploded off the face of the server's racket.

Fiona hit the ball full tilt on the forehand, creasing it down between the tramlines. Peter back-pedalled, top spin sending it Liam's way, low and hard. To his surprise Liam hit it, scooping it up off the grass.

On the far side of the net Peter's partner leapt like a gazelle, arm extended way way above her head for the smash. It seemed to Liam that the moment was frozen in time. The sunlight shone through her Airtex shirt, throwing her heavy breasts into stunning silhouette. For a split second he imagined she was naked. Leaping lifted her skirt. Liam swallowed hard, cemented to the grass.

The ball, flying back, razored through the air beside his cheek. The sound that brought him back to reality was Fiona screaming, 'You stupid, stupid bastard! What the bloody hell do you think you're playing at?'

Liam tried to say something but the only thing that came out was an odd throaty mewl.

Fiona flung her racket down. 'Their game, their set,' she snapped furiously.

Liam mumbled an apology.

Fiona picked up her cardigan. 'I've got to go, can we play the rest of this tomorrow night?' She glanced at Liam. 'Maybe my partner will have found his form by then.'

Peter laughed. 'Hoping to find yourself a new partner over the next twenty-four hours, are you Fi?'

Fiona stuffed her racket and towel into a bag. 'Sounds like a bloody good idea to me.'

She was bending down. Liam tried not to look at her legs and then wondered if there was anything he could take for his mind.

'I'm going to go as well,' said Peter's partner, who was called Liz. 'Can hardly play with three of us, can we?' She skipped across to Peter and snuggled up against him. Peter's body had already broadened out into the man he would eventually become. He grinned and kissed her lightly, whispering something Liam couldn't quite hear. Whatever he said, it made her giggle. She jogged over to the sidelines, smiling still.

'See you later,' she called back over her shoulder.

Liam didn't think she was talking to either him or Fiona.

Peter grinned and pat-a-caked the ball on the grass.

'Are you clearing off as well, Liam? We could have a knock-up if you like.'

Liam nodded. He didn't trust himself to speak. Fiona was pulling on her sweater, her breasts jiggled, straining against her shirt. He turned away quickly and swallowed hard.

'Sure, why not,' he managed in a strangled voice. Peter grinned at him and drop-served the ball over the net as the girls called their farewells and let themselves out of the court.

When they had vanished into the trees Peter jogged up to the net. 'Fancy a fag?'

Liam sighed. 'Too bloody right. Jesus Christ.' He ran his hand back through his hair.

Peter pulled a cigarette packet out of his sports bag and lit two from a single match.

'You've really got to ease up,' he said, handing Liam one.

Liam shook his head. 'Easy for you to say.'

Peter nodded and slumped on the warm grass, legs

apart. 'Got anywhere yet?' He nodded towards the gate, blowing out an impressive smoke ring.

Liam rolled his eyes heavenwards. 'With Fiona? What do you think?'

Peter sniffed. 'In my humble opinion? Ice queen. Great legs though, and those boobs –' he made an obscene noise in his throat and gestured weight with open cupped hands.

Liam groaned. Great everything, but completely and utterly untouchable.

Peter rolled over onto his belly. 'Do you know Linda Bremner? She comes from Maglington too, I think.'

Liam took a long head-spinning drag. 'Is there anyone who doesn't.'

Peter pulled a face. 'Tut-tut. Very non-PC, Liam, they tell me she's this free spirit, a wild woman, creatrix, a hunter-gatherer.'

Liam snorted. 'They also say she's a complete and utter dog.'

Peter grinned. 'Not bad looking though. Whatever, apparently she fancies you like crazy, has for ages, though God alone knows why.'

Liam stared at him. 'Oh right, working her way through the whole of the sixth form is she?'

'I gave her a lift into town this morning and she asked me to tell you that she's going to the dance tomorrow night at Maglington village hall. Home turf, home boy,' Peter said with a grin.

Liam stared at him. 'You're just winding me up.'

Peter stubbed out the butt of his cigarette. 'As if I would. I'd take a bottle of cider along if I were you, Linda loves cider apparently.' He paused and then lifted an eyebrow. 'It'll improve your tennis no end.'

Chapter 2

Alone in the house, Mim stripped the bed, remade it with clean sheets and duvet cover and then sprayed air freshener around the bedroom to disguise the smell of cigarette smoke. Fisher wasn't very keen on smoking.

Once you had been unfaithful there was really no way to undo it. There was no perfume that she could waft around to mask the odour of adultery. When she'd finished tidying Mim sat down heavily on the edge of the bed and stared into the dressing-table mirror; wondering whether she ought to feel more guilty, feel more anything. Something. As it was she had been left with an odd unnerving sense of nothingness.

Forty. Mim had been looking forward to her fortieth birthday as a rite of passage. A seminal moment that somehow marked her having arrived, having achieved a high watermark on life. There was a birthday card from her mother standing on the dressing table, a whole week old now, alongside one from Harriet that she'd made in art class and another with a slightly risqué cartoon and joke from Liam. Behind them, back in the ranks, were cards from friends, relatives and acquaintances, even one from Doreen, the woman who ran the local post office.

Mim hadn't deliberately intended to leave the cards on display, but some part of her had hoped that Fisher, né Frank, would have noticed his glaring omission and bought her one, however belatedly, bought her something to fill what she felt was an obvious gap. By leaving them out she was making a silent accusation of neglect, fourteen small cardboard accusations that so far had brought no response whatsoever. Once the day was over and done with, Fisher appeared to think any obligation had passed.

She picked up a brush and then tugged the little caterpillar-fluffed band out of her hair. A dramatic fall of teak and copper-coloured waves dropped silently onto her shoulders, though she noticed today that there seemed to be considerably more silver threads in amongst the autumn-coloured curls. Perhaps now that she was forty it was time to think about having her hair cut short. Reuben Harnwell hadn't got a single grey hair on his head, she had looked. Very hard.

On the morning of her fortieth birthday, at the breakfast table, Harriet had carried in the post in an almost ceremonial way. There had been a rash of brightly coloured envelopes shuffled amongst the brown ones.

'I haven't forgotten,' Fisher said, lifting his hands in surrender, as she started to sort through them. 'I do know that it's your birthday.' It appeared that knowing was meant to be enough. It was sufficient excuse for not making a fuss, not sending a card or buying her a present. Mim took a deep breath and stared into the reflection, aware of her eyes. It wasn't even that she felt sorry for herself, it was more a sense of resignation, tinged with annoyance maybe.

Allowing herself to be seduced by Reuben Harnwell might easily be interpreted as an act of revenge. A pay-back for years of neglect. Or perhaps something to do with wanting to feel special again for a little while, special and important enough to be desired and pursued. An act to announce that whatever Fisher might think about Mim, she was still very much alive. Mim studied her reflection more closely, looking at the soft lines around her eyes, and wondered why it was she didn't know exactly why she had screwed Reuben. It was hardly the most sensible thing she'd ever done.

One of the girls she'd gone to school with, who worked in the bank now, had gone for a hot air balloon ride on her fortieth birthday. Her husband had treated her.

Mim gathered up the birthday cards and opening the top drawer of the dressing table dropped them inside. She'd made her point even if Fisher hadn't realised it. Free now, score settled, she dragged the brush through her hair and then tugged it back into a bleak, utilitarian ponytail.

It was just after five – which meant that even if Fisher had left at the usual time and was on his way home she still had a little longer to scour the remaining stains of Reuben Harnwell from the house. She picked up the ashtray from the bedside table, last seen nestling amongst the thick dark hair on Reuben's chest, and hurried downstairs.

The state of the house was something else Fisher knew all about and hadn't forgotten. The door to their bedroom cupboard was propped up against the wall, one side was stripped down to warm grainy old pine, while the other was still covered in chipped orange gloss. There were no carpets on the landing, down the stairs or in the hall and the last tread of the staircase was broken. Where the carpets had been taken up tank traps of carpet retainer lay in wait for the unwary. The stairwell was down to the lath and plaster in places and, in the hall below, the wall by the front door was striped with a dream coat of paint samples.

Mim's bike stood beside the coat rack, primly balanced upside down on saddle and handlebars, its gears, pedals, chain and other oily sprockety things all carefully stored in plastic ice-cream tubs alongside it. No door in the house had a set of handles that matched, and there were vast uncharted areas where Fisher had taken off lengths of skirting board to address a long forgotten electrical problem and then simply not put the boards back.

There were quite a lot of tools around too, remnants of Fisher's countless projects, fads and fancies: a clawed hammer and an adjustable spanner tucked into a Waterford crystal vase on the hall stand, an open box of screws and three Phillips screwdrivers settled in the dust amongst the family's discarded shoes. A tape measure, two brown rawl plugs and a pair of safety goggles resided as a permanent feature, a still life, on a raffia mat in the centre of the kitchen table. There were more, quite a few more, little outcrops of DIY equipment about the house but Mim chose to ignore them.

Once upon a time she used to dutifully tidy them all away, but now, like the birthday cards, they were left as a silent accusation, though to be fair she hadn't set out at first to apportion blame. Mim had thought that if she didn't clear the tools away eventually Fisher would have to do it. He had proved her wrong.

The one outcrop of peace and quiet, the one area that Fisher had not been allowed to tamper with was a small room at the back of the house that overlooked the garden. Here was where Mim worked. Inside, the room – once the old wash house – was calm and tidy, white emulsioned walls reflected the best of the available light, a wooden bench ran all the way round at just above waist height. There was a sink, a broken kettle and mug out on the work surface and below them neatly labelled cupboards and drawers. The only pieces of furniture that were not built-in were a bright red filing cabinet, an adjustable stool, an easel on which was propped an A2 art board and a potter's wheel tucked up in the corner. Mim Pilgrim's own private kingdom.

On the windowsill that ran the length of the wall opposite the door, basking in the warm summer sunlight, was a cascade of variegated ivy tumbling recklessly out of its pot, and arranged around it in swirls and rills were rows of beach pebbles, sea-washed wood and shells. The wall facing the window was dominated by a fantastic collage of images and ideas that had caught her eye, cards, photos, magazine cuttings, fabric, clippings and snippets, carefully arranged on cork tiles that covered the wall.

Mim smiled; the collage always made her smile – it was a tiny glimpse of the richness that made up her dreams. How long was it since she had had that thought? She'd done a ceramics course when the children first went to school and since then had slowly built up, if not a large, then at least a self-financing little business.

Pulling on an apron she settled herself at the bench. Swathed in a plastic bag was the piece she had been working on before Reuben Harnwell arrived – which seemed like a very long time ago now. Very carefully she eased away the cover to reveal a set of tiles on which Mim was very carefully building up an image of a handsome old house and mature country garden, a stylised copy of the photo Blu-tacked to the wall above her.

Although it didn't exactly pay a fortune, Mim usually had a steady stream of commissions, customers looking for the personal touch. She pulled a lug of clay from the bag alongside her and began to work it into shape. The sensual delight of the cool wet clay between her fingers made her shiver.

She knew that people always assumed when they came to the rambling shambles of a house, tucked away at the end of Priory Lane, that somehow it reflected her true nature, an artistic temperament, one of the world's natural bohemians, untrammelled and untouched by life's practicalities. Nothing could have been further from the truth. Mim had always much preferred things to be calm, serene and tidy and had a strong natural sense of order.

She'd just got tired of fighting the battle with the rest of the house.

Selecting a tool from one of the jars, Mim began to work the clay's surface, stippling it until it resembled tree bark. She glanced down at her watch, wondering again if Fisher would be coming home, and if he did, whether he'd have eaten or not. Harriet would be having chips and be bringing supper home for Liam, which was a relief. Despite a very strenuous day Mim couldn't find the energy to be hungry.

After the tiles, which were going to have a house number set into them, Mim's next commission was for the local bee-keeping association's annual general meeting and dinner dance – six bowls, with tiny bumble bees on the rim of each – to be presented as trophies. Her fee included two complimentary tickets and six jars of honey. Small beer. As she picked up another modelling tool the phone rang in the hall. Maybe it was Fisher saying he was going to be late.

Wiping her hands Mim picked up the receiver.

'Hello, this is Yolande Burke, I wonder if I could possibly speak to Miriam Pilgrim please?'

'Speaking.'

Mim teased a notepad and pen closer to the phone; the name rang a loud bell but it didn't quite deliver the whole image.

Meanwhile the woman had already carried the conversation on a yard or two more. 'Good, I'm so glad I caught you. I picked up some of your cards at Isaac's Mill today. At the craft shop there, do you know the ones I mean? Little cards with mermaids and fish on them.'

When commissions were slow Mim hand-printed and then painted greetings cards for Maglington village's one and only tourist attraction. Alongside the cards she also made a few inexpensive ceramic pieces, mostly mermaids and a selection of bowls, mugs and jugs for the display cabinet there which sold slowly over the long hot dusty summer.

On the phone the woman continued. 'I hope you didn't mind my ringing, but I wondered if you take private commissions?'

'Certainly, what sort of thing have you got in mind?'

The woman cleared her throat. 'I'd prefer to come and talk to you about it. It would be for quite a large piece. Perhaps life-size? Torso, I thought –'

Mim suppressed a sharp breath. 'That is large,' she said, wondering how the hell she'd be able to fire it.

'But would you be interested?'

Mulling over the possibility, Mim glanced up at the hall ceiling. It was stained with a bouquet of sepia blossoms, the result of Fisher's efforts at plumbing earlier in the year. They really needed a new boiler and a proper plumber before winter turned up, and two complimentary dance tickets and a few of jars of honey were not going to pay for it.

'Er, yes,' she lied. 'Although I should point out that it isn't really my speciality.'

'But you do do some large-scale work?' The woman sounded almost insistent.

'Oh yes,' said Mim, with a surety she did not feel. She had made a lot of enormous garden pots when she was at the local college doing her ceramics course.

'Good,' said the woman. 'Now, would you prefer me to come to you or would it be easier for you to drive out here and take a look at the site that I have in mind?'

Mim doodled on her pad. 'Whereabouts are you?' she said, weighing the idea of a long journey in her ageing VW.

'Ganymede Hall? I don't know if you know it? It's up behind the school?'

Mim nodded, and as she did the pieces and the name all slotted together.

'Oh yes,' she said slowly. Everyone in the village had heard of Ganymede Hall, and now she knew that she was speaking to Yolande Burke, the wife of Sam Burke, award-winning novelist, scriptwriter, columnist and raconteur and now – almost by default, for having moved into Ganymede Hall – a newly installed local dignitary.

On the far end of the line the woman laughed without humour. 'So, you know all about us, then?'

'I'm so sorry,' Mim blustered. 'When would you like to meet?' she said quickly to cover her embarrassment.

'I wondered whether it might be possible for you to come out to see us tomorrow? Shall we say eleven? I do appreciate that it's short notice. If it's not convenient –'

'No, that will be just fine,' said Mim hastily. 'I've got to deliver some work in town first thing. I could call in on the way back.'

'Wonderful,' said Yolande. 'I'll look forward to it. If you drive up to the main house, there'll be someone about.'

After Mim hung up, she tried to figure out what she might be able to charge for something so large. Realistically she would probably have to decline the commission or maybe pass it on. The biggest thing Mim had tackled before were three Ali Baba pots for the terrace. Hardly life-sized sculpture, but, driven by curiosity, she would definitely go and have a look.

Ganymede Hall had been the home of an ageing colonel, last of a long line of squires and minor gentry, whose history had been tied up with Maglington since the Peninsular Wars. Since the new owners had arrived in the autumn, the comings and goings at the big house had been the subject of an awful lot of gossip in the village shop.

People were naturally curious.

Mim went into the kitchen and plugged in the kettle. It would be interesting to see what had been going on up there.

The new owners of Ganymede kept themselves very much to themselves, which in an odd way had endeared them to the local population. Norfolk village people have no time for showy displays of wealth or hollow city bonhomie. They understood people quietly getting on with their own business. There had been speculation as to whether the Burkes would follow the colonel's example and open the house on May Bank Holiday for the village fête. No offers had been forthcoming so the committee had used the playing field instead.

No one made a fuss, if anything there had been a sense of relief.

The hall was a long mile from the village centre, up past the school and then out along a single track road. In previous years it had been a gruelling relay race, trekking back and forth with tables and tea urns and tombolas.

Mim dropped a tea bag into a mug and sat down at the kitchen table; it would be good to see what the Burkes had done with the old house.

'Hello, Mim? Are you there?'

She looked up in surprise. Fisher, dressed in that ridiculous denim shirt grinned at her from the open back door.

'I didn't hear the car,' she said, mind still elsewhere. 'Do you want some tea? Have you eaten?'

He held the grin. 'I've cracked it.'

It came as no great surprise to Mim. 'I'll go and get the brush and dustpan,' she said, getting to her feet distractedly. 'What is it?'

'No, no,' said Fisher angrily. 'Angela is planning to try and get me a full-length programme. Of my own. A programme all of my own. God, isn't that wonderful? She took me out for lunch at this really trendy little bistro so we could talk product, throw a few ideas around – do you know what this means?'

Mim considered and then said with a smile, 'That we could just have beans on toast for tea?'

Fisher took a deep breath. 'Oh very funny. Aren't you at least going to congratulate me?'

'Congratulations. I'm really pleased for you. That's great.' She tried to sound as if she meant it and not confrontational. She was pleased but the last few years with Fisher had been exhausting and as she watched him pluck a mug from the sink, Mim realised, if she was honest, she'd got nothing very much left to say to him. The thought took her by surprise. She wondered if it had anything to do with Reuben Harnwell, although, thinking back, she had had nothing very much to say to him either.

Fisher sniffed. 'I thought you'd be pleased for me.'

Mim fixed on a synthetic smile. 'I am, love, it sounds wonderful. Have they said how much they're going to pay you?'

Fisher, kettle in hand, swung round furiously. 'Oh, that's right, I might have guessed. It always comes down to money with you, doesn't it? Money this, money that –'

Mim flinched. When he had first been made redundant she'd applied for a part-time job as a technician in the art department at the High School, and that had been his first question.

'I just wondered,' she began, aware she sounded defensive. 'I mean, the thing you do for them at the moment isn't exactly well paid. Maybe you should get an agent – someone to negotiate for you. I'm sure that they should be paying you more.' It wasn't the right thing to say but she needed to say something. On the kitchen dresser was a rusty spanner, and tucked under the spanner was a pile of unpaid bills.

Fisher stared at her, waiting for some act of appeasement she suspected.

'Frank, with the best will in the world, seven minutes a week on TV just doesn't cover what's going out of here each month. And the renewal notice for the room you hired in that holistic clinic came through this morning. They seem to think that being on the telly means they can double your rent. I wondered if you'd thought about putting up your fees?'

Fisher didn't move. 'Angela says this could be the start of something big; she's already thinking about merchandising, self-help books, tapes – videos even.'

'Angela?'

His face hardened. 'She is totally committed. We all are. Part of a team. She's going to pitch it to Sven.'

'Do they know you did the counselling course by correspondence? It's not that I'm criticising you, Frank, please don't think that. It's just that I sometimes worry that you're getting out of your depth. Twelve written assignments and a day's workshop over at the Natural World Holistic Centre doesn't make you – doesn't make anyone – a world expert on the human condition.'

'Always the same with you, isn't it, Mim? I might have known you'd try and scrape the bloody gilt off the gingerbread. I think it's fate – karma.' He pulled out a chair and sat down heavily. 'It's a fantastic opportunity.'

'You're right, it is.' She couldn't help herself. 'But you're not Sigmund Freud, Frank.'

Fisher glanced at the bills. 'I'd prefer it if you called me Fisher, Angela always says –'

'Oh, bugger Angela. I'm just worried that you might be getting yourself into something that you can't get out of – overreaching yourself. If that bloke hadn't come looking for a chiropractor, you'd still be listening to people whine for thirty quid an hour.'

'But he did come, didn't he? That's exactly what I meant about karma.'

While they were talking Fisher casually adopted a counselling posture and matching voice that infuriated Mim.

He took a deep breath. 'To be perfectly honest I find all this hostility really unsettling,' he said, leaning forward with a solicitous expression on his face. 'Is there something you feel we need to talk about?'

Mim glanced down at the washing machine. The sheets had begun to rotate very slowly as the machine refilled. Above them, on the windowsill, was the little bowl from beside her bed that Reuben had used as an ashtray.

Fisher lowered his voice to an unctuous purr. 'I think what we're talking about here, Mim, is synchronisity. I've got a really good feeling about this whole thing. I've got to take things at the flood. That's Shakespeare, you know – Lily, the astrologer who does the slot before mine, told me about it.' He pulled a crumpled sheet of paper out of his back pocket and read: '"There is a tide in the affairs of men, Which, taken at the flood, leads on to fortune." *Julius Caesar*. That's how I feel – in full flood.'

Behind him the washing machine began to rinse.

Harriet glanced down at her watch. Reuben Harnwell had dropped her off at the vet's at the bottom of Railway Terrace. It was a brisk ten-minute walk up into the town centre from here. Harriet took a deep breath. There was a distinct lingering odour of tom cats and she wondered if maybe Babe had sprayed her, although as the veterinary nurse moved away with the cat basket the smell seemed to fade a little.

'May I wash my hands?' she said. Better to be safe than sorry.

The plump woman, cradling Babe's basket as if it was the Holy Grail, nodded. 'Certainly dear, first on the left down the corridor.'

With the door safely locked Harriet had a good sniff of her clothes. Her skirt smelt of damp chamois leather but other than that she seemed to be blessedly odour free. She washed her hands with surgical scrub from the dispenser on the wall and then opened her shoulder bag.

Inside were the pickings from a few weeks' dedicated shoplifting, a pearlised lipstick, two eye shadows, a clutch of eye pencils and a tester bottle of perfume. She drew a ragged line around her eyes and then blended it with a damp fingertip into a grey slubby arc, before drawing an oval of pale mauve lipstick around her lips. The perfume was a little overpowering and made her sneeze. Flicking her fingers through her hair, Harriet smiled at her reflection – not bad, not bad at all – and then unlocked the door.

The receptionist looked up from her computer screen. 'If someone would like to ring tomorrow about three. Babe will be going down to have his operation first thing tomorrow morning. You should be able to collect him around tea time.'

Harriet nodded and blinked – and as she did a little slick of make-up found its way into the corner of her eye. She blinked again and wrinkled up her nose. The stinging sensation made her eyes fill up with tears.

The woman smiled benignly. 'Oh, now then, don't get upset, poppet. He'll be just fine. Don't you worry, we'll take very good care of him, I promise.' She pulled a tissue from a box on the desk. 'He'll be right as ninepence, lovie, really. Here.'

Harriet bit her lip, annoyed that the woman thought she was getting sentimental over her mother's manky old cat, but accepted the tissue and dabbed her face anyway. Outside she checked her reflection in the surgery windows. She couldn't be certain but it looked as if she now had one grey-rimmed eye and one naked eye. She'd have to put it right once she got to Goldes and hope none of the girls saw her before she had chance to repair the damage.

Denham Market was already almost deserted. Harriet took the opportunity to watch herself walk by in the plate-glass windows.

Despite the fact that the rest of the little market town was already closing down for the day, Goldes was half full with teenagers. Most were grouped around the video jukebox, drinking coffee and toying with the rigours of insouciance. Harriet slipped into the ladies to patch up her make-up. As she opened her bag, a girl emerged from one toilet, followed an instant later by another. They looked at Harriet and grinned.

'Made it then?'

Harriet nodded and pulled a face at her reflection in the mirror so she could paint on a few new lines. 'Piece of cake, but I've got to get the ten-past seven bus back.'

'Yeah, me too. D'you have drama today?'

Harriet shook her head. 'Nah, tomorrow, first lesson, why?'

Her two companions giggled and rolled their eyes.

'What?' demanded Harriet.

The first girl snorted. 'You haven't met the school's new super stud yet, then?'

'What are you on about?'

The second girl boosted herself onto the vanity unit beside the sink. 'You know old Tinker has had some sort of thing – heart or something – well, they've got a supply teacher in to cover for him, but my God, drop dead isn't in it – he is . . .' She looked heavenward, searching for an adjective, pursing her lips and blowing hard as if there were no words adequate.

Harriet busily fixed her life belt of lipstick. 'I might not get him, what teaching group are you in for drama?'

'Did you get Tinker before?'

Harriet nodded.

'Well, you'll get him then, Rob Grey. Trust me, he is bea-u-tiful. Got any money?'

Harriet reached into her handbag and brought out the ten-pound note Mim had given her for fish and chips.

Her companions' eyes lit up with avarice. 'Stand me a burger?' said the first.

Harriet shook her head. 'Nah, but you can have a coffee if you like. So, what's this Rob Grey got that's so special?'

The second giggled. 'Jesus-H-Christ, everything. Great big blue eyes, ponytail, hippie shirt, open down the front, really tight Levis. Tight little bum.' She narrowed her eyes and then leered obscenely. 'Nice little bum. Yum, yum, yum.'

They both giggled. Harriet dismissed them with a wave. 'I've got no time for posers.'

The girls drifted back out into the sugar candy colours of Goldes café and ordered a round of coffees. Open less than a month, cliques had already staked out the territory. Two other friends were holding a table by the window and looked up at Harriet and the other two girls as they sauntered over. They settled themselves down with their drinks and lapsed into the private jokes and shared secrets that cemented the group together.

Harriet glanced round the other tables. Theirs wasn't the prime group, but came a pretty close second. The top table was over by the jukebox and comprised four girls. They were all smoking hard and chewing gum.

Harriet sipped her cappuccino; she'd seen enough wild-life programmes to know that she was watching social hierarchies at work. She was an important part of the group she was in. If she ever wanted to join the top table she would have to hang around on the edge, listen, fetch and carry, and even then they might not let her in. The four girls on the top table had truly mastered the art of insouciance.

'So d'y reckon you'll be able to come then?'

Harriet looked round realising she had missed a bridge-head in the conversation. 'Uh, what?'

'Friday night? We thought about going to the dance at Maglington. Everyone's going to be there. What do you reckon?'

Harriet shrugged, wondering whether her mother would let her go.

'Shit,' murmured the girl closest the window. 'Don't look, don't look. It's him. It's *him*.'

Harriet, having no idea who 'him' might be, swung round and looked straight into the eyes of the guy wandering aimlessly down the precinct. He had his hands tucked into his jacket pockets, and dark hair slicked back into a ponytail. Harriet stared. They were right, he was absolutely gorgeous. She felt a strange little flutter somewhere deep inside her and blushed. The sensation was as primeval and basic as anything she had ever experienced and it took her totally by surprise.

The guy grinned and lifted a hand casually. Harriet was rigid, she didn't think she would ever be able to breathe again. Next to her, one of the girls from the toilet raised a hand in response and instinctively Harriet knew, without looking, that her companion was blushing furiously too.

'Rob Grey,' someone hissed. Harriet hadn't really needed telling, his name was irrelevant.

'Is he coming in here?'

Harriet prayed that he wasn't. She didn't trust herself to speak. They drew a collective sigh of relief as he turned and made his way past the window.

'What did I tell you?' whispered one of the girls. 'Gorgeous or what?' But Harriet wasn't listening. She was watching Rob Grey walking away, her heart firing up into a tango rhythm. All she could think about was the way he had looked into her eyes and grinned, and the fact that she had double drama the next day, straight after registration.

The sense of anticipation was broken by the sight of another figure sloping down the precinct towards Goldes; her brother Liam, still in school uniform but without his tie, sports bag hoisted up onto one shoulder, pushed open the door. She groaned. The last thing she wanted was him around cramping her style. Waiting to be served he looked round, unfocused, and then spotted her.

'Shit, isn't that your brother,' hissed a girl across the table, hastily stubbing out a cigarette. 'Did you know he was coming here?'

Embarrassed, Harriet shook her head, wishing the earth would open up and swallow her whole. The only softening blow was the arrival, a second or two later, of Peter Feldman. Unaware of the complex intricacies of social boundaries, Liam and Peter headed towards the table behind Harriet, making her colour deepen to scarlet.

'What are you doing here?' Liam said, through a mouthful of burger. 'And what's all that stuff you've got on your eyes? Does Mum know you're here?'

Harriet squeezed her way out from the place by the window. Any conversation with her brother was best done *sotto voce*. Across the room, the prima group were already glancing in their direction and giggling madly.

'No,' Harriet muttered furiously. 'And if you tell her, I'll bloody-well kill you.'

Liam savaged off another bite of burger. 'Are you catching the ten-past seven?'

Liam knew nothing at all about *sotto voce*.

Harriet felt her colour intensify. 'Yes,' she snarled, 'why did you have to come in here?'

33

'Free country, besides we were hungry and it's either this or standing outside the kebab van.'

Peter grinned up at her as if to confirm their hunger.

'Got any money on you?' Liam continued. 'Only I could do with some chips.'

Harriet shuffled her purse out of her bag and gave Liam a handful of change, hoping that he might consider it hush money.

Liam grinned and pushed himself to his feet. 'Great. We thought Mr Grey was going to come in here. We were going to see if he'd stand us a coke.'

Harriet felt the nervous little flutter returning. 'Mr Grey?'

Liam nodded. 'Yeah, the new drama bloke. He's taking over the school play and wanted volunteers to help him clear up the back of the stage. We said we'd give him a hand. Thought he might shell out for a couple of drinks out of gratitude.'

Peter Feldman snorted. 'Fat chance of that,' he said with his mouthful. There was a gobbet of tomato relish clinging to his chin.

Harriet looked away, there was just no way she could stay in Goldes now her brother and his mate had arrived. She picked up her handbag, trying to ignore the little nip of hunger in her stomach. She'd have to go to the chip shop after all.

'Fancy a walk?' she said to the girls around her table. No one moved. Harriet sighed. She knew at least two of them thought Peter Feldman was extremely fanciable.

'See you later,' she said, without looking back.

All's fair in love and war.

Nibbling her lip, she headed back into town towards the chippie. At the corner of Church Street, just off the market place, she saw Rob Grey looking in one of the shop windows; without thinking she walked up to him.

He turned and smiled, with a slightly puzzled expression as if he felt he ought to recognise her but couldn't put a name to her face.

'Andrea? It is Andrea, isn't it?' he said.

She shook her head.

He laughed easily at his own mistake. 'Sorry, I thought you were a girl in one of my classes.' He looked at her again, more closely now, and although it made her blush, it also stirred the little flare in her stomach into a brighter flame and she had a very strong sense that a teacher shouldn't look at her quite like that.

She coughed. 'No, I'm Harriet Pilgrim, I'm in the GCSE drama group, you haven't taught us yet. First lesson tomorrow.'

He looked surprised. 'Really? Christ, I thought you were part of the A-level media studies bunch. God – right. So what's that then? Fifth form, year ten?'

She was in year nine, but didn't bother correcting him.

He still looked deeply amused. 'I'm going to have to watch myself with all you lot around.'

Harriet stared at him. Teachers weren't meant to say things like that.

'Are you going to stay at Denham High?' she said, in an effort to find a conversation.

He shrugged. 'Shouldn't think so, I'm really just filling in for Bob Tinker. I used to know him – I've been working in London, with a youth theatre project.' He paused. 'But I'm sure you don't want to hear this.'

Harriet nodded towards the market. 'I was going to go and get some chips.'

Rob Grey's smile returned. 'Funny that, me too, mind if I join you?'

He seemed far too comfortable and easy with her to be a real teacher, but without hesitation she fell into step beside him.

Chapter 3

Next morning Mim Pilgrim took a pint of milk out of the fridge and set it alongside the breakfast cereal on the table. Harriet stood beside her nibbling a slice of toast into a work of art.

'LIAM!' Mim was tired of having to try and persuade the children to get up in the mornings. 'Come on, love. The bus will be here in a few minutes.' She handed Harriet a mug of tea. 'Who did you say brought you home last night?'

Harriet coloured slightly. 'Mr Grey, he's our new drama teacher. He's just moved to the village.'

'That was very nice of him, but I'm really cross that you missed the bus, Harriet. You ought to have rung. I could have driven in and fetched you.'

Harriet nodded. 'Sorry.' She sounded genuinely contrite.

'You were lucky he was passing. LIAM!' Mim upped the volume as she glanced at the kitchen clock, willing her son to appear. She wanted to get ready to go into town, but more than that, wanted to get ready to meet Yolande Burke at Ganymede Hall.

Liam slouched in cradling an armful of books, on top was his PE kit, a tennis racquet tucked under one arm and a CD clenched between his teeth. Without pausing he leant forward and slid the whole ensemble into a cavernous school bag. He looked up and grinned. 'Tea?'

'I'm getting fed up with this every morning, Liam. I've got better things to do with my time than chase around after you. Do you want cereal?'

He nodded and dragged out a chair, as if he had all the time in the world.

Less than ten minutes later they were both gone.

Fisher – who had a private client booked in at ten-thirty – had yet to appear, although Mim had set the alarm clocks, one for her, one for him. She stacked the dishes into the sink. Despite his non-appearance her plan was to leave well alone in case he suggested they share cars or came up with some complex scheme that involved her dropping him off in town, collecting something he had forgotten, running it back, and then picking him up again later. It wouldn't be the first time. No, today she wanted the whole of the morning clear, to herself. A vacuum. Table cleared, Mim went back upstairs to get ready.

Get ready for what, though? she thought, turning the shower on full and stepping into the tidal surge. Mim moved the idea around in her mind. She was as curious about Yolande and Sam Burke and the house as she was about the commission.

'Mim?' Fisher's voice bludgeoned its way in through the bathroom door snapping her thoughts off. 'Are you going to be long in there?'

She thrust her head beneath the prickling, tickling, searing torrent.

'Why don't you use the other bathroom, Frank?' she called, eyes closed, sliding her hands back over her head, the deluge slicking her hair down into a glistening pelt.

The coursing water might, she hoped, snatch away any reply or protestation. The door to the en suite bathroom in their bedroom didn't fit. Fighting it open, incising an arc of pure aggravation across the carpet, set her teeth on edge and since Fisher had mended the shower the tray leaked, which meant there was an odd rotting smell coming from the drains and the water pressure was extremely patchy, dangerously so if anyone else was in the house and turned a tap on downstairs. She was now using what Fisher grandly referred to as the family suite.

Outside the door Fisher refused to be ignored. 'Come on, Mim. You know that I've got a client this morning,' he said, knocking furiously. 'And I need to go to the library.'

Mim conceded defeat. 'Just a few more minutes,' she answered in a flat voice. They passed on the landing; Mim wrapped in a bath sheet, Fisher in pyjama bottoms and a scowl.

'You've got all morning to get yourself organised,' he snapped before slamming the door. 'Why did you let me lie in? What time did you get up? Why didn't you call me?'

Mim said nothing. He reappeared in their bedroom ten minutes later, swathed in a bathrobe and began to raid the drawers whilst she sat at the dressing table doing her hair and putting on make-up.

'Clean shirt?' he said, rifling through the tallboy.

'They're hanging up in the wardrobe.'

'Underpants?'

Mim opened the underwear drawer, the drawer in which she had put his underwear for the best part of twenty years, and took out a pair of navy-blue boxer shorts and matching socks. He took them without a word and dropped onto the unmade bed to put them on.

'What've you got planned for this morning? Only, if you're not busy –'

Mim beaded him in the mirror, feeling one of Fisher's invasive and highly complicated transport plans coming on. 'Actually I am busy. I've several odds and ends to get finished before I pack the kiln and then I've got a new client calling round later,' she lied.

Fisher sniffed. 'I thought maybe you could run me into town. I had a hell of a job starting the Volvo again yesterday and I'm not sure how much petrol I've got

38

left. You know what that gauge is like. What time did you say your client is coming?'

Mim held up her hands in a gesture of apology. 'No idea. They said they'd drop in some time during the morning.'

Fisher frowned. 'For God's sake, you ought to get yourself organised, Mim. It's ludicrous. I've told you about that before. Messes up the whole morning if people don't specify a time. How would I manage the practice if I let my clients show up whenever they felt like it?' He paused thoughtfully. 'Mind you, if you're going to be home all morning I could take the VW, couldn't I?'

Mim winced as her lie rebounded and hit her squarely in the back of the neck. She picked up her bag from alongside the dressing table. 'I've got ten pounds you can have for petrol.'

Fisher was busy buttoning himself into one of the new denim shirts he had taken a shine to. There must be at least half a dozen in his wardrobe now, two still in their cellophane packets. 'No, you're all right,' he said tugging at the lapels and then straightening the shoulders, checking his reflection at every stage. 'I'll take the Beetle. It's more economical on short runs, anyway.'

Mim swung round and slapped the ten-pound note alongside him on the bed. 'No.'

Fisher looked up in surprise. 'No?'

Mim nodded. 'I'll need the car later.'

Fisher sniffed, still watching himself in the mirror as he ran his fingers back through his hair. 'You can always use the Volvo.'

Old turf; she had saved up and bought the car herself, kept it taxed, insured it, road tested and fuelled, on the road sometimes against all the odds. It was hers, one tiny piece of territory, the significance of which was totally lost on Fisher.

'No, I won't,' she said, 'because you'll be in town in it.'

He pocketed the ten-pound note without another word.

At school, Harriet Pilgrim slipped into the changing rooms just before drama and added the tiniest hint of eye make-up to her morning-white face. She checked the mirror, rubbing the grey line into the softest blur and then tugged a few tendrils of hair out from the ponytail to frame her face and jaw. She tried out a few expressions on her reflection.

Rob Grey looked up and smiled as she walked into the hall.

'Hi,' he said casually. 'And how are you this morning?'

Harriet coloured slightly. 'Fine,' she said, but she didn't feel fine. She was struggling to remember the French word for dead cool, while Rob handed round a pile of dog-eared text books.

'As you've probably all heard, I'm standing in for Mr Tinker for the rest of this term. My name is Rob Grey and although I do have a post-graduate teaching certificate in Drama, I hale from the bright lights of theatreland – I've been directing youth theatre in inner London for the last five years and before that I was involved in –'

Harriet's attention was wandering. Rob Grey moved with the liquid feline grace of a jungle cat, all the while his bright eyes moving hungrily around the group, drinking in faces until finally his eyes settled back on hers. Was it her imagination or did he reserve a special smile for her? She swallowed hard, struggling not to blush.

'Okay,' said Rob in a low voice. 'Well, this morning we're going to read a little bit of Good Ole Mr Shakespeare. Amongst Mr Tinker's many tasks was to put on a play at the end of term and I thought we'd use that as the core activity of our time together. A way to explore the dizzy heights of the dramatic arts, but this morning it's going to be the lovely Will – so, who'd like to start us off?'

For one awful moment Harriet thought Rob was going to ask her to read, but very slowly his gaze moved on and she made very little effort to contain a sigh of relief.

Across on the other side of the school Liam was slung between two chairs in the senior common room, like a volunteer in a levitation act. He was thumbing through a magazine. First two periods Friday morning were, in theory, private study.

'All arranged,' said Peter Feldman, dropping his bag onto the table under the window.

Liam looked up. 'Huh?'

Peter had passed his driving test first time and drove to school every day in the bright red Mini his parents had bought him. Since he'd passed his test he always arrived late.

Liam stretched. 'What's all arranged?'

Peter pulled the chair out from under his feet. 'Tonight, you and the lovely Linda Bremner. All set up.' He rubbed his hands together to imply the deed was already done.

Liam tidied himself back up into a sitting position. 'I'm not with you.'

Peter grinned. 'Shit, you can be so bloody slow sometimes, Pilgrim. Dance, tonight, Maglington village hall, half-past seven, you, Linda, and a bottle of cider? I've just seen her over by the canteen.' He leant forward and rapped his knuckles sharply against Liam's forehead. 'Hallo, is there anyone in there?'

Liam nodded. 'Cider, I remember. So what did you say to her then?'

Peter pulled out a packet of cigarettes. 'That the interest was mutual.' He looked heavenwards and pulled a face that could have implied anything.

41

Liam mimicked it so that he might appear as if he understood. 'And what the hell do I do if Fiona and her friends show up?'

Peter shook his head. 'Fi? At Maglington village hall? Not her scene at all, I wouldn't have thought. So you've got an open goal, mate – time, methinks, to score.'

Liam reddened. 'And what about you. Are you going?'

Peter snorted. 'Don't worry about me, mate. I'm going babysitting. Big comfy sofa, couple of videos, me and Liz, all alone for the evening. Oh yes.' He grinned and then glanced down at his watch. 'Shit, I'm late for chemistry, got to go. See you on the tennis court lunch time, yeh?'

Liam nodded and wondered what exactly it was he had let himself in for.

Mim dropped off a box of hand-painted tiles, set into little wooden frames so people could use them as pot stands, at the craft shop in Denham. She left a small selection of mermaids at the mill, and was now heading through the village and up the narrow lane towards Ganymede Hall.

As she got to the gates Mim was very tempted to abandon the car and walk the rest of the way. The morning was bright and clear, with just the odd remnants here and there of a haze rapidly being burnt off by the warming sun. The year was already rich and ripening with the promise of a beautiful summer.

Ganymede Hall stood at the end of a long avenue of mature trees. There were oaks, hornbeams and horse chestnuts interspersed with the dramatic maroons of copper beech, while the house itself was tucked down amongst a deep green velvet pleat of parkland.

The last time Mim had made this journey she had had a Punch and Judy booth strapped precariously to the roof of the Volvo, with Harriet and Liam in the back, moaning about being roped in to help, and had arrived feeling hot and fraught and much put upon. This morning couldn't be more different.

Ahead of her, morning sunshine rippled through the trees, dappling the drive with great patches of golden light and pools of deep, liquid shade. Last time there had been an air of genteel shabbiness about the long drive up to the house, but the Burkes appeared to have whipped the estate back into line. The ribbon of roadway was newly gravelled, the verges trimmed back, hedges clipped into neat lines. On her right the lodge cottage gleamed with new paint, glittering windowpanes reflecting the sunlight like polished jet. The whole place looked like some model of rural estate management.

On the final bend it was possible to catch a glimpse of the main house if you knew where to look. Mim slowed the car down to a crawl and searched it out between the trees, Ganymede Hall, its soft, almost Mediterranean, red roof caught in the soft light of morning rays. It seemed to be dozing in the sunlight. With a real glow of expectation Mim slipped the VW into second and guided the car around the broad arc that led round to the front door. The first thing that struck her was the serenity of the old house. The new occupants had cleaned up the fascia, stripping away a shroud of bedraggled Virginia creeper to reveal the warm almost feminine lines of the original Elizabethan house beneath.

Amongst beds of flowers and a tumbling profusion of green foliage a classical full-sized statue of a cupbearer stood sentinel to the main doors. Mim smiled. She'd made a point of looking Ganymede up in Harriet's encyclopedia before she left, he was the symbol of Aquarius, cupbearer to the gods.

Mim parked in the shadows, locked the car, and then, carrying her portfolio, headed off to find Yolande Burke. She was halfway across the gravel when a man – maybe

43

in his early thirties – appeared, pushing a wheelbarrow. He was tall and slim with thick dark hair brushed back off a suntanned face, and was dressed in faded jeans and a grey T-shirt. Lifting a hand in greeting he abandoned the barrow and walked over to meet her.

'Beautiful morning, isn't it? You must be Miriam Pilgrim. Yolande is expecting you,' he said pleasantly in a soft Irish accent. Big blue eyes looked her up and down from under strong arched brows.

She nodded and then stared at him, the warmth of his greeting suggested that perhaps she ought to know him.

He smiled, rubbed a hand over his jeans and then extended it towards her. 'Jack Tully, I'm the head gardener here. If you'd like to follow me.'

'I'm sorry, do I know you?' she asked hesitantly.

Jack grinned. 'No, Mrs Burke asked me to keep an eye out for you. This way –' Mim followed him. 'Yolande tells me that you're an artist. Do you live locally?'

She nodded. 'Yes, in the village,' and as she spoke she wondered about Jack Tully's swing from the familiar to the formal and back.

'Must be wonderful to be able to record your thoughts and feelings, capture that sense of immediacy – explore your imagination, bring things out, allowing them to become whole, real.' He looked out across the gravel. 'It takes years and years to do the same thing with landscape. If you paint with trees it'll be your children or even your grandchildren who get the real benefit of the view you imagined.'

Mim looked across at him; it was quite an extraordinary opening speech. To her surprise when she met his gaze, attempting to fathom out exactly what he was trying to do, Jack Tully looked back with undisguised interest, and then, just as the look reached the point of becoming too long and far too intimate, in those uncomfortable seconds

44

when she felt her colour rising, he pushed open the heavy front doors and beckoned her to follow him.

What lay inside surprised Mim almost as much as Jack Tully's frank appraisal. She remembered the house as being a dark, musty place, full of shadowy corners, muffled sounds and stuffed with a discordant mismatch of battered furniture.

It couldn't be more different. The Burkes had changed all that; the huge hallway – although it retained its heavy oak panelling – was now nearly empty and washed with a mellow golden light. On the flagstones in front of a huge open fireplace was a faded red rug and set either side of the hearth were two period chairs, almost thrones, artfully draped with matching throws. Mim felt she ought to say something complimentary but nothing came to mind. It didn't look like a home at all, more like a film set or something out of the lifestyle pages of the Sunday colour supplements.

'Have you ever been to the hall before?' Jack's voice hijacked her thoughts.

Mim nodded, finally finding a voice. 'Couple of years ago. It's changed an awful lot since I was here the last time. It's –' she hesitated, still unable to find an adjective. It was elegant and artfully arranged but also uninviting and cold in a way that went beyond words.

'Money,' Jack murmured, standing to one side as he opened another door for her. 'It makes a huge amount of difference, although of course wealth and good taste don't always walk hand in hand. One of Yolande's friends came up with the idea for the conversion. The outside has a preservation order on it but we've got permission to change quite a lot of the inside.' Mim noticed his unselfconscious use of the word we. He pointed upwards; a light well extended up through the various floors to a distant glazed roof. From the centre of the hall a sweeping staircase rose up on the sunlight, twisting like smoke towards the ceiling.

Mim shivered. 'It is lovely,' she said, after a second or two, unhappy with the word, instinctively lowering her voice in the presence of so much well-mannered, heartless beauty.

'Glad you like it,' he said casually. 'Yolande's office is just down this way. If you'd like to follow me.'

'Delighted that you could make it,' said the cut-glass voice from their phone conversation. Ahead of her, Yolande Burke stood framed by a set of ornate double doors. Mim had the distinct impression that Yolande knew exactly what kind of impression she made. She was tiny – no more than five foot if that – but in perfect proportion, with sable blonde hair caught up in a soft knot. It was difficult to guess her age, she could have been anywhere between late thirties and late forties, although the latter seemed more likely. She had high well-defined cheekbones and large almond-shaped eyes, the colour of dark toffee, all of which gave her an unsettling feline quality. Her skin was clear and she appeared to be wearing no make-up, although Mim knew from experience that that bare faced wholesome natural look took a hell of a lot of work to get right.

Yolande was dressed in a cream slub silk kaftan that reached from jaw line to ankle and wore leather sandals, her only jewellery a narrow wedding band and small gold earrings, which glowed in the half-light. The impression Mim felt she was meant to get was one of elegance and a spiritual serenity, though what struck her the most was the way Yolande's eyes moved hungrily, albeit briefly, over Jack Tully's muscular body.

Stepping forward she took hold of Mim's hand, and shook it in a two-handed presidential hold, looking into Mim's face with an intensity that was unnerving. Her hands were tiny, bony, and cold as ice.

'Delighted to meet you, Miriam. It was very good of you to come at such short notice. Would you like a drink, coffee or tea, we have decaffeinated? Or something cold? I'm sure we could probably rustle up some homemade lemonade, couldn't we, Jack?' Her gaze shifted again.

Mim nodded. 'That sounds lovely, thank you,' she said, turning to thank Jack only to discover he had already vanished into the shadows.

Indicating that Mim should follow her inside, Yolande continued, 'What do you know about Ganymede?'

Mim shook her head. 'Nothing that isn't gossip,' she said, hoping the woman might appreciate her candour.

'It's a shame that Sam isn't around this morning,' Yolande continued. 'We've been up to our eyes in renovations for the last year or so. Still nowhere near finished but it's coming along. It's my plan to use part of the house as a centre for holistic and complimentary medicine eventually.'

'Really?' Mim said politely. 'That's interesting. I've got friends who are –' But Yolande Burke had already moved on, totally disinterested in whatever it was that Mim was going to say.

'The energy here is so unspoiled,' Yolande continued. 'We might even build a temple at some stage.'

Mim said nothing.

Yolande's office had a long open view over a lawn that fell away towards a stream. The room was painted off-white, the only touches of colour were full-length dark green velvet curtains that framed the French windows and a wall lined with green leather-bound books. Whatever it was that happened in this room it was very well hidden.

'Oh yes, the energy at Ganymede is really quite exceptional. We had a man dowsing here earlier in the year – there is a major ley line running right through the drawing room down to the stream apparently and then it goes up

47

into the woods. Very potent.' Yolande indicated a chair beside the desk.

How could anyone follow a statement like that? Mim didn't feel inclined to say anything, despite being interested in all sorts of alternative things she doubted that her opinion was of any interest at all to Yolande, and made a noise that she hoped might imply approval or agreement.

Yolande smiled. 'Now, about the commission for the woods.'

Although Mim wasn't altogether certain what she had been expecting from her meeting with the Burkes, she knew that this certainly wasn't it and made a decision, based on a gut reaction to Yolande, to back-pedal.

'To be perfectly honest, I'm not certain I'll be able to take the commission on at the moment. It's a question of scale and time really –' She chose her words carefully.

Yolande Burke looked up, eyes alight with amusement.

'But you don't know what I'm going to ask you to do yet,' she said with something approximating a smile.

Everything about Yolande made Mim deeply uneasy, she didn't like the woman at all although she couldn't quite work out exactly why.

'At least let me show you the site, take a look around the grounds, get a feel for the place before you turn me down.'

Mim reddened. She already had a feel for the place and it was making the hairs on the back of her neck stand up.

'Aren't you in the least bit curious about us?'

It was an odd way to phrase the question. 'Yes, but so is most of the rest of the village. To be honest I'm not certain that curiosity is a particularly good motive for taking on a project.'

Behind her the door opened and Jack reappeared carrying a tray with jugs and glasses.

Ignoring her discomfort Yolande poured them both

a glass of lemonade. 'We're redesigning the gardens at the back of the house. They need to be different. I've always thought it important to understand the power of contrast and I like to patronise local craftspeople if at all possible.' She fixed her gaze on Mim, and as she did Mim realised that what was so unsettling about Yolande was that she sounded as if she was reciting something rather than saying it or meaning it – as if the whole speech belonged to someone else.

'After all,' Yolande was saying, 'how impotent light would be without the darkness. Can you imagine summer heat without the glories of a sudden winter snow? I suppose that as an artist you must be aware of those things. Sam is the same. We wanted something instinctive and earthy – and when I saw those little figures that you make and the cards, I sensed that we'd found exactly the person we were looking for.'

Yolande offered her a plate of biscuits; they looked homemade.

'I think Ganymede needs your passion,' she continued.

Mim stared at Yolande. Under different circumstances she might well have laughed. 'Passion?' Mim planned to protest, not sure that she had got any passion, at least not any more. Her mind was about to compose a reply but her voice faded as she remembered the raw, mindless, instinctive, all-engulfing sensations of making love to Reuben Harnwell and the way her body had responded, meeting like with like. Fire with fire. Passion. Yes, perhaps she did have some after all, perhaps she was finally rediscovering it.

Mim felt her colour deepen. She had been far more surprised by the way her body responded than Reuben appeared to be. And what had she thought about before she had thought about him? What had her mind done with all those fantasies and desires and possibilities?

Across the room Yolande said, 'If we're not careful there is always the risk that we intellectualise ourselves away from the core of what we truly are, away from the essence and end up living purely in our imagination. I've said that so many times to my husband, Sam. He lives his whole life in his head, crawls up inside and pulls up the ladder so that no one else can reach him. I keep telling him that it's the most terrible form of neglect, it almost borders on abuse. It's fortunate that I am such a self-contained person and have so many other interests. I think a lesser woman would have died from lack of attention. Sam's fictional families are far more real to him than any of us out here in the real world, and far more important. No, there are definitely times when we all need to step back and replenish ourselves. I think your work will be perfect.'

Mim took an enormous bite of the biscuit she was holding, wondering if it was possible Yolande was really talking about the things she made. Maybe the woman at the craft shop had mixed the labels up. Finally, when it was painfully obvious that Yolande was expecting a reply, Mim said, 'I make mermaids,' through a mouthful of crumbs. 'Mermaids and pot stands.'

Yolande nodded, 'I know and I love them. Really. Why don't you bring your drink with you and we'll take a look at the site I have in mind. It's in a most beautiful part of the new garden.'

Outside was warmer than in. The two women walked in virtual silence down through Ganymede's formal gardens, and then out along a narrow winding path that grew wilder and less defined with every step, although Mim quickly realised that even the wildness was a glorious illusion created by careful planting. It was very cleverly done, each feature subtly drawing the eye and the attention to the next curve, the next twist or turn.

Finally the path took them up over a terraced bank, set with rough pine-log steps, and from there into a stand of trees, through which Mim could glimpse a clearing. Beyond that, in a great arc of dappled shade, was a small squat building, a tiny brick-built cottage with a pantiled roof that swept down over the windows like a protective red wing. It was impossible to tell whether it was original or another of Ganymede's clever optical illusions, although for some reason Mim couldn't quite shift the idea of *Hansel and Gretel* out of her head. She shuddered as they got closer.

'There we are, that's Sam's office over there –' Yolande said, in a voice barely above a whisper. 'I'd like you to make something for the woods here. Something really special, spectacular.' She indicated the central clearing. 'I'd like something that would reflect the energy of this space. Can you feel it? I thought we could put honeysuckle in, to clamber over whatever you make to soften the lines. Give it an organic feel as if whatever it is grew here.'

Yolande turned away as she spoke, almost as if she was afraid her voice might carry across the open ground and disturb Sam, wherever he was. Mim shivered again. It felt for all the world as if they were creeping up on a pride of lions or a family of wild gorillas or possibly a family of carnivorous trolls.

'The very essence of woman. An instinctive combination of the corporeal and the spiritual – flesh and intuition – addressed as an archetypal image.'

Mim took a deep breath. It took a lot of courage to find the right words and even more to speak them aloud, even if it was only in a murmur. 'I'm sorry, but I'm not sure that I'm really up to this.'

Yolande looked genuinely surprised. 'Oh come on. I thought once you saw the wood you'd realise what a wonderful opportunity this is for you. We're terribly excited

51

about the whole idea.' That word we again. Yolande lifted a hand as if to embrace some vast unseen concept. 'Don't turn it down without giving yourself time to consider the possibilities. Perhaps you could do some sketches, a few designs. Something on paper that we could look at.' Mim was surprised how anxious the other woman sounded. 'I'd be interested to see what you think might work in this space, even if you don't actually take the commission.'

As she spoke the door to the cottage swung open, the gesture so big, the noise so loud in the clearing that it seemed as if it had been blown off its hinges. Sam Burke appeared or at least that was who Mim assumed it to be. It seemed as if he had to squeeze out of the tiny opening. Despite him being six foot six if he was an inch, with shoulders like a sawhorse, and a ruff of stubble that hadn't quite made it into a beard, the thing that struck Mim most about Sam Burke was his expression – which suggested he might well be contemplating murder.

Instinctively Mim took a step back behind Yolande, convinced now that whatever it was they wanted, she most definitely didn't want to be part of it.

'Bloody sodding fucking radio,' Sam threw back his head and roared into the morning air. 'Why can't I get a signal, all I want to do is listen to the fucking news, and what do I get? What do I get?' He swung round, fists clenched, knees bent and looked from face to face, apparently surprised to see them standing there and then – as they were there – as if he genuinely expected some kind of answer. When none was forthcoming he continued, 'This weevily insidious sodding little crackle at the back of every word, every note of incidental music, even the chimes of Big-fucking-Ben, this nasty little crackle pushing its way forward, shouldering its way through the words until that's all I can hear. Me, me, me. Crackle, crackle,

crackle. Do you know what that does to me? Do you know how fucking irritating that is? It's driving me mad. Mad.' He caught hold of his hair and shook it in some great melodramatic theatrical gesture of encroaching insanity.

Yolande said, 'Darling, this is the sculptor I was telling you about. Miriam Pilgrim? The woman who made the mermaids. I showed you the cards she'd painted?' She spoke very slowly as if Sam might not be quite bright enough to follow the words.

His eyes narrowed. He blinked sharply, once, twice like he was coming to, and then, as if dictated to by some instinctive nod towards good form, extended a hand. 'Charmed I'm sure,' he said, without a shred of sincerity and no apparent gaps between the words, and then moved his attention back to Yolande.

'I've already said I don't want any more disruptions this week. I've had it up to here with golden boy and his sodding projects, the water features, the pergola, and the fucking bluebell walk. He was out there yesterday with a chain saw. What is he doing planting bluebells with a chain saw? How can anyone make so much noise putting in half a ton of sodding bulbs? Don't tell me, your guru, Swami-what's-his-fucking-name, told you it would enhance the energy, light up the ley lines. Whatever the reason I don't give a tin shit, Yolande. What I need is peace and quiet so that I can get on with some work, to pay for all this stuff, that's why I'm stuck out here in the fucking woods in the first place.'

He turned towards the shed and just before he disappeared glanced back at Mim. 'Nice to have met you.'

Yolande paused for an instant as if weighing up whether the outburst merited some explanation and then said, 'Sam is an extremely passionate man – he's passionate about everything. Jack and I are disciples of the Harani Joshe, it's an eastern philosophy embracing and beautifying Mother Earth, Sam is a little skeptical.

'That was how I met Jack, he was such a find. It was at a celebration in Hyde Park to mark the rising of the seventh star. It was quite, quite beautiful. Very moving and Jack was there arranging the hibiscus for the return of the powers of celestial light. I was there as an observer on the committee sent to see if the Harani's activities contravene the convention on human rights and – well, I fell in love with the whole thing, the whole doctrine. It was breathtaking and Jack is such an absolute marvel with the garden, in fact everything he touches is renewed and revitalised.'

Mim got the distinct impression Yolande wasn't just talking about the flora and fauna. Perhaps if she had patronised the local window cleaner she might have saved herself the trip to London.

'My new commitment to the planet and the healing centre disturbs Sam, I mean I suppose it would disturb me if my mind was as closed as his is. The Harani suggested we try to realign him with visual stimuli, which is where you come in, Miriam. I want something that touches his heart, his instincts, subverts that great intellect that divides him from himself. Do you understand?' Yolande's eyes were bright with pure excitement and something else. Mim nodded, oh yes she understood all right – Yolande Burke was barking mad, it was obvious now.

Chapter 4

Fisher's final client of the morning was a wealthy middle-aged woman who seemed to have a highly developed fear of almost every object known to man. Animal, vegetable or mineral, organic or synthetic there was no classification or genus that had not terrorised the buxom and expensively maintained Ms Coldwell. Her list of allergies, phobias and aversions reached out way beyond the extensive to something verging on the global. The list of animals alone read like a medieval bestiary. Fisher glanced down at the pile of notes about her case and numerous treatments she had tried, which was currently stacked on his desk. The receptionist told him that the rest of her file was out the back in the store cupboard.

Ms Coldwell – currently making a great play of taking off her jacket and hanging it on the bentwood stand in one corner of the consulting room – had been coming to see him at the practice once a week for nearly three months now. This was despite his suggestion that once a fortnight, even once a month, might be better, to allow her subconscious to process the information and instructions being fed into it. Before being treated by Fisher she had done two months past life therapy with a colleague down the hall – a man who put a great deal of emphasis on hands-on healing – and a crash course in teach yourself reflexology with another who came in on Friday afternoons, who didn't. Still there were no signs of remission.

Once one animal was culled, or another inanimate

object consigned to the nether regions of the collective consciousness, like the dragon's teeth up would spring another phobia, as virulent as the last. If it wasn't for the fact that Ms Coldwell always paid in cash, and that she was a very forceful woman, with an aggressive and extremely intimidating manner, Fisher would have suggested that they had gone as far as they could with her problems and called it a day.

She settled herself on the couch with much wriggling and smoothing of clothes followed by fluffing and flicking of her long curly dyed auburn hair. She and Fisher were currently exorcising marmots and county council wheelie bins, while dealing with some residual issues left from curing an aversion to Jeremy Paxman.

'I saw you on the television again yesterday, Dr Pilgrim,' Ms Coldwell said. 'It was an interesting programme this week.'

She always insisted on calling Fisher doctor despite his protests.

'Is that the same shirt you're wearing?' Ms Coldwell continued as she slipped into a deeply relaxed but receptive state between waking and sleep. Fisher couldn't help but notice that she had undone the top two buttons of her blouse again and was wearing one of those tight-fitting clingy skirts with a slit right up the side. He didn't realise that women still wore stockings.

Fisher glanced at his watch before unleashing his deep supportive voice, the one designed to slither in under the watchful guard of his client's consciousness. Angela had said she was going to ring him and let him know how her meeting had gone. Across the room he caught sight of his reflection in the glass doors of the bookcase. Angela was right. He was ready for the big time, ready for the spotlight, in fact there was a very large part of him that wondered why it had taken so long for his genius to be recognised. How much longer would he have to put up with thirty quid an hour and Ms Coldwell resting her hand on his knee as she lowered herself experimentally onto his couch?

'Just relax and breathe with me,' he said in a low even tone. 'Let my voice guide you into a warm safe place.'

On the shiny black leather Ms Coldwell moaned softly. Her eyelids fluttered.

'The real problem with Fisher Pilgrim is – do you want me to be frank?' asked the man who headed up Eelpie's PR machine. He was clutching a canary yellow folder that he seemed reluctant to lie flat on the table as if there was a risk, some very real risk, that Angela might crib the answers.

Wearily Angela nipped the bridge of her nose trying very hard to hold a headache at bay. 'Yes, of course I do, Oliver, that's what you're being paid for.'

It had been a long and difficult week. She certainly wasn't spending a Friday afternoon with this nauseating little cretin because it suited her. She had planned to leave straight after lunch with the 4×4 and the pretty little new boy in reception for a weekend at her cottage in the Cotswolds. Instead she was here with Oliver – that could not be his real name – who'd said that the only time he could fit her in between now and Wednesday week was three o'clock, over a late houmous and chargrilled red pepper baguette in Eelpie's conference suite.

Completely glazed and facing south, the office, overlooking a grey moribund Thames, was like an oven. Across the table Oliver sniffed and surreptitiously whipped one grubby finger under his nostrils to wipe away any residual traces of snot. From experience Angela knew that he had hayfever not a habit. She remembered him sucking on an inhaler halfway through a particularly grim afternoon in the sack late last year. She screwed up her eyes and looked at him again to check that it was the same guy.

For one supposedly immersed in the sublime mysteries of public relations Oliver had scant acquaintance with the niceties of personal hygiene and his teeth were positively grey.

Angela played a couple of fortissimo scales with her acrylic nail extensions on the slate table-top to underscore her impatience.

Oliver stopped sniffing. 'He isn't anywhere near dangerous enough, petal. Public opinion, fickle beast. When we say Fisher Pilgrim to our target demographic what we're seeing is gentle, a little dull, slightly comfy – solid team player. The kind of man you'd trust with your au pair and your teenage daughter and a bottle of tequila. Our demographics show that what we really need from Fisher is more raunch, more pizzazz, more meowwww.'

Angela looked at him, her sense of weariness not lifting; she could barely manage an eyebrow. Oh yes, and Oliver from PR really looked like the sort of man who'd recognise meow if he saw it.

'And?'

He looked alarmed. 'And? And what? I'm not with you.'

'And what, in your infinite wisdom, Oliver, do you suggest we do about the meow thing?' Angela, who could feel her headache shift up a gear, tried very hard to be patient. She tried to keep the venomous sarcastic tone out of her nicely modulated voice, a voice that had taken a lot of money and considerable effort to carve out of a flat front of house West Midlands burr.

'I have to convince Sven that Fisher can hold the audience share. I need to know from you how we can make that happen. I need you to make Fisher Pilgrim more popular, more ratings friendly.' It was not a request.

The expression on Oliver's face suggested the very idea had totally blind-sided him. Where did Sven get these people?

Angela held his gaze, not giving an inch. 'What *exactly* can I do to make Fisher Pilgrim more popular?'

'Meow,' Oliver said after a few seconds' pause and much adjusting of his tie, which was narrow and black against a blood-orange red shirt.

'Meow? Is that the best you can do?'

'The meow factor is terribly important. We need to feel that despite the wholesome little boy lost quality there is still a slightly roguish quality to him. It's a gypsy in the soul thing. We need to know he's held life in the palm of his hand and squeezed hard.' Oliver paused and narrowed his eyes as if visualising the picture and then added, 'They like his shirts.'

'Who do?'

'Our sample. They rather like that soft washed-out, well-worn denim look, man of the world sort of thing, although you and I are aware it's passé. And he came up well on soulful eyes. Maybe Fisher could concentrate a little more on upping his stubble and possibly adding a wicked little twinkle from time to time?'

Angela swilled the last of the coffee around the polystyrene beaker she was holding and then drained it right down to the cold and bitter dregs. 'Did anyone ever tell you, Oliver, that you are a complete and utter wanker?'

It took him a few more seconds to frame a reply. 'Only I feel, in an ironic way,' he said, flushing slightly behind his Buddy Holly spectacles.

Angela leaned forward and lifted the report out from between his fingers. 'I'd look at my definition of irony if I were you. I'll read this over the weekend and get back to you Monday morning. Think of Fisher Pilgrim as my baby, Oliver, my own special child prodigy. I want the very best for him, I want this idea to work. I've got a good feeling about Fisher, we just need to package the package properly. You follow me?'

She could sense Oliver planning to add another meow and met his gaze steadily, daring him. He remained blessedly silent.

In the pottery Mim carefully covered the tiles of the house mural she had been working on with a sheet of polythene to keep them from drying out. Although from the outside she appeared totally rapt in what she was doing, Mim was actually busily composing the telephone conversation she planned to have with Yolande Burke.

It wasn't going to be easy. Thinking about what she was going to say had occupied her mind on and off for most of the afternoon. The most important thing was not to let Yolande get a word in, not let her have her say, not give her any opportunity to talk about ley lines, cosmic forces, angels or extra-terrestrials. All of which had cropped up during their conversation on the walk back to the house. Mim's plan was to not let Yolande say any more than 'Hello' and 'Oh what a shame'.

Most of all she didn't want to hear any more about Harani-what's-his-name and his thoughts on celestial alignments. No karma, no spiritual guidance, no channelled voices. There was just no way back from acts of incarnated gods and nothing Mim could say that sounded in any way relevant if that was the way the conversation turned. It was going to be very tricky.

Mim wiped down the workbench, packed away her tools and then rinsed her hands, all the time her mind busy elsewhere. Liam and Harriet were due home from school at any minute, Fisher too. Maybe it would be better to ring first thing Monday morning, a brisk no nonsense business call. There was something infinitely more mellow and concessionary about late Friday afternoons that would make it much harder to be cut and dried. Even on a Monday morning conflict and assertiveness were hardly Mim's strong points.

There had been many occasions over the years when Mim had heard herself saying, 'Oh, yes of course, I'd be delighted, no trouble at all,' while inside her skull her brain was running around, maniacally, much as Sam Burke had been in the woods, clutching at its hair screaming, 'No, do you hear me? For Christ's sake say no. Say no now, before it's too late. You'll spend weeks regretting this, worrying about it, resenting all the time it takes, cursing yourself for being such a bloody pushover. Are you mad? Say no for God's sake while there's still a chance to claw yourself back from the edge –' While on the outside she would be nodding and smiling and taking the lists and the instructions, just as later she would be taking the flak.

Mim sighed. It was her own fault that the Yolande Burke thing had gone this far really. The woodland walk back to the house was lovely, all bark chippings and interesting little byways set with ferns and hidden loveseats, and in an effort to resume some sort of normal conversation Mim had asked Yolande exactly what it was she had in mind for the woodland clearing outside Sam's office. Worse still, when Yolande began to wax lyrical about nymphs and dryads and elementals of the mittel earth as described by her guru and god-incarnate, the glorious Harani Joshe, Mim had heard herself making polite, interested noises, while her head first began to growl a warning and then frantically begged her to consider the long and extremely sticky business it would be extracting herself from the situation if she was stupid enough to agree to do anything for Mrs Burke. But, even before the thought was fully formed, Mim heard herself saying that perhaps she could manage a few preliminary sketches after all. Of course she would, although Mim had stressed that this was not a commitment to take on the commission. Oh no, just a sop to make Yolande shut up and stop bullying her. Mim glanced up at the studio clock, maybe if she rang Yolande before five, kept it brief, refused to be drawn, she could still back away quietly with no harm done.

In the hall the front door slammed shut. It made the jars of tools on the windowsill rattle.

'Mim?' Fisher's voice was there in her mind almost before the sound of the door had had time to register. 'Where are you?'

'I'm in the –' she was about to reply as the door into the studio swung open.

'Are you making tea? God, I've just been talking to Angela about the new programme.' He looked past her out into the garden and then pulled a scrap of paper from his pocket. 'What do you think dangerous means? This man in PR wants me to up the risk factor. This whole image thing is complete madness. I mean, am I sexy? What do you think? Really?'

Hoping it would turn out to be a rhetorical question Mim got to her feet and headed through the hall into the kitchen with Fisher following right behind her. He was so close it felt as if he was breathing her air before she got the chance to. What upset Mim even more was that because of his intrusion into her space she felt furious, instantly, as if all her fur had been brushed up the wrong way.

'I was wondering if going to the gym might help,' Fisher said, still talking, trying to catch sight of himself in the glazed door to the garden. He was sucking his belly in hard, folding his arm across his chest, making an effort to lift his jaw line towards something approaching chiselled splendour. Mim plugged in the kettle and got two mugs off the draining board.

'Maybe I could just build my upper body a bit, broader

62

shoulders. Angela said that Eelpie might be able to run to a personal trainer.' Fisher paused for a few seconds as if considering the possibilities, turning this way and that to examine his profile. 'Seems such a lot of effort to me. I wondered if shoulder pads might work just as well.' He bunched a fist up and slid it under his shirt to see what it looked like. 'You wouldn't think people would be so shallow. I mean, I'm a counsellor for goodness sake not some kind of sex god.' Mim noticed he paused again after the word god, as if expecting her to protest. 'Although of course,' he continued, 'appearance is terribly important on TV.'

He was talking – in the main – to himself, letting the words string together, long bright glittering beads of self-obsession. Although at least, with his current trend towards the stream of consciousness monologue, Mim felt excused the need to make conversation or answer any of the more difficult questions. Whatever it was Angela had said it had obviously upset him a great deal.

Fisher took the mug Mim offered without a word and sat down at the table, mind and eyes fixed on the middle distance.

'Meow,' he murmured under his breath, which reminded Mim that she had forgotten to pick the cat up from the vet's, which meant she hadn't got time to call Yolande, which – at least short-term – came as a relief.

Fisher suddenly focused on her face. 'According to Eelpie's audience survey, I'm not dangerous enough. Would you say that I'm too safe?'

He had opened the biscuit tin, one hand dithering back and forth between the digestives and the chocolate bourbons. Mim looked away; it was hardly an image that conjured up an impression of recklessness.

'I've got to nip out for half an hour, the kids should be home in a little while. I shouldn't be long, but if I don't collect the cat before five they'll charge me for an extra night in the cells.'

Fisher screwed up his eyes. 'Can't it wait until they get back? You've had all the time in the world to fetch the damned cat. I've had one helluva day one way and another. I've got things to do, I need to think strategy. I need to centre myself.'

'Can't you do it before they get home? You've got fifteen minutes.'

Fisher scowled. Mim decided that forty was the ideal age to stop being intimidated by facial expressions and picked up her car keys from the hook by the door. 'Anyway, don't worry, Liam is meant to be mowing the lawn and Harriet needs to tidy her room and put the washing-up away. I'll be as quick as I can.'

Fisher didn't respond. She wondered fleetingly if it was too much for him to remember, but then his eyes refocused and he swung round to face her.

'What about if we got one of those gardening programmes in. You know, the ones that give the place a complete makeover over a weekend. You could look surprised, couldn't you? I could hang around, help out – maybe take my shirt off, although I'd need to do a bit longer on the sunbeds. Perhaps if I just undid the buttons. What do you think?' He struck a pose and then continued, 'The fallible expert, you know the sort of thing, even if you're on TV doesn't mean to say you're a natural with the decorative edging. It would be a good way to get across the man behind the smile, and you've got to admit, Mim, that the garden could do with a bit of work. Cutting the lawn is the least of it.'

Mim felt a cold chill trickle down her spine. 'You're not serious?'

Fisher nodded. 'Absolutely. Angela co-produces that gardening programme on ITV on a Wednesday night. The one with the big blonde girl in wellingtons. Nice smile. I can see the front of the *TV Times* now, me and her side by side, leaning on spades, sharing a mug of tea, it would look great.'

Mim thought of the tangle of lazy old gold roses, clematis and honeysuckle laced through with a great mane of ivy that meandered over the tumbled-down wall at the bottom of the garden. There, a riot of self-sown sweet peas seemed to spill everywhere, creating exquisite archipelagos of carnival colour in the beds and borders of claret and yellow night-scented stocks spilling colour and perfume all over everywhere. In one corner there was a ramshackle greenhouse, off limits to everyone but a raucous vine that blossomed and then fruited as if there was no tomorrow, a bacchanalian explosion of obscenely large grapes. Closer to the house were fruit trees and a fig which although long past their best, set amongst a daisy and buttercup-strewn lawn, looked beautiful on long summer days. Here and there in sheltered corners were some of Mim's work, a great pot full of herbs, amphoras in a pile stuffed with climbers and creepers and just outside the back door a series of bowls stacked with pebbles that filled with rainwater for the birds.

The notion of letting some bright spark straight out of horticultural college, or worse still some lanky great prune with a second-rate degree in media studies, loose in amongst its mature gentle splendour was so awful it was almost more than Mim could bear.

'I might ring her later tonight and suggest it,' Fisher was saying, dunking a bourbon into his tea.

'But is gardening really sexy and dangerous?' Mim asked, trying very hard to sound neutral, in case her very reluctance spurred him on, while fighting equally hard to hide the murderous expression on her face.

Fisher sighed. 'Sexy maybe, there's all that earthy hoary

handed sons of the soil thing, but no, not dangerous in the way Angela means.' His face contorted with the effort of thinking while Mim sighed with relief at the reprieve.

At the vet's Mim wrote the cheque from her clay account. Angry as a punch-drunk wasp Babe lay coiled in the cat basket, sore and dopey and ready to bite the hand that fed him if it was foolish enough to come within striking distance.

Upstairs in his bedroom in Maglington Liam sniffed the armpits of his best shirt, should have put it out for a wash really. He picked up a can of deodorant, sprayed it, waited for the fog to clear and then sniffed again. It was better, not perfect but not bad. Maybe if he hung it outside on the line for a bit, or stuck it in the tumbler with one of those perfumed tissue things it might help.

'Mum said you'd got to mow the lawn,' said the voice of his conscience from outside the bedroom door.

'Bugger off, Harriet. I'm doing my homework.'

'If you don't mow the lawn you can't go out,' his sister added in an irritating whine.

'So?'

'So, I've done the kitchen and tidied my room already.' There was an exposed raw edge to her voice that was impossible to ignore.

'And if I don't go tonight then you won't be able to go either? Maybe you ought to get your arse outside and cut the lawn yourself if you're that desperate.'

Harriet growled and then made another higher sound, somewhere way up in the top of her throat that suggested she wasn't at all happy with the idea or him.

'Mum said –' she began in the same shrieky, whiny tone.

'I know exactly what Mum said. Keep your knickers on, Harri. I'm just getting changed.'

'What's taking you so long?'

'What the bloody hell has that got to do with you? Piss off.' The words sounded far harsher than he intended.

Harriet yelped as if he had bitten her.

'Dad'll hear you.'

Liam looked heavenwards. Harriet must be really desperate if she was invoking the spirit of the great Fisher-bloody-Pilgrim. Liam couldn't remember the last time his dad had noticed anything without being provoked. Not that it was a new development. Even when he had been called Frank, Fisher had been the same, although once he'd finished the counselling course he had a name for it: a state of passive receptivity. In Liam's unsolicited opinion bone idle and totally indifferent were a lot closer to the mark.

He pulled a pair of trainers out from under a pile of clean clothes his mum had brought up and asked him to put away. Some of the other kids at school wanted to know what living with Fisher was like. They were envious in a non-specific way about what being the son of someone on the telly might mean. Liam couldn't be bothered to point out that whatever perks they thought it might bring, whatever doors it might open, none so far had benefited anyone other than Fisher.

When Liam had arrived home from school, there was a notice written in red felt-tip and Blu-tacked on the study door that read, 'Be quiet, I'm meditating'. Curious, Liam had taken a quick look inside before going up to his room. He had stood outside for several seconds before opening the door, paying token respect to the notice. Hanging around outside had confirmed his suspicions. He opened the door very slowly; inside Fisher was sprawled out full-length on the sofa in an altered state of consciousness, snoring like an elephant seal.

Mowing the lawn would without a doubt wake Fisher up. His mum had bought an old petrol mower from an auction at the village cricket club. It made a sound like an English motorbike, a big Norton or a Lee Enfield, a deep, meaningful throaty chug that gave Liam a sense of power and a warm kick in the bottom of his belly when it fired up. The idea of ripping Fisher out of the soft cocoon of meditation gave Liam a great sense of pleasure. Short-term it kept his thoughts away from the Linda Bremner hornets' nest that was buzzing and stirring into life in the dark moist corners of his mind – not that it wasn't tempting to go there, not that fantasising about Linda wasn't horribly darkly appealing.

He'd seen Linda at morning break; she had raised a hand in greeting, the gesture discreet but unmissable. She wasn't tall, maybe five feet two inches, with brownish hair that was chewed off just under her chin, but with this warm well-rounded, soft, girlish body, and big . . . Liam stopped abruptly and swallowed hard as the image of Linda Bremner's breasts, ripe and heavy as grapefruit, moving under her blouse as she jogged up the stairs to the science block pressed down hard on his mind.

'Cut the lawn,' he murmured in a choked monotone, a breadcrumb trail of words that led him safely back out and away from the fantasy.

He felt hot and uneasy and tried very hard not to look at the bottle of cider that was standing on the dressing table. Alongside it was his lucky bear, Ruey, which his Granny Mo, his mum's mum, had given him on the day he was born, and beside that the last model he had made out of Lego Technic and which he couldn't quite bring himself to break up. Life generally had been a lot simpler when his main concern was whether he had any live AA batteries to make it work.

Across the landing, Harriet, who was peering into the mirror, screwed up her nose and braced herself to pluck

68

out one single eyebrow hair from a ragged arc of what must be, what? A thousand? God, why did women do this to themselves? What was the point, really? A tiny red patch raised almost instantly where the hair had been. She pulled out another bringing tears to her eyes. On the hanger at the end of her bed were her clothes for the dance, pink strappy top, and matching angora cardigan, denim pedal pushers and sandals. She was going to paint her toenails and fingernails once she'd had a shower and washed her hair.

From the garden the mower engine ripped once, and grumbled at the effort of starting, twice and it coughed and then on the third attempt belched, wheezed and finally roared into life.

Harriet smiled. Cinderella would be going to the ball after all. Over the sound of the cutter she heard her mother's car reversing into the driveway and then the back door slamming.

Harriet licked her finger and pressed it down hard on the little red patch where the eyebrow hairs had been and made her way downstairs to greet her. Besides needing Liam to go with her as a chaperon, she also needed a hefty sub from her mum to get into the dance in the first place.

'Right, I want you both home by eleven,' Mim said, handing Liam the money for the tickets. Harriet screwed up her nose but Mim was ahead of her, 'And don't you dare moan, madam.'

Harriet's expression didn't alter; Mim's face hardened but neither of them spoke.

'And make sure you keep an eye on her, Liam.'

Brother and sister looked levelly at each other. They both knew how they felt about that piece of advice.

'And Harri, you do what Liam says, all right?'

Even Mim knew that there was fat chance of that. Watching them walk off towards the village hall she suddenly felt terribly old and tired.

'Mim?'

Fisher's voice from the study. They had had vegetable pasta bake for supper with salad. Fisher had wanted his taken in to him on a tray. Now he wanted her.

She pushed open the office door. He had been tidying. The transformation was shocking although only superficial. The curtains were open and tied back – for weeks he had had them shut and worked by lamplight. Gone were the piles of dusty paper, envelopes, newspapers and circulars, what was left in their place were outlines of fluff and dust and biscuit crumbs recording their passing with uncanny accuracy. Glancing round the room Mim couldn't quite work out where he had put all the things that had been stacked on the floor, the desk, every flat surface.

Fisher stood against the fireplace and struck a pose. 'So, what do you think?' he said.

Mim didn't speak, knowing from experience that she was damned if she did and damned if she didn't. Fisher frowned. 'Maybe you're right, sitting at the desk would be a better image. I was thinking perhaps I could get Angela to do a through the keyhole piece. Celebrity relaxes at home – little feature on the morning show. You know the kind of thing, an insight into my life, a candid behind the scenes peek at Fisher Pilgrim at home with the family. You'd have to have a good set to on the house. Obviously.'

Still Mim said nothing although her outrage didn't need words. It shone bright as the morning star.

Fisher sighed. 'Oh come on, Mim. You've got to admit the place is a bit of a mess. It's not been the same since you started the pottery.'

It was all Mim could do to keep her hands off his throat.

There was an intense silence and then from somewhere in the room came a peculiar little stirring sound; muffled at first it grew in volume until seconds later one of the doors to the sideboard flew open and a great cascade of papers spewed out all over the carpet.

'See, that's exactly the sort of thing I mean,' snapped Fisher.

'We'll meet out here at half-ten, all right?' Liam said, pointing at his watch in case Harriet might miss the point. They were standing outside the village hall. On the walk there he had told her about his planned trip to the pub but hadn't mentioned Linda Bremner.

Harriet nodded. 'Half-ten.' It suited her just fine to be out from under Liam's insensitive gaze. 'Here.'

'Right,' said Liam.

Through the open doors, beyond the trestle table set up with tickets and raffle prizes, Harriet could see the rest of her mates. She stood back while Liam went in and paid, trying very hard not to look like anyone's little sister.

'And what've we got here, then?'

Harriet ignored the voice until she became aware that the speaker was talking to her – and was standing next to her, smelling of aftershave and beer.

Reuben Harnwell leered down at her. 'Well, if it isn't little Miss Pilgrim. Want another lift, do we?'

Harriet shifted her weight onto one foot, and did her best to look hard and cool and totally unflustered.

'Hello Reuben,' she said, making a point of not meeting his eyes. Without the restrictive framework of him being the window cleaner and her a customer's daughter, Reuben totally unnerved her. She regretted showing off and bumming the lift now and wondered, uncomfortably,

71

whether he had mistaken her need to get into town as a need to get off with him.

He grinned at a couple of other lads standing near the notice boards, and leant alongside her.

'Hello yourself, want to come down the Swan with me an' the other guys? I'll buy you a drink if your pocket money won't stretch.'

The two boys laughed and Harriet felt her colour rise. Quickly she stepped out from under his shadow and hurried into the hall.

'There you go.' Liam appeared with the tickets and a handful of change. 'Half-ten, remember.'

Harriet nodded. Reuben had backed off, and although she wouldn't have admitted it, for once in her life Harriet was really pleased to see her brother. He stuffed his hands in the pockets of his jacket. 'See you later and make sure you behave yourself.'

Harriet turned to watch him leave. Reuben and his friends were still there, hanging back.

'Your mum's not so stuck up,' Reuben said as she glanced back nervously over her shoulder. 'Ask her when you get home.'

The lads giggled again. Harriet shivered, although she didn't really have time to consider the implications of what he'd said as the next person through the hall doors was her drama teacher, Rob Grey.

Harriet smiled but he didn't seem to notice her. Coming up behind him was a tall slender woman with a face like thunder.

'For Christ's sake Rob I'm getting sick of this. I asked you to be home by six, if it was one of your bloody friends you'd be there on the button. You totally piss me off sometimes.'

The woman was wearing a wedding ring. She was pale, with wispy dark hair, a pink leather basque and a very long floral shirt under a studded biker's jacket. She had tartan DMs and long dangly earrings and Harriet knew enough about body language to know that this was Rob's wife, and that this tall, painfully thin creature was most probably a dancer. She was also very, very angry.

Harriet looked away, not wanting to embarrass Rob by letting him know she had witnessed him rowing with his wife, although some other part of her – the woman part that was just budding – was pleased. Very pleased indeed.

Chapter 5

Liam loped off back towards the middle of Maglington, not comfortable, not easy, not even sure now that he wanted to meet up with Linda Bremner at all, but most of all not certain that he could convince the landlady at the Swan that he was eighteen.

The village pub was on the river opposite the Spar shop. A family from London ran it. It had hanging baskets outside and trestle tables and blackboards with lists of supper-time specials hanging up on the wall. At this time of the year there were half a dozen pleasure boats tied up outside boosting local trade. Not that Liam took too much notice. He planned to nip into the loo and then buy a packet of cigarettes from the vending machine in the lobby, although on the walk down from the village hall his mind had been busy concocting a far more ambitious plan.

What if he suggested to Linda that they have a quick drink before going back to the dance? In his mind's eye he settled her down in the big veranda overlooking the river at a table tucked out of the way by the jukebox. She'd smile up at him. He'd ask her what she wanted to drink and nonchalantly he'd head over to the bar. All of which seemed like a great idea, except Liam had this horrible feeling that they wouldn't serve him, the landlady would demand to see some ID, explain to him the dangers of underage drinking and then laugh him right out of the place.

It was a horrible, horrible thought and fantasy or not, Liam reddened furiously, before reminding himself that he had no need to go into the pub at all. He'd got a bottle of cider inside his jacket pocket, the weight of which was dragging his coat down so hard that he had to support it in the crook of his elbow to stop the lining from ripping. He'd just get some fags and leave, no sweat. Liam was so preoccupied with what might happen that he didn't notice a figure stepping out from the bus shelter until he practically fell over her.

'You look as if you're in a bustin' hurry to get somewhere,' Linda Bremner said, nonchalantly chewing gum. 'Meeting someone special are you?'

Liam jumped. He couldn't help himself. Why was it that girls always sounded as if they knew exactly what to say, as if there was a whole script already written and unrolling inside their heads? He'd noticed that his mum, and his tennis partner, Fiona, even his little sister, Harriet did it, though it was probably not the right time to think about Fiona at this precise moment. Without further invitation Linda Bremner fell into step beside him.

'I thought you weren't going to turn up, or that maybe Peter was having me on or that you'd chickened out. Another couple of minutes and I was going up the hall on my own.'

She was so close he could smell the heat of mint on her breath although it couldn't quite disguise the underlying smell of cigarettes.

He mumbled an apology, unsure whether or not one was necessary. 'I was just nipping down the pub to get some fags.'

'Oh, right,' she said, pulling a packet out of her shoulder bag. 'My mum slipped me twenty before I came out. Want one?'

He nodded.

At least it was a start.

They walked down to the Swan. He wasn't sure whether

or not he was supposed to hold her hand or quite how to go about it if he was and wondered if he ought to try that brushing-up-against-each-other-by-accident thing.

Linda waited for him outside, leaning up against the wall, sucking hard on her fag while Liam went inside.

'Don't like the landlady in there,' she said, as Liam reappeared. Unselfconsciously she slipped her arm through his, which solved a lot of problems. 'Chucked me and my mate out last time we went in there. Told me to come back when I grew up a bit. We only wanted a coke and stuff, you know, chocolate and crisps and that. Cow. Mind you she doesn't say a bloody thing if I go in there with someone older.' Linda giggled and handed him a strip of gum. 'What do you fancy doing then? Do you want to go straight up to the dance or what?'

It was almost exactly what Liam was thinking. He shrugged, wishing he had spoken first, wishing he had made her have to come up with the answer, and hoping the shrug made him look cool and not just indecisive.

'Come on, you must have some ideas,' she said.

He had lots of ideas but none he wanted to talk about out loud.

'I don't mind. How about we go for a walk?' he said after a few seconds' deliberation. Inside his head it sounded as if he was talking complete gibberish through a thick swirling fog. 'Or, if you like, we could go back up to the village hall. Band sounds good. There's a lot of people there already. I've got us some tickets.'

She stepped in front of him, blocking his path, eyes alight. 'You got me a ticket? Wow, that's brilliant. I thought I was going to have to blag my way in.'

Dry gulched by Linda it gave him a chance to study her. She came up to his shoulder, and was wearing a little pink T-shirt with a matching cardigan and a pair of tight denim pedal pushers, which left very little to

76

the imagination. It looked as if her clothes had been sprayed on.

'You know, you're a real sweetie,' she said, and as she spoke Liam realised with a peculiar sense of foreboding that she was expecting to be kissed. She wanted to say thank you for buying the ticket and that involved him kissing her or her kissing him or some combination of the two. He swallowed hard, wondering if his breath smelt, wondering if it was too late to palm a mint.

While his brain was busy trying to untangle all the possible permutations, Linda Bremner stepped into his space, into the place where no one had ever been before except for his mum and his imagination and Fiona for a few minutes when they danced at last year's Christmas party. Linda tipped her face up towards his and before he had quite fathomed it out she kissed him. It wasn't his first kiss but it felt like it, this was certainly the first one that contained any promise of the things that might follow.

He swallowed again and almost choked, nearly spoiling it. It was a bit clumsy, an exploratory questioning kiss as if she was asking him what it was he wanted, what he expected for her dance ticket and a bottle of cider, the token in his pocket, a price as yet unpaid. She tasted of Juicy Fruit and nicotine and other less definable things that sent a terrible shiver up his spine.

Liam felt the heat rising low down inside his belly and kissed her back, with his mouth more open this time, more confident, maybe harder than he intended. Their teeth banged, unguarded by lips. She pulled away giggling, dragging the back of her hand across her lips. 'Whoa, Peter should have warned me that you were hot stuff.'

She giggled some more and then caught hold of his hand, Liam blushed crimson, but Linda appeared to be delighted. She kissed him again, this time standing on tiptoe, pressing her breasts into his chest, moving her whole body closer and wriggling against him. It was wonderful. He slipped his arms around her and very carefully set his palms flat on her back, one above the other just above her waist.

Inside his coat the bottle of cider dropped like a stone in his pocket and tugged at the lining. Inside his head, amongst everything else, he could hear the stitches ripping and popping or maybe it was his body that was doing those things.

It felt good to hold her, she felt so tiny and so alive, like a wriggly little bird. He could feel the heat of her, smell her perfume and the subtle waft of something slightly sweaty, slightly musky that he knew was the scent of her body. It made his mouth water and at the same time made him feel dizzy. He tried hard not to think about the other things it made him feel.

The kiss seemed to go on for ever and ever. Liam felt as if he was drowning. Desperate, clawing breath into his lungs, he finally pulled away, holding his jacket closed over his growing embarrassment and whipped out the cider as quick as any magician.

'How about we walk up the playing field and have a drink?' he said, delighted by the immediate sense of recovery.

Linda grinned. 'Yeh, all right then, if you want to. We could have a go on the swings – you can hear the music out there. Go in later, yeh? When it warms up a bit.'

Liam nodded. He didn't like to tell her that he was quite warm enough already.

Mim switched on the lamp in the sitting room and settled down on the sofa with the radio, a sketchpad, pencils and a mug of coffee. Her idea was to work on some sketches, and, yes, maybe some of the things Yolande Burke had suggested; after all they were images that interested her.

Mim had always been interested in magic and mythology. Even if she didn't use the ideas at Ganymede she could use them for herself. Perhaps it was time to move on from making mermaids. Mim wedged the sitting-room window open with a book, letting the night air waft through scented by stocks and honeysuckle.

So far Mim had drawn a dragon, all curled and coiled and ready for flight and realised as she coloured in its great knowing eye with a yellow felt-tip, that it was reminiscent of another dragon she had seen very recently. The thought stopped her dead in her tracks. Was it possible to commit adultery and it not spill over into other areas of your life? In some ways it felt as if the time spent with Reuben was in a box, tucked away somewhere on a shelf up in the back of her head.

Mim stared into the middle distance, letting her mind run free, thinking about the way it had felt to touch and be touched by a strange body that desired her, even if it was in the most basic and most instinctive of ways. She wondered if it was perhaps a one-off thing and realised with a start that Reuben Harnwell had helped spark a hunger that she didn't even know she had.

Screwing him, making love to him, sleeping with him, fucking him – how would you best describe the physical coupling that had happened between them? Whatever it was it had been like helping herself to a big slice of cake. There was a sense of having gorged but it was not accompanied by any sense of regret. In fact in a way, Mim thought, carefully drawing in a rake of scales along one heavily muscled flank, it almost felt as if it had happened a very long time ago to someone else, as if she had been a spectator rather than a participant.

Watching her intently from the big armchair near the hearth Babe the cat, still dopey from the anaesthetic, lay stretched out, still angry, still sore, growling and dozing on an old blanket. It seemed as if he knew exactly what she was thinking about, although he had no plans to spill the beans.

At around nine, Fisher pushed open the door. 'Where is everybody?' he asked. He sounded surprised and a little indignant that he and Mim were alone in the house together and she hadn't told him.

'The kids have gone to a dance at the village hall. I did tell you about it.'

Fisher hesitated and then said petulantly, 'Oh right,' in a way that suggested she was lying, and then closed the window and locked it before continuing, 'You'd think I'd get invited to those sort of things, you know, cutting ribbons, garden fêtes, prize-givings. I would have thought they'd be pleased to have someone local.' He sat down opposite Babe, steepled his fingers, turned them out and then cracked his knuckles to spectacular effect before continuing, 'Although you can never be a prophet in your own land, that's what Lily the astrologer told me. I've rung Angela and mentioned the garden makeover and the through the keyhole idea. Got her machine, which was a pity. But I suppose she's probably out on a Friday evening. I'd have liked the chance to talk things through with her really. I'm hoping she'll ring back, you'd think someone like Angela would pick her messages up fairly regularly, wouldn't you?'

Mim nodded. Answering Fisher only annoyed him; she added a sharp predatory beak to the griffin she had been working on. From what she remembered it looked a lot like Lily, Eelpie's astrologer.

'Right,' said Fisher, 'well, that's it then, no kids to decide which programmes we can watch, turn up the music or demand our attention, liberty hall,' and picking up the remote control turned on the TV, ignoring the gentle burble of the radio. He flicked from station to station catching the gist of what was going on before changing channels again.

Mim tried to concentrate on the drawings, making every effort not to get ensnared by the two or three minutes of show time Fisher took to get the hang of what was going on. She knew that the minute she was hooked into the programme he would move on.

Although they had been together for twenty years, when Mim looked closely at Fisher now she found it hard to believe that this was same man she had married. Or was that something everyone said? The man she had known and fallen in love with seemed to have been lost along the way. Over the last few years she began to wonder whether goblins had come in the night and swopped him. But which night? When had he stopped being the man she remembered, the man who was her friend and who she wanted to share the rest of her life with, and become this, this . . . her train of thought paused for an instant as she made a real effort to get a fix on whatever it was Fisher had become, which adjective best summed him up, and found none. No single word covered the transformation. Once he had been funny and fun to be with and now he was arrogant, self-centred and insensitive. How had that happened? And how had she changed? Did he have the same kind of thoughts about her?

Across the room Fisher flicked through the channels backwards and forwards, remonstrating with the presenter of one, shaking his head at another and then, after maybe ten minutes, got up without a word and left, leaving the TV on. Mim watched his going, wondering whether she should switch it off, in which case he was bound to reappear and demand to know why she'd done it, or leave it on and suffer the cacophony of a late-night chat show.

*   *   *

At the village hall the evening was really starting to warm up.

'And now, last but by no means least, let's all put our hands together for Maglington's king of karaoke, the man himself – the one, the only, Bert Hendley.'

There was outrageous and riotous whooping and stamping from the audience as a fat balding man took the microphone from the evening's master of ceremonies. At the back of the hall Harriet reddened with the sheer embarrassment of it all.

Beside her, her best friend, Kate, was sipping from a can of coke. 'Much more of this and I'm off,' she said sullenly.

'But I thought your mum and dad were coming to pick you up at half-past ten?'

It was totally the wrong thing to say, Harriet knew it the instant the words were out of her mouth. Kate glared at her. They were within earshot of a gang of sixth-form boys, most of whom had played in the band they'd been dancing to earlier, and who were now busy taking the rise out of the guy wailing 'Wonderwall' into the mike.

'Oh yeh, me too,' Harriet said, in what she hoped was a really insouciant way, hoping to redeem herself. Harriet was about to add that she thought the whole evening was total rubbish when Rob Grey shouldered his way through the crowd that was horse-shoeing around the doorway. Seeing him made something tighten sharply in the pit of her stomach.

He smiled. 'Hi, I thought it was you. How's it going? Having a good time?'

Harriet suppressed her first impulse, which was to giggle madly and run away. 'Yeh,' she said, busy painting on a smile. 'Okay.'

He looked back towards the hall. 'These sort of things are totally amazing, aren't they?'

She held on tight to the smile wondering whether he really meant that or whether he was being ironic. They'd just been talking about irony in English. The best bet, she thought, was probably to nod and say nothing.

He smiled at Kate too but it didn't seem the same. 'See you later,' he said lifting a hand and then winking at her. 'And behave yourself.'

Harriet watched his progress to the gents, her pulse had quickened, her stomach was still knotted.

Kate sniffed. 'He is such a total poser, a real creep.'

It was like splash of cold water.

'Uh?'

'Rob Grey, and I think he's a crap teacher, spending the whole time lying around on the table at the front trying to look sexy.' She pulled a face and rolled her eyes. 'It's so pathetic at his age.'

Before Harriet could consider what Kate had said, or leap to his defence, Rob's wife appeared from the hall. If anything she looked even angrier than when Harriet had seen her earlier and was even paler, hair escaping in wild Medusa tendrils. Rob ambled out of the toilets, spotted his wife standing there, and stopped dead in his tracks. Her expression hardened up and then, as their eyes met, she indicated that he should follow her outside.

Kate and Harriet looked at each other and without a word headed outside after them. Rob and his wife moved out across the car park into an arena created by the floodlights. Harriet had to press herself against the wall to make sure that they didn't see her.

'I've had enough of this,' snapped Rob's wife.

'Oh come on,' said Rob, in a soft conciliatory tone, catching hold of her elbow. 'I've already said that I'm sorry.'

'You're always bloody sorry,' his wife hissed. Somehow

the words sounded all the more aggressive for the lack of volume. Harriet shivered.

'Sorry just doesn't cut it any more, Rob. I'm going home.'

'Wait a minute, I'll go and get my jacket,' he said. 'I'll drive you.'

She spun round. 'You've had too much to drink. I'll take the car, you can walk home later. After all, they need you.' She put a lot of sarcastic heavy-handed emphasis on *need you*.

'Look, I can tell them –'

'Tell them what? You piss me off Rob. You promised me it would be different, I should have known. It's always been the same, it's always you and everybody else and then last of all me and Paddy. Isn't that how it is?' She was walking across the car park, head down, pausing every few feet to turn and glare at him.

Rob kicked up the gravel in frustration. 'I'll be home in about an hour,' he called to her retreating back. 'I promise. I won't be long. Really.'

'Yeh, right,' she shouted over her shoulder.

The girls moved back towards the hall doors while Rob watched his wife's progress across the car park. Less interested in the outcome Kate was well ahead of Harriet, who couldn't shift the peculiar feeling of triumph that glowed inside her. She was so absorbed in her thoughts that she bowled straight into a group of lads having a smoke out in the foyer. Her first thought, after a hasty apology, was that it was the sixth-formers waiting to play their next set. She was wrong.

Reuben Harnwell grinned down at her, eyes red and beer bright. 'Well, if it isn't you again. Little Miss Pussy-Cat. Yum, yum, yum.'

Harriet froze and took a step backwards but not quite quickly enough. He grabbed hold of her wrist and jerked her closer. She snatched her hand back in horror. He smacked his lips and then licked them salaciously. He leaned forward and before she realised exactly what was happening, tried to kiss her. His lips were wet, there was something horribly reptilian about him, his breath smelt and his clothes reeked of beer and aftershave.

Harriet shrieked and pulled away, staring at him in complete horror, and before she really thought too hard about what she was doing, Harriet balled up her fist and punched Reuben Harnwell as hard as she could in the side of the head.

To her amazement he staggered sideways, face contorting in pain. He swore, blinked once, twice, his eyes filling with tears and then he made another wild grab in her direction. For an instant time seemed to freeze and then all of a sudden, Harriet ripped herself free of the shock and instead of running past him and his friends back into the hall, made a dash for the exit and the great outdoors before he recovered enough to come after her.

Harriet ran out into the twilight, out across the car park, past Rob Grey and small groups of teenagers hanging around smoking and snogging. Outside, over by the gates, beyond the potholes and puddles and the village play bus she stood very still, listening hard, unsure quite what to do or where to go next. Her heart was thumping frantically in her chest and she struggled to grab hold of the next breath.

Maybe running away hadn't been such a bright idea after all, she'd left herself nowhere to go. No retreat. Harriet glanced back towards the hall, after such a spectacular exit she could hardly go back in and what on earth would Reuben do if he caught her? Harriet bit her lip, hardly daring to think about it. If she could just find Kate or Liam.

'Are you all right?' said a familiar voice. Harriet let out a tiny shriek of fear and swung round.

Rob Grey stood by the play bus, looking anxious.

'Yes, I'm fine, thank you,' Harriet lied, lungs still searching around for more oxygen. She was surprised to see him there. 'Just –' she fumbled for the words to describe what had happened with Reuben and realised that she didn't want to tell Rob about it. It was too sordid, too unpleasant to repeat.

She waved a hand as if to dismiss her fears. 'Nothing really, I don't feel very well, that's all. I think I'm going to walk home now.' It was as much news to her as it was to Rob.

He nodded. 'Yeh, me too. My wife left a few minutes ago, she's got a bit of a headache. Maybe it's the weather. I don't want her to be on her own for too long.' He paused as if waiting for Harriet to contradict him. She said nothing. He indicated the lane that led back to the village. 'I'll walk home with you if you like.'

It wasn't all that late. Night was gathering around them but hadn't quite landed yet. Harriet fell into step beside him a little embarrassed, a little self-conscious but all the same hoping that Kate might look out of the door and see them walking off together.

'Have you lived in Maglington long?' Rob was asking. 'I didn't realise it was your dad on the TV. Must be where you get your talent from.'

It crossed Harriet's mind that it would be nice if he held her hand and wondered if she ought to try that brushing-up-against-each-other-by-accident thing.

Liam had been getting extremely flustered and deeply uncomfortable out on the swings on the back field behind the village hall. He and Linda and another girl whose name he didn't know, and now couldn't remember, had drunk most of the cider between them.

At some point they had moved off the swings onto a bench under the trees, and the other girl had gone – God knows where. Then he and Linda had settled down on his coat on the grass and done a lot of kissing and touching and cuddling. The touching had been nice, amazing really, to have the chance to explore those big warm breasts, to feel their weight in his palms, with the promise of more. Linda had made odd little noises in the back of her throat. To begin with Liam thought she might be choking but apparently it meant that she liked the things he was doing to her, which was even better.

Touching her had stirred up all sorts of feelings that he wasn't sure had a name but most certainly had given Liam a driving sense of purpose. He could barely bring himself to think about what had happened next. It was just so awful that Liam was afraid he might never be able to live it down.

It was ten minutes before he dared to come out of the toilets. He'd washed his face, tidied his hair with his fingers. At the door Liam paused and looked himself up and down in the long mirror by the sinks, he didn't look all that different, which surprised him – although there was a big wet patch on his coat where he'd had to sponge it down, and on his jeans too. God, how the hell would he ever be able to look Linda in the face after that?

In the main hall the band had started up, a driving rock beat hitting him squarely in the chest as he made his way back out of the gents. A lot of people were on the floor dancing. Maybe this would be a good time to go and find Harriet. It must be getting late. Easing his way in through the circle on the edge of the dance floor he let his eyes adjust to the gloom before trying to pick her out amongst the crowd.

Kate was there, dancing with a couple of other girls and as she saw him she picked up her handbag and headed in his direction.

'Hiya, seen Harriet?' he asked, running his fingers back through his hair.

Kate looked uncomfortable. 'Not for a while. There was a bloke in the foyer –' she said, shouting to make herself heard above the driving drum solo. She glanced over her shoulder as if there was some chance whoever it was might still be lurking close by. 'He was talking to her and then they went outside together, I think. I'm not sure really, but you know what Harriet's like,' she paused, '– I've been to look for her since but I can't find her anywhere.'

Alarm bells went off in Liam's head, not least because he was supposed to be keeping an eye on Harriet and he had no idea what she was like at all.

'Do you know who it was?' Surely his little sister was more resourceful than to be bullied into going outside with someone she didn't want to go with? And what if she did want to? God, how old did you have to be before this stuff caught light? He knew girls matured quicker than boys and all that but had never considered how his sister fitted into that equation. Linda wasn't that much older than Harriet. Liam shuddered. The events of the last couple of hours were so fresh in his mind, the idea that his little sister might be engaged in the same kind of fumblings made him feel sick. He stopped, refusing to let his mind stray any further down that path.

Meanwhile, Kate was trying to work out who it was Harriet had gone off with. 'I don't know what his name is, but I think he cleans windows. He's got long dark curly hair and an earring.' She was miming him as she spoke. 'Do you know who I mean?'

Liam nodded, he knew all right. That bastard Reuben Harnwell. There was something about that guy that annoyed

88

him, although he had never been able to quite put his finger on it. The cider was still bubbling busily around in his bloodstream, firing him up, all thoughts of Linda Bremner vanishing amongst his anger and the intense flash of anxiety and annoyance about Harriet.

He exhaled hard in an effort to clear his head. Maybe it would be better to take another walk around, see if he could see her, not overreact. Liam stepped back into the foyer, the brightness of the lights making his eyes water. He made his way outside, trying to ignore how the cold air made his head spin, wishing that Peter was there to back him up.

Squaring his shoulders Liam eyed up the couples arranged in a straggling row around the back of the hall. They were curled up tight against each other, bent over to exclude the rest of humanity, tight little twosomes, snogging and cuddling and worse. For a moment Liam wondered how it would feel if he found Harriet there, pressed up against some bloke, and then with a growing sense of horror he saw her. Up the end in the shadows, by the wheelie bins. She had her face turned away from him, head on one side, lips firmly engaged with Reuben-sodding-Harnwell. Liam felt his anger flare. He would have recognised those pedal pushers and the pink top anywhere and before Liam knew what he was doing he grabbed hold of Reuben Harnwell's shoulder and pulled him away from his sister. He was about to draw back his fist when he realised with a rush of horror that he had made a mistake and instantly dropped his guard.

It was Reuben Harnwell all right but it wasn't Harriet he was with at all – it was Linda Bremner. It struck Liam then just how much Linda looked like Harriet and how odd that they were both wearing pink tops and cropped denim jeans. The moment of shock and revelation was blown apart by a glimpse of something hurtling through the air towards him. He had a strange out of space, out of time realisation that it was Reuben's clenched fist and then felt the most awful explosive pain on the side of his jaw.

A flurry of stars lit up the darkening sky, a great flare of something detonated noisily in his brain and Liam fell back as if he had been taken off at the knees.

The next thing he was aware of was Linda's worried face peering down at him against a backdrop of the night sky.

'Are you all right?' she said, in an anxious little voice. 'I've sent Reuben to go and get some ice. He thought you were one of my brothers. I wondered where you'd got to after you were sick. I did come looking for you. I thought maybe you'd gone home.'

Liam blushed furiously in spite of the pain and made a valiant attempt to get to his feet, even though Linda told him to stay exactly where he was.

The memory of those last few minutes on the field were coming back to him in glorious Technicolor. He had rolled over on the damp grass, Linda had been lying on her back on his coat. Very slowly, in case he startled her or in the rare event that there was some happy possibility she might not notice what he was doing, Liam had slipped one hand, palm down, under the waistband of her pedal pushers. They were too tight for him to do much more than press his fingertips into the soft warm skin of her belly and so he'd changed position and tried – very carefully – to undo the buttons. As he did he had been hit by a great wave of nausea, something unstoppable and unfathomable and bitter sweet lifting in his guts that roared up from the depths.

Linda had leapt out of the way just in time, whisking his coat away with her, but not quite quickly enough for him to miss it completely. He had retched his guts up, splashing his jeans, heaving and heaving until there was nothing left to heave with until, eyes streaming, he thought his stomach would turn itself inside out in an effort to get rid of the last traces of the cider.

But that was then, this was now. It seemed that by getting laid out by Reuben, Linda had forgotten all about it. She looked down at him, brushing his hair back off his face, her eyes wide and sparkling with a mixture of admiration and emotion. 'You're so brave,' she said, in a peculiar choked little voice.

Brave? Liam was about to ask what she meant and then realised with a start that Linda thought he had been trying to rescue her from the clutches of Reuben Harnwell. A knight in shining armour. He would have grinned if his face didn't hurt so much.

Chapter 6

'Hi there, Fisher, darling,' said Angela at the far end of the line. 'Just picked up your messages. Haven't disturbed your evening, have I? Can you still hear me? The signal keeps breaking up. I know what you country types are like, probably tucked up in bed alongside Mrs Fisher, all that bucolic bliss, a little cocoa and a little cosy-cosy.' She laughed, although the sound seemed devoid of any humour.

Fisher cradled the phone tight up under his chin and reddened furiously. 'No, no actually I was er – er,' he fumbled around for something sophisticated and urbane to say that might suggest when he wasn't at the studio he pursued an interesting and hectic social life. 'I was getting ready to go out, actually. Popping down the pub with some friends for a late supper, you know,' he lied. It was hardly an invitation to the Café Royal but it would do at a push.

'Oh okay, in that case I won't hold you up; this shouldn't take long.'

Fisher kicked himself for putting the pressure on. Now he felt he was rushing her.

'What we want is meow apparently, Fisher. Gardening won't cut it unless we could get Titchmarsh, in which case we wouldn't be needing you, darling. We want women to send their knickers in and offer you all manner of sexual favours – I was wondering if you were busy this weekend?'

Fisher hesitated, considering exactly what the right answer

was. 'Why?' he managed after a few seconds of painful deliberation.

'I'm staying up at my place in the Cotswolds for the weekend, it's tucked away at the edge of the village, lovely spot. I thought maybe we could get together, roll a few ideas around, gel, chill, brainstorm, whatever. I've got some things that I'd like to run by you. Or are you completely chocka?'

Fisher paused, 'Chocka?'

'Uh-huh. I quite understand if you are. I have friends to stay usually but er – er – their au pair was, was er, was er . . .'

Angela sounded as if she was struggling for an explanation. Fisher waited to hear what it was that the au pair was, but nothing seemed forthcoming, so he said, 'Well, actually no, I'm free all weekend, as free as I ever am, obviously.' He added a hearty little laugh which he hoped would once again underline the fact that he was normally in great demand, engaged in a social whirl that demanded far more than the odd spin.

She sounded relieved. 'Right, so how about tomorrow then? Perhaps you'd like to stay over? There is this great pub in the village, fantastic food. We could have dinner, split a bottle of house red? Talk a little shop. Assuming you don't mind working at weekends, that is? Have you got a pen? I'll give you directions.'

Fisher paled, caught on the hop. 'In principle, Angela, it sounds like an absolutely excellent idea. Fine by me, obviously, but I'd need to check with my er, my er . . .' an enormous gap opened up in the air between them. Why was it he found it so hard to say wife?

'Partner?' Angela suggested.

Fisher almost thanked her, 'Yes, that's it. My Mim, my partner. Can I call you back in a few minutes?' There was not a single breath between any of the words.

'Sure, not a problem. I'll look forward to hearing from you.'

Fisher pulled his shoulders back and looked at his reflection in the mirror above the fireplace. Not in bad shape for a man his age. Brainstorming in the Cotswolds with his producer sounded a damned sight more fun than heading off round the supermarket with Mim, although it always gave him a little thrill when people came up and asked for his autograph.

Across the hall, in the kitchen, Mim – who had been crushing up painkillers for the cat – was busy talking to Harriet who had just rolled in.

'Where's Liam got to? This is not good enough, Harriet, I expected the pair of you to come home together,' she said anxiously, trying hard not to sound cross although she was annoyed that, despite all her best efforts, Harriet had managed to end up walking home alone. She was worried too, Liam was usually responsible where other people were concerned.

Harriet slung her handbag onto the sink unit and shrugged petulantly. 'I don't know, don't have a go at me. It wasn't my fault.'

Mim relented a little. 'Sorry, love, I'm just worried. It's a parent thing. So, did you have a good time?'

Harriet pulled a face. 'No, and I don't feel very well, and anyway once the band and the disco finished it was really naff. They had karaoke, some bloke singing.' She sounded whiny and tired, looked heavenwards, her voice cracking a little for all her apparent bluster. Her eyes were shiny, edged with the suggestion of tears.

Mim felt a great wave of sympathy, sighed and reached out a hand to stroke her daughter's hair. Harriet looked pale and tired, her make-up emphasising the little girl still hanging on in there by her fingertips. Harriet made no attempt to move away from her touch.

'Never mind, sweetheart, do you want some hot chocolate? I've just boiled the kettle.'

Harriet nodded and slumped down at the kitchen table.

'Did all your friends turn up too?' Mim asked brightly, trying to lift her mood.

Harriet nodded. She seemed much quieter than usual, and strangely tense. Mim wondered whether she had fallen out with Kate or one of the others. 'Did you walk home on your own?'

'No,' Harriet snapped, angrily, defensively, it was hard to tell which. Mim decided not to push it. It was thin ice, and difficult enough trying to learn and then second guess the social rules, traverse the wilderness without a map, without having a mother cross-examine you at every turn.

Mim felt as if she was in a similar place, puberty revisited, a place where anything could happen, anything was possible and yet the sense of not knowing where life might lead, the uncertainty, was nearly unbearable.

Across the table Harriet sighed as if crushed, accepted the mug Mim offered her and then got up and strutted off into the hall, carrying her drink and her bag, struggling to look cool and sophisticated in her strappy sandals, little girl-woman.

Watching Harriet's progress made something deep inside Mim ache. Transition was such a hard and unforgiving place to be, one slip here, one wrong move now and it might take years to recover if you ever recovered at all.

With the hall door open Mim could hear Fisher talking in the study. It sounded as if he might be working on the script for his segment of next week's show or maybe he was just talking to himself.

Upstairs Mim heard Harriet kick-start her life with

95

music whose heartbeat momentarily pulsed through the whole house before she turned the volume down.

Mim picked up her mug and let her mind work slowly through the sense of discontent and disillusion that was fuelling her own desire for change. There had to be more to life than sitting out here in the sticks watching the children grow up and herself go grey. Even though she was angry with Fisher for not seeing how unhappy she was, she didn't assume that there was any possibility or responsibility for him to help her put things right. Not that she'd trust him with her dreams, those days were long gone. He was too shortsighted and much too self-absorbed to see beyond those things that he wanted and needed to get him through the day. No, she needed to do it for herself. Perhaps this was her chance to recover, reclaim, and begin again too. Mim glanced down at the sketchpad on the table, perhaps she ought to try drawing a phoenix.

'Want me to drive you home, then, mate?' Reuben asked Liam. 'Least I can do under the circumstances.' It would have sounded a lot more convincing if Reuben hadn't been grinning and rolling himself a fag at the same time, Liam thought.

He was about to say no, but forming his face into the words still hurt like hell. Liam was sitting on the damp grass now, leaning forward, legs apart, trying to master the next bit of the trick which involved him standing up. He felt sick again.

Reuben trickled smoke as he continued, 'Sorry about making a mess of your face, mate. It was a reflex, you know, wham bam, thank you, ma'am.' He mimed some kind of soft ineffectual punch that wouldn't have ruffled Liam's hair let alone floored him.

Liam guessed Reuben had only apologised to impress Linda and encourage her to get her up off her knees. Left to himself Reuben would probably have stepped on his neck to finish the job off.

Turning down Reuben's offer of a lift would mean an unsteady walk home but better that than clambering into the back of the van amongst the buckets, sponges, squeegee and rags, and Reuben, for all his apparent contrition, looked annoyed at having to save face in front of Linda not to mention Florence Nightingale. The idea of the smell of damp rags, stale water and the company of an angry tattooed window cleaner made Liam feel worse not better.

Very gently, with an arm under his, Linda helped Liam to his feet, brushed the mud and grass clippings off his back and then they all walked round into the bright lights of the village hall. Liam caught a glimpse of his reflection in the glass door. It was not a pretty sight.

Safely back in the gents Liam ran a sink of water and washed his face and hands and sponged the mud off his coat and jeans again. It was getting to be a habit. One of Reuben's mates came in to bring him one of the towelling runners off the bar to dry himself down with. Liam winced as he patted the livid navy-blue bruise that was forming around one eye. Anxious to be away from Reuben and his friends, Liam said, 'Thanks, but I've really got to go and find my sister.'

The youth nodded towards the door, drawing hard on a roll-up. 'She's gone home already. Well, walking back into the village anyway. Saw her meself not more 'an fifteen minutes ago with that new teacher from the High School. He was talking to his missus outside and then they all went off. I reckon they're probably taking her home. I know cos your little sister had a few words with Reuben just a'fore she went home. Straight up.'

Liam nodded, not for an instant considering what Reuben and Harriet might have had to say to each other, quite the reverse, it was a relief to know exactly where she was, or at least where she had been. Now all Liam wanted was to get home himself and smooth over any rough edges.

He looked hard into the mirror. Washing his face really hadn't made a lot of difference. He'd lost his comb somewhere and didn't feel he could ask Reuben's friend to lend him one, and anyway even with his hair brushed, Liam wasn't going to look good. He blew out his cheeks and wondered what the odds were on his mother having already gone up to bed.

Outside the sanctum of the gents the band were just settling down into the late-night slow smoochy numbers and Reuben Harnwell and Linda were there waiting for him, Linda looking anxious, Reuben lolling up against the notice board surreptitiously picking his nose.

'All set?'

Liam stopped dead in his tracks. He had assumed that once he knew that Liam was all right Reuben would vanish back into the hall, or go outside with Linda.

'No, thanks, you're all right,' he said.

The window cleaner spun his key ring over and over on his index finger. 'Any friend of Linda's is a friend of mine and all that,' he said. It was not the most convincing statement in the world.

Liam turned up the collar of his jacket against an imagined chill. Reuben indicated the dark, the night and the distant contours of his battered Escort van.

'Cheers,' Liam managed and without another word the ill-matched threesome headed out across the car park.

'He's sort of my boyfriend,' Linda said, glancing back nervously over her shoulder while Reuben went for a pee in the bushes, when Liam asked, as lightly as he could manage, how it was she had gone from lying down on his coat on the back field to throwing herself into an enthusiastic snog with Reuben Harnwell under the lee of a county council wheelie bin.

'Sort of?' Liam asked, pressing the wet bar cloth up against his throbbing temple.

'Yeh, sort of.'

It wasn't the most satisfactory of answers he'd ever had.

Checking his flies Reuben emerged from the shadows and undid the back doors of the van.

'In you get,' he said, standing to one side, with an unpleasant grin on his face.

Liam smiled, swallowed hard and did as he was told.

Mim made herself another coffee and settled down at the kitchen table to wait for Liam to come home. Her eyelids had begun to droop as the back door swung open. It was barely quarter to eleven but it felt like the early hours.

'Hiya, I thought you might be in bed.' Liam ambled in through the back door, clutching something up against his head. Mim gasped, all the things she had planned to say to him instantly gone. He was wet, his hair was all over the place, his face was pale, puffy, bruised and it looked as if he was going to have a black eye if not two. Mim wasn't sure what to say and in the end got to her feet and just stared at him in horror.

'Hiya,' he said again with a wan smile. 'Harriet get home all right, did she? Any chance of a coffee?'

'For God's sake, what the hell have you been up to? Are you all right?' she managed finally, a stupid thing to say if ever there was one.

Liam shook his head. Mim wasn't sure whether Liam was saying he wasn't all right or whether he was shaking away her anxiety. 'It was an accident.'

'You fell?' she suggested.

'No, Reuben Harnwell hit me.'

99

'Reuben? You mean the window cleaner?' Mim felt uneasy and uncomfortable wondering what on earth had brought the two of them to blows. All sorts of dark thoughts shaped and reshaped themselves in dusty, fetid corners of her imagination. 'But you just said it was an accident.'

'Yeh, it was, he thought I was some girl's brother.'

Mim waited.

Liam grinned, the swelling around his eyes and chin gave him an odd Quasimodo, Charles Laughton look. 'Unfortunately it was the wrong girl and the wrong brother.'

It was then that Mim spotted Reuben skulking about outside on the doorstep. He looked up, smiled, eyes bright. She felt an odd and totally inappropriate kick of desire in her belly and was about to speak when Fisher pushed open the kitchen door. He took one look at Liam and Mim and snapped, 'What in God's name is going on here?' as if there was some chance that Mim might have hit him.

Fisher paused, and for a few awful moments she thought he was going to strike a counselling pose and suggest they all sat round as a family and talk it through; instead his expression clouded over and he barked, 'Jesus, Liam. What have you been up to? I'm ashamed of you. What the hell do you think you're playing at? Have I taught you nothing at all?'

Mim assumed it was another of Fisher's famous rhetorical questions.

'What on earth will people say?' he continued. 'You really ought to think about that. We have a reputation to think of. You know what people in the village are like.'

He glanced across at Reuben, who had stepped into the light and was doing his trick with the ignition keys, spinning them round and round on one long finger.

'Thank you for bringing my son home. It was very good of you.' Fisher sniffed the air theatrically, pulled a disapproving face and looked Liam up and down. 'Drinking as well, for God's sake? My parents wouldn't have tolerated this kind of behaviour, I can tell you. I bet Reuben didn't get himself into this sort of state when he was your age. I know I didn't. How about you, Reuben?'

It was a preposterous thing to say. Besides anything else it was quite apparent that Reuben was as drunk if not drunker than Liam and whatever else Liam had been up to, or was contemplating, Reuben Harnwell did on a regular basis. Liam and Mim both stared at Fisher in astonishment.

Reuben grinned and said nothing, but instead turned slightly and looked Mim straight in the eye. She felt herself reddening and was suddenly furious with all three of them.

For an instant she caught a glimpse of the glorious mistake she had made going to bed with Reuben. She saw the great divide between the family she was part of, the sort of man Reuben was and the sort of good and gentle man her son would eventually grow up to become. In some ways it was a glimpse into the abyss.

Oblivious, Fisher continued, 'Anyway I just came in to tell you I've been talking to Angela about the new programme idea. I'll be out tomorrow all day and possibly overnight. She's invited me to stay at her cottage in the Cotswolds, which is rather nice. I didn't think you'd mind. Has Harriet got back yet or did Liam manage to lose her on his drunken foray around Maglington?'

Mim watched his mouth opening and closing and then nodded.

'Good, so have you got something that you want to give Reuben?'

Mim didn't move. She had no idea what Fisher was talking about and didn't dare guess.

Fisher jerked his head towards the window cleaner in a gesture meant to galvanise Mim into action. 'A drink, a little something for bringing Liam back home safely, you know.' His tone was more emphatic, and he was mouthing the words as if there was a chance she might be deaf and then, when it was obvious she hadn't understood, rubbed his thumb and forefinger together to emphasise the point.

Out on the doorstep, great clumping moths flew around the bare lamp directly above Reuben's head like a noisy halo. His expression hadn't changed.

'Nah, you're all right, really, Mr Pilgrim,' he said in an even tone, although he made no attempt to move away. 'Very least I could do under the circumstances.' He didn't quite tug his forelock, Mim noticed, but it was a close run thing. As he looked at her he winked. There was something about him that was barely tame, and most certainly not pompous like Fisher, who was currently standing in the kitchen like Lord Bountiful, chest thrown out, the master of all he surveyed. Mim quashed the wholly inappropriate desire to giggle and turned her attention to the Welsh dresser.

Apparently Fisher was adamant. 'No, no, I absolutely insist. Mim, give Reuben a fiver, will you, for petrol, for a drink, for something. A gesture.'

With her back to them all, Mim got her purse out of the top drawer and then wandered over to Reuben. As she handed him the money he ran a finger slowly across her palm. She shot him a disapproving glance but it did no good whatsoever. His smile just broadened.

'Thank you, Mrs Pilgrim. Hope Liam feels better soon,' he said pleasantly and then added, 'See you bright and early Monday morning. You know me, satisfaction guaranteed or your money back.'

It was such an artful thing to say that it was all Mim

could do to stop herself from smacking him, except that she had a sneaking suspicion Reuben might quite enjoy fighting with her.

Although Reuben was far from the only catalyst there was no doubt in her mind, bad boy, bad influence, big bad mistake or not, that Reuben Harnwell had helped her to see herself clearly for the first time in God knows how many years. He had helped her rediscover all sorts of things that she thought were long dead. All that banter and flirting and teasing over tea in the kitchen; God, he was good.

Reuben had talked but more than that he had listened. It was an irresistible combination. All this had taken her back to a place where minds stand still and there is only sensation. There had been a moment when she had found a rhythm that made her forget everything else. Reuben – for all his obvious failings – had made her body ache with pleasure. She could still feel the touch of his fingers on the small of her back and the lightest caress of lips on her breasts. He had made her body feel more alive than she ever could remember.

All these thoughts were over and done with in the time it took for him to pocket the fiver. Mim looked at him with a warm if knowing gratitude for exactly what he was, well aware of the clever trick he had managed to pull off – not that it came as that much of a revelation, it was just this was the first time she had seen all the pieces of it glittering in one place at one time. Without a shred of doubt Reuben had used the same sleight of hand over and over again, doubtless to the same effect.

It was tempting to speculate how many other bored lonely women on the window cleaning round he'd had, and then Mim smiled at him again, acknowledging the game and somehow in doing so forgiving both him and herself.

'Mum-m-m?' Liam's voice brought her back to reality. 'I've got the most terrible headache.'

Mim turned, and as she did chameleoned effortlessly back into her role as a mother. 'I'm not surprised. Sit down and I'll get you some paracetamol. Do you want me to have a look at that eye for you?'

Fisher hadn't left and was obviously, by his expression, reconsidering his position. 'I think you ought to go straight up to bed and sleep it off,' he said, tone more conciliatory. 'The thing is, Liam, I do understand this need to push the envelope, try the boundaries, explore the masculine side of your nature. All those boys' games, all that drinking, and fighting for your position in the social hierarchy. I just wish that as an intelligent young man you could perhaps rationalise those needs and understand it is a primal instinct and sidestep it completely. I did. It certainly didn't do me any harm.'

Once he got into the flow Fisher used exactly the same tone as the one he used on TV.

No one said a word.

In the uncomfortable silence that followed Fisher picked up Mim's sketchpad from the top of one of the kitchen units. Normally he wouldn't have bothered, her work had never been of much interest to him. She waited for a verdict or a comment, instead to her surprise he flicked back through the pages to where she had stapled the original enquiry sheet, a little note with the address and basic details scrawled on a page from a reporter's notebook. 'Yolande Burke?'

Mim nodded. 'She wants me to do some work for her.'

'There was a message on the phone from her, she said she could up the offer if that would make a difference to your decision over the commission. She seems very keen to have your work. Who is she anyway?'

He was reading the notes as he spoke and then said, 'Ganymede Hall? She's not married to Sam Burke, is she?'

Mim felt icy fingers track down her spine. Her expression must have given her away.

Fisher grinned. 'Sam Burke, the writer? Christ, I bet they're absolutely loaded. I should ask for twice whatever it was they offered you.' His avarice glowed like a beacon. 'How much did she offer you?' He looked down at the sketches on the pad. 'What's it for, one of these fawny, animally things?' He flicked back through the pad again. 'Amazing what people will pay good money for.'

Mim decided not to say anything.

At the back door Reuben Harnwell coughed and made his farewells. He lifted a hand in salute to Liam, reserving a sly smile for Mim and this time – without a shred of guile – she drank it in.

Harriet could hear the low drone of voices downstairs even above the sound of the CD player. She was tempted to go down and see what was happening until she happened to glance out of the window and noticed Reuben's van parked up on the kerb under the street light.

Christ, now what did that creep want? Without thinking she rubbed the back of her hand across her mouth.

She didn't like the way he looked at her or the things he said or the way he made her feel. Strange how by contrast she loved the way Rob Grey looked at her with those twinkly starry eyes. It gave her a peculiar warm glow right in the middle of her chest, which felt really nice and at the same time ached. She had walked as close to him as she dared on the way home, so close that she could smell his aftershave, feel the heat of his body and just about pick out the pulse in his throat.

Harriet did think there was a remote chance he might

hold her hand, although she would probably have run a mile if he had tried to. At one point on the way home she had stumbled over the ragged verge and he made a grab to stop her falling over. His arm flew out to steady her and for an instant she had imagined what it might be like to kiss him, to feel his lips on hers. The thought, the image, gave her a peculiar feeling inside. As it was it had been no more than a fleeting touch, his hand moving away almost as soon it had landed on hers.

Chapter 7

Fisher stood in front of the dressing table. He was naked except for his underpants – a pair of red silk boxers that a client had given him as a Christmas present. He was posing in the lamplight, moving the mirrored panels in on themselves so that they formed a triptych of images. Turning first this way and then that it was as if he was trying to discover and then capture some likeness of himself that no one else had ever seen.

Mim, who was sitting up in bed reading, finally took off her glasses and put her book down.

'Please,' she said gently. 'Why don't you come to bed, Frank? It's getting late. You'll want to be up early tomorrow if you're driving to the Cotswolds.' She had the most terrible temptation to laugh and would have done if it wasn't so obvious that Fisher was quite beside himself with worry.

'I don't want to mess this up. It's my big chance. And how many times do I have to tell you, Mim, please, call me Fisher.' He paused and sucked his stomach in. 'Do you really think I need to work out?' He had another shot at breathing in and swallowing his paunch down whole. 'What do you think? Maybe I should get my hair cut. What do you think?' He sounded truly desperate.

There were times, even after all the things he had done and after all the things he had neglected to do, that Fisher's boyishness and his sheer naiveté made Mim's heart hurt.

'I think that you look fine, really,' she said, slipping a bookmark in between the pages of her novel. 'And Angela offered you the opportunity. She wouldn't have suggested it if she didn't think you were up to the job – why on earth should she? I'm sure Angela knows what she's doing, I'd trust her judgement if I were you – and your own. Just go up there with an open mind, listen to what she's got to say tomorrow and then decide for yourself what you ought to do. I'm certain it will all turn out fine.' It was the kind of thing she would have said to Harriet or Liam. In fact maybe it was the kind of thing she ought to say to Liam about whatever it was that had provoked Reuben to punch him.

Fisher continued to stare into the mirrors on the dressing table.

Mim patted the bed alongside her; still he hesitated, looking uncertain and not a little pained, as if leaving the mirror might rob him of a potential solution, some great insight into what would make things go well. Or possibly he was worried that the instant he looked away the answer might appear and he would have missed it. But, before he could slide under the duvet, Babe, who must have moseyed upstairs from the sitting room without anyone seeing him, leapt onto the bed in a single seamless bound and took up residence alongside Mim.

He was obviously feeling better. He arched his back and immediately broke into a chainsaw purr. Babe was a huge, muscular cat with a great broad head and acid yellow eyes. While his back was deepest, sunniest ginger, underneath, his belly glowed so brilliantly white it seemed unnatural. Mim had got him from a family down the road who planned to move and consign him to the local rescue centre. It was such a terrible fate for so handsome a village tiger. Mim smiled, he reminded her a lot of Reuben; their eyes reflected the same degree of amused certainty.

The anaesthetic must have worn off and the painkillers taken effect, the cat certainly seemed perky enough and obviously not as sore as she had anticipated. Mim ran a hand along the full length of his sinuous spine, from the pink wedge of nose to the very tip of his luxuriant tail. He responded in kind, pressing himself up into her caress, muscles rippling under her fingertips like shot silk.

As Fisher went to climb into bed, the cat beaded him and then yowled provocatively. It was a low dark angry sound that rolled up from somewhere deep in the cat's gut, a sound that promised violence, scratched arms and a lot of swearing. Fisher, instead of playing the man and swatting the cat off the bed, hissed back at him – which sounded like the opening salvo over the question of territory.

'Stop it, for God's sake,' Mim said with surprise, the remark aimed at both of them. The cat looked up at her, eyes benign and generous – as if he would ever do anything to upset her.

Still Fisher hadn't moved. 'That cat hates me,' he said.

Mim laughed. 'Don't be so daft, he's just a dumb, good-looking animal who wants your half of the bed and who can blame him?' So much like Reuben it was almost unbearable. 'He thinks it'll be a lot cosier up here under the duvet than stuck downstairs in his basket in the kitchen.' She shooed Babe away. Reluctantly he sashayed across the counterpane and silently dropped onto the carpet, somehow managing to imply that he was a heavyweight, a cat to be taken seriously. He vanished around the bedroom door, tail up, muscles rolling, but not before giving one last over-the-shoulder look of disdain for Fisher's benefit.

'I wish you'd asked me before having that cat in the house.'

'I didn't think you'd mind. And they were going to send him to the pound.'

'You see, that's one of the problems with you, Mim. Communication in this house has always been a one-way street. I like to be consulted about those sort of things. I feel that you constantly undermine me.'

Mim laughed. 'What?'

'I'm just saying I would have preferred to have been asked about the cat, that's all. It's an issue that I think we need to discuss.' He paused, settling down under the covers and stared up at the ceiling. There were polystyrene tiles covering about two-thirds of it – the centre section shaped like North America – while strips of discoloured lath and plaster made up the rest.

'Perhaps we ought to get a dog. A dog says solid family values.'

From experience Mim knew that dogs said piles of crap all over the lawn and fur, fluff and paw prints all over everything else an awful lot louder, but let Fisher carry on uninterrupted.

'Perhaps we should get a golden Labrador or a Retriever or maybe one of those mongrels with a good face, you know the sort of thing I mean, hairy, full of character. A dog makes a house into a home. It implies a kind of earthy instinctive back-to-the-soil sort of character, sensitive but playful. What do you think?'

'But you always hated Ollie.'

'Ollie?'

'The mongrel we used to have when the kids were little. Hairy, full of character, you know the sort of thing I mean,' she said, with barely a trace of rancour.

Fisher gave her a sharp look. 'Maybe a Lab or a Retriever then. Pedigree dogs say stability.'

Mim couldn't hold back any longer. 'Whatever else they say, Fisher, they're also a huge responsibility, take a lot of seeing to and a lot of clearing up after. I don't want a dog.'

'The children'll help you with him. It'll help them develop a sense of responsibility.'

Mim rolled over and stared at him. 'Come off it, Frank. It never worked with the rabbits. They're not interested in having a dog now and neither am I. What about when they leave home? My dad's Labrador was sixteen when it finally gave up the ghost. Harriet would be thirty at that rate. No, I don't think a dog is a very good idea at all, however good it would look on the front cover of the *Radio Times*.'

Fisher's eyes were still firmly fixed on the ceiling while his mind was quite obviously ruminating over the question of his new image. Mim wondered if perhaps he might ask her for a pony next.

But no.

He sniffed and then said, 'Perhaps we could just hire one for the photo-shoot. For the day. They must have agencies that rent those sorts of things. What about a Wolfhound? I've always thought they were sexy – and rather dashing and handsome.' He began to mug for an imaginary camera with his eyes closed.

With a sigh, Mim turned over and switched off the reading lamp.

Across the landing Liam was still wide awake and lying very, very still while visualising a long cool crystal clear glass of water, so cold that the outside of the glass was fogged and rivulets of condensation trickled down the outside. He swallowed hard, trying to imagine how refreshing it would taste. So cool, so clear. The image was meant to hold at bay the terrible waves of nausea that kept rolling through him every few seconds.

His head throbbed, his breathing was shallow and the spasms in his belly were so violent that he thought that there was a very real possibility that one might nip him in half. Then – out beyond the immediate pain and the dull ache of a black eye blooming – came the feel, the smell and the taste of Linda Bremner. He groaned.

The evening hadn't gone exactly how he had imagined, although Liam had had no cast-iron plan just a series of unlinked, unrelated possibilities, with no idea how one might lead to the other, tableaux rather than narrative.

In the drawer of his bedside table, along with a tumble of change, the dance tickets, a mangled packet of cigarettes and a glow-in-the-dark skull lighter that he'd got on a school trip to France, was the packet of three he'd bought in the gents at the Swan when he'd gone in to buy cigarettes. Maybe he'd been a little premature.

Just as he began to feel a little better, the universe seemed to rock violently. It took Liam a few seconds to realise that it wasn't Armageddon but the cat jumping up alongside him. In the half-light Babe stared down at him with those great glowing eyes and purred raucously.

Liam swallowed hard; the cat's breath smelt of something rich, dead and very, very fishy.

Gagging, with one hand he swatted Babe off and at the same time struggled to reinstall the picture of the ice-cold glass firmly in his imagination.

In the room next door, Harriet lay in bed, staring up at the mobile hanging from her ceiling, although she couldn't actually see it. She was wondering what Rob Grey was doing now. Were he and his wife still fighting? Had she walked out crying, swearing that she would never come back? Harriet imagined them downstairs either side of the kitchen table, pale and shaking, fists clenched, faces contorted with sheer fury.

On the walk home, Rob had told her that he and his wife were staying in one of the cottages near the church so he must have got back home by now. Or maybe he had decided to take another walk around the block, trying to clear his head and let his wife go to sleep before he got back. Or had he opened the back door to find the long thin creature contrite and oh so sorry, had she burst into tears, had they gone up to bed all forgiven and forgotten, kissed and made up? It was an image Harriet decided to overlook and headed back instead to a more palatable fantasy where Rob let his wife rage at him, while he made placating noises until finally, hurt and defeated, he crept away into the wintry wastes of the spare room. He might be married but Harriet knew in her heart that it was unlikely to last. Oh no, not if his wife kept on treating him like that.

Harriet's eyes were heavy with sleep, she turned over onto her side and curled up. One of the last thoughts Harriet had before the dark claimed her was how much better she would treat Rob Grey if he was hers. It was such a radical thought that it nearly shook Harriet back to consciousness, but then Babe plopped gently onto the bed beside her, as if he had fallen from the sky rather than sprung up from below.

She felt him circle a time or two before curling tight into the small of her back. The warmth of his body and the soporific sound of his purr lulled her out beyond all thoughts of Rob Grey into a fine deep blue-green sleep.

Meanwhile, on the edge of a village deep in the Cotswolds, Angela was lying naked on her futon, stretched out under the stars in the master bedroom of her baby barn conversion. The architect had designed it so that, at the rear of the property, a great deal of the roof and part of the back wall on the sheltered, tree-covered side were glazed and had French windows which opened up onto a little deck that overlooked the garden.

On warm summer nights like these she left the blinds

open and so it appeared that Angela was sleeping under a heavenly canopy. She could see her body reflected against the indigo expanses of the night sky. At least, that's what the architect had whispered as he had pulled her down amongst the sacks of cement when the builders had gone home for the day the year she'd bought the barn. It had been totally open to the elements then, little more than a shell, with no roof at all. They had made love on the rough board floor, under a darkening sky, there in amongst the rubble and the dust and debris, to the sounds of the birds in the trees, the distant rumble of cars and children playing somewhere close by.

It was such a vivid satisfying memory that Angela often replayed it on lonely nights alone at the cottage, and sometimes even when she wasn't alone she spliced the raw images into the current action to add fuel to a flagging fire.

She just thanked her lucky stars – which might very well be circling above her even now – that it hadn't been loft insulation under the polythene sheet that she and the architect had rolled and wrestled and rutted on. She would probably still be picking glass fibre fragments out of her arse if it had been. As it was she had had one or two splinters that needed attention, not to mention a few friction burns. A cool milky smear of Savlon on anything these days always made her think of sex.

As it was, the barn conversion and her delight with it had stood the test of time far, far better than the relationship with its architect. As he had been ripping the buttons off her blouse, dragging her bra off, his hot wet, hungry mouth nuzzling and nipping and biting and sucking at her aching nipples, there had been one glorious instant when she had imagined herself sharing a future with him, in some stunning London town house. Completely gutted, the house would be painted white from top to bottom, obviously by someone fashionable, and hung with lots of good art and a few well-chosen sculptures by little-known artists, in some trendy up and coming area while what's-his-name . . .

Angela froze the frame and reran the fantasy one more time. What exactly *was* his name? Names and faces were getting a little grainy with the passing of time. Edwin? Albert? George? Whatever it was, he had been called something terribly stolid and respectable sounding, that her friends would laugh about behind his back, at least until they got to know him better. As she had lifted her hips to give him more freedom and the encouragement to explore he had plunged into her, baying and yelping, his fingers working all sorts of magical and quite unexpected tricks.

And while he amused himself Angela had imagined for a few minutes what it might feel like to see him off to his office every morning, him wearing canary yellow braces and matching silk boxer shorts under his navy-blue Italian hand-tailored suit. She would be in the kitchen reminding the au pair to check on what time the caterers were arriving for their later-that-night dinner party, oh and not to forget to drop the twins off at nursery.

And then, just as Angela was deciding between encouraging him to buy the little baby, soft top Merc or the sexy metallic grey Alpha for her birthday, he had rolled off her, sweating hard, face red, belched and then said, 'God you were good, sweetie, but I really can't stay long, I live with my mother you know, and she frets most dreadfully if I'm late home. You know how it is. I really don't know how I'd manage without her if I'm honest.'

Usually Angela finished the memory a little earlier – although obviously not until all the manoeuvres and the changing position and lickings and touchings and moanings and thrustings had been rerun. Usually she finished up replaying it until just after the point where, with astonishing ease he had brought her to a breathtaking, yowling, whimpering, sobbing orgasm. Quite impressive for a man with so little hair.

Around her on the futon Angela had arranged her clipboard, TV, video and hi-fi remote, her Palm Pilot, mobile and a notebook and one of those pens in brushed stainless steel that would write in any position even under water. Alongside the tools of her trade was a tray scattered with Chinese takeaway cartons and what remained of a bottle of Australian Chardonnay; pride of place, however, on her pillow, was Oliver's canary yellow dossier on Fisher Pilgrim.

She had been giving Fisher an awful lot of thought over the last couple of weeks, since he'd done the extended segment on how men should learn to listen to women, how the new man should be able to reach out to women in a truly caring, mature way. The new woman might be strong and self-determining but maybe more than ever she needed a man to hold her in his arms all night long. It let Angela see a different side to Fisher, one that she would quite like to lick all over.

Summer was on its way and she needed something special to convince Sven that Fisher was really worth investing in. She needed a new idea, something sexy and different – but obviously not too different.

Angela had been letting her thoughts bubble up during the drive to the barn and had already scribbled the first few breaths of a half-decent idea down, bare bones, barely born but interesting and potentially gratifying in all sorts of ways.

What if they had a problem-page road show? Had Fisher heading up a panel of experts who then moved around the country – a sort of counsellors' progress. What Angela needed was the chance to get Fisher away from home, wrong-footed and all alone, and this idea existed as a subtext to any other of the ideas she had. It wasn't just the shirt Angela liked the look of. She bit the end of her pencil, the wood gave under the pressure in a very satisfying way.

All her life Angela had been looking for a real man who would recognise the soft vulnerable little girl lurking beneath that cool businesslike exterior. She stretched and poured herself the last of the wine. It seemed that in Fisher Pilgrim she might finally have found what she had been looking for. How nice it would be to have a man in her life who would listen to her, understand and take care of her when she needed it, be a shoulder to cry on and have the patience and the ability to cure all those little tics and hang-ups we all develop through life.

Oh yes, Angela had plans for Fisher Pilgrim. As she settled down under the stars she imagined lying in his warm strong arms, her head on his shoulder, nestled comfortably up against faded blue denim. She had bought him eau de toilette for his birthday – a warm woody, crisp little number by Ralph Lauren that made her mouth water. If she closed her eyes she could smell it now and the way it broke down after an hour or so into something softer and even more inviting.

She shivered. God, it would be good to have him on her turf.

Fisher struck her as such a strong, honourable and supportive man, a man who was big enough to take advice, listen and then having balanced what he believed with what needed to be done, would make a wise and informed decision. He also had a beautiful little bum. She was salivating at the very idea.

'What do you think I should take then, Mim? What about this shirt? Or this one? What time is it? I really ought to be on my way if I'm going to get there by lunch time. Mim, what do you think? You're not listening. Please, just tell me for Christ's sake.'

Fisher was standing in his underpants and socks, his shirt open down the front to reveal his pale porky little paunch. It was a few minutes before seven o'clock. Mim had set the alarm for six. The children were still in bed, sound asleep, and although Fisher claimed to have been awake all night tossing and turning with worry his snoring had kept her awake until nearly three. As soon as Fisher had gone off to the Cotswolds Mim planned to go straight back to bed.

It was a long while since she remembered going back to bed. Maybe the last time was when she was pregnant with Liam and had given up working at the bookshop. They had bought their first house, a tiny two-up two-down, Number 18 Victoria Walk, their first real home. It had been furnished with all sorts of oddments and bits and pieces and they had decorated it after work and at week-ends. Odd how back then Frank had been keen to finish a job off. She remembered how Frank had banked the fire down at nights so that when they got up in the morning the tiny sitting room would be warm and snug. On cold winter mornings Mim would sit beside the hearth and he would make her tea and toast and they would snuggle up awhile before he had to head off into the dark. Anything had seemed possible then. She had loved him with all her heart and couldn't imagine a future that he wasn't part of.

How could Fisher be that man, how could he be the Frank that she had been so sad to see leave in the mornings? He would stand in the hall of Number 18, coat on, and he would kiss her, hands sliding under her dressing gown so that he could run his hands over her body, torn between the delight at her swelling belly and a huge hungry lust, and then finally – regretfully – he would tear himself away and she would head back upstairs feeling robbed that he was gone.

They had been together about two years by then although looking back there was still a sense of unfamiliarity about their relationship then, new ground: marriage, the house, the whole idea of having a baby. With hindsight Mim had this feeling of mystery, of not quite knowing who Frank was, and she had liked that, the feeling that there was more to him that she had no access to. A huge piece of him that was competent and strong and existed without her. She remembered thinking how lucky she was to have such balanced whole man in her life. Seemed very strange now.

Mim folded two clean shirts into the suitcase she'd got down from the wardrobe.

'I've got a headache,' said Fisher.

She handed him a pair of cream chinos.

'There's paracetemol in the bathroom cabinet.'

'And diarrhoea.'

Chapter 8

When Fisher got downstairs the battery on the Volvo was flat. So after getting Mim to give him a jump-start from the VW and much fretting it was nearly ten o'clock before Fisher finally reversed the Volvo out of the drive and drove away from Maglington, heading across country towards Tiny Netherton. The road map lay open on the passenger seat, alongside the instructions Angela had given him and a little brochure Mim had about Bourton-on-the-Water and Stow-on-the-Wold that she thought might help as they had how-to-get-here maps on the back. Before he left she had mentioned the idea of him taking sandwiches which had annoyed him. There were times when Fisher felt Mim treated him like a child. He just needed a garage now to fill up with petrol and buy some nice sweets for the journey.

Mim spent what remained of the weekend drawing dragons and satyrs and all manner of mythical and magical beasts, while trying not to think about the time she was wasting working on sketches for a project she'd swore blind she wouldn't take.

On the drawing board in the pottery the Burkes' woodland glade had begun to take on a life of its own. In slow moments when Mim wasn't ruminating over how glorious it would be to build pieces so dramatic and so large and so full of magic, a part of her was still planning the polite but firm speech declining Yolande's commission. In the next breath she was considering who she knew who might be able cast the figures in resin or fibreglass. Bronze was out of the question, it was expensive beyond belief, but glass fibre coloured, treated to look like bronze, complete with weathering and verdigris was a different matter altogether. Maybe she ought to have a shot at making one of the figures whether she did it for Yolande or not. She'd ring the college first thing Monday morning – although Mim couldn't work out whether that was going to be before or after she had spoken Yolande. It would be useful information to have anyway Mim decided, sitting back to admire the latest sketch.

It would be magical to feel the forms grow beneath her fingertips, taking shape, taking on a life of their own. It seemed such a long, long time since Mim had found herself in that glorious place where she wanted to make and build and lose herself in the textures and shapes and the tactile delight of the clay. Half a dozen bowls with a few bees on them and the odd commission for wall tiles hardly fed the artist in her soul.

Mim carried a bag of clay in from the shed and began wedging it up into grapefruit-sized balls, a process designed to knock any air bubbles out of the clay to stop it from bursting or blowing in the kiln. It took a while to do the whole bag but the physical effort felt wonderful, a wholesome act of preparation, a readying for the moment when the creative impulse became totally irresistible.

It seemed wonderfully quiet and very calm without Fisher at home.

Liam stayed in bed until lunch time on Saturday, waking occasionally with a start from violently erotic and then just violent dreams.

By the time he got up he was completely exhausted. So, once he'd showered, dozed on his bed and read a couple of magazines that Peter had lent him and played on his computer until his eyes ached, he was bored. Liam would have given Peter a ring but couldn't think of what to say to him.

Harriet – who seemed a little preoccupied to Mim – got up just after Fisher left and cleaned out the rabbits without being asked.

A weekend without Fisher was sheer bliss.

'How about if we go out for lunch?' Mim suggested, washing the clay off her hands. It was Sunday lunch time and she'd been busy in the pottery all morning, working up the new figures while firing a kiln. Outside the day was warm and bright.

'We could walk down to the pub.'

Harriet, who'd been lying outside in a hammock slung between two of the apple trees watching the world go by, thought it was a great idea. Liam, who'd been upstairs doing God only knows what, agreed.

The Swan was busy but they managed to find a table out in the veranda.

'That's Mr Grey, over there,' said Harriet, lifting a hand casually in acknowledgement. Mim smiled in the general direction of a young couple sitting out on the river bank, a baby buggy wedged in the space between them.

'Were they the people who brought you home on Friday night?'

Harriet nodded and Mim wondered if she ought to go over and thank them, but then the food arrived and everyone started to eat and the thought got lost amongst a dozen others.

Fisher arrived home just before tea time on Sunday by which time Mim had come up with several other possible design ideas for the Ganymede woodland clearing, made a couple of small-scale prototypes, and was still struggling with what she was going to say to Yolande Burke. Harriet was upstairs finishing off a project for school and Liam was engrossed in something on Channel 4.

Fisher didn't have much to say for himself when he got in, other than that the meeting with Angela had gone well and no, he wasn't hungry, and then he'd disappeared into his study to organise things for the show on Radio Washland first thing on Monday morning.

His coming home was almost anticlimactic.

Mim was asleep before Fisher came up to bed, her head jam packed full of nymphs and dryads.

Babe, who had found a place to sleep on a pile of clean sheets in the airing cupboard on Saturday morning, just after Fisher had left, stayed there all weekend, leaving briefly for comfort breaks and light refreshment.

On her way back from the Cotswolds Angela rang Sven at home to remind him that they had an early meeting at Eelpie. The weekend hadn't gone exactly to plan but she wasn't a person who gave up easily.

On Monday morning the heavens opened at first light and gave no sign of letting up.

'I wasn't expecting you. It's raining,' Mim said, wrapping her dressing gown tight around her.

Reuben Harnwell stood outside the back door carrying an empty bucket with a chamois leather slung over the side. He smiled at Mim. It was nothing lecherous, nothing overtly suggestive but even so it made her shiver just the same.

'It's only a shower. Don't worry, it'll clear up by lunch time. How are you today? How's your boy? I'm really sorry about the, you know.' He indicated his eye. 'I had no idea it was him. It was an accident.'

Mim shifted her weight so she was blocking the doorway. 'So Liam said. It's all right. These things happen.'

The school bus had left ten minutes earlier. She had watched it leave. Fisher had followed it out of the village on his way to Radio Washland. Mim was all alone in the house and at the moment felt it most keenly.

Reuben held her gaze, eyes dark and glittering, and for the briefest of moments Mim felt nervous. For her adventure, her foray into adultery, she ought to have chosen someone from further afield, a faceless stranger whom she could have screwed and then never seen again.

One of her friends, Maggie Hutchins, had fallen into bed with a man from Croydon on her first day at an Open University summer school, slept with him all week and had never clapped eyes on him since. It had been a perfect reintroduction to the restorative power of passion.

Maggie had arrived home a changed woman, three months later she had left her husband, Trevor, and gone off to teach English to students in Madrid. Mim had had a postcard saying that she was having a lovely time and wouldn't be coming home in the foreseeable future, but if Mim was ever in Madrid to look her up. Mim still had it tucked away somewhere; maybe it was pinned to the cork board. Briefly Mim wondered if she ought to find it, keep it at hand as a touchstone.

It wasn't the act of adultery that had changed Maggie but the fact that along with it she had undertaken some arcane act of reclamation, of pulling together all those parts of herself that she had left and lost and lent, back into the middle.

She had told Mim that over coffee in the pottery one morning, just before she left. There was snow on the ground and the light in the studio had been outrageously bright, a spotlight picking out Maggie's new-found confidence. By that time Maggie had lost a stone, had blonde highlights put into her mousy grey-brown hair, and taken to wearing a huge amount of eyeliner, and although at the time it had seemed like gibberish, Mim now knew exactly what it was that Maggie had meant.

Out under the porch Reuben was still looking at her. He was wearing that lazy self-assured smile that suited him so well. Mim was the first to break eye contact. He made her feel hot and self-conscious.

He hung back from the door, leaning nonchalantly up against the trellis, under the overhang, out of the weather, not encroaching on her space, as if she was some wild animal that might bolt or bite if he made a sudden move. She was aware for the first time of how much taller he was than her.

'Would you like me to go?' he purred.

God, what sweet torture this was, and how clever of him to give her the choice, the power, let her appear to call the shots so that whatever happened next it would appear – true or not – to have been her choice, her responsibility. Mim managed a smile. He was a canny little bugger.

He was wearing faded jeans that emphasised long legs and lean hips, and a white cotton granddad shirt, tucked in, with the sleeves rolled back, which made a lot of his broad shoulders and tan. Dark hair curled in the open V, the dragon asleep but not invisible.

'I could always nip back later and do the windows when the weather clears if you like.' He looked fleetingly at the great ripe drops of water that had gathered on the fretwork of the overhang.

So, if she liked he would provide the service she paid him for, if not he would let her have the one he provided free. Taking him to bed once, Mim could persuade herself – if she needed to – had been a mistake, a heat of the moment thing, but twice? More than twice?

That was premeditation, that was a considered act, complicity. Knowing. The edge of a summer storm crackled past them.

Mim looked up at him. The moments seemed to drag out into months as she weighed the pros and the cons. Inviting him over the threshold into the cool quiet chaos of the kitchen was tantamount to agreeing to all those things that he was offering her. Agreeing to the touching and the persuasive kisses, and all those questions that lips ask, all the demands that they make. Suggesting he came in for coffee until the weather broke meant she was agreeing to leading him through the house, up the stairs in the silence of anticipation to the bedroom, where she guessed from the last time that he would very slowly undress her, gently and with surprising tenderness so as not to frighten or startle her, reassuring her at every turn.

Oh, Reuben Harnwell was terribly good at what he did, and if later, in the weeks or months to come, these liaisons turned into something raw and hungry, furious ripping and biting and other things that she imagined him well capable of, at the moment there was only tender coercion. Although, even then she had felt him driving the game, a silken thread wrapped around a steel core.

Mim wasn't stupid enough to think that her seduction had been some happy accident, there was absolutely no doubt that she was part of the plan Reuben had tucked away in the recesses of his mind, behind those bright predatory eyes, although, whether it was purely a numbers game or just the desire for another conquest, Mim had no idea.

Outside, still his smile held.

Perhaps this time he wouldn't be so bothered with the niceties and the persuasion. Perhaps this time he would have her there in the kitchen in the warm sunlight, only taking off what was totally necessary, a reckless fiery animal fuck hunched over the table, voices plaited into gasps and moans and guttural sighs of desire.

The intensity of the image stopped Mim in her tracks and made her shiver, hoping that none of the thoughts showed on her face but guessing that they did – at least the broad sweep if not the details.

Even then Reuben's expression did not falter. It was as if he was breathing her in, and like a snake waiting to see which way his prey moved.

Mim focused on all the things she knew about the consequences of her actions and said, in as even a voice as she could manage, 'Later then, Reuben.'

He didn't move. 'Sure,' he said lightly

There was not one shred of resentment, no attempt to persuade her, no pressure. It was a masterly ploy, Mim thought with a flicker of admiration. Did he perhaps see this moment as an opening gambit, or was he just giving her the opportunity to change her mind?

'What time will you be back?' Mim heard herself asking over the drumming pulse in her ears. Something inside her winced. She shouldn't have said anything else, she shouldn't have asked. She should have waited for Reuben to turn and leave.

'What time would you like me? I haven't got any more calls until the weather breaks and you're top of my list.'

Mim daren't look him in the eye.

They seemed to be caught inside a glittering prism of silence; outside the water dripped, cars drove by and yet under the porch was a silence so sharp, so deep, so well defined, so ripe with anticipation that Mim could almost see it.

'Would you like a coffee while you wait for the rain to stop?' she said in an undertone.

He grinned. He'd won. Mim didn't see Reuben grin

because she wasn't looking at his face but she knew just the same.

'Don't mind if I do,' he said and stepped into the kitchen. He left his bucket and chamois outside.

Fisher always got to the studio well ahead of the time they were due to begin broadcasting. Currently he shared studio two and the three-hour Monday morning slot with Billy-Boy Wilder, a wonderfully good-natured man, addicted to country and western, who always did the programme wearing a Stetson and crocodile-skin cowboy boots.

Between all the talk about depression and agoraphobia, Billy-Boy would say, 'And now then, for all o' you out there with the blues, let's have a little Willie Nelson to lift your achin' heart. Over to you Willie.'

Every Monday morning Fisher parked the Volvo outside Radio Washland, and before booking in would go for a stroll around the block and have a cappuccino and blueberry croissant at a trendy little café he'd found in Berbeck Passage. Today it was raining and grey and so he sat inside and breezed through the notes for the programme. Fisher planned to talk about the menopause. He thumbed through a brochure he'd picked up at the surgery when he'd nipped in to see the doctor about his bad knee – it was called 'Supporting Your Partner Through the Menopause'. Fisher just wanted to check that he'd got the gist of it.

After the traffic round-up and the weather report – specially extended on a Monday for farmers and growers – he and Billy-Boy would be hosting the live phone-in. Fisher really liked working at Washland, although it was nowhere near as high-powered as Eelpie and the TV slot; he liked the people, and the way that Billy-Boy, if he could see Fisher was struggling, would say, 'And now we'll lift the mood with the lovely Dolly Parton. You know, Fisher, I've always thought that woman should have been a philosopher.' And he would fade up some piece of rustic homespun nonsense that would give Fisher time to gather his thoughts.

The woman who manned Fisher's phone was called Irene and had a good nose for weeding out nutters and time wasters and called him petal when they weren't on air. Maybe he ought to talk to her about the menopause. She wouldn't mind, very broad-minded was Irene.

Fisher spooned the froth off his coffee, heavy with cinnamon it was delicious. Irene didn't make him feel uncomfortable, she didn't threaten him or make him feel inadequate. Not like Angela. Fisher stiffened, the thoughts about Angela had surfaced unbidden from somewhere in the dark recesses of his mind. He took a quick look round in case anyone could see what he was thinking.

The trip up to the Cotswolds had been a lot more difficult than he anticipated. He'd found the village all right, and hadn't been too late arriving. So, he had missed lunch, but he was certain that something else had upset Angela, although he couldn't quite put his finger on what exactly. He'd taken her a pot plant as a little present, along with his notes with the ideas for the new programme. She had some good ideas too, ideas that he had been very happy to discuss.

Her house was lovely – Fisher had enjoyed the guided tour, unpacked his things in the guest room – and then they had walked down to the pub, had a bottle of house red with dinner and come back for liqueurs. She had slipped her arm through his on the way home, which he didn't mind at all. It felt companionable, after all they were friends, colleagues and he was a married man and was certain Angela was seeing someone, although she had never mentioned it at work. There were lots of men's things at the barn. Aftershave in the guest bathroom cabinet and a Barbour and a pair of wellies tucked up in the bottom of the coat cupboard.

It wasn't that Fisher didn't drink but he thought Angela was rather heavy handed with the measures when they got back from the pub, and then she had suggested they went upstairs and had brandy and some more coffee out on the deck. Watch the sun set she had said or was it the moon rise? He watched her roll a joint. It wasn't his sort of thing, but what the heck it was a free country.

It was late; he was tired. Angela didn't seem best pleased that he had fallen asleep on one of the sun loungers – and then when he finally woke up a mosquito had bitten him right on the end of his nose, and she hadn't got any StingEze or first aid stuff or anything, so he'd had to make do with a cold flannel.

Sunday morning the atmosphere had been a little less convivial but then she'd got a long week ahead, and he didn't think she'd slept very well because he had heard her walking past the door to his room at least half a dozen times during the night. So, what with one thing and another they had barely scratched the surface of her plans for him.

'How did it go, then? And what the fuck happened to your face?' asked Peter the next morning at school.

Liam slid his bag under the table in the common room, and shrugged in what he hoped was a man of the world way.

'Jealous boyfriend,' he said casually, slipping off his jacket.

Peter grinned and threw an arm around his shoulder. 'He shoots, he scores –' with the other hand Peter made a fist and punched the air triumphantly.

Liam shook his head, 'Uh-uh. He didn't.'

'What? But I thought you'd got an open goal there, mate.'

Liam was getting sick of the soccer metaphors. 'Linda's bound to tell you anyway. I got completely and utterly wasted and then I threw up.'

Peter laughed. He laughed so hard that Liam thought he might choke. He laughed way beyond any possibility that what he was laughing at was funny. Way, way beyond that point. Out to a point where Liam wanted to punch Peter's lights out for being such a complete and utter dickhead.

There was a bright yellow flyer pinned up on the notice board outside the gym. In one corner was a little picture of two masks, one happy, one sad. The poster read:

Roll Up, Roll Up!!
Auditions being held at lunch time on
Thursday & Friday
for parts in the end-of-term play.
Everyone welcome.
Enthusiasm way more important than
experience.

It was naff, but it was signed by Rob Grey. Kate glanced across at Harriet.

'Suppose you're going?'

Harriet shrugged. 'Dunno, maybe, might do. Probably, why not? You get time off during lessons for rehearsals.'

Kate snorted. 'Yeh right. You're totally crap at the whole cool thing, Harriet, you know that, don't you?'

Harriet reddened and hefted her rucksack up onto her shoulder.

Kate hadn't moved, 'And even if he does fancy you there is no way anything is going to happen. He'd lose his job.

It's against the law. It's not going to happen, Harriet. Get real. And anyway it's sick.'

'I know,' Harriet snapped. 'I know.' She said it, but she didn't believe it. Not a word.

'I want him,' Angela said, slamming her fist down on the palm of the other hand for added emphasis. 'And I intend to have him, Sven. Fisher's new, he's fresh. He's got my name stamped across his arse in big red letters. And we've got to be careful here, Sven, we've only got him signed up on a short contract. Don't make the mistake of thinking he's safe, I can see another independent snapping him up. Making him a better offer. It's in the wind, Sven. It's in the wind.'

She waited to gauge his reaction, nothing made a bone more attractive than knowing that another dog was eager to carry it off.

Sven sucked thoughtfully on the earpiece of his sunglasses. 'We should take a long hard look at the demographics on this one, Angela, but I do trust your instincts. And you say there are other people after him?'

Angela held her hands up as if to defend herself. 'It's what I've heard,' she said non-comittally. Better not to be caught out in a barefaced lie.

Sven nodded and looked again at the notes she'd made. 'Maybe we should go with the pilot. See how it shapes up.'

Angela tried to hide a smile of triumph.

It had not been an easy weekend. She had thought long and hard about Fisher's apparent indifference to her. Not towards the business stuff obviously but that whole man–woman thing. Angela had considered and reconsidered the way he had blatantly ignored what she had to offer as if he didn't understand what was going on.

And then, while driving back to town it had occurred

to her what a wonderfully honourable thing it had been to do. After all Fisher was a married man, he'd said so more than once. By pretending that he didn't know that she was after him they could both leave the barn with their dignity intact, without him having to actually turn her down and make a fool of her or risk hurting her feelings. He hadn't *wanted* to turn her down, obviously, but because of his sense of loyalty to whatever-her-name-was he just couldn't follow his natural instincts. Obviously. Angela had felt the power of the attraction between them, to be able to fight that was real strength. God, the man was deep. And sensitive? She'd never met anything like it.

On the far side of the desk Sven was scratching his fingernails through a dappled covering of designer stubble. 'Okay,' he said slowly. 'Okay. Let's see where we can go with this.'

Angela smiled. 'I'll go and sort it out with the rest of the team.' She picked up the folder and turning on her heel, headed smartly towards the door. Sven was notorious for encouraging pitchers to linger and just as they thought they were being invited onto the inside track he would – as if he had been ruminating all along – say perhaps it would be more prudent to rethink, reassess. Better not to give him the chance.

Angela was out of the double doors and halfway down the hall before Sven had had time to take another breath.

She'd go downstairs and work up the idea with Andy and Nicole, and then ring the media desk at the *Daily Argos* to get Fisher a mention. A line or two in the gossip columns would be excellent – if only there was something they could use. Angela paused for a few seconds at the water cooler, maybe it was time to find something to add that little frisson to the Fisher Pilgrim package, maybe it was time to seed a little meow.

'TV's Top Agony Uncle in rural love nest
with mystery Blonde.'

Regretfully Angela shook her head. She hadn't got any
pictures and realistically Fisher wasn't big enough yet for
anyone to bite and run with that particular hook, but he
would be soon and then Angela would ensure that bloody
Oliver in PR would be waist deep in meow.

Chapter 9

Mim had remembered to switch the answering machine on while she was busy with Reuben Harnwell.

Yolande Burke's voice was as clear and as hard-edged as good crystal. 'I had hoped that you'd ring me over the weekend. Perhaps you would call me today if you get this message. Obviously if you don't want to take on the work we'll have to look elsewhere.' There was a weighty pause and then Yolande said in a more conciliatory tone. 'I would really like you to work on this project, Miriam. I truly feel that we've been guided to you.'

Trying to ignore the effect the otherworldly tone of the last sentence had on her, Mim picked up the working drawings stacked on the bench and looked through what she now considered to be a fair representation of what the finished articles might look like. Drying on a rack were two little figures – a dryad and a satyr. It would be a fantastic challenge to build any of the pieces.

Mim turned the pictures towards the light and took a long hard look at her doubts. Realistically you didn't have to like your customers to take their money, and on an artistic level there is no development, no progress, without risk.

Creating pieces as complex as the ones she had drawn would mean Mim working at the very edge of her talent and abilities, pushing the boundaries of what she had accomplished. The challenge both excited, delighted and terrified her.

What Mim visualised was a whole series of almost

life-sized figures, some mythical, some magical, some almost human, any of which could be integrated into Yolande's woodland garden – some of the component parts were meant to be seen in the open against a back-drop of rich complex greenery whereas other pieces were meant to be partially hidden or mounted in or on the trees. It also meant that Yolande could pick and chose from the various forms and faces and animals to make up the kind of tableau she had in mind.

Mim slipped the finished sketches into large polythene wallets and then picked up the phone. Yolande answered on the tail end of the second ring as if she had been sitting by the phone waiting for Mim to call.

It didn't take her long to get to the point.

'So, when can you come over and show us what you've done,' said Yolande briskly. 'I'm very keen to get started. There are certain astrological alignments that I would like to integrate into the garden's creation.'

Mim slid her diary closer and picked up a pen. In small neat block capitals alongside Monday she had written 'Window cleaner 8.45'. It was hardly a cryptic clue.

Reuben had had her from behind, on all fours, like a dog, on the bed. Was *had* the right word? It most certainly wasn't making love but screwing, shagging, sounded too hard and too sordid. Was there a middle ground, a middle word that described what it was they had done and why it was that Mim felt obligated to find one? Was it perhaps best described as sex, just that, sex, a bare, functional word?

Sometimes his hands had been on her hips pulling her back onto him and at others his fingers were busy in other places. But throughout it all there hadn't been a single moment when in some way Reuben hadn't encouraged Mim on with words or fingers or lips, biting the back of her neck and nipping and licking, cupping her breasts in his hands or brushing his body up against her spine and buttocks until Mim thought she might go mad with the sheer pleasure of it.

'Actually I'm free tomorrow afternoon,' Mim said to Yolande evenly.

'What time?'

'Any time after midday. I usually try and work in the studio in the mornings.'

There was a moment's pause and then Yolande said, 'Would you like to come and discuss it over lunch?'

It had taken Mim and Reuben a long time to make it to the bedroom. She had spent an age downstairs in the kitchen wrestling with the dilemma of whether or not to call a halt, whether or not to allow herself this exquisite forbidden fruit or just to make Reuben a mug of coffee and wait for the rain to stop.

He had leaned casually against the Welsh dresser before accepting the invitation to sit down. Watching him while the kettle boiled, trying to make some pretence of conversation, Mim was stunned to realise that her body had another mind that was entirely its own, a subtler, simpler, more instinctive structure that bypassed the whole intellectual process, short-circuited morality, and while she was busy weighing the good and the bad and guilt of it all, this pretender had already worked out a plan and was glowing with desire, desperate to feel Reuben's hands and lips on her body.

And then he had moved closer and she'd kissed him.

They stayed upstairs for a long while too – a long, long while – time enough for Mim to lose herself in the pure physicality, the sensation of what they were doing. Odd that in those most intense moments she had felt totally alone, losing Reuben along with the rest of the flotsam and jetsam of her life. Finally she had rolled over amongst the tangle of sheets, sated, exhausted and lay totally still, listening to the pounding of her heart while Reuben smoked a cigarette and stroked her hair. It was a tenderness Mim had not expected let alone felt she deserved.

If this wasn't love – and it most certainly wasn't – then it was lust and what place had such an intimate tender gesture in amongst the sharp unforgiving lines of lust? She imagined the scent of her body on his and wondered if she ought to offer him a shower before he left to go and get on with the rest of the day, or was there some pleasure for him in the way her perfume lingered?

And then, while she was thinking and enjoying the sleepy embrace he offered her, downstairs the phone had rung, once, twice. Mim knew from experience that there wasn't time to get downstairs to pick it up before the machine cut in. The noise was invasive, slicing into the odd sense of peace she had found.

'So, what shall we say then? One o'clock?' Yolande was still talking.

Mim hesitated, accepting an invitation to lunch meant that she wouldn't easily be able to escape Yolande's clutches.

'The thing is,' Yolande continued. 'I'd really like it if Sam could see the drawings before any work begins and I can't persuade him away from his shed except at meal times. He likes it there – his sacred space he calls it. I suppose I understand to some extent. No one ever goes inside except him. God forbid that anyone should touch any of his precious things.' There was more than a hint of resentment in her voice.

'We'll eat out on the terrace if it's fine. I'll get Jack to put the awning up,' said Yolande Burke.

'I'll see you next week,' Reuben had said.

*   *   *

138

'I just wanted to say that I had a really nice time on Friday night.' Linda reddened up a touch and toyed with the straw of the carton of orange juice she was holding. Liam and Linda were standing outside the mobiles near the science block. It was lunch time.

'It was nice to talk,' Linda said, not quite catching his eye. 'You know, just talk and hold hands and snog and that. Reuben always wants – well, you know, a lot more, most older blokes do, so it was nice to be with you. I just wanted to tell you that.'

It wasn't the most coherent of sentences. Linda Bremner looked down and did something with the toe of her shoes that seemed a lot like scribbling. 'And not feel pushed, you know. Like you wanted to be with me for myself not what you could get. That was nice.'

A crowd of year sevens pushed past on their way to lunch. It was like having a herd of sheep driven through the middle of your conversation, but at least it gave him a minute or two to think. Liam really didn't know what to say to Linda. First of all it was only true by default and secondly he'd been so busy avoiding Peter all morning that it hadn't occurred to him to avoid Linda as well, so he was a bit surprised to find himself outside the mobiles with her.

Liam was supposed to be playing tennis with Peter but he wasn't sure he could take much more undisguised derision.

'I'm on early lunch today,' Liam said, nodding vaguely in the direction of the canteen. 'I've got tennis practice.' It sounded churlish and unchivalrous.

'Sorry, I didn't mean to stop you or anything. I just wanted to say how nice it was.' Eyes downcast she was already backing away from him nervously. This wasn't how he had expected their next meeting to go, nor what he expected from Linda of all people. She was almost coy.

Liam felt a complete heel. 'You want to come?' he said, reaching out in a gesture of invitation, wondering how he could persuade the dinner supervisor to let her in.

Linda held up the carton of juice. 'Nah, you're all right. I'm packed lunch.'

It felt as awkward as shoes on the wrong feet.

'I'm not that hungry actually,' he said, just as she said, 'You can share my lunch if you like.' They both laughed. For a few seconds it felt like they were okay and at ease and everything would be all right and they were like real boyfriend and girlfriend, not some horrible fit up.

'My mum always packs me up loads,' Linda finished. 'She doesn't want me to waste away, you know, get anorexic or anything. She's always on about it. Fat chance of that.'

He grinned at the bad joke and Liam also realised that amongst many other things Linda was really quite sweet, and he liked the way her eyes lit up with mischief and amusement when she giggled.

'So, do you want a cheese and pickle sandwich, then?'

'Yeh, okay,' Liam said. If nothing else it would keep him out of Peter's way.

'We could go and sit up at the pavilion if you like,' she said. 'It's nice up there, under the trees, out of the way. Have you got any fags?'

'Uh-huh', he said and hurried to catch up and walk alongside her, carrying his bag over one shoulder, for some reason feeling big and cool and okay about the whole thing. He wondered how she would feel if he held her hand.

'And now for our final caller on line three. How can we help you?' Fisher said.

It had been a very harrowing morning one way and another at Radio Washland. The menopause had opened up a whole can of worms. Fisher had no idea it would be so traumatic, he was totally exhausted. At one point Billy-Boy had had to play three Dolly Parton tracks back-to-back while Fisher caught his breath and Irene sent out for an espresso and a chocolate éclair.

After half an hour on the menopause they had opened the lines up for more general calls. Relationships, divorce, dieting, you name it, although thankfully after the news and weather and the traffic round-up things had settled down and Fisher felt he was finally getting back on form.

'The thing is I really love this man, Fisher,' said the woman on line three. 'It's so intense, it hurts. I don't know how to let him know how I feel. I don't know how to make him want me.'

The voice sounded very familiar. Fisher smiled into the mike. Regular caller probably, if he could just remember who she was. She hadn't wanted to leave her name so Irene dubbed her Lucy. Billy-Boy had told him after the first week that listeners hated it when you called someone caller one or just caller, they needed a name to fix the voice to.

'You're not alone in this situation, Lucy. It's a matter of believing in yourself and being brave enough to stay with what you feel for a while until the right moment comes along. And it will. Trust me. What have you got to lose? If he wants you then this opens the door and if he doesn't then at least you know exactly where you stand. How did you meet him, Lucy?'

'We've been working together for the last few months. I'm his boss.'

Fisher struggled to put a name to the voice. It was on the tip of his tongue. He pressed his fingertips together. Although the gesture was lost on the listeners it always gave him a good feeling. It was a pose that the facilitator on the course he had been on had always used. He called it considered listening. Under pressure the course leader would steeple his forefingers and press them to pursed lips as if summoning up some special wisdom from the deepest recesses of his mind. One of the women, who called herself Anouska and had been to find herself in New Mexico a month before the course, said it looked more like playing for time.

If Lucy was this guy's boss, she probably wasn't that woman who always served him at the Co-Op.

Fisher took a long breath. 'I can see that that might put you in a difficult position, Lucy. A lot of men would find that intimidating, a lot would find it difficult perhaps to see their boss as a woman – do you think he really sees you as a woman, Lucy?'

She sniffed, it sounded as if she was struggling to hold back a well-stream of tears. 'Oh God, Fisher, I do hope so. The thing is he is such an honourable man, so sensitive, so caring. I know that he wouldn't ever do anything to jeopardise the great working relationship we have and – and . . . then this weekend. Oh my God . . . it was just so difficult, so frustrating. We'd finally got some time alone and even then – even then – I've been thinking about it all morning, that's why I rang –' The sniff degenerated into a little sob.

'What is it, Lucy? You can tell me – I'm here for you – we all are,' Fisher said in his gentlest, most encouraging voice.

At the control desk Billy-Boy was scribbling something with a felt-tip pen onto the back of a cake packet. He tipped it towards Fisher. It read, 'He's married.'

Fisher struggled to hide his surprise and then said, 'Let me run something by you Lucy. Is this man you love married? This man you're in love with, is he already in a steady relationship?'

Lucy sobbed so loudly that Billy-Boy had to fade her out before she sent the sound levels off the meter.

'You bastard,' she wailed. 'You've known all along, haven't you? You know all about me, oh, Fisher. I don't think I can go on like this. You bastard.'

Thanks to Billy-Boy's quick wits she was talking off air, but before Fisher had a chance to reply she hung up.

There was no time for another Dolly Parton, but it didn't do to end the programme with incoherent sobbing and wailing, so Fisher pulled the mike a little closer and dropped his voice to an almost seductive pitch.

'The thing is, before you reach out to someone else Lucy, it's important, imperative, that you learn how to love yourself. Maybe you're choosing men, unattainable men who you can't have, as a way of punishing yourself? It's a common pattern with clever, powerful, modern women. That desire to please daddy and make him love you. I'd really like you to think about that, Lucy. We produce a booklet here at Washland, part of the Fisher Pilgrim self-help programme called *Loving Yourself First*. I'll send you a copy and anyone else out there who would like one, if you'd like to send in a stamped addressed envelope and a cheque or postal order for £3.50 to the usual address, we'll get those out to you as soon as we can. Is that okay, Lucy?'

Billy mugged a strangled yes to cover the potentially yawning silence.

Meanwhile at Denham High School Harriet had settled herself down at the back of the classroom – it was double maths – and let the sunshine and the ambient warmth lull her into a comfortable stupor where waking dreams were easy. The sun shone in through the windows and her eyelids felt increasingly heavy.

They were revising for end of term exams and the

143

teacher, Mrs Millburn, was discussing the whole concept of revision strategy. Normally Harriet sat near the front and – even though maths wasn't her best subject – made an effort to answer and join in, but today she felt sullen and silent and hard done by, although she wasn't altogether sure why. Maybe it had something to do with the things Kate had said. Harriet made a point of not sitting near her. Kate was over by the door with Anne Bell and the rest of the goody-goody girls.

'So,' Mrs Millburn was saying, running the pointer down a white board full of notes. 'Half an hour – even fifteen minutes – of regular, concentrated, structured study is far better than hours of last-minute cramming. Boring but true. Now, let's have a look at the next topic on our list.'

Something caught Harriet's attention and tempted her away from the board, away from the list and well, well away from the soporific monotone of Mrs Millburn – although it wasn't much of a contest.

Outside on the playing field a group of year ten boys were pretending to sword fight on one of the grass banks that edged the running track. They were armed with reeds cut from the wildlife garden by the look of it. For a few seconds Harriet struggled to stay focused on whatever it was that Mrs Millburn was droning on about but it was pointless.

The boys were holding sheets of paper in one hand and were sword fighting with the other. Rob Grey was there, dressed in jeans and a bright yellow T-shirt, directing operations. He was grinning, encouraging them on, while the boys seemed to be shrieking Shakespeare at each other. Seeing Rob made Harriet smile. Something in her belly kicked and tightened, making her hungry for something she didn't have a name for. Rob moved with an easy confidence, up on his toes miming the parry and thrust of a real sword fight. The boys around him laughed and catcalled, totally caught up in what they were doing.

Without thinking Harriet leant a little closer to window and pressed her fingers to the glass – was it her imagination or did Rob look up and see her there watching him. Was that a wave? Was that smile meant for her? Harriet shivered. Was there any possibility that this feeling really could be mutual? Surely teachers didn't do that sort of thing? It was a thought that at the moment haunted her every waking hour. Her mouth was dry, her pulse racing, it was all she could do to stop herself from calling out to him – and all the while the voice of reason told her not to be so ridiculous, so stupid.

'Harriet Pilgrim, are you with us?'

Reason was louder than she thought. Harriet swung round, reddening furiously and with a great backwash of horror realised that everyone else had stopped working and was looking at her. She swallowed hard, struggling to regain her composure

Mrs Millburn had her hands on her hips and a grim expression on her face. 'So, Harriet, would you like to tell the class what is so interesting out on the field?'

Harriet bit her lip and looked down at her rough book, so far the only thing she had written was the date.

'Well?'

'I'm sorry, Mrs Millburn.'

The woman's expression didn't soften. 'Sorry won't cut it when the exams come up, Harriet. You need to concentrate and revise. Now let's get back to the list. Number eight –'

Harriet stared blankly at the board wondering where her brain had been while they'd been running through points one to seven. With a great show of compliance she picked up her pen and began to write. Mrs Millburn nodded her approval.

Surreptitiously Harriet took one last look out of the window. Rob Grey had sprung up onto the bank and, grabbing a reed from one of the boys, took up a fighting stance. Harriet sighed, crushed under the weight of the nameless thing.

It seemed insoluble and horribly, inescapably painful. First of all there was no one she could really talk to about it and secondly Harriet was afraid that if she didn't say something to someone soon her heart might burst.

Across the field, some way away from the running track and Rob Grey's Shakespeare re-enactment, Linda Bremner settled back amongst the tangles of goal nets on the pavilion floor, lit another cigarette and then blew out a great plume of smoke. Liam had had no idea where the spare keys to the pavilion were hidden, even that there were any spare keys, but Linda did.

It felt nice lying there together in the gloom eating and talking and smoking. In the shadows she seemed softer and less intimidating, the whole being together thing seemed a lot less frightening.

Liam glanced down at his watch. He had a free period first thing after lunch and then chemistry. Time yet to enjoy this intimate softness.

Linda caught the gesture. 'It's all right,' she said, as if there was a question in the slight flick of his wrist. 'I was going to bunk off the rest of the afternoon anyway.' She took another long pull on the cigarette and then handed it to him. 'We've got history and then textiles.' The words were punctuated by a great rolling boil of smoke.

Several times since they had clambered in over the piles of sports gear and found a place to nest amongst the musty piles of netting, Liam had caught himself watching her. Presently she had one arm tucked behind her head, hand cupping the base of her skull, hair spread out around her like a dark halo. Her skin was pale, almost translucent in the shadows. It took him a few seconds to realise that she was watching him watching her, and when he did she grinned and he blushed furiously.

For a few seconds everything felt wonderfully still and calm in the gloom. Liam leant closer to breathe her in and she craned up and somewhere between those two things their lips met. As they kissed he felt as if he had been electrocuted.

Linda moaned softly and stretched up for more, while Liam felt something tighten low in his belly along with another more basic stirring. Any sense of peace, any sense of stillness was instantly lost, torn away as Linda sat up, their lips still locked and, taking the cigarette from him, stubbed it out and began to undo his shirt. Gasping for the next breath, Liam – expecting at any minute to have her pull away and ask him what the hell he thought he was playing at – reciprocated by starting to undo the buttons of her school blouse.

Simple it most certainly was not, his fingers, which had worked perfectly while peeling clingfilm off the cheese and pickle sandwiches now seemed to be as big and clumsy as ripe bananas. She tugged his shirt out of his trousers and back off his shoulders, her tongue and teeth and lips all working overtime. He flinched, he shivered, it felt amazing – and then he gasped as one of her hands slipped down to his belt buckle, while far, far away in the distant land of somewhere else he could still feel his fingers trying hard to make sense of her buttons.

Linda stopped and pulled away from him. Liam sighed, his hands – hot and desperately sweaty – dropped back into his lap. The sigh was partly one of relief. There was a bit of him – an anxious, scared bit – that almost hoped that it was all over and would stop there, while the rest of him was baying for more.

Edging away a little, just enough so that Liam could watch her, although she needn't have worried she had his full attention, Linda took over the complicated business of undoing her blouse, a button at a time, so slowly that for an instant it crossed Liam's mind that she might be having problems too.

It was like some heady unveiling. Liam began to salivate. Snuggled up inside her school blouse were the heavy soft warm objects he'd been trying to get his paws on for most of Friday evening and now it appeared there was no struggle needed after all. She was wearing a white lacy bra. It brimmed full with pale creamy flesh. There was a shadow in the deep valley between her breasts that emphasised their shape and others that highlighted the contours of her collar bones. She shimmied the blouse back over her narrow shoulders, slid it down her thin arms and then dropped it onto the netting.

Liam groaned. Would she take off more? Was he supposed to touch her now? Applaud? Would he suffer permanent brain damage from the lack of oxygen because of the gallon and a half of blood needed to sustain the erection that he was no longer trying – or able – to hide? Whichever it was there was a good chance he might just drown in drool before doing anything else. God, this sex stuff was tricky. Wasn't it supposed to all be instinctive and come naturally and even if the urge was, what about all the details?

Amongst a lot of other things Linda appeared to be able to read minds. She took hold of both his hands and held them up under her breasts. She was warm and soft and very scary.

'Don't worry. It'll be all right. I won't bite,' she purred as she guided his hands round to the hooks and eyes at the back. Liam wasn't totally convinced.

Chapter 10

At her office in the Eelpie building Angela sat back with her feet up amongst the debris of the morning, crumpled tissues, a notebook and an empty packet of Maltesers, and flicked through the Rolladex. Her eyes were far too puffy to bother with the minute screen on her electronic organiser and anyway flipping through the cards gave her some sense of being busy. The smell of lasagne wafted in under the door and up through the AC vents, although instead of making her feel hungry it made Angela feel nauseous.

The phone on the desk buzzed like a discontented wasp. It really needed putting back in its cradle. It was tired and had had enough. It wanted to go home.

Maybe today she'd send out for sandwiches, pastrami and wholegrain mustard on rye, instead of going to the trendy little restaurant that fronted Eelpie's reception area. She didn't feel up to the crush and flap of it all. She wanted a chance to be quiet and mull things over, have a chance to rethink her plans which she couldn't do elbowing her way towards the trough with all the other media lunch-timers.

The card index was open at Fisher Pilgrim's details. There was his home number, his practice number, the main reception number and the show call-in number for Radio Washland, all written neatly in Angela's carefully controlled hand. He ought to have a mobile. Maybe she would buy him one for his birthday. Just how long did it take to drive back to his house from the radio station? Did he go straight home? Was he having lunch with a client? Or that idiot he shared the show with? Or was he in bed with someone else, his wife or that breathy little receptionist who took the calls for him at Washland? Bitch. Angela made a big effort to strangle that thought before it had chance to suck in another breath. Worst of all why didn't she know these things about him? The frustration was almost more than Angela could bear.

'Hiya, can we come in?' The words were accompanied by a knock at the office door, snapping Angela's attention back from the edge of the abyss. She opened the desk drawer and slipped on a pair of shades before calling the visitors in.

There was no excuse, no are you busy, no polite introduction, no preamble: 'We've found some really cool venues for Fisher's first road show.'

'He's from Norfolk right, so how about we haul hard on the country boy connection.'

'There's Sandringham, so there's a royal connection, always popular with a day-time audience.' Andy and Nicole – joint heads of the team who had been working up the Fisher Pilgrim project – spoke one after the other as if they had rehearsed this speech. It was quite possible that they had. They were excited and sounded extremely pleased with themselves in a Tweedle-Dee, Tweedle-Dum kind of way. Nicole was holding a large-scale map, Andy a sheaf of notes and sketches.

'There are some great old-fashioned seaside resorts over there,' said Andy, flapping in a generally eastern direction while encouraging Nicole to spread the map out on Angela's desk. 'Very family values, very kitsch, very cute – end of the pier kind of stuff. I've been pulling all sorts of things off the net all morning – golden beaches, old world charm – God, it's absolutely per . . .'

He froze as Angela slid the dark glasses down far enough to reveal beady red-rimmed eyes.

'Norfolk?' she said. Where in God's name do they keep the meow in Norfolk?

The two of them nodded in unison.

'Uh-huh. Bear with me. It's perfect. And the bonus ball is that Sven loves Hunstanton,' said Andy not quite able to keep the defensive tone out of his voice.

'Absolutely adores it,' continued Nicole. 'You must remember, he kept going on about it when Fisher came down for the interview. Salt of the earth, country fisherman type of thing.' She pulled a face as if willing Angela's memory into action.

Angela sucked hard on the end of her magic biro. She had been thinking Salcombe, or that Sunday supplement village in Cornwall, maybe Southwold at a push, somewhere picturesque, and stylish, somewhere that beat the living meow out of all comers. She had imagined a place with character and a half-decent restaurant, far enough away so that the crew would have to stay overnight at some nice quiet little hotel. The crew and Fisher of course. Angela certainly didn't want him slithering back home to the wife and kids after a day's filming. The idea ran for a moment or two before Angela jerked on the leash that would bring it to heel.

'Okay,' she said carefully. 'Norfolk.'

If they filmed the pilot on Fisher's home turf she would have lots of reasons to spend time with him location hunting. It was a start, a way to lull him into trusting her. And what better guide to the area than the host himself? Softly softly catchee monkey. If they made the first show close to home and all went well then next time they could travel a little further afield. Maybe it wasn't such a bad idea after all.

'Okay, let's go with that. You know the ropes, make

sure the press know what's going on, see if we can't create a nice little buzz.'

Nicole nodded and made a note. 'Local TV, radio. Tourist board, local council, local papers – all the usual sort of thing?'

Angela grimaced. 'Uh-uh, but please, do let's see if we can't stir up something a little less parochial. We're aiming for national coverage not end of the pier. Fisher's profile is on the up. Let's all be aware of that.' She remembered her conversation with Fisher over the weekend. 'Maybe we should try for an at-home-with-your-friendly-TV-shrink feature in one of the women's magazines. Although the tits and knits pages in the tabloids would be better.'

Nicole and Andy scribbled down a flurry of notes on matching leopard-skin-print clipboards. It did cross Angela's mind that they could be scribbling anything, the gesture of apparently writing down every word she said being meant purely to placate her. If that was the case, it worked every time.

Once they'd left, Angela arranged to have sandwiches and decent coffee sent up and then picked up the phone again and composed her opening sentence, after all now she had any number of reasons to call Fisher at home.

'Hello?' A woman answered.

Angela froze. 'Hello?'

'Can I help you?' said the woman.

Angela took a moment or two. 'Could I speak to Fisher Pilgrim please,' she said guardedly.

'I'm afraid he's not in at the moment. I'm Mim, Fisher's wife. Can I help?'

Angela sucked her teeth, composing her thoughts. 'This is Angela, from Eelpie TV?'

How was it they had never spoken before or was it that she hadn't minded so much before?

The woman's voice warmed. 'Oh hello, Fisher talks

about you a lot. I'm afraid he won't be back until later this afternoon. He does a radio show from nine till twelve and then he likes to eat with Billy-Boy, the guy he does the show with.'

Angela didn't like to say that she knew Fisher's schedule almost as well as her own, instead – realising that some part of her had persuaded itself that Fisher's wife was a fiction, a mythical creature, an obstacle that was purely a figment of her own imagination – she said, 'Right, well if you could tell him that I called,' and without waiting for a reply hung up.

So that was Mim Pilgrim, a living breathing woman who sounded warm and humorous and bright. The Mim that Fisher dropped into conversation occasionally. Mim, the potter. Mim, the mother of Fisher's children. Mim, the woman who shared the bed and the life of the man she loved. Angela felt quite undone and reached for the tissues. What made it all a hundred times worse was that Mim Pilgrim sounded really nice. The bitch.

It rained on and off all day. At nearly four o'clock, Fisher, soaked through to the skin, scurried into the kitchen dripping water all over the floor. Mim found him a towel out of the linen basket. In the corner of the kitchen the tumble drier was making an odd heavyweight grinding noise.

'You ought to get out of those wet things,' she said.

Fisher grunted.

Mim switched the tumble drier off and pulled out a plait of sheets.

'Angela rang.'

'Uh?'

'Angela. She rang earlier on. I told her you'd call back as soon as you got in.'

Fisher threw the damp sweater he was wearing over the back of a chair.

'Did you hear the show today?'

Mim smiled. 'No, I was busy this morning, how did it go?'

Already on his way to the phone Fisher didn't bother to answer her.

Liam leaned against the wall under the lee of the bus shelter and watched the raindrops explode into the puddles. It was cold and wet and his hair was plastered down like a skullcap, but it didn't matter a bit. In every other way it had been a totally magnificent afternoon, a great recovery after the fiasco on Friday night at the village hall. He had considered catching a later bus, going down into town for a coffee and a burger with Linda but she'd told him that she'd got to meet someone straight after school. Liam didn't ask who.

At the other end of the bus shelter Harriet was reading a magazine, ignoring him, and apparently ignoring Kate and the rest of the people too.

'. . . I thought we could take a drive round and scout out possible locations later in the week,' Angela was saying. 'Can you recommend a good hotel close to you where I can stay? I was thinking about driving down late Thursday after we've wrapped up the show.'

Fisher, clutching the phone, stared unseeing around the hall's interior, a huge boyish grin splitting his face. 'So Sven really went for it then? That's absolutely marvellous. What did he say?'

'He was enthusiastic but cautious, Sven is always cautious. If an idea works he loves it and takes all the credit, and if it pans then he can genuinely say he had his reservations about the whole thing right from the start. It's just his style.'

'God, this is brilliant – well, wonderful news.' Fisher

ran his fingers back through his floppy fringe, grinning like an idiot, lunch bubbling up inside. Swept away by his own enthusiasm, he continued, 'Look, why don't you come and stay here with us? I'm sure that Mim wouldn't mind at all. You could stay Thursday night and Friday and then go back on Saturday, stay for the whole weekend if you like. Meet the family – the children. I'll go and ask her now – God, this is wonderful.'

But before he could close the thought, Angela snapped, 'No thank you, Fisher. It's very kind but really there's no need to put your wife to any trouble. A hotel will be fine.' She sounded very certain.

Fisher glanced around the hall. It needed a lick of paint and a few things sorting out here and there, but nothing that he couldn't do in an afternoon and people didn't come to see the place, did they? They came to see him or Mim or the children, although obviously he wouldn't have time to sort it out between now and Thursday.

'Maybe that's not such a bad idea, Angela. It'll give you a chance to unwind and if you were here we'd only talk shop –' He didn't like to add that Mim wasn't much of a housewife, although she tried and she was a good cook but since she'd started on the pottery the house always seemed to be a mess. Never tidy. Maybe he should have a word with her about it. Obviously they were going to be entertaining a lot more if the show took off.

'We could all go out to supper instead,' said Fisher warmly. 'I'll book a table. Anyway, tell me, what else did Sven say? Did he like my ideas? What did he think? Did he want me to come down for a meeting? I'll go and get my diary, shall I?'

Fisher told everyone the good news at supper time. He was going to have a programme of his own. It annoyed him intensely that no one seemed that impressed. Mim couldn't wait to get back to her blasted drawings and finishing off some bee bowls or so she said. Harriet looked as if she was sickening for something and cried off straight after they'd eaten to go upstairs and read through a play her class were doing and Liam seemed to be on a different planet. Perhaps it was time to remind him about the dangers of drugs.

Fisher was hurt that they all seemed so blasé about the programme. It was right about familiarity breeding contempt. Fisher took a mug of tea into his study; maybe they were just a little overawed. Realistically what could anyone, even his own family, say beyond congratulations, well done, bravo? Although they could have at least said that.

He found it impossible to believe that they weren't impressed, or perhaps they were and were jealous of his success? It made sense. If the shoe had been on the other foot he would have been the same.

Fisher settled down on the sofa, wriggled the flex on the angle-poise lamp until it came on, and then began making notes about some of the subjects that he thought would make good programmes and a list of things he wanted to talk about with Angela and Sven, after which he planned to meditate.

It was almost two in the morning before Fisher woke up.

The following day Mim tucked the portfolio up under her arm and locked the VW. It was just after quarter to one and in her mind Mim was still working out how best to handle Yolande Burke. She didn't usually work ideas for projects up so quickly, and was deeply aware of the paradox of being excited by the subject matter and yet repelled and unnerved by its originator.

Mim glanced into the wing mirror, licked a finger and

smoothed her eyebrows. It was a mistake to appear too keen. Maybe it was a mistake to have come at all.

Across the driveway Ganymede Hall was still and warm, curled up amongst the trees in the early summer sunshine. As Mim crunched across the gravel the sounds of a peacock calling raucously on the midday air picked out a steady counterpoint to the rhythm of her footfalls.

Mim took a long slow breath as she reached the door. Calm, collected, casual. Say nothing, commit to nothing. Mim was wearing jeans and T-shirt and a great big shapeless cardigan to emphasise just how casual she was feeling about the whole meeting. It had taken her hours to decide what to wear.

She didn't have to like a client to take their money. No really, said a calming voice in her head. Even if in the end nothing came of it the experience and the renewed sense of passion for her work was worth it. Yes really, she murmured to something about to reply with heavy sarcasm and derision. Everything would be fine, just fine. Honest. Maybe she ought to have worn a suit. Deep breaths.

Mim rang the doorbell expecting Jack Tully to appear at any moment from the ether.

Nothing. She rang the bell again.

Still nothing.

From the lawn came the sounds of the peacock gloating.

Mim checked her watch. True, she was a bit early, maybe it would be better to wait in the car for a few more minutes. Or come back bang on one. Maybe Yolande was a stickler for time or some celestial alignment had come up and taken her by surprise. Mim would ring the bell again, one more time, and if nobody answered it would definitely go back to the car. Definitely.

Mim pulled the bell chain and heard the sound echo through the cavernous interior of the house in a distant

157

softened rolling way. She waited, counted to thirty and then stepped out from under the portico, and as she did the heavy front doors opened an inch or two.

'What?' snapped a male voice.

Mim swung round. The door opened a fraction wider. Sam Burke stood framed by the shadows. He had bare feet and was dressed in khaki combats and a crumpled white T-shirt. In one paw he was cradling a large blue china mug. He looked like an unkempt bad-tempered bear and peered out at her from under a great range of eyebrows.

'What do you want?'

Mim refused to let herself be intimidated by him, after all she had been invited.

'I'm here to see Yolande,' she said. Mim thought about adding 'your wife', but felt that despite appearances Sam Burke probably would know who Yolande was.

He didn't move.

She tried out a smile on him. 'We met the other day. My name's Mim Pilgrim, I'm the potter? Yolande has asked me to do some work for her. Design a sculpture for the woodland garden?' She floated the words out towards him as if there was a very real possibility that he had forgotten everything about her.

He sniffed. 'And?'

God, the man was a complete pig.

'And I've done some preliminary sketches for her to take a look at; she invited me to come over and show her what I'd done. Today. For lunch.' Mim was rapidly running out of steam.

Sam scratched his belly and then looked heavenwards as if considering what to do next. After a few more seconds he said, 'I've got absolutely no idea where she and that cretin Tully have got to. You'd better come in and wait,' and stepping back from the doorway waved her inside.

Mim accepted the grudging invitation and followed him.

Sam looked totally out of place against the cool elegant backdrop of the hallway.

As if reading her thoughts he said, 'I can't stand this bloody room. You can't use it for anything and those chairs are so bloody uncomfortable that anyone with an ounce of common sense would sit on the floor rather than plant their arses in either of them.' He paused and then added, 'I liked it better as it was, all dark, dusty and cosy, womb-like, not so elegant maybe but at least it felt like a real place, like someone's home, not a fucking museum – but what do I know? I suppose you want coffee.'

Against all the odds Mim felt herself warming to Sam Burke.

'I wouldn't mind,' she said, falling into step alongside him. This time he didn't direct her into any of the public rooms but through a heavy wooden door, down a set of steep stairs and along a dingy corridor that led – eventually – into Ganymede's kitchen.

Obviously Yolande hadn't got as far as refurbishing this part of the Hall or perhaps she never ventured that far into its depths. Whichever was the case Ganymede was hardly geared up for any sort of large-scale entertaining. There was an ancient range tucked into the fireplace, alongside that stood a battered propane gas stove splattered with carbonised grease and assorted orange and yellow splashes. Dwarfed by the high ceilings the remaining walls were lined with a range of mismatched units and cupboards. In one corner was a vast pantry into which Sam promptly vanished.

'Stick the kettle on, will you?' he said from the shadowy depths. Nonplussed but amused, Mim did as she was told. Moments later Sam reappeared carrying a slab of roast beef on a dish in one hand and a jar of homemade pickled onions in the other, which without ceremony he slid onto the table before vanishing back into the gloom to rescue a loaf of bread, a tub of Flora and a jar of horseradish.

'Shouldn't we wait for Yolande?' Mim asked, taking two mugs down from the rack above the draining board.

Sam stared at her as if she was totally mad. 'Whatever else we've got in this godforsaken bloody hole we've only got the one kitchen. All the hired help appears to have pissed off into the great beyond for the day. If Yolande had remembered you were coming to lunch trust me someone would be in here stuffing something with cream cheese and smoked salmon. No, she's out there somewhere communing with trees or chanting with Jack-fucking-Tully. Here –' He thrust a jar of Nescafé in her general direction, took two faded seersucker napkins out of a basket on one of the units and settled himself at the table.

'Yolande's got plans to turn this whole place into a retreat, you know.' He tucked a napkin into the neck of his T-shirt. 'She doesn't think I know but she and Swami what's-his-face have got it all sussed out. In most films the loonies get locked away in the attic but Yolande's planning to bang me up in the shed out in the woods, churning out potboilers to keep her and the rest of the commune in veggie burgers and incense.'

What was most odd about Sam's speech was that there was little or no malice in his voice. He jerked open the table drawer and produced a carving knife and fork.

'You're not a vegetarian are you?' he said, making it sound as if it was a capital offence.

Mim shook her head.

'Good, then get some plates.' He waved towards the sink, and without a word Mim did as she was told.

He cut great slabs of beef off the joint followed by doorsteps of bread, sat down and waited while Mim boiled the kettle, tracked down the milk and sugar, and made the coffee. Lunch, apparently, was served. While struggling to open the pickle jar, he nodded towards her portfolio and said, 'Is that what you brought to show Yolande?'

'Uh-huh.'

'In that case I'd better take a look at it while you're here, then, hadn't I? Don't want your trip to be a complete waste of time.'

Mim eyed him suspiciously and to her great surprise he grinned at her. It was the first halfway pleasant thing he had done since opening the front door. The change of expression did something magnificent to his heavy dark features and for an instant Mim caught sight of what it was that might attract a woman like Yolande to a man like Sam. Behind the protective mask of a bad-tempered, ill-mannered ogre was a mischievous little boy. The transformation startled her.

His amusement lingered. 'I'm not a complete philistine whatever you may think. I designed the new gardens here, not our friend Tully, he's just putting my ideas into action.' He held out a paw towards her. 'I employed him because Yolande told me he was a natural. A natural what remains to be seen. He's been here for nearly a year, good wages, all found, Land Rover, cottage in the grounds and I'm still waiting for his bloody references to arrive.'

Mim handed him the sketches. 'Is he a good gardener?'

Sam shrugged. 'Christ only knows. Probably. And Yolande likes him. He's company for her. I'm a self-centred, cantankerous old git living in a world of my own in case you hadn't noticed.'

Mim couldn't think of anything to contradict and so said instead, 'Do you follow this guru's teachings too?'

Sam laughed and this time the impression that he was a far gentler soul than he liked to appear lingered for a little longer. 'Do I look as if I live on bloody lentils and the word of some minor Asian deity? No, not my scene at all. But if it makes her happy –' He paused, pulled a lump of meat off the slice on his plate and dropped it into his open mouth, continuing to talk through the whole process. 'Yolande has always been a powerful woman. She needs a purpose, a cause, been the same ever since I first met her. It used to be me – I was her project. Her *raison d'être*. Without her I would still be scraping a living as a hack on a local paper or maybe churning out short stories for a small press. She said I'd got talent and then set about proving it to me and everyone else.' He extricated a length of string from the joint that had got wedged between his teeth.

'She's done the whole thing, animal rights, women's rights, vegetarianism, you name it. Then along came this Indian guru guy. Apparently he does some amazing work with orphans and women's stuff. There's some educational programme they're helping to fund, a "trade not aid" programme, long-term conservation. You know the kind of thing.' He paused and then looked up at Mim. 'We didn't have any children. It makes a big difference.'

She nodded. Without Harriet and Liam, God alone knows what she and Fisher would have done.

Sam fished a pickled onion out of the jar and crunched through it. 'Yolande didn't want kids when she was younger – it was one of those do it later things – and then when she did we couldn't. Tried all kinds of stuff, all the doctors. Pills, potions. I think we just left it too late, but she wouldn't have it.' He stared Mim down, as if defying her to say something trite and placatory.

Mim pulled one of the smaller slices of beef off the pile, refusing to lower her gaze. 'Life would be so much simpler if foresight was as clear as hindsight, don't you think?'

It seemed to be the right thing to say.

'Too bloody right.' Sam popped another pickled onion into his mouth, opened the portfolio and looked down at the first sketch. It was of a dryad amongst trees, ivy curling up and over her, softening the outline and the junction between tree and woman. As the sketch progressed, her hair became part of the foliage. The next figure, set on a tumbled log, was a satyr stretched back and staring up into the heavens while playing pan pipes. Other pictures were of torsos and faces and animal masks hung and hidden and disguised by and amongst the branches and climbers. The effect was intended to suggest having stumbled across a magical pagan gathering. It was all Mim could do to stop herself from getting to her feet to explain each image but she knew instinctively that if the ideas didn't speak for themselves then the project wouldn't work anyway.

Sam turned the page.

Mim slipped off her cardigan, hung it over the back of the chair, got up to put the kettle back on, found a knife for the butter amongst the washing-up draining near the sink, almost anything rather than watch Sam thumbing his way slowly through the pictures. Finally she couldn't contain herself.

'I thought that we could use fibreglass for the figures, pieces of that size are not naturally suited to ceramics, having said that I've seen some wonderful things made from fibreglass and resin coloured to look like bronze. I've already rung the college and they will let me –' she stopped, aware that Sam wasn't listening to her, instead his full attention was focused on her work.

'This one is Yolande,' he said in surprise, pointing at one of the sketches.

Mim nodded. 'Not a particularly good likeness I'm afraid but I thought we could do a series of photos, although the idea was to get the feel of her rather than a portrait –'

'And this is me?'

She nodded again feeling hot and self-conscious that he was so drawn to the pictures. 'I found an article about you in one of the Sunday supplements.' Mim wondered how well she was doing, having prepared herself for Yolande's otherworldly coolness rather than Sam's earthy passion.

'And these?'

Mim felt her colour deepen a shade or two more; amongst the satyrs and fawns was a sketch of Reuben Harnwell. 'Just faces, people I know,' Mim said as casually. 'But there's no reason why they can't be people in your life.'

Sam snorted. 'You mean like Jack Tully and the bloody Swami.'

Mim laughed. 'If that's what you want.'

His concentration shifted back to the portfolio. 'I really like them,' he said slapping the pages with his hand. 'I can see that they'd work – and if we lit them properly at night too they'd look amazing. I've got plans for a pool in the clearing, maybe we could have one of these female torsos coming up out of the water. What do you think?'

Mim, who had imagined making just one of the figures, nodded. 'Sounds wonderful.' It would be fantastic to do a group or maybe some of the other smaller pieces to put in the trees along with one of the larger figures.

Sam got to his feet. 'Do you want to go and have another look?'

'Now? What about lunch?' Mim indicated the shambles that littered the kitchen table.

'Bring it with you,' he said, folding a wedge of beef into one of the slices of bread and tucking her portfolio up under his arm. 'Maybe we'll meet Yolande en route and she can tell us what the fuck she'd got planned for you to eat. You never know, we may have narrowly missed a finger buffet somewhere.'

Mim laughed, and picking up her coffee followed Sam through the kitchen door and back out into the warm sunlight.

The air was heavy with summer heat. Ganymede Hall appeared to be totally deserted, a green and fertile island oasis afloat in an ocean of farmland; the only sign of life was a black cat who sauntered on silent pads up the garden path and then dropped down into the shade beneath an abandoned wheelbarrow.

Mim and Sam walked out through a walled vegetable garden, passed banks of salad crops, herbs and strawberries, fruit trees and raspberry canes, down a path between the main house and outbuildings and then across into a finger of woodland that snaked up close to the house. This way into the woods was more direct, and the planting far rawer and newer than the route that Yolande had taken Mim on. It felt odd, almost like coming upon the back of a carefully constructed illusion.

Stepping out into the clearing, the shed where Sam worked was hunkered down in the dappled shade, as if curled and ready to pounce. Mim hesitated as they reached the door – hadn't Yolande implied that this was the holy of holies? Sam's inner sanctum. Surely he was supposed to deny her entry.

Sam banged the door open with a shoulder charge.

'Sticks like buggery,' he said by way of explanation, 'even in the good weather. I reckon the frame is wracked, but Tully won't have it. In the winter when the wood swells up it's a bastard, but I'm loath to plane any off because of the draughts. Can't abide draughts.'

He beckoned her inside. The lintel was so low that Sam had to stoop to get through. He looked like a giant wedged in the entrance to a doll's house.

Inside, the main room, his office, consisted of a large bright space with a big shabby old red sofa, desks, computer, a wood-burning stove in one corner with a neat stack of logs piled alongside it. There was nothing particularly odd or outrageous about either the layout or the contents. There were filing cabinets and bookcases, beside which books and magazines of all descriptions were stacked on almost every available surface but even then it was not unduly untidy – there was an air of quiet industry rather than an uncontrolled maelstrom of creativity. Mim instantly warmed to the space; she would be happy to work here.

Sam dropped her sketches onto one of the desks and then – after a minute or two's searching – pulled a cardboard tube out from beside one of the bookcases. Inside was a set of plans. Setting aside his makeshift sandwich Sam unrolled and then weighted one of them down on his desk. It turned out to be a scale drawing of the woodland garden.

'There,' he said, indicating the clearing through the window, and then tapping on the corresponding spot on the plans. 'Pond there, where the markers are – pool sounds nicer though, doesn't it? Then the trees around the back, over there with somewhere to sit, I thought I'd like nice shallows a bit like a shallow pebble beach. And then over there a marginal area with blue irises and stuff.' He looked across to make sure Mim was following him. 'What do you think?'

'It sounds beautiful.'

He nodded. 'That's what I thought,' and he began to roll the print up. 'Take this home with you. Might help you to have a sense of the place and scale.' Seeing Mim was about to protest he added, 'It's all right I've got several other copies. Now, if we take a little look outside –'

'I've brought a camera. It's a shame Yolande isn't here. Do you want me to leave the drawings for her?'

'Yeh, that would be great.' He stopped and then said carefully, 'Don't take any notice of Yolande – I don't mean *no* notice, I mean try and ignore her idiosyncrasies. She's been through an awful lot. She had a shit childhood, a lousy first marriage and then me, and if that wasn't enough all the trauma of trying to have kids. It's not been that long since she finally admitted it wasn't going to happen. Every new thing, every new development – that bloody woman in Italy, all that stuff kept her hanging on long after she should have given up –' Sam stopped again and when he spoke it was more slowly, in a more considered way. 'Even without any of the way-out experimental stuff, the things they do to women are barbaric and to go through all that and still – well –' he reddened. 'You know. Yolande and I have been together for as long as I can remember. She believed in me when I was struggling and depressed and all alone and then I couldn't help her get what she wanted. It doesn't seem fair or right –' It was a huge speech that left an enormous silence in its wake.

Mim glanced up at him, part of her mind curious about the details and stories that she knew must lurk behind the words although she had no intention of pressing him to reveal any more.

Meanwhile Sam was standing to one side to let her out.

The tour of the clearing didn't take long – ten minutes, fifteen maybe – before Mim had a sense of him wanting to be back in his shed, back at work. She slipped her camera into its bag. 'I'll ring Yolande later today if that's all right.'

Sam nodded. 'Bloody good idea, ask her what the hell she thinks she's playing at not showing up.' He grinned.

'I will. There's no need to come to the house, I can find my own way.'

Sam nodded once and without shaking her hand or thanking her was gone.

As Mim headed off through the trees, carrying the plan, half a mind on the pool and the possibilities it created, she remembered she'd left her cardigan in the kitchen.

It did cross her mind to go back and tell Sam and then she thought it would be easy enough just to slip in through the kitchen garden and back door and pick it up. It wouldn't take more than a couple of minutes.

As Mim drew level with the range of outbuildings that were set against one wall of the vegetable garden she heard noises. It took her a while before she registered exactly what it was and exactly what it meant. And then Mim had it. There was a low throaty moan, followed by laughter that was more about pleasure than humour.

The sound stopped Mim dead in her tracks, all her attention instinctively craning to pick up more sounds and more information. She held her breath until she thought her lungs would burst. The noise was more distinctive now and Mim knew with a horrible certainty that what she was hearing was Jack Tully and Yolande Burke and they certainly weren't talking about plants or planning a religious event.

Chapter 11

Liam lay very still, enjoying the sensation that his mind was melting. Up until seconds before every molecule, every single thought had been focused like a laser on Linda Bremner's compliant little body and the feelings it gave him and the great waves that threatened to drown out every other thought. Exploration and pleasure. God, this moment felt so good, so very, very good and there had been lots of moments like this over the last few days. All that was left now was heat and tiredness and the scorch-marked memory of a frantic overwhelming sensation that had driven him on and on until Liam thought he might just die, and finally he felt as if he had.

Linda's skin was the softest thing he had ever touched. Running his hand over her belly was such a wonderful feeling that it almost made him want to cry. How odd. Snuggled up beside him Linda grinned and settled back, languid and warm in the crook of his arm.

They were upstairs in her bedroom. In her bed. Everything smelt of sweat and bodies and an earthy oceanic scent that made Liam's mouth water. It was lunch time and they had spent most of the day up there in her room, listening to music, talking, curled up in each other's arms, snogging, touching, snuggling up. God, it was bliss, a kind of rancid, animal instinctive bliss that he suspected might very well end in tears but was worth it. Probably.

Linda's mum was at work. She was a line supervisor at a vegetable trimming factory and wouldn't be back till half-past six, later if they were really busy, Linda said. Her brothers worked there too.

Liam had told his sister Harriet – on the walk to the bus stop on Tuesday morning – that he was on study leave. He said he was going round to meet up with Peter to revise at his house, and not to mention it to Mum because she'd want him in school, or at home. Definitely not naked in Linda Bremner's bed. For once Harriet hadn't said a dickie-bird, not a peep.

He'd watched the bus leave and then walked round to Linda's house all week, arriving a few minutes before nine, knocking on the back door, waiting for her to answer. She had still been in her dressing gown this morning.

Occasionally, out on the periphery of Liam's thoughts, school arced through his mind like a solar flare, but then Linda would roll over and smile at him and the thoughts would dissolve like morning fog under summer sunshine. All day long there were only the immediate things, like touch and hunger and thirst and those thoughts that pressed up at the very front of his brain, and then Linda would hand him a cigarette, pad downstairs in a T-shirt to make toast or coffee or get packets of crisps or a can of Dr Pepper or just press herself up against him and giggle and wriggle and as she did all thoughts of school sank without a trace.

Liam felt like a king and for a moment wished that Peter was there to see him or at least there to tell.

It was Thursday lunch time. Or was it Friday?

While Liam was revelling in the afterglow, at Denham High School Rob Grey was holding auditions for the end-of-term play.

'Okay, that was great, Lizzie, Stuart. Next pair up are . . .' Rob glanced down at his list. He was leaning against a table that stood a little way back from the stage. He was cradling a mug of coffee, sleeves rolled back, looking suntanned and very slightly windswept, and waited as a queue of would-be Desdemonas and Othellos, Juliets, Romeos, Hamlets and Ophelias, and Macbeths, of both sexes, went through their paces at the lunch time auditions.

He'd hand out a pile of laminated script pages at the beginning of the session and let them read whatever came up off the pile – and to make it easier and quicker and to add a little edge to the proceedings had arbitrarily arranged them in pairs.

It was day two of the auditions. Harriet – who had decided to play it cool and play hard to get by not going to Thursday's session, even though the suspense had nearly choked her – walked out onto the stage along with Ben Tierman, a tall thin spotty boy who was in year ten.

Harriet had worked it all out beforehand. She wouldn't look at Ben and definitely wouldn't look at Rob Grey, she'd compose herself and then gaze out into the hall towards the double doors at the back. Hold up her laminated sheet, take a deep breath and . . .

'For Christ's sake, get on with it, will you,' hissed Tierman through the wires on his brace. He had something green and wet wedged above one of his eye teeth.

Harriet glared at him and took another second or two to settle herself.

'Oh, for God's sake,' Tierman said.

Harriet hated him, hated him more than she thought was possible.

Rob Grey leaned forward, one hand cupping his elbow, the other his chin, all attention was fixed on the stage. As their eyes met Harriet felt the heat rising in her cheeks, followed by a peculiar tightening sensation in her chest that just looking at him gave her. He grinned which made it worse.

Finally she started to read. The words came out as a squeak, a high-pitched squeak that carried out towards the back of the hall like a party trumpet.

'God, this is ridiculous,' said Tierman, slapping his thigh with the text. He had played Azdak in the *Caucasian Chalk Circle* at Christmas and got reviews in the local papers. 'You don't have to audition to work backstage you know, just put your name down on the bloody list.'

'Who died and made you Kenneth Branagh?' Harriet snarled.

'Is there some sort of problem?' Rob asked from the floor of the auditorium, looking from one face to the other. 'Let's go again, and Harriet, relax, you've got a great voice. Come on. Let's go from the top –'

Harriet blushed, shook her head and taking another breath began again, trying hard to project tragedy and something Desdamonaesque into her tone, '"My lord what is thy will?"'

'That you fuck off out of it,' snarled Tierman under his breath, while pretending to do something Moorish with an imaginary cape.

Harriet flinched.

Everyone knew he was expecting Natalie Smith to get the female lead opposite him and if Natalie hadn't gone off to the toilets to do her hair just before going into the hall, chances were they would have ended up reading together.

Well tough shit, Tierman, Harriet thought, eyeing him angrily.

Natalie Smith was watching them from the back of the hall, she was standing with Kate.

'"Pray you, chuck, come hither."' Tierman's tone was murderous.

'Good, this is good,' said Rob from the floor, taking a swig of his coffee as Tierman finally got into the lines on the page. 'There's a really nice buzz between you two. Let's have a little more, shall we –'

Fisher had cancelled all plans for Friday to accommodate Angela's location hunting. It had been another long day.

'Sandringham House is over there,' he said to Angela, pointing down an avenue lined with what he thought might be Cedar of Lebanon although he wasn't certain, maybe they were Douglas fir. Mim would know, if only she was here; part of him really wished that she was. Ahead of them stood the gates to the main house, so enormous and so outrageously over the top that it was impossible not to be impressed. 'We could go there for lunch if you fancied it,' he said, waving in their general direction.

'You know people at Sandringham?' she said in a tone both incredulous and at the same time delighted.

Fisher reddened. 'No, no, that's not what I meant, but there's a visitors' centre with a shop and restaurant – and,' he was a little flustered, '– and they do organic things, honey and plants. If you drive down here, take the first on the right.' He was floundering and blushing now in case Angela thought him too mousy, too tame, too domesticated with no contact amongst the landed gentry.

Angela did as he said and a few minutes later they pulled over under an impressive canopy of conifers. So far they had made an early morning sortie to Wells-next-the-Sea, Holkham, Old Hunstanton, Hunstanton and several places in between. Fisher was absolutely ravenous and had a sock full of sand.

Angela yawned. 'How about we stretch our legs and then go and eat,' she said. 'Are we going to eat here? We could go back to my hotel if you'd like to?'

Fisher was about to clamber out of the Jeep – there was a definite hint of gravy on the air – when Angela swung round and pounced on him. It was stunning, in fact Fisher was so stunned that he froze like a rabbit caught in the headlights. She had wanted to hold his hand and snuggle up against him on the beach, which struck Fisher as a little odd but all right, although he hadn't said anything because he was afraid she might take offence.

'Do you feel it?' she gasped. 'The madness, the wild frantic passion, the obsession. Oh Fisher, tell me that you feel it.' Her breath was so hot it was like a blowtorch in his ear. Maybe she was sickening for something.

'Do you feel it, Fisher?' She was insistent.

He could feel the seat-belt digging into his shoulder because she was kneeling on the strap, could feel her watch rubbing up against his arm but to be honest he couldn't feel a lot else. But before he could come up with any sort of answer Angela kissed him. It was a big wet kiss that smacked him on the lips and held him tight by suction so that for an instant Fisher felt as if she had swallowed half his face. Finally pulling himself away, gasping for breath, Fisher had to resist the temptation to drag his hand across his mouth.

'Please,' he stammered. 'For God's sake, Angela. I've already told you I'm a married man. It's not that I don't find you attractive.' Which was a complete lie. Fisher had never thought of Angela as anything other than his boss, but he knew that wasn't the right thing to say. 'But I've got a wife, Angela, Mim and the children.' He dragged the emotional wagons into a circle.

Angela, eyes as bright as coal, ran a hand up over his chest and pressed a finger to his lips. 'I know, I know – and you're such a good man. That's why I love you so much, Fisher. God, this is so painful. Please don't say anything, Fisher, not a word. I want to relish this moment.'

Fisher, tactfully, leant as far away from Angela as he possibly could. It wasn't far enough. Venezuela wouldn't have been far enough. She dropped a hand onto his thigh and squeezed it tight just as his stomach rumbled angrily. It proved to be his salvation.

'Oh, how sweet, you're hungry,' she said, in a high-pitched cutesy little voice more suited to sweet-talking a lapdog. 'Better go and get our special boy some lunch then, hadn't we?'

Looking at the way Angela was writhing around in the driver's seat perhaps a cold shower might be more appropriate.

'They do a very good toad-in-the-hole here, I read it in the local paper – dish of the week, I think,' Fisher said, scrambling out of the Jeep. She was round his side of the vehicle in an instant and slipped her arm through his, pulling him close.

'I'm hungry too,' she purred, resting her head on his shoulder. Fisher swallowed hard. He wasn't altogether sure they were on the same wavelength. He'd get her a big main course – maybe a starter as well, then something with two veg and a lot of potatoes and a pudding, that ought to fix it.

In Maglington Mim had been busy working in the pottery all morning.

'Are you going to let me in, then?' snapped Sam Burke angrily. 'I've been ringing that frigging front doorbell for ages.'

He was standing under the porch by the kitchen door and appeared to be dressed in exactly the same clothes as Mim had last seen him in on Tuesday. There was an extra stain on the front of the T-shirt that looked as if it could be dried horseradish.

He might appear angry but Mim was furious and glared right back at him. She had great gobbets of clay smeared all over her hands and halfway up her forearms, there were splashes in her hair, on her face and even more on her apron. She'd been throwing the last of the beekeepers' trophies when Sam had hammered on the pottery window, making her jump so high and so hard, that she'd ruined the bowl she was working on and gone from calm focused introspection to adrenaline-charged fury in seconds.

'You are so bloody rude. You frightened the life out of me. What the hell do you want?' she growled.

Sam flinched. 'I was just passing and wondered how the plans for the garden were coming along. The sculpture – you know.' He sounded flat and hurt and unconvincing.

'Oh, all right, you'd better come in,' Mim snapped, after a moment's hesitation. 'I'll put the kettle on. I called Yolande two or three times in the week and left messages. I had expected her to get back to me.'

Mim made a point of avoiding Sam's gaze. It was true, she had rung. It was also true she'd been relieved every time when Yolande hadn't answered. If it had been hard to talk to Yolande before their aborted lunch date it would be close to impossible now. Listening to her voice on the answering machine, all Mim could see was Jack Tully and Yolande screwing like rattlesnakes out in the tool shed in the kitchen garden. Warm bodies entangled and entwined, moving like oiled silk against each other in a way that suggested that this was far from being the first time they'd danced this particular gavotte.

Every time Mim opened the sketchpad to work on the plans for Sam's woodland clearing it was Yolande and Jack and not the plans she saw. It wasn't so much the physicality of it – although for some reason the daylight had made the two of them seem all the more naked; the contrast of pale eager flesh against the rough brick walls had stayed in her mind – it was more the way Jack had been looking at Yolande. He was totally and utterly besotted with her. Jack Tully loved Yolande, a fire that burned that bright left nothing over for any-one else.

Mim couldn't have been in the shed for more than a handful of seconds, drawn by the sounds, terrified that the two of them might realise she was there and yet at the same time quite unable to resist the temptation to look, and having looked, realising she had the answers to all sorts of questions.

'Want me to make the coffee?' Sam said, indicating the clay on her hands.

'Why not,' Mim said, distractedly.

'I rang the doorbell.'

'It's broken.' She turned on the taps and started to wash the slip off her face and arms.

'Not the only thing round here, is it?' He was looking around the kitchen.

For a few brief seconds Mim saw the room as Sam saw it. There seemed little point being anything other than honest with him of all people, the man who had a degree in being up front and totally tactless. She elbowed the tap off.

'I'm sick of it, sick of the mess, sick of not being able to afford to do anything about it. I hate the place being in such a state,' she said flatly.

Sam took two mugs off the drainer. 'I'm not surprised. It must be soul destroying for someone like you to live like this.'

Mim felt tears prickle up behind her eyes. How was it possible that a man, a man as apparently obtuse as Sam, could be so sensitive to her pain?

'I haven't done that much more to the plans.'

Sam shrugged. She had a feeling that it didn't matter, that the drawings had been no more than an excuse to be away from Ganymede.

He made the coffee and followed her meekly out to the

pottery. She showed him the work she'd done since they last spoke. They drank the coffee and played at making small talk, or at least as close as Sam ever got to small talk, while all the time Mim sensed that there was something else he wanted to say, or ask or wasn't telling her. At first Mim thought that her sense of unease was because of the things that she knew.

Surely if Sam wanted to say something he would? But he didn't. It was like pulling teeth. Finally, after he had made a string of inane comments about how nice the studio looked, how light it was and complimented her on the pots and tiles and mermaids that were drying on racks, Mim was at boiling point.

'What the hell are you doing here, Sam?'

To her surprise his eyes instantly brimmed with tears. 'Yolande.'

There can be an awful lot of emotion wrapped up tight in a single word. Mim looked away in case her face revealed something Sam didn't want to know.

'I need to talk to someone, I just don't know where to start,' he said.

Mim wished that he wouldn't start at all but didn't have the heart to tell him so. 'Do you want some more coffee?' Not waiting for an answer she marched out of the studio.

'Something's wrong,' he said following her. 'She's not talking to me, and she's acting strangely – well, stranger than usual. She's distracted, distant.' Sam carried on talking, dogging Mim out to the kitchen, crowding her, walking no more than a footfall behind. Mim couldn't bear to look at him. How it was that this great bear of a man – so sensitive to her frustrations moments before – was so dense as to miss the obvious. Or was it that he didn't want to see what was staring him straight in the face?

'Sam, I don't know what help I can be, I barely know

either of you. Isn't there someone else you could discuss this with? Friends or –' It struck her that if there had been he would have been talking to them.

'I've tried talking to her. I don't know what to do. She's shutting me out. All my life she has been there. I'm not sure I've been much of a support to her, but I thought that we'd always been friends not just a married couple or lovers – I – I think she might be having –'

The phone rang. Sam stopped speaking and Mim was grateful. Anything had to be better than this. She hurried into the hall leaving him in the kitchen holding the coffee mugs.

'This is the High School here,' said an officious-sounding woman on the far end of the line, after the most basic social niceties had been exchanged.

Mim felt a little buzz of apprehension.

'Liam hasn't been in school this week and we wondered if there was anything wrong?' It was artfully worded, the tone lifting at the end of the sentence to emphasise the question.

Mim took a moment or two to collect her thoughts. Liam had left for the bus every morning and arrived home at the usual time. It was hard to believe he was skipping school, though it did occur to her that presumably most truants' parents thought the same. After the initial stab of shock Mim decided she had no intention of colluding with this woman against her son and said in an even voice, 'He'll be back next week.'

Even if she had to take him there herself and watch while he went in. And where was the little bugger if he wasn't in school? Her sense of surprise and shock was rapidly replaced by anger. All sorts of plans, thoughts and possibilities ricocheted through her head, along with disbelief and outrage and what she was going to say to Liam when she laid hands on him.

'Right, that's fine then,' the woman continued. 'Obviously this year is terribly important, with exams and –'

'Don't worry. He'll be there first thing on Monday morning,' said Mim, with a warmth and certainty she most certainly didn't feel. Her mind was still performing a series of back flips and tangential problem-solving exercises. Peter – Liam's best friend – was bound to know where Liam was, always assuming that Peter wasn't bunking off as well. Mim had picked up her handbag and car keys before she realised that Sam was still standing in the kitchen.

Not meeting his gaze, Mim said, 'I've got to go, family crisis.'

Sam looked as if he might be having one all of his own. Pale and forlorn he was still holding the coffee mugs.

On impulse Mim said, 'Do you want to come with me?' It was a stupid thing to say and by rights he should have said no. Except of course that this was Sam Burke, a man who had no idea what 'right' was. He brightened visibly.

'Right-i-o,' he said, and they both headed outside to Mim's VW.

Peter Feldman was in the sixth form common room when Mim got to the school. He had his feet up on the desk. He was eating a jam doughnut and didn't bother to empty his mouth before answering Mim.

'I've got no idea where Liam is. I assumed he was off sick. He's been looking a bit peaky lately.' He sounded smug and Mim wanted to slap him for knowing things that she didn't.

'Peter, this is serious. I need to find him.' She beaded him with the same expression she used on Liam and Harriet. He held up well for a few seconds until Sam tripped over the aerial of the TV set Peter was watching and jerked it clean out of the socket. The screen filled with a sea of angry white noise, and by some quirk of interpretation unplugging the TV appeared to be some sort of strong-arm tactic.

Peter blanched – he most certainly wasn't expecting a henchman. He looked Sam up and down and then looked back nervously at Mim.

'Well?' she asked, implying that another word might just be enough to unleash her heavyweight companion.

Peter flinched. 'I think he's with a girl.'

Mim kept her expression reined in. 'A girl? Which girl?'

Peter shrugged. Mim was really beginning to get annoyed, part of her wishing that Sam *would* pick him up and shake him till he squeaked. She leaned forward so that her face was no more than a foot away from his and hissed, 'I've just about had enough of this nonsense, Peter. Which bloody girl?'

Sam, bless his heart, leaned forward too, adding the required extra emphasis.

Peter looked from face to face and then said quickly, 'Her name's Bremner, Linda Bremner, she lives in Maglington I think, but I don't know where, not exactly.'

Mim nodded. 'Thank you.' Her tone was icy. She would have quite liked to have smacked Peter's smug little face anyway, he looked so very arrogant, but far worse she was hurt and horribly annoyed that Liam had lied to her.

'So, how was school today?' Mim had asked Liam every night that week as he wandered in while she was sorting out supper.

'Fine,' he'd said, heading upstairs, bag slung over one shoulder.

'Make sure you do your homework,' she had called up after him. God, she'd even given him a clean PE kit that morning.

'Come on,' said Mim to Sam. 'I have to find him.'

Sam caught hold of her elbow. 'Why don't you leave it until he gets home?'

Mim frowned. 'I don't really know. Because it's instinctive, because I'm furious now, because I don't think it can wait; and if I do I might blow a fuse, and short circuit something in my brain. And if I brood I'm just going to get angrier and angrier. I need to drive round frantically.'

'Fair enough,' he said, opening the common room door.

Mim had a feeling that the idiosyncrasies of women came as no great surprise to him. She smiled; against all the odds it was strangely comforting to have Sam there.

'And have you got any idea how you're going to find this Linda Bremner?'

Mim unlocked the VW. 'Local telephone directory and if that fails then the village post office.'

'Very Miss Marple.'

Mim smiled.

He looked very sweet folded up into the front seat of the VW.

Harriet wasn't altogether surprised to get the answering machine when she phoned home. Mim was probably in the pottery and had switched the phone off so she wouldn't be disturbed.

'Hi, Mum it's me,' she said brightly, 'just rung to say I'm going to be late home tonight. I've got to stay behind for a drama club thing. The teacher asked me to stay for an audition, I didn't think you'd mind. Don't worry, I'll catch the later bus – the one at quarter to six – it's all right I've got my bus pass with me.'

Harriet made every effort to sound casual and self-assured. One of the school secretaries looked as if she might be listening. After the lunch time audition Rob Grey had suggested she might like to come along after school and join in another read through with about a dozen others. Ben Tierman was beside himself with rage.

Fisher was pleased to get home. He was tired, tense and had a throbbing headache. Very quietly he closed the front door behind him and leaned against the wood, his back to it, holding it shut.

A slice of bacon and onion quiche, green salad, a baked potato and an apricot Danish had subdued Angela for a while but the cease-fire hadn't lasted. They were finishing their coffee when he saw Angela start to rev up again. Just as she was about to reach across the table and grab hold of his hand Fisher announced he had to get home for the children. Home by four, he said firmly, so they'd have to leave pretty soon to pick up his car that he'd left parked at her hotel.

For a moment Angela had looked nonplussed and then nodded with an odd little smile that suggested resignation. 'I suppose I should have guessed that you'd share the parenting.' She sighed.

Fisher nodded. 'I've got to get back for them. Mim's, um, Mim's busy sometimes . . . she has her own, her own –'

What was it Mim had? He struggled to find an explanation that sounded both plausible and big enough to wedge into the rolling machine of Angela's passion but she was already way ahead of him.

'I think it's wonderful that she's got her own life, Fisher. I do – really – and the way that you support her in that,' she murmured. 'What more could any woman want? A family, a satisfying and creative career and a man who loves and understands her.' Angela was apparently filling in the blanks for him.

Fisher had nothing to add about the state of his home

life. 'I've booked a table at the Swan for tonight so that you can meet them all, Mim, the kids, the whole family.'

Angela's eyes unexpectedly filled up with tears. 'Oh Fisher, how could you be so heartless.' Angela started rummaging around in her bag for a tissue. It sounded as if she might choke.

So, all in all it felt good to be home. The house was quiet and still, a blessed sanctuary. All this nonsense with Angela was really spoiling things. Why couldn't she control herself? Fisher glanced around the hall. He wasn't sure whether he ought to say something to her or play along, try not to upset her. He really wanted this opportunity, this chance.

Tricky though.

Mim would've known how to handle it. Fisher pulled off his jacket, slung it over the banister and headed for the pottery. He'd tell her all about Angela and she would come up with something, she was very good like that. As he reached the door he hesitated for an instant, unable to remember whether he'd told Mim that the family were going out to dinner with Angela or not. He must have done, surely.

'No, I'm sorry about that Mim, there's no one called Bremner, that I know of,' said Doreen, the woman in the post office. 'It doesn't even ring a bell. But then again these days there's no telling, is there? Her mum might have got married again or be living with someone else, or maybe she's living with an auntie or adopted, or something. Could be anything.'

Mim had come clean to the woman in the post office.

There were no Bremners listed for Maglington in the local directory or on the electoral role, and as Mim had looked down the columns, the rage slowly ebbed away to be replaced a sense of sadness and betrayal.

Behind her, Sam Burke handed the woman a giant Mars Bar and a chocolate milk shake from the minimarket.

Catching Mim's look he took a step back. 'What?' he asked defensively. 'I'm hungry. You want one?'

Without a word Mim headed back to the VW.

Fisher was not best pleased. Mim's workshop was like the *Marie Celeste*, wheel smeared with clay, tools abandoned, a dirty apron by the sink. He wanted Mim to be there. He needed her to be at home so that he could talk to her, and she wasn't. No note, no explanation and an Alpha Romeo parked in the drive. Very odd.

To try and compensate for the sense of neglect he had made himself a mug of tea and settled down at the kitchen table with the local paper when the phone started to ring. Mim probably.

'Hello?'

It was a woman but it wasn't Mim.

'Hello, I wonder if you can help me?'

Fisher fumbled round to try and put name and voice together.

'It's me, Ms Coldwell. I do hope you don't mind my ringing you at home.'

He did.

'I just wanted to share something with you. You don't mind do you?'

He did.

'Well, actually Ms Coldwell . . .' he began. It took Fisher fifteen minutes to get another word in, by which time she had given him a blow by blow account of her life since Friday. Not that she mentioned Friday by name, it seemed since they had last spoken she had developed a phobia relating to days of the week. In desperation Fisher hung up. Seconds later the phone rang again. It crossed his mind not to answer it but it might be Mim. If it was Ms Coldwell again he'd pretend to be a wrong number, or the answering machine.

'Hello, I wonder if you can help me.'

Fisher grimaced. It was a woman but it wasn't Mim. The only good thing was that he was ninety per cent certain it wasn't Ms Coldwell either.

'I'm trying to contact Miriam Pilgrim.'

He was about to suggest, curtly in the aftermath of Ms Coldwell, that she rang back later when the woman continued, 'This is Yolande Burke. Miriam's been doing some design work for me? I'm afraid I've been busy all week and didn't have chance to get back to her.'

Yolande Burke, Sam Burke's wife. Rich, famous Sam Burke, Sam Burke who now lived at Ganymede Hall and whose face had graced the Sunday colour supplements the length and breadth of the country and details of whose latest advance always made the tabloids. Sam Burke who had won the Booker. Sam Burke whom Mim knew.

'Hello,' Fisher said again, this time his tone several degrees warmer, 'Mim's mentioned you. I'm Fisher Pilgrim, her husband.'

And then a very funny thing happened, Yolande Burke laughed nervously and said in a high-pitched, slightly breathy voice, 'Oh my God, not *the* Fisher Pilgrim?' And then she laughed again, sounding genuinely impressed.

The Fisher Pilgrim from the lips of a woman whose husband was practically a household name? Fisher straightened up, not hesitating to claim his rightful place up there with the universally adored. His smile widened a little and he said, 'Yes, that's right.'

'My God, that is amazing. I watch you religiously every Thursday morning, never miss, I didn't realise that you were married to Miriam.'

Fisher felt a foot taller. 'I'm afraid Mim's not here at

the moment,' Fisher said, but Yolande was still suffering from terminal astonishment.

'What can I say?' she said. 'Perhaps you and Miriam would like to come over some time for supper. Sam would be so pleased to meet you. We know so few people locally.' She paused, when she spoke again the tone had changed a fraction. 'It would be nice to meet you. I suppose you're busy this evening? Are you busy?' She sounded desperate.

For an instant Fisher caught a glimpse, albeit fleeting, of a crock of gold. He recognised that tone. Yolande Burke needed to talk. Yolande Burke needed someone that she could confide in. The door to a whole new world opened a fraction wider and Fisher knew instinctively that this was one of those moments that cried out to be taken at the flood.

'Actually, my producer is staying at the moment and we were all going out to dinner tonight at the Swan – all of us – Mim, myself the children as well. Why don't you and Sam join us?'

Yolande laughed. 'That's very kind of you but Sam isn't very good at those sorts of thing.'

Fisher felt the moment slipping away and was about to say he could pop round another night when Yolande said, 'Why don't you come and eat here instead? I'm afraid as it's short notice it would be something simple, salad from the garden, fruit, a little wine. What do you think? Shall we say eight?'

Fisher smiled triumphantly; this was going far better than he could have possibly anticipated. 'Are you sure?'

'Oh, absolutely, I feel that we've been brought together. Guided.'

'You are truly an amazing woman,' Fisher said, his voice as warm and comforting as a woolly sweater in November, '– and we'd be delighted to come.' He took a breath and shifted the tone of his voice just a fraction, something he had been taught at Norwich, something his tutor said he had a natural gift for. 'Although I feel you need to talk to someone on a different level, without the pressure of playing hostess, don't you, Yolande? I feel you need someone who will really listen.'

It was an outrageous and presumptuous thing to say, but it worked like lucky heather.

'Oh my God,' Yolande whispered in an undertone, her voice tight with emotion. 'Is it that obvious?'

'No, not at all,' Fisher reassured her. 'I think that you've learnt to hide your pain and your distress well, Yolande, but I've been trained to pick these signal things up.'

Yolande sighed. It was the sound of a woman ready to bare her soul, to set down her worries at the feet of the master. 'Do you do private consultations?'

'Of course,' he said.

'And what about house calls?'

Fisher smiled. 'If the situation demands,' he said.

Yolande sniffed. 'When can I see you?'

'When do you want me?'

'I'll get my diary,' she said.

It was all Fisher could do to stop himself from whooping with delight.

Chapter 12

'Where have you been? I've had the most amazing day.' Fisher started talking as soon Mim got in through the back door. She had seen the school bus turning round and heading back into town as she had pulled up in the driveway.

'Is Liam here?' she asked, dropping her bag and keys onto the table.

Fisher pulled a face. 'No, neither of them is back yet. Anyway, don't worry about them. Let me tell you about my day. To be honest I don't know where to start. I got a call from Yolande Burke this afternoon, actually it was you she wanted to talk to, but anyway. She wants us to go over there to supper this evening. You'd better ring up and cancel the table at the Swan. I did mention we were going out for a meal with Angela tonight, didn't I? My instinct is that dinner isn't what Yolande wants at all, not really and Angela, well, the day I had with her – she –'

Mim swung round to confront him, seething with a strangling sense of frustration. 'Fisher, please shut up. Both of the kids ought to be home by now. Have you got any idea where Harriet and Liam are?'

He shrugged. 'No,' he said, in such a dismissive way that it was all Mim could do to stop herself from punching him.

Behind her Sam Burke sloped in through the back door. Fisher stared at him, there was a double take when his face registered some glimmer of recognition and surprise and then his mouth dropped open as Sam meanwhile emptied the tea pot and then picked up the kettle and refilled it.

Fisher frowned. 'Who the hell is that?'

Sam looked up as if noticing Fisher for the first time. 'You ought to do something about the state of this kitchen, you know. The whole bloody house come to that.' He spoke casually without any particular malice. He nodded toward the sink. 'Taps leak, grouting's shot to shit. How long would it take to put that right? Couple of hours. I couldn't live like this, it'd drive me totally nuts. Mim deserves better.'

Fisher reddened and then pulled himself up to his full height. 'Bloody cheek. Who the hell do you think you are?'

Sam stuck out his hand. 'Sam Burke, you must be Fisher? I haven't heard much about you but I think I can fill in the gaps.'

Mim suppressed a grin. Fisher's dilemma was painfully obvious – whether to follow the path of outrage and indignation that was obviously broad and well lit or veer off into something more conciliatory and sycophantic. It didn't take Fisher long to decide which. He pumped Sam's hand enthusiastically.

'Sam Burke, well, good Lord. How very nice to meet you at last. Small world. Funnily enough I was talking to your wife this afternoon. Mim mentioned that you were quite a character. Quite a character. So how are you?' Fisher punctuated his speech with not one but two totally false laughs.

Sam resumed filling the kettle while Fisher babbled on. 'Yolande suggested that we pop over for supper this evening. Did Mim mention that the TV company I work for are location hunting in the area? We're looking for somewhere with a strong sense of place and character, somewhere a little bit special. I hear you've been doing a lot of renovations on the old Hall.' He kept eye contact with Sam as the words unrolled and Mim instantly saw that Ganymede Hall had already passed like a comet through Fisher's mind. Sensing where his thoughts were going and at the same time angry that he didn't see their children's non-appearance as important, Mim snapped, 'For God's sake Fisher never mind your bloody television programme, where exactly are the children?'

Fisher's expression hardened as if she had snatched some precious moment away from him. 'How the hell should I know, Mim, you're the one who is supposed to be at home all day.'

Speechless, Mim went out to the hall. First she would ring the school to see if Harriet had missed the bus. Family rules stated that in case of emergencies the kids should go back into the school and phone home.

It was a relief to see the light on the answering machine flashing, even more so when Mim pressed the button and heard Harriet's voice, slightly defensive and yet at the same time defiant, telling her about drama club. Fine. A little of the tension in Mim's shoulders eased.

Now there was just Liam to deal with. From the kitchen she could make out Fisher talking in his best Sunday voice, although as she walked back in she could see Sam appeared to be far from impressed.

'Tea?' said Sam, handing her a mug. 'Have you managed to track them down yet?'

Mim murmured her thanks and then said, 'Harriet's stayed after school to go to a drama thing.' The tea was strong and hot and exactly what she needed.

'And what about your boy?'

'No idea. I don't know what to do about him.'

Sam took a long slurp of tea. 'Don't worry. He'll be fine.'

Mim laughed. 'Not when I get my hands on him.'

Odd that it was a man who barely knew any of them who was most concerned about her children. On the other side of the kitchen table it appeared that Fisher was hanging on to Sam's every word and yet quite obviously hearing none of them.

As soon as Sam left, Fisher rang Angela's hotel.

'Angela,' Fisher whispered, 'I think I may have found the perfect solution to the location situation.' He cupped the receiver before glancing over his shoulder to see if he could be overheard or whether Mim had followed him out into the hall.

Angela sighed. 'Your dedication is amazing, Fisher. Maybe you could come by the hotel early and have a little drink before dinner? I think there are still some points that we have to mull over.' Her voice was soft and suggested everything except business. 'We could meet up with your family later. At the restaurant.'

Undeterred Fisher pressed on. 'That's what I wanted to talk to you about. Have you heard of Sam Burke? The writer? He's a novelist? He won the Booker. He's been in the Sunday colour supplements and wrote that series for Channel 4 – and a film I think?' Fisher wondered how far he would have to go before Angela knew who he meant.

'Yes, yes. Sam Burke.' She didn't sound that interested or that impressed.

'The thing is he lives in the village in a great big pseudo-Elizabethan pile. He was round this afternoon. Yolande – that's his wife –' Fisher daren't risk Angela not having heard of her, 'has asked us to go over for supper tonight. Mim has taken on a commission for a sculpture for their garden, and I happened to mention the programme and that we needed somewhere special as a backdrop for the pilot.'

He left a pause, enough of an opening for Angela to fall

in head first. He sensed that he had Angela's attention. 'It's a fantastic house in its own grounds.'

'We are talking about *the* Sam Burke, aren't we?'

It was the same tone that Yolande had used about him not more than two hours earlier.

'Uh-huh.'

'The same Sam Burke who refuses to be interviewed and punches reporters?' Angela was beginning to sound interested, actually a lot more than interested, she sounded excited. 'It's his home, right? God, that would be great.'

Fisher felt a slight ripple of unease as if he had inadvertently lit the fuse to a bomb he didn't know existed.

'I suppose it must be him –' Fisher began, aware that he had already taken a colossal leap into the void between truth and faith by implying that the location was as good as in the bag.

'Sounds extremely promising. Did you say he's invited us over for supper this evening?'

'Yes, well, his wife did.'

'Wonderful, look I need to talk to Sven about this one.'

'What about?' said Fisher, but he sensed he had already lost Angela's attention.

'What time are we eating?'

'Eight, but I thought –' he began. He planned to suggest they went for a drink first at the Swan.

'Okay. I'll come over and pick you and the rest of the family up. This may be just the handle we need to get Sven on side.'

'What do you mean? I thought you said he was really keen?' Fisher's voice quivered. 'Do you mean that he isn't?'

'Er, oh no, that wasn't what I meant at all, no,' said Angela dismissively. 'I'll see you at around eight.'

'But we have to be there by eight.'

Angela laughed and hung up.

Fisher stared at the receiver and wondered what fashionably late actually meant.

Sven was still in his office. Since talking to Fisher Angela's brain had been working overtime. 'The way I see it Sven, is that we could do the whole show in a different celebrity home each week.' Angela made no attempt to keep the excitement out of her voice, Sven liked enthusiasm even if it wasn't his natural territory.

'There have to be hundreds of washed up, dried out has-beens and also-rans out there who would leap at the chance of a little free exposure. We'd make sure they came across as big wounded human beings, braver and wiser but still unbroken. You know the kind of thing. The press'll eat it up. I see us doing a little cameo piece, how I coped with . . .' Angela was about to say rehab but remembered just in time that Sven's latest live-in bimbette had checked into the Priory and both his kids had been in and out of every detox, de-stress, get-clean-in-a-hundred-and-one-different-ways clinics the length and breadth of the known world.

'. . . their latest break-up, or whatever. We could cover a different area every week. Depression, dependency, dipsomania. We already know Fisher would be perfect and then after we've talked to the celebrities we bring in the punters. People who've gone through the same things as the rich and famous, ordinary grubby little proles talking about how they coped. Money doesn't divide or protect you from that kind of thing. I really think it'll fly, Sven. I can see us generating some really powerful TV here.'

There was an intense little pause and then Sven said, 'Tears?'

'Without a doubt.'

'Sordid revelations under stress?'

'I hope so.'

'Fights?'

'If we're very lucky,' said Angela.

'Sounds on the button to me. Although starting off with some middle-class, arty-farty writer might be a bit upmarket for the target audience.'

'He looks like a bad-tempered pirate and punches reporters.'

There was another little pause and then Sven said, 'Although obviously we do have an obligation to widen our viewers' horizons and stretch them intellectually. And maybe between now and air time we could up the ante a little, generate a little excitement. A little press attention maybe? See if the boy still bites?'

'My thoughts exactly.'

The silence that followed was positively gleeful.

Harriet settled back in the bucket seat of Rob Grey's dinky little sports car and wondered if any of the others had seen her leaving with him. The second stage of the audition had gone really well, or at least a lot better than the one at lunch time. She hadn't had to read with Ben Tierman for a start, although Rob had said that he was anxious to explore the tension between the two of them, whatever that meant. As they were packing up to leave he had offered her a lift home.

Rob gunned the engine. Harriet strapped herself in and then settled back, closed her eyes. God, this was wonderful. They could be going anywhere, just the two of them. He was so good-looking. It felt as if her whole body was trembling. What would she do if he leaned over and kissed her now, or ran his hand up her thigh? What would she do if he . . .

'Are you feeling all right?'

The sound of Rob's voice made Harriet jump and her eyes snap open.

'Sorry?'

They weren't even out of the school grounds yet. She blushed furiously.

'It was just that you'd closed your eyes, I wondered if you were feeling sick or something? Do you want me to open a window?'

Quickly Harriet sat up and began to tidy herself. 'No, no, I'm fine, thank you,' she said, 'just, just – a bit tired that's all. It's been a long day.' She could have kicked herself, it was the sort of thing that her mother might say.

He nodded. 'At your age you need to make sure you're eating a balanced diet. Not just burgers and fries down at Goldes. You need protein, vitamins –'

Harriet stared at him in surprise; it sounded like something her dad or mum would say, although then again he was older, and she was touched that he was concerned about her welfare.

They drove in silence towards Maglington. Harriet wasn't exactly sure what to say and Rob appeared to be deep in thought. It wasn't an uncomfortable silence though. Harriet was careful not to close her eyes again but it didn't stop her mind from running through all sorts of interesting ideas.

Finally, as they pulled up under the trees near Harriet's house and she was about to get out of the car, Rob said, 'There is something I've been meaning to ask you for a while now. I hope you won't be offended.'

Offended? Her heart skipped a beat. There was almost nothing she wouldn't have agreed to. Harriet swung round, heart thumping out a samba rhythm and found herself quite unable to speak.

'The thing is –' he began.

She could feel his eyes on her. Harriet hung on tight to every single word.

'My wife and I don't know many people in the village and I wondered if you would consider baby-sitting for us? We'd pay you the going rate, obviously. We need to have someone to look after Paddy that we can trust.'

Harriet's mouth rushed to the rescue while her heart sank without trace beneath the waves of disappointment. 'Sure, yeh. But not school nights though, I don't think my mum would let me do school nights,' said a distant voice she vaguely recognised as her own.

'That's great,' Rob said, 'only my wife is getting cabin fever stuck in the house all the time with our little boy. Not that he's any trouble. I'd drive you home obviously.' And then he grinned up at her. It was a warm, lazy, open grin that made her heart tighten. Harriet held his gaze for an instant too long. And then she saw it. Baby-sitting would mean that she would see more of him, have more reason to talk to him, see him off-duty, away from school, see him when he drove her home.

Harriet's heart warmed to a degree off boiling point. 'Thanks for the lift.'

'You're welcome, fair lady. Oh and don't forget drama club tomorrow, senior hall three till five if you can make it, new members are always welcome,' he said, winking and tugging at an imaginary forelock.

Harriet blushed. Maybe this wasn't such a bad move after all.

And then he leaned a little closer and brushed her cheek with his fingers. 'You're a real sweetheart.' Harriet thought she might just die.

Any alarm bells that might have rung were silenced by the sheer joy she felt inside. Rob Grey liked her, he really liked her, it wasn't just a figment of her imagination.

Harriet practically skipped up the path.

Inside in the kitchen things couldn't have been more different.

'Hiya love, I need you to get yourself upstairs, have a shower and get ready,' said Mim, who was doing the washing-up. 'And bring your uniform down for washing. Dad's boss is picking us up around eight and I'd like you out of the bathroom before I want to get in there.'

'I know, I know, best dress, no cheek, no spitting or swearing.' Harriet grimaced. 'To be honest I don't know why we've got to go at all.'

'Frankly, me neither,' said Mim, handing her a glass of milk shake. She paused and then said quietly, 'I need to talk to you about Liam and before you leap to his defence or his rescue I do know that he hasn't been in school this week.'

Harriet coloured slightly, wondering what else Mim might know.

'Do you know a girl called Linda Bremner?'

Harriet sighed with relief. She hadn't asked whether Harriet had caught the bus, or who had brought her home if not, or anything. 'Is there anyone who doesn't?'

'Me,' said Mim slowly. 'There's a good chance that Liam has been skipping school to be with Linda. Does she live in the village?'

Harriet was incredulous. 'Yeh. Up at the Backs on the council estate.'

'And what's she like?'

Harriet felt uncomfortable. This wasn't what she'd been expecting at all. 'You know,' she said waving a hand dismissively.

'No, I don't know or I wouldn't be asking you.'

Harriet's felt her colour intensify. 'A bit, well, you know –'

Mim was still staring at her. God, how do you tell

your parents this sort of thing. 'Easy, Linda's a bit of a tart.'

Mim had known, she'd just wanted someone to say it out loud.

But Harriet had found her voice now. 'I'll kill him, the little pig. He told me he was on study leave with Peter, and that I wasn't to tell you because you'd want him to go into school instead. I didn't know about –' she stopped and then said carefully. 'You know, her. So, has he been with Linda Bremner all week?'

'Your guess is a good as mine, but yes, probably. He certainly hasn't been in school.'

'And is that where he is now?'

'I really don't know.'

Mim saw Harriet moving effortlessly into the role of the good child. 'Don't worry Mum, I'm sure he'll be all right. I'll go upstairs and get ready.' She stopped at the kitchen door. 'What did Dad say about Liam and Linda?'

'I haven't had a chance to talk to him about it yet –' Mim began and as she spoke the phone rang and Fisher, as if he had been waiting in the wings for his cue, leapt out of the study and snatched up the receiver.

'Hello?' he said in the silky smooth man-of-the-world voice, and then, 'Oh it's you,' in a tone altogether more work-a-day.

Whoever it was on the far end of the line, Fisher's disappointment was obvious. 'All right I'll tell her, hang on.'

Some sixth sense made Mim scurry past Harriet into the hall.

Fisher said, 'It's Liam, he said he's going to be late, he's helping out at some after-school club.'

The words were barely out of his mouth before Mim had snatched the receiver out of his hand and snapped, 'Liam,

I'd like you to say goodbye to your extracurricular activities and get your arse home now. Do you hear me? Now!' The tone was emphatic and brooked no contradiction.

Fisher stared open mouthed as Mim slammed the receiver down and headed back into the kitchen.

'Mim? Mim?' He scuttled after her. 'What on earth is the matter with you? Is there a problem? Do you need to talk about this? Surely you must realise that Liam needs other activities besides home and the family. He ought to be allowed to help out at the youth club. We both have to accept that they will eventually grow up and leave the nest – as people we all –'

Mim swung round. 'Fisher, for God's sake shut up, will you?' she growled. 'I've been trying to talk to you about this since you got home but you've too been busy smarming around Sam Burke, talking on the phone to your precious bloody Angela and holed up in your sodding office doing God knows what –'

'This level of aggression is –'

Mim rounded on him. 'Is perfectly justified, Fisher. Liam has been skiving off school all this week. From what I can gather he's spent most of it in the company of some girl called Linda from the council estate and if that isn't justification enough he's also been lying through his eye teeth to both of us. Mostly to me, mostly first thing in the morning. I ironed his bloody tennis whites last night.'

She saw Fisher's expression change and then to her astonishment he said, 'You know, Mim, it's terribly wrong to judge people by where they are being brought up, just because this girl lives on a council estate doesn't mean for one moment that she isn't a perfectly decent person.'

Mim stared at him in complete amazement. She thought she might swallow her tongue in pure fury. 'Fisher, I don't care if Linda Bremner is one of the crowned heads of

Europe, she and our son have spent all week bunking off school doing God knows what.'

'Well, exactly,' said Fisher in a calm oily voice.

'What?' Mim said. The reply felled her.

'Exactly. God knows what. It could all be perfectly innocent. Here you are jumping to all sorts of premature conclusions, Mim. Before getting in such an emotional turmoil about the situation I really feel we need to discuss this whole thing with Liam. In fact I think perhaps we ought to have a family conference about how we relate to each other and how we respect each other's emotional space.'

Mim was murderous. She had three thoughts layered like angel cake in her brain. They surprised her. The first thought was how was it she had ended up married to such an idiot. The second was what Yolande Burke might or might not manage to conjure up for supper, and the third was how hard you would have to hit someone with a baseball bat before they didn't get up again, and how very nice it might be to find out.

Fisher smiled at her. He had no idea what danger he was in.

'I'll be in the study if anyone needs me,' he said. 'And let me know when Liam gets back.' He hesitated and then said, 'It's early yet, why don't you go and have a little rest before we go out for dinner? I was reading in that booklet I picked up that pre-menopausal women get overtired and that can affect their judgement.' Before Mim could think of a suitable reply, Fisher slipped back into his office.

Harriet, having read the storm warning in her mother's eyes, beat a hasty retreat upstairs leaving Mim all alone in the hall to wait for Liam. Mim wasn't altogether sure exactly why she was quite so angry but it felt strangely satisfying, like finding a part of herself that she had had no idea existed up until that moment.

* * *

In the privacy of her hotel room Angela stretched full-length on the bed and glanced down at the notes she had started to make on her clipboard. Fisher was such a sweetie.

'Yes, that's right, *the* Sam Burke. I've just been chasing up the facts and figures with the guys back at the office. He won the Booker, wrote the screenplay for the film about – er – can you still hear me?'

The hotel phone had an irritating little buzz on it but it had to be better than wandering round playing chase the signal on her mobile. What did these people *do* out in the sticks?

She and Mel, the guy who ran the media desk on the *Daily Argos*, went back all the way to a tumultuous affair at film school that had ended badly. Very badly. He owed her and she had no hesitation at all in using the rope to haul him in when the situation demanded. Not that the lovely Mel had much to complain about or needed much hauling. She had given him some juicy little tit-bits and a couple of really decent exclusives in the years in between now and then. And slept with him when he was between marriages.

'The plan is to feature Sam Burke on this show but if I have it my way this is going to be the first of many. I thought we might possibly do a piece on male aggression, the whole machismo thing or maybe if he won't talk, then his wife might – you know, what it's like to live with the rumours of violence, reputations influencing expectations – I'm not sure yet. I need to talk to the two of them but it could be very sexy. Sam Burke's a good-looking bunny, dark and brooding with nice stubble and a petulant expression.'

'Uh-huh and the angle for me is what exactly?' Mel said, sounding tired and grumpy. 'Your Fisher Pilgrim is pretty small beer; happily married family man solves people's problems. I could probably get him a nice little photo feature on the women's pages promoting sweaters if you fancy it – oh no, he's the guy with the denim shirts, isn't he? We could probably réchauffe the denim industry single-handed. How about a button-down collar give-away?'

'Oh, come on, Mel, run with me on this one. You have to admit it's a great idea for a format. The chance to spill your guts on national TV with a guy who could listen for England. The guests get the chance to set the record straight publicly. It's pure dynamite if you ask me. I'll let you have some names of other possible guests after the weekend when we've had chance to put some feelers out. Why don't you put someone onto it? Go on, Mel. Sam Burke has a reputation for being volatile, I shouldn't think you'll have to stir too hard or push too far to get a story out of this one.'

'And you're definitely all set to use him and his house for the pilot episode of what's-his-face's new show?'

Angela bit down hard on the end of her pencil, considering her reply. Fisher sounded pretty certain that Sam would play ball and besides, if they didn't get Sam Burke's country house as a location because the story had been leaked to the press then it would still make good copy. Volatile novelist in U-turn on new TV agony programme. If they could just get him to punch someone. Maybe Fisher.

Mim heard the back door close very quietly and waited for Liam to come and find her. She had started to clean up the pottery while waiting for him to come home.

The door opened very slowly.

'Hello,' Liam said. He made no attempt to meet her eyes, but there wasn't a shred of defiance in his body language.

'Hello,' said Mim, rinsing her hands. 'You want to sit down and tell me what the hell you think you're playing at?' She spoke in the gentlest of voices.

He was still staring at his boots. 'No, not really.'

'Do I have to lecture you?'

'No.'

'Right, well go and get washed and changed, we've all got to go out to this dinner with your dad tonight but after that you're grounded. Do you understand? Do you need me to take you into school every day to make sure you get there?'

Liam's ears were bright red, and although she couldn't see his face she did see him shaking his head.

'And about this girl. Linda, isn't it?'

Liam looked up, his eyes were brimming with tears that made him look closer to seven than seventeen.

'I'm certainly not going to ask you what you've been up to or say that you're not to see her again because I was your age once too, believe it or not, and I know all about this stuff. Just make sure you see her after school. Maybe you could invite her to come here to tea.'

'What?' hissed Liam.

Mim sighed. 'You can invite Linda to come round here tomorrow for tea so that we can all meet her. What I am saying though, Liam, is that this is all about growing up and being treated like an adult. Although I do understand, I don't want you bunking off to be with her. If you do that then you can get your arse out of sixth form and into a job.'

He blanched. 'A job?'

Mim nodded. 'If you're not studying then you're wasting your time at school, playing around, and I'm not paying for you to play around.' She picked up the local paper and gave it to him. It was open at the situations vacant columns. 'Here we are. Halfway down, they want a full-time fisher fryer at the Big Chipper in town, twenty pence an hour above the minimum wage, uniform provided; if not, then they're looking for people at the vegetable trimming place. Free bus service from all the outlying villages.'

Liam stepped back as if she'd slapped him.

Mim's expression remained totally impassive.

'But I want to go to university,' he said in a sad little voice.

'Fine, then in that case you better get your act together. You're too old for me to lay down the law, Liam, by now you ought to be able to work out the consequences of your actions for yourself.' Mim folded the newspaper up and handed it to him. 'Your life, your choice. And by the way, if you want the job in the chip shop the applications have to be in by Monday lunch time.'

For a moment their eyes met and they both grinned. All anger gone Mim smiled. 'Go and get changed, and then you can ring Linda and see if she can come round tomorrow.'

'Ah, there you are, I thought I heard the back door go,' Fisher said to Liam as he came bowling into the pottery. 'Now, I'd like to talk to you about what's been going on. Oh and I've found this leaflet on teenage sexuality that I thought you might find useful.'

Mim and Liam both burst into laughter at the same time.

Fisher was outraged. 'What, what?' he blustered. 'Tell me, what is so bloody funny?'

Chapter 13

Everyone made an effort for Fisher's big dinner. Harriet wore a dress, Liam wore a tie and Mim spent a long time on her make-up.

They all looked good, even Fisher in his trademark denim shirt, despite Mim thinking that perhaps he was overdoing it as a motif. At half-past seven everyone was in the sitting room ready and waiting for Angela to arrive. The minutes ticked by.

By quarter past eight Mim suggested that she went ahead with the kids in the VW and that Fisher and Angela followed on later. After all they were all ready. More than ready.

Fisher said no. He was absolutely adamant. They would all go together, with Angela. They just had to be patient, it wasn't easy. Fisher checked his appearance one more time in the mirror above the fireplace and smiled at his reflection. Again.

By half-past eight Mim didn't think she could take much more. The clock tick-tick-ticked the minutes away. Unhappy at being ignored the cat was busy hacking up a fur ball on the kitchen floor. Harriet and Liam were past bored, fidgety and beginning to bicker.

'I really think we ought to leave now Fisher, or at least ring up and tell Yolande and Sam that we're going to be late.'

Fisher frowned but said nothing.

Mim hadn't dare mention that it was quite likely they would arrive at Ganymede only to discover Yolande had forgotten she'd invited them at all. Cleaning up after the cat with a handful of kitchen roll Mim had a vivid but fleeting vision of the five of them wandering in through the open front doors to discover Yolande Burke and Jack Tully *in flagrante delicto* across the dining-room table.

By twenty-five to nine Fisher's agitation was finally beginning to show. The combination of him picking at his collar, pacing and pretending to be relaxed and unconcerned in combination with the children's grumbling and grimacing was almost unbearable.

At quarter to nine Angela finally rolled up outside the front door and blew her horn not once but three times in succession, three short blasts that suggested she wasn't a woman to be trifled with.

Mim was nearly killed in the rush to get out of the front door.

Angela didn't bother to get out of the Jeep to greet them, instead she reached across to pop open the passenger side door. Fisher was up on the running board and inside the Jeep like a rat up a drainpipe, leaving Mim, Harriet and Liam to let themselves in and clamber up into the back seats which were strewn with all kinds of folders, boxes and bags. The footwells were full of empty fast food wrappers, crisp packets, burger boxes and lidded plastic beakers.

Angela kissed Fisher enthusiastically on both cheeks before nodding at the rest of them. She was dressed in a turquoise halter top, tight cream capri pants and pink kitten heel mules. She had a pair of wrap-around sunglasses on top of her head keeping her hair back and adding a little extra something to the whole ensemble. Mim noticed the details when she got to her feet to try and find a comfortable place to sit on the rear seat which felt as if it been made out of pre-cast concrete.

'I've talked to Sven this evening,' Angela said by way

of conversation, completely excluding Mim and the kids. 'And he is knocked back by the whole idea of using Sam Burke, I mean really. I think we're looking at the potential for some really powerful TV here. Where exactly is this place? Do I need to go back the way I've just come? Shame I didn't bring Jimmy with me really – you know, Jimmy the outside broadcast guy? He's so good on location. I was wondering whether we should ring and get him down here first thing tomorrow morning to look at Sam Burke's house.'

Mim had to run the words through again to make sure she was sure of what she'd heard. Pilgrim had told Angela that she could use Ganymede for his new show.

Meanwhile Angela pulled out without a backward glance, ignoring the squeal of brakes and furious horn work of the red saloon she cut in front of. Mim winced and couldn't help wondering if Fisher was in way over his head with this woman.

Angela talked all the way there.

Ganymede Hall was – as Mim had feared – in complete darkness when they drove up to the front doors although Angela was extremely impressed by the neatly trimmed verges of the estate road and gatehouse she saw on the drive up. It was easy to tell she was impressed because she kept bobbing up and down, leaning forward and peering out of the windows, murmuring, 'Oh yes, oh yes, this is perfect. I can see how this will work. Sam Burke, rich but emotionally bankrupt. Great, great. People enjoy seeing the rich in real pain, the kind that even money can't insulate you from, it's that kind of serves-you-right factor.'

Beside her, Fisher squirmed, as if trying to vanish into the depths of his leather bucket seat.

As the Jeep jerked to a halt amongst a spray of gravel

Angela framed a shot with her short stubby fingers. 'I can see it now – Sam Burke walking up from the stream down there, moving slowly through the mist. Head bowed, hands in his pockets. A broken man. I assume he is broken, isn't he? We'll need a Barbour. Do you think he's got a Barbour? A dog would be nice. Did you say his wife had a drink problem or is it drugs?'

Fisher blustered. Mim suspected that he was trying to avoid any sort of answer in front of his family that revealed just how little he knew about the Burkes. Mim felt herself observing Fisher with a growing sense of disgust. What the hell had he told Angela, and more to the point what was it that he had promised her? To deliver the heads of Sam and Yolande Burke side by side on a silver platter?

There was a pregnant pause and then Fisher clapped his hands and said, 'Right, fine. Then, okay let's – let's – go in, shall we?'

He stopped and looked helplessly back at Mim who refused to meet his eye and instead shooed Harriet and Liam out of the vehicle and set off towards the main doors. It was obvious that Fisher had implied that he was bosom buddies with the Burkes when – as far as Mim knew – he had met Sam for a very strained twenty minutes or so in their kitchen that afternoon and hadn't met Yolande at all.

However, nothing about the way he had treated Mim, nothing that he had said since he had told her about the invitation to supper inclined her to support him or buffer his passage.

As Mim and the children got to the door a security light, presumably triggered by movement, flashed on, catching them in a cool halogen glare, and an instant later, just before they were plunged back into grey evening gloom, the ornate double doors of Ganymede opened a fraction and Sam Burke peered out.

'She's pissed off,' he said.

Mim stared at him. 'What do you mean pissed off? Gone? Yolande's gone?'

'No, not pissed off, she's pissed off with me. That's what she told me tonight when I came in. Although, actually what she said was that she felt that our vibrations were in astral conflict. Do you think that's bad? That's bad, isn't it?'

Mim sighed.

'And then she said she needs to talk to someone on a different level, without the pressure of playing wife. Someone who will really listen. She told me that was why she asked Fisher over here tonight.'

Their eyes met and a wealth of knowing and understanding and amazement was exchanged.

'It was a spur of the moment invitation, Sam, has she cooked anything?' Mim said, imagining sending Angela and Fisher down to the chip shop for a fish supper. It was a thought that had surfaced several times en route.

Sam nodded. 'Yeh, yeh. She and Tully have been stuck in the kitchen for hours.'

So at least there was food, the kids were ravenous. Then Mim reconsidered. An earlier image of the pair of them resurfaced, maybe it was hasty to jump to any conclusions – maybe Yolande and Jack Tully were round the back shagging like spaniels under the kitchen table amongst an explosion of rocket and raducchio. Mim took a deep breath and snuffed the image out like a candle flame; all this sexual imagery was really going to have to stop if she had any chance of getting through the evening.

Meanwhile Harriet was staring up at Sam with undisguised interest.

Sam glared back at her. 'What?'

Harriet wasn't in the least bit fazed by his rudeness.

'My mum said that you are a famous writer. What sort of things do you write?'

Sam didn't hesitate. 'Books where everyone says fuck a lot.'

Harriet and Liam both attempted unsuccessfully to stifle a laugh. 'Cool,' said Liam.

Sam nodded in the direction of the Jeep. 'See you brought Mr TV and his evil sidekick, Blondie, with you. What does she look like in that top?'

Liam and Harriet both laughed again, Mim fought the temptation and very nearly succeeded.

Fisher and Angela were still picking their way across the gravel. Angela's mule heels made the going tricky. As they reached the trigger point the light came on again and Fisher smiled up into its icy eye.

Sam turned and disappeared inside. Mim followed with the children but not before she saw Angela grin impishly and Fisher mouth 'Artistic temperament,' his lips working overtime to make sure Angela didn't miss a single syllable. Mim also noticed, before the light went out, that despite Fisher's apparent bravado, he had a tight little tic lurking in the corner of one eye and a distinct pallor around the gills.

Once inside everyone was impressed by the entrance hall, but much less so by the odour that was emanating from one of the corridors. It was a fishy, gutter-like, drainy, oceanic smell, that refused to be ignored and made everyone swallow hard.

None of the adults said a word.

'Jesus, what on earth is that?' said Liam, pulling a face, quite unable to contain himself, as Sam led them down through the bowels of the house. If anything the smell was getting steadily worse.

'Kelp, I think,' said Sam, directing them through double doors into an old-fashioned conservatory overlooking the grounds. The room was as warm and moist as a laundry, with vines and tumbles of rich greenery falling out of the troughs that lined the wall.

'Yolande boils it up with onions and soy sauce, and something else. It's very rich in – in, something or other that's really good for you.'

'And people eat it?' said Harriet aghast.

'People do, I don't,' said Sam, pouring himself a large whisky from the bottle on a side table that was concealed amongst the undergrowth. It seemed that leading them through the labyrinth was the extent of Sam's hostly duties.

When in Rome. Mim picked up a glass and helped herself to a small brandy, topping it up with coke and ice. It tasted really good.

'Oh my God, are we going to have eat it?' continued Harriet, her voice unnaturally loud and – not quite sure whether she was the butt of some terrible adult joke – filled with a genuine horror. 'I'll puke.'

Mim felt no urge whatsoever to rein her daughter in or to remind her of her manners, despite frantic messages being semaphored across the room by Fisher's eyebrows.

Angela joined Mim by the drinks table, poured a tall glass of Evian over ice and added a lot of vodka; they might have to get a cab home.

'So, Sam,' Angela said, lighting up a cigarette. 'Exciting place you've got here. Filming shouldn't take long, though obviously at this stage I've got no idea of what sort of schedule we'll be working to. Standard rates obviously – I'm not trying to rip you off. We'll need to see the kind of response we get from the ads for participants before we can really work out exactly how the show is going to work. What I'd really like to do is go over the whole place with Jimmy, talk about what we want to achieve visually, what we're looking for. Where is your wife at the moment

– I mean, can we talk frankly in front of her? Have you got an agent who deals with all this sort of thing? I presume you have?'

There was a silence that opened up, into which the Empire State building and possibly the *Titanic* could have vanished unnoticed leaving lots of room to spare.

Sam looked across at Mim who shrugged.

'What are you talking about?' he said to Angela. Although, before Angela had chance to answer, Sam turned to Mim for help. 'What the fuck is she talking about?'

Mim looked across the room. 'Fisher?'

Fisher looked from face to face, pale and desperate like a man slipping slowly, inexorably over the edge of a precipice.

'Well, I was um, um, talking to Yolande about the, the um – the thing is . . .' He took a deep breath and puffed his cheeks out.

Every eye in the room was on him.

But, remarkably, salvation was at hand. Before Fisher had chance to compose the rest of his reply there was a terrifying scream from somewhere deep in the house that echoed horribly up through the corridors.

'Yolande. Oh my God – quickly,' yelped Sam and scurried out of the room, followed for some reason by Fisher and the children. Mim considered her options and then poured a little more brandy into her glass. She hadn't eaten since sharing a Mars Bar and a milk shake with Sam at the post office at around three o'clock. The alcohol swept through her bloodstream like a bush fire.

Perhaps she ought to go and help Sam. Fisher was useless in a crisis and sometimes much worse than useless, catching the panic and flapping round, making stupid suggestions and getting in the way. Finally, pricked by a nosey conscience, Mim set her glass down on a little wrought-iron table under an overenthusiastic rubber plant. Angela, it seemed, was torn between the call of the vodka and the need to be seen to be concerned and involved.

'I'd faint if there was any blood,' she said, draining the tumbler, as Mim headed after the main party, wondering if she would be able to track them down in the rabbit warren of corridors.

'I've had therapy, two years, you know.'

Lost for words Mim set off in the general direction of the kitchen. The smell led her the rest of the way.

It was not a pretty sight. A large plastic bowl of something grey-green and unpleasantly fetid had melted or possibly exploded all over the inside of the microwave and was now dripping down the unit underneath. Yolande appeared to have scalded herself retrieving whatever was left, although it was obvious Jack Tully had the whole situation under control.

Sam, frustrated at being edged out of the role of rescuer and unable to help in any practical way, shifted from foot to foot and – in his role as observer and recorder – repeated what had happened for Mim's benefit.

A woman, who wore the apron and long-suffering expression of hired help, was busy mopping the floor, Yolande had her hand under cold running water, while everyone else stood around the periphery looking like ghouls who'd turned up to stare at a car crash.

On the floor, outside the arc of the woman's mopping, were the remains of what looked as if it might once have been an alien life form that had been blown to pieces. Mim blinked in an effort to clear her head; the brandy was maybe not such a good idea.

Beyond the carnage, set out on the kitchen table were various bowls of salad, plates of sliced cold meats, a selection of cheeses and two huge dishes of new potatoes.

'We were all ready to call you. Yolande and I were

just putting the finishing touches to the soup,' Jack said. 'Shame about spilling it but there we are.' As he spoke he caught Mim's eye and winked.

Yolande, despite everything, elegant in a pale blue, floor-length kaftan covered in a striped butcher's apron, looked from face to face and then smiled with all the composure of the good hostess trained to cope with every eventuality.

'Nice of you all to come. We thought we'd have supper in the breakfast room, it's much more intimate, why don't you show them through, Sam, and get everyone a drink? I'll be there in a moment –' As Sam went to lead them out Mim noticed Yolande nodding towards Fisher with an expression bordering on adoration.

The breakfast room was candlelit and overlooked a small terrace, a smooth stretch of lawn and beyond that a stand of mature trees – another tail of woodland wrapping itself artfully around the shoulders of the old house.

Once inside Sam touched Mim on the arm, then prodded Harriet and pointed out into the fading light.

'What?' hissed Harriet, her curiosity immediately attracting Liam's attention. The four of them stared out into the velvet-edged gloom.

Mim was puzzled and then as her eyes adjusted to the fading light she saw that under the skirts of the woodland a tiny monkjack doe and her fawn were tippy-toeing their way across the grass, stopping every few yards to nibble at the tender tops of the freshly mown lawn.

On the periphery of her consciousness Mim registered the fact that Jack Tully had followed Sam and the Pilgrim family into the breakfast room and, usurping Sam, had begun to serve drinks and that Yolande arrived seconds later and was busy introducing herself to Fisher. Even then Sam and Mim hung back in the pleat of silence they had found and watched the deers' silent progress until mother and child finally vanished like ghosts into the inky blackness of the night wood.

Mim shivered, thinking how wonderful her sculpture would look in those secret night time places, sharing the darkness with the deer, and how they would witness all kinds of things that she would never see.

Jack handed her a glass of white wine spritzer and no one resisted when Yolande asked them all to take their places at the table. As soup was off the menu they waded straight into the first course which had appeared along the length of a refectory table. The place settings were arranged so that Yolande and Sam sat at either end of the table. Fisher and Jack Tully were on Yolande's right and left respectively, then Liam and Harriet sat opposite each other, next to Liam Mim, and then finally Sam.

There was very little ceremony. Despite the lingering smell of par-boiled alien everyone was hungry. The children were ravenous. Fisher had to ask Liam to put back some of the potatoes he had piled up on his plate. Mim poured herself a glass of wine, wondering if the cold beef was off the same joint she'd seen earlier in the week. It was a while before Mim realised that they had completely forgotten about Angela.

She was still waiting in the conservatory, drunk, and very maudlin, sitting between two big pots of something dark green and tropical. Mim wasn't sure why she was the one who had felt obliged to go and find Angela.

Angela looked up through the gloom, panda-eyed with smeared mascara. 'Is she all right?'

Mim nodded. 'Yolande? Oh yes, she's absolutely fine. Soup's off though. We've just started dinner.' It would be a gross untruth to say that they were about to start. Liam was on his second helping.

'To be honest I'm not that hungry.'

'Better come and have something. It's not a very good idea to drink on an empty stomach.'

Angela looked thoughtfully into her glass. 'My big chance this, you know, first major project. My future is in Fisher's hands.'

Mim didn't like to point out that he'd always been clumsy and prone to dropping things.

Angela looked up at Mim, eyes misted with Smirnoff. 'You don't know how lucky you are having a man like Fisher in your life. I can't imagine what it must be like to share your life with someone sensitive, and perceptive.'

Mim couldn't imagine either and very gently helped Angela to her feet; she probably still believed in the tooth fairy and Father Christmas as well.

'Come on, up you get,' she said, cupping Angela's elbow. 'You really ought to come and meet Yolande.'

Angela nodded, some residual spark of professionalism finally taking control. 'Oh, absolutely, you're quite right. Fisher told me she was very, very –' Angela screwed up her nose in an effort to order her thoughts. 'The thing is I don't actually know what it is she is. I realise that he's not keen to break the whole client/counsellor confidentiality thing but can you tell me what the hell is wrong with her?'

Mim smiled, wondering what clinical euphemism Fisher might use for mad as a badger? She pulled a face that she hoped would imply that either she knew nothing of any consequence or possibly that the moment Angela clapped eyes on Yolande she would have the nous to guess exactly what ailed her.

What remained of the supper party wasn't easy. Between them Angela and Yolande vied for Fisher's attention like cats on heat. Angela insisted that Liam move round so that she could sit next to Jack Tully and thereby be closer to the man of the moment, who – with his harem around him – was waxing lyrical about the modern family, religions, child-rearing, childbearing and most probably raising the dead. It seemed there was nothing Fisher didn't have an opinion on or a solution for.

Sam could barely bring himself to say a civil word to Jack, Liam had been at the wine and looked as if he might fall asleep or be sick and Harriet was tired and bored and stared unfocused into the middle distance. Dessert was a selection of fruits from Ganymede's walled garden served with heavy cream and Amaretti biscuits. Even that didn't lift the mood.

While the hired help carried a tray of coffee out on to the terrace Sam showed Liam and Harriet into a room adjoining the one in which they had eaten that had an enormous TV and a pool table in it.

Jack Tully sidled up. It was the first time he had spoken to Mim since they had arrived. 'You're looking wonderful this evening.'

Mim peered at him and didn't edit the words that came fresh into her mind. 'Feeling a little left out are we?'

Even she was surprised by just how much spite there was in her voice; there was some part of her that felt a totally disproportionate sense of outrage and indignation at Jack's cuckolding Sam. Through open doors she caught a glimpse of the gentle harmless man who was playing with her kids and laughing like a drain. He deserved better than this. He deserved a woman who loved and wanted him, one who didn't just see him as a bankroll for whatever scheme was fashionable.

Mim looked back over her shoulder into the breakfast room. If Angela and Yolande got any closer to Fisher they'd be on his lap.

Jack caught her look.

'Jealous?'

Mim snorted. 'Of what? Those two? No, Jack, if you think that you're sadly mistaken and read me completely wrong. They're welcome to him if that's what they want.'

Momentarily she saw his expression change and, aware of how dangerous was the territory into which she was straying, said, 'You're in love with her, aren't you?'

Jack's face reddened. 'Does it show that much? I thought I'd got it better hidden than that. I'd like to think she loves me too but there's no way she will ever leave Sam.' He paused and looked at Mim as if he expected her to comment. Mim shrugged.

Jack took another pull on his drink. 'Thing is I could understand some misplaced desire to do the right thing. But her motives are a lot less admirable, though more honest. She enjoys this lifestyle, being married to someone famous – and who can blame her? She helped make Sam, put her life on hold to get him established, build his career – and now she fully intends to reap the benefits.'

Mim smiled. 'The two of you sound like a match made in heaven.'

He laughed. 'You're right. Part of me admires her for having that kind of blatant self-interest, and understanding herself so well, not to mention having the courage to tell me straight up, right from the start that she had no intention whatsoever of leaving him for a gold-digging gardener.'

'And what was your plan?'

Jack laughed. 'When I first met Yolande? Move in, move close, graze in lush green pastures for a year or so and then move on. It certainly wouldn't be the first time – only this time I fell and fell real hard – crazy, huh? I suppose you could say it's an occupational hazard.'

Mim heard herself saying, 'Yolande would be entitled to half.'

'I know that, and I'm certain Sam wouldn't fight her for it. He's an incredibly decent guy. But as far as Yolande is concerned half is nowhere near enough,' Jack said thoughtfully. 'She is mean and shallow and petulant and quite, quite amazing.'

'And totally crazy?'

He grinned and drained his glass in a single mouthful.

'Oh yes and then some. Would you like coffee?'

Mim nodded. 'White no sugar.'

'How about a liqueur to go with it?'

Mim lifted her hands to indicate a state of indecision. Jack grinned. 'Leave it to me.'

He had no sooner gone than Angela appeared from the shadows and lit up a cigarette. She seemed to have sobered up considerably since Mim found her in the conservatory.

She took a long drag on her cigarette before turning her attention to Mim. 'Well, well, well, amazing isn't it? Adultery, greed, lust, organised religion, cults, infertility, insanity, coping with fame and depression, interior decorating and landscape gardening? We could do the whole series right here. In fact we might just about be able to fill the current schedule if only she could cook.'

Mim laughed, although she was concerned about how much of the conversation with Jack Tully Angela might have overheard. Surely she couldn't have been there for more than a minute or two.

'Did you ask Yolande about using Ganymede as a location for the show?'

Angela looked surprised. 'I thought that was already a done deal?'

Mim shrugged. 'If you say so.'

'Seems to me that Fisher and Yolande have already got the whole deal sewn up.'

Mim looked back into the breakfast room. Yolande was so close to Fisher that it looked as if they might be sharing the same lung, her expression unnervingly intense, hands moving rapidly to emphasise some point or other. For an instant Mim saw Fisher look up with an expression of total panic on his boyish face. Oh, it might be that the whole deal was sorted out but Mim doubted very much that it was Fisher doing the sorting.

Chapter 14

Mim rang for a taxi despite Angela's insistence that she was quite capable of driving them all home. It was close to midnight and Mim was more than ready to leave. She had spent the last hour or so sitting out on the terrace watching the world go by. The night was warm and fragrant and part of her hoped that in the intimate rustle of the darkness she might see more of the secret woodland things. Sam said that they had foxes and a badger set on the estate.

Harriet and Liam were watching a video in the play-room, Fisher and Yolande were still installed in one corner of the breakfast room deep in animated conversation while Jack, Sam and Angela were playing pool.

It was not as convivial as it might sound. Sam and Jack had both had enough drink to prise apart the thin veneer of good form and the tension was slowly building. Angela – halfway down a bottle of vodka and still going strong – appeared to be oblivious to any of the undercurrents between the two men, and constantly appeared and reappeared on the terrace to check on any developments between Yolande and Fisher. She was getting increasingly annoyed at being excluded.

Fisher had finally found his form and retreated behind a classic counselling pose, adopting an air of benevolent, almost paternal interest in his hostess, fingers knitted in a loose basket over his belly. Occasionally when there was a hiatus in the proceedings he would nod and make an odd noise in the back of his throat. From where Mim was sitting it sounded like a cross between a purr and a growl that somehow inferred he was considering a reply or maybe requesting that Yolande carry on. Mim couldn't help admiring his recovery, and it really was a useful little noise. By contrast Yolande, who earlier had seemed so composed, was a writhing mass of uncertainty, indecision and tension, gesticulating, eyes flashing, talking in a fierce hungry whisper, although odd words broke through and rippled out into the darkness.

'I just can't do it,' she hissed wiping away a tear and then a few moments later, 'Do I need to explain? Karmically the whole thing was a complete disaster,' and then, 'the Mercedes – something, something, something, when we were in New York, I mean, I ask you, who could . . . ?' Her voice sank back beneath the waves and then burst through with, 'I couldn't, I just couldn't, Fisher, I mean, surely you of all people must be able to understand?' And all the time Fisher nodded, and made his useful noise while her waves of pain and confession rolled on and on and on.

It was tortuous and yet impossible to ignore.

Sitting in the darkness, watching and listening, Mim felt as if she was trying to put a giant crossword puzzle together with hardly any of the clues and none of the grid, and longed to either move closer or ask Yolande to speak up. It was all contributing to the beginnings of a headache.

'How much longer are we going to be, Mum?' Harriet sidled out from the playroom and sat down alongside her on one of the benches, shoulders slumped forward.

'Film finished, love?'

Harriet nodded. 'Uh-huh.' She looked tired and terribly young, any pretence of insouciance long gone. 'Liam's playing the pinball machine. I want to go home now,' she whined.

'Have you had a good time?'

'Okay. It's a great house, and I really like Sam. Not so

223

sure about the rest of them though. I just want to go home now.'

What a wise child, Mim glanced down at her watch. 'Not much longer. I've asked the cab to pick us up at quarter-past twelve. Better get your things together and tell Liam, I'll go and tell your dad.'

Harriet yawned. 'I'm totally bushed.' She pointed towards Fisher and Yolande. 'What's Dad doing?'

'What he does best. Yolande needs someone to talk to. That's your dad's job.'

Harriet didn't look convinced.

The taxi arrived bang on twelve fifteen.

Reuben Harnwell was driving it.

When Angela opened her eyes she had absolutely no idea where she was, only that the daylight seemed horribly bright.

'Good morning.' The voice sounded vaguely familiar.

Angela made an effort to focus on the figure standing in the doorway while somewhere in the back of her head the events of the last twelve hours flashed by in monochrome fragments.

Fisher, Fisher and a hotel, Fisher and lunch and Sandringham – and then in rather less detail snippets of dinner, of a dinner party with, with – Fisher and his wife and their kids and . . . who? It took a while . . . Sam and Yolande Burke. Yolande Burke, yes that's who she was.

'So I stayed then?' Angela asked, well aware that she was stating the obvious. She made some effort to smile. It hurt. She screwed her eyes up to aid concentration and instantly regretted it. She had a headache, a terrible malevolent angry headache that was very annoyed at being disturbed.

'I hope you slept well,' Yolande said in that clipped cultured voice. She peered down at Angela from under beautifully plucked eyebrows. She was immaculately dressed in expensively cut casual weekend clothes. By contrast Angela felt as if a ferret had nested in her mouth, and looking down, was aware that she had slept in her clothes, in fact, as she tentatively stretched to encourage the blood to flow, Angela realised there was a very real possibility she still had her shoes on.

'It's nearly ten o'clock, I thought perhaps you might like some tea or coffee?' Nothing in the way Yolande spoke implied she was pleased to have Angela as a house guest.

Angela constructed a smile from the remnants of her brain. 'Right, thank you. Coffee would be great.'

But Yolande wasn't ready to let her off the hook so easily. 'Mim suggested that you went home in the taxi with the children, but –'

'But?'

'But you said you didn't want to leave. He is a very special man, so sensitive, so very intuitive. I feel privileged to have met him.'

They both knew exactly who Yolande was talking about.

'When Fisher said that he was going to stay for a little bit longer – we had just reached a very important point in the conversation – you insisted on staying as well. I'm surprised that you don't remember. You made quite an impression on Jack and Sam.' Her tone was icy.

Angela glanced fleetingly at the bed in case by some miracle Fisher was there and she hadn't noticed him, although if Fisher spent the night surely she ought to have remembered? She wasn't sure whether to be pleased or disappointed that the bed beside her was empty.

'He went home,' Yolande said as if Angela had asked. 'I didn't think you were in any fit condition to drive and you couldn't remember the name of your hotel.'

Angela made an effort not to wince. 'Right, well, it was

very kind of you to put me up. I hope it wasn't too much trouble. I'll – I'll be off as soon as I'm, I'm –' it was pointless to say dressed. 'And,' she said, gathering her wits back together in an untidy pile, 'we really need to talk, Yolande, maybe not at the moment but –'

Her hostess was already ahead of her. 'Fisher explained to me that he wants to make his programme here. At Ganymede. His new series.'

'*Our* new series.'

Something that up until now had been almost hidden crackled furiously between the two women.

'Right. I felt that the energy here would be perfect for him. He is a quite remarkable man.'

Angela smiled slyly. 'My remarkable man.'

'Meaning what exactly?'

Gloves off.

Angela squared her shoulders. 'What do you need, Yolande, a diagram? I found him, I discovered him, I believe in him.' None of this was strictly true but then what did Yolande know? 'I've encouraged and nurtured Fisher's talent. I know that Fisher trusts me to take care of his future.'

Yolande's expression hardened. 'Really? Well in that case the sooner I get him signed up the better. It seems that we both have a gift for recognising talent. Fisher told me last night that he hasn't got an agent.'

Angela felt a little ripple of alarm. 'Well, no, he hasn't but then again at Eelpie we are . . .'

Yolande cut her off. 'Sharks just like the rest of the media. Don't tell me you're out to promote Fisher's career as a philanthropic exercise? I'd be interested to see what kind of deal you've got on the table for him. I've already said that I'd be delighted to represent him if he wants me to. He's very keen. He needs someone who knows the ropes, someone with his best interests at heart.'

'And that would be you, would it? I've got the whole of the Eelpie PR machine behind me, we've got people who will make sure Fisher goes all the way.' Angela glared at her, two bitches fighting over a single juicy bone. To think that just twelve hours earlier Angela had been convinced that Yolande Burke was two slices short of a loaf.

Yolande snorted. 'All the way where exactly? To ensuring Eelpie climbs the ratings, cleans up on the merchandising – self-help tapes, videos, books. It doesn't take a lot of imagination to see where you're going with this. He needs me, I can see that. Like you, I have got a real eye for talent. Fisher is my big chance too.'

Angela swallowed back the reply she had right there on the tip of her tongue, the reply which included Jack Tully and the things she had overheard out on the terrace. Ganymede would make a great backdrop for the new show, Yolande and Sam great subjects, and Fisher could hardly have signed a contract since the previous evening, surely?

'I'd love a cup of coffee,' she said from behind a nice polite little smile.

A matching smile crawled reluctantly over Yolande's face. 'Fine. I'll have some sent up.'

Before she had drunk the coffee, half a cup of something lukewarm and pale grey, Angela had concocted a strategy that would promote the show and also scupper Yolande Burke.

She rang Fisher to thank him for a lovely evening and see if he was free later in the day. They needed to talk, although she wasn't sure when – not yet. He was free and keen. And then she phoned Mel, the journalist at the *Argos*. As she tapped in Mel's number her eyes reduced to bright pinpricks.

'We need to meet and you need to be up here. Now. Yes,

really. I'm going to up the ante.' Angela knew a rival when she saw one and wasn't planning to roll over that easily, after all Fisher was hers not Yolande-bloody-Burke's.

She glanced down at the list she'd made between sips of coffee. 'First thing: Yolande Burke is having an affair with her gardener, we can use lots of Chatterley references and before you say it, I do know Lady Chatterley was shagging her gamekeeper, but it's got the same flavour. Lady of the manor playing fast and loose with the hired help – and then there's this whole Indian, hippie, religious cult thing.'

Mel made a noise implying agreement. Angela knew that he knew better than to interrupt her when she was on a roll. 'You get the shots and I'll give you the copy. What time can you get up here?'

'You're joking, Angie. What, today? Not today?'

She didn't bother to answer, until grudgingly he told her how long it would take him to drive up to Norfolk.

'I still can't see where we're going with this one, Angie,' he said in the middle of the goodbyes.

'You don't have to worry about that, just trust me and get your hairy little arse up here.'

Now she knew what time Mel was likely to arrive, Angela called Fisher back and suggested they meet for afternoon tea at her hotel.

It wouldn't take very much, she'd done it before – a couple of long shots of her and Fisher through a bedroom window, one big wet kiss in the car park, Fisher carrying her luggage out to the car. TV's new agony uncle at hotel with mystery blonde. She'd show Yolande exactly what the score was and blow the hippie bitch right out of the water.

Mel with his long lens and an eye for impropriety, and she with a few sharp headlines could imply all manner of goings on behind the scenes of their new TV series. Angela even might be able to work up a tangled love triangle as a shoutline. Triangles were always good for sales. Like most reporters Mel had never knowingly let the facts get in the way of a good story.

As she let the ideas take shape Angela didn't give Mim Pilgrim a second thought.

At around the same time on the other side of the village Mim was handing Harriet a mug of tea. 'So, they've asked you to baby-sit?'

Harriet nodded. 'Yeh, Mr Grey and his wife.'

'Do you know when they want you?'

'No, they just asked if I'd be able to, you know, see if it was all right. I said I'd ask.'

'Sounds fine. I used to do a lot of baby-sitting when I was your age and it's not so far away that if you have any problems I can't help. Yes, fine, you can tell Mr Grey that it's okay with me.'

It had taken Harriet a while to get around to having the baby-sitting conversation with her mother. She had run it through in her mind more times than she cared to think about so that it sounded casual. She didn't want to talk about it while Liam was around in case he had heard about her and Rob. Under the circumstances he was probably in enough trouble without causing her any, although if things had been the other way around she wouldn't have hesitated to defuse her own guilt by getting him into trouble.

'And you've got drama club at school this afternoon?'

Harriet nodded. 'Yeh.'

'I'm glad you're taking an interest in drama. I loved it when I was at school. What times does it finish? I'll come in and pick you up. I've got to get a few bits and pieces from town.'

Harriet had already anticipated Rob driving her home, but although everything about her longed to protest,

Harriet was afraid to push it too far in case she blew it. 'Five, I think.'

Mim nodded. 'Okay.'

Harriet went back upstairs, at least she would see him soon. On the landing she caught sight of a car outside their house and for a minute Harriet wondered if it might be Reuben Harnwell. God, it had been awful him turning up in the taxi, she had been so angry and uncomfortable. Bloody man. Harriet shivered and pushed her mind firmly in the direction of baby-sitting and Rob Grey.

Outside Liam was finishing off the far end of the lawn. The noise of the mower was invasive, bubbling in through the kitchen window like a swarm of angry bees.

Mim stood by the kitchen window and watched him work, wondering what he had been up to with Linda, as if she couldn't guess. Odd to think of her son with a girl, as a sexual creature doing those things that boys and girls do. It had been a good idea to invite Linda over for tea. Mim closed her eyes; and instantly saw Reuben Harnwell. She had no idea he drove cabs as a sideline.

Mim had sat in the front seat of the taxi on the way home from Ganymede. The atmosphere had been so tense that Mim almost asked him to stop and let them all out. Reuben chatted to her and the kids all the way home, grinning from time to time, eyes moving over her face and body in an unsettling almost proprietorial way. It was absolutely torturous.

At the gate, when Liam and Harriet had hurried up the path to unlock the front door, he had leant towards her, taken the fare and then said in an undertone, 'Not going to invite me in for coffee then?' in such an intimate tone that Mim had flinched, feeling vulnerable and angry as he stepped boldly across some invisible line.

* * *

Liam braced himself against the handle of the mower and pushed hard. The long grass at the far end of the garden round the apple trees was coarse and always a struggle compared to the soft lawn grass up near the house. The only consolation was it would probably build muscle, give him shoulders. For some reason the idea of broader shoulders instantly fired an image of Linda running her hands over him, kissing him, wriggling closer.

This was worse than when he hadn't screwed anyone. Sex was on his mind all the time, no longer abstract thoughts but intimate exciting details. Without any effort at all he could feel her head snuggled up under his chin, and the soft smell of her body. He swallowed hard and pushed violently against the handle and as he did the mower hit a clod and spewed gravel and nuggets of dried earth all over the place, pinging off the shed and his calves and up into his face. It stung. He wiped away the mixture of sweat and dirt with the back of his hand, still careful of his black eye despite the fact that it was fading.

Christ, fancy running into Reuben Harnwell of all people. He was the last person on earth Liam had expected to see driving the cab. There had been a moment when their eyes met and they acknowledged each other with a slight inclination of the head, when Liam wondered if Reuben was going to say something. He had been careful to keep his expression neutral – no fear but no cockiness either and – thank God – the moment had passed.

Linda had giggled when he'd rung up and asked if she wanted to come round for tea. 'You're such a sweetie,' she said. 'I'll just go and tell my mum.'

It felt nice and a bit weird at the same time. His mum had arranged to pick Linda up and bring her round. Weird. Liam shook his head and flexed his muscles. He needed to get the lawn finished and have a shower.

*　　*　　*

Yolande rang Fisher at ten and eleven and twelve o'clock. Angela rang him from her hotel room on the half-hour. Fisher had never been so popular, although after the second phone call from Angela, Fisher decided it was going to be very difficult not to break the client confidentiality thing wide open.

'This is very irregular,' he said, struggling to keep Angela off him. 'Yolande is a very complex and sensitive woman, she sees me as a confidant, someone in whom she can trust. I can't just tell you what we talked about, it breaks all kinds of unwritten rules.'

'What the hell do you mean you can't tell me? I'm your producer, for Christ's sake,' Angela growled. 'We're going to broadcast your precious Yolande's idiosyncrasies, addictions and general overall weirdness across the sodding country as soon as I can get the show up and running.'

Fisher didn't know what to say. Of course it was true but some part of him hadn't quite registered exactly what it meant. Maybe he ought to ring Yolande and warn her.

'I want you to nail Yolande Burke,' said Angela, over her second double espresso in the hotel bar. It was nearly three and she was expecting Fisher at around four.

Mel had arrived a few minutes earlier, dressed in a faded khaki jacket with many pockets, uniform of press photographers everywhere. He sniffed and took the address that Angela slid across the table.

'If you ask me this Yolande Burke bird is hardly worth the effort,' he said, spooning the cream off his hot chocolate.

Angela's eyes narrowed. 'Maybe, but it'll certainly help promote the new show, and it will help me. I'd like to show Yolande flaws and all.'

'But I thought the idea was to get you and golden boy,

232

all cosied up, bit of a snog – you know. Hotel hideaway stuff.'

'We are and then we get her. Two birds with one stone, *capiche*? Me and Fisher, and then Lady Bountiful and the gardener, and maybe it would be worth keeping an eye on her old man too. We need to whip up a little froth.'

Mel turned his attention back to the overextravagance of whipped cream. Angela suspected that he had more sense than to argue with her.

'Mim, Mim? Where are you? Are you in there?'

Fisher burst into the kitchen as if his hair was on fire. 'I need to borrow your car. Now. The battery on the Volvo is totally dead. Nothing.' He held out a hand for the keys.

Mim had written a thank you card to Yolande and Sam, and then, sitting alone at the kitchen table, had been considering all manner of things. Reuben Harnwell, Liam and Linda, Jack Tully and Sam, Yolande and the two of them, her own marriage and, in amongst that and the sketches for Ganymede, wondering if she would ever get the chance to make the sculpture for the wood. Her head was quite full and her consciousness a long way away. It took her a few seconds to make out what it was that Fisher was saying.

He wiggled his fingers at her. 'Come on. Car keys,' he pressed.

'I'm sorry but I can't. Harriet's gone to drama club, I've got to go and pick her up and then I've promised Liam I'd go and collect Linda and bring her home for tea. And I need to get a few groceries.' How long did the list need to be to get Fisher off her back? And how was it that Fisher could make her feel that his inability to buy a new battery was somehow her fault?

His shoulders slumped forward. 'But I need to be in King's Lynn by four.'

'I could run you down to the railway station if you like.'

It was obviously not the answer he wanted.

'I told Angela I'd meet her at the hotel at four. We're having afternoon tea. Scones and things.'

'You could ring her and say you're going to be a little bit late. I've got a train timetable in the pottery.'

It was still not what Fisher wanted to hear. He was not amused.

'All right,' said Mim, after enduring a moment or two's intense prickling silence. 'Give me a second and I'll take you into Lynn.'

'But I'm already running late as it is,' Fisher whined.

Ten minutes later they were out on the Lynn road, with Fisher glancing down at his watch every fifteen seconds to emphasise her tardiness. Mim, not the most confident of drivers, kept within the speed limit and refused to overtake unless she was certain it was clear, two bones of contention that today Fisher left buried.

Mim dropped him off in the hotel car park and was about to drive away when it occurred to her that she could pick up the odds and ends of shopping that she needed while she was in town. The hotel car park was free to patrons – surely she was a patron by proxy? Mim pulled up under the lee of a People Carrier and headed off towards the shops.

The town centre was busy, people dressed in bright clothes milling around in the early summer sunshine. All of sudden it felt good to be out, summery, warm – a nice place to be. Mim stretched and let the weight of Fisher's disapproval slip silently to the ground. Maybe she'd take a quick look in Marks and the Body Shop before going round the supermarket. Shouldn't take her more than half an hour and then she could drive back to Denham and pick up Harriet.

It actually took thirty-nine minutes, which was fateful.

'Can you help me take the luggage out to the Jeep?' Angela asked Fisher, finishing off the last of the smoked salmon sandwiches, just before stubbing out her cigarette in a saucer.

It had been an odd meeting. Fisher was a little confused as to why exactly Angela had invited him; they had barely spoken over tea and he felt that she had rushed him through what he thought was going to be a leisurely get together.

Fisher didn't feel he could refuse to help Angela carry her luggage down, even though they had hotel porters to help with the bags. She had seemed a lot more interested in what Yolande had said to Fisher at the dinner party than any plans for the new show, and when he had suggested Angela might like to run him back to Maglington after the meeting she seemed positively hostile.

Then, when they had gone upstairs Angela had dragged open the net curtains in her room and insisted that he take a look at the view from her window. Well, there was no view to speak of, although Fisher couldn't work out whether she was complaining or genuinely thought that the car park and the social security buildings that backed it were truly picturesque. He was a little concerned that she was being ironic and he'd never been too sure what it was exactly that constituted irony.

So, their afternoon tea had been a rushed affair and then he'd had to carry her bags out to the car park – and just as they got the tailgate open she had made a grab for him. Again. He was going to have to talk to her about this whole thing. It wasn't comfortable and it wasn't fair. She'd played the advantage, he had had both hands full. Fisher hadn't even had the time to protest, there was a great rush of perfume and then she kissed him. Hard, hungrily, hands all over him like a rash and then less than a minute later, with the bags safely installed, she had carried on talking to him as if nothing had happened.

'Angela,' he protested, 'I've already told you about this, I'm married.' She looked at him sadly and then with a hand resting on each shoulder smiled. 'I know,' she said. 'Your sense of fair play is the only thing that keeps me going.'

He wasn't sure what that was all about but he was damned certain it wasn't irony.

Unable to drive him all the way home Angela had dropped him at the railway station. He'd rung home but Mim didn't seem to be there which was bloody annoying. It had to be at least a mile walk from the station to their house.

Liam stepped out of the shower and wiped a broad reflective arc in the condensation on the mirror on the back of the bathroom door so that he could admire his body. He'd got a sprinkling of dark hair on his chest, not a lot but it was coming along, and another more defined line ran up over his belly. After towelling it dry Liam brushed it thoughtfully and didn't fight too hard when the thoughts strayed back towards Linda, who had said, after she'd called him a sweetie, that yeh, she would really like to come to tea but she'd got to go by nine.

The house was empty. Liam had got the stereo cranked up to boiling point and he felt, if not good, then okay. He knew that his mum would be kind to Linda and make the effort to understand, and if he was really lucky then Fisher would be busy in his study and not bother to come out. Harriet was so moony there was no way of second guessing which way she would roll. It felt weird to think that in less than an hour he and Linda would be sitting side by side on the sofa, with their thighs so close that they touched. Maybe when they had tea in the kitchen she would look for his hand under the table. Liam grinned. Perhaps it was going to be all right after all.

In the senior hall at Denham High School the drama club were clearing the chairs away and putting the benches back on the stage. Ben Tierman handed Harriet her cardigan and grinned. 'Not so shabby after all. Do you fancy going down to Goldes for a coffee?' His voice echoed around the senior hall.

He'd changed his tune. Harriet made a show of not catching his eye, tucking the script into her holdall and shaking her head. 'No thanks, my mum is coming to pick me up.' She did make an effort not to sound sharp though.

Tierman nodded. 'Right, okay, yeh.' He looked a lot better out of school uniform, not fanciable or anything but a lot better.

They were amongst the last three or four people to leave the drama club.

'That went really well,' said Rob Grey, wandering over towards them. 'Do you want a lift?' His question was aimed squarely at Harriet who could feel her colour lift a little, despite the fact that she had been waiting all afternoon for him to ask her.

'No thanks. My mum's coming to pick me up.' She had practised it a few times so that it came out warm – not a brush off or a put down – it would just make him realise she wasn't a pushover, not easy or anything, and that she had people who cared about her.

'Okay, I'll make sure all of you get the rehearsal schedules as soon as I've organised them and meanwhile I suggest you both make a start on the lines. But don't rush them and don't get in a panic, we've got plenty of time yet. It's important with Shakespeare that you understand what you're saying. It can so easily end up as nonsense, and I'm not just talking about finding the literal meaning, but the feel – the mood.' He grinned at Harriet. 'Don't look so worried. It'll come, promise.'

'He's a very good director, better than Tinker by miles,' Tierman said as they walked back out into the sunshine.

Harriet blinked, not altogether sure how it was they had come out together. Mim was sitting in the VW under the shade of the horsechestnut trees. She lifted a hand and waved.

'That yours?' said Tierman, staring at the car and sounding impressed.

'My mum's.'

'Cool,' said Tierman, 'I've always wanted one of them or a Mini Cooper, real cult cars. Classics. You know, retro.' And for some reason his avarice was reason enough to follow Harriet over to the car.

Mim rolled down the window. 'Hi love, how did it go?'

'Okay,' said Harriet.

Mim smiled at Tierman. 'Hi, do you want a lift?'

Tierman blushed. 'Well I'm er – I was – yeh, okay. I live in Wimblington. My name's Ben Tierman.' He shook her mother's hand through the open window.

'Pleased to meet you. You're in luck, Wimblington's on the way home. Harriet, let Ben in, will you?'

Harriet's earlier feelings of live and let live where Tierman was concerned rapidly ebbed away. How dare he cadge a lift?

What made things a hundred times worse was that just as Tierman was clambering in the back of the VW, Rob Grey pulled out of the car park and waved. God, now he would think she was going out with Tierman. Harriet could feel a great bubbling plume of annoyance hiss up inside her like the roar of a geyser. And then to cap it all Tierman gabbled on and on and on all the way home to her mum about the bloody Beetle.

*　　*　　*

Mim was really relieved to see Harriet and even more pleased to talk to Ben Tierman. She had a funny cold dark sliver stuck somewhere inside that she couldn't seem to shift.

Harriet pulled a carrier bag out of the footwell and peered inside. 'Is this for me?'

For a moment Mim couldn't remember and then after a few moments it came back to her. 'Yes,' she said. 'A top. It was on the sale rail in New Look.'

Harriet opened the bag and made a noise of approval.

Mim had just been coming back to the car when she'd spotted Fisher in the car park with Angela and was about to call out – after all it appeared as if their meeting was over and this way Mim could give Fisher a lift home – when all of a sudden Angela had leaned forward and kissed him. Hard. A long, slow, wet, lover's kiss.

It had taken Mim completely by surprise, what she saw sucking the breath right out of her lungs. She was stunned, she had no idea at all that Fisher was having an affair. How long had it been going on? How was it she hadn't guessed? Mim was almost more perturbed by the fact that she didn't know than by the fact that Fisher was involved with his boss. Questions that couldn't be answered filled her head.

Fisher, laden down with bags, had made no effort to fight Angela off, in fact he had looked totally bemused when she pulled away, but Angela had just laughed and helped him put the luggage in the back of the Jeep.

And so that was it, was it? Her own adultery was now no more than a featherweight on a scale already heavily tipped in her favour. It was all over. Her and Fisher. The thought hit Mim like a great blade slicing her right through the middle, first of all ice-cold and steely and then, closing in behind, Mim felt relief. A huge rolling wave of relief. Finally she was free of him. Finally her life could begin again. Fisher had found someone else, or more accurately

Mim suspected, someone else had found Fisher. And as it sunk in Mim felt almost elated.

As Mim went to put the shopping in the boot – which was at the front of the Beetle – she practically stepped on a man skulking around behind the People Carrier. She did wonder for an instant if she had caught him having a pee but when he turned round Mim saw that he was carrying a camera and smiled at her in a non-committal, disinterested sort of way.

'Lovely day,' he said, without meeting her eye.

'Ummm, yes, lovely,' Mim said, struggling with the boot catch and the things that she had just seen. But now, on reflection, his presence struck her as very odd and these two images kept flooding up and demanding attention. Fisher and Angela and the man with a camera.

'Here will do,' said a voice in her head, only it wasn't in her head this time, it was Ben Tierman leaning over between the seats.

'Just up here on the left.'

Mim's mind headed back into the present. She pulled over on the side of the road and smiled inanely while Harriet said her goodbyes and let him out.

'Ben seems like a nice boy,' said Mim conversationally, as Harriet clambered into the front seat.

Harriet looked heavenwards and groaned theatrically.

'My mum works at the vegetable trimming place over near Swaffham,' Linda said, between mouthfuls of lasagne. 'Shift work. She's a supervisor.' A little trickle of sauce rolled down her chin and plopped silently onto the front of her cream blouse. 'She said she'd seen you on day time TV. Must be great being famous. Do people come up and want your autograph and that?'

Fisher nodded and smiled. 'Occasionally.' The smile was purely superficial.

'Would you like some more salad, Linda?' asked Mim.

Linda nodded. 'We don't get none at home 'cause my mum's sick of the sight of it, they do all sorts of lettuces and spring onions and that sort of thing where she works.' She piled her plate higher.

Linda had appeared quite nervous and shy when Mim first picked her up, but had thawed rapidly once it was apparent Mim wasn't going to read her the riot act about encouraging Liam to bunk off school.

On the other side of the table Liam appeared to be torn between some kind of blind puppyish delight at having Linda in the house and red-eared self-consciousness. Harriet looked sulky and Fisher could hardly contain his derision for the jolly little mongrel that was sitting at the kitchen table talking with her mouth full, blouse undone a button too many and shiny grey trousers that looked as if they had been sprayed on.

Mim thought Linda was beautiful in a strange way. She had a real ripeness and self-assuredness about her that was both delightful and oddly unsettling.

Linda sniffed and rubbed a finger up under her nose to deal with any potential running. 'It's a lovely dinner, Mrs Pilgrim.'

'I'm glad you like it. Why don't you call me Mim? Everyone does.'

Fisher pushed his chair away from the table. 'If you'll excuse me I have some work to do.'

Mim watched him go, and felt the tension ease, although some part of her was expecting him to say something about Angela, now that she knew, as if her knowing shifted something. What would he say? 'Hello, I'm leaving?' 'Hello, I'm in love with someone else.' Or would it be that he just wouldn't come home one night? It seemed the most likely, Fisher had never been the bravest of souls.

'We're going to go and watch a video,' said Liam.

Mim nodded. 'Okay.'

Linda started to help clear the table.

It was obvious from the way she worked that this wasn't something Linda was doing to be polite.

'Thank you.'

'No, that was lovely. Did Liam say about me going home? I've got a lift organised, I hope that's all right. Do you want a hand with the washing-up?'

It didn't take very long. In spite of everything Mim liked Linda, who followed Liam into the sitting room. Harriet went up to her room. Mim stayed in the kitchen and once the clearing up was finished, settled down at the table with a book.

When the phone rang at quarter to nine and no one else hurried out to answer it, Mim did. She wondered if it might be Angela. It turned out to be Sam Burke.

There were no niceties, no preamble.

'Did they send a photographer down for this TV thing? I should have been asked.'

'Who? I'm not with you, Sam.'

'Her and him. Fisher and that TV woman. I was walking in the woods and I came across this bloke with a camera. I've tried talking to Yolande but I can't get any sense out of her. I was going to leave it but it's driving me nuts.'

Something made Mim's scalp prickle.

'What did he look like?' she heard herself asking.

Sam made a noise that implied something and nothing and then said, 'Pretty nondescript, got one of those jackets with endless pockets. Frightened the bloody life out of me.'

What were the odds on two men fitting the same description being near Sam and Fisher within hours of each other?

Mim felt her sense of expectation shifting. 'I don't know Sam, Fisher hasn't said anything to me. I would have thought the TV company would need your permission before they could do anything, certainly on your property. What did the man say?'

'That he was fucking lost.'

'Perhaps he was.'

'Yes and I'm the Queen of Sheba. He'd walked right into the woods – I mean, you stay in your car, don't you? Reverse up? You don't go wandering around – there are signs everywhere on the fences that say it's private property.'

Mim heard the sound of a car horn and put her hand over the receiver. 'Liam, I think Linda's lift is here.'

Nothing.

'Sam, can you hang on for just a minute?'

He grunted.

Mim went into the sitting room. Liam and Linda, who had been sitting side by side on the sofa, sprung apart as if jet-propelled. Mim smiled, and then turned away as she heard a knock on the front door.

'Your lift's here, Linda.'

Linda got up, tidying and patting herself as she did. 'I'll go and get my coat.'

'Okay, but I'm on the phone, don't be long.'

Mim went to answer the door, conscious of Sam hanging on the far end of the line.

'Evening,' said a familiar voice as it swung open. Reuben Harnwell stood on the step, framed by the porch light. He grinned down at her. 'Linda here, is she?'

For a minute Mim was totally speechless and peered past him expecting to see the taxi he had been driving the night before, instead she saw his window cleaning van curled up under a street light.

'Are you Linda's brother?' she asked experimentally.

'Nah,' Reuben said, shaking his head, grin broadening as Linda appeared from the sitting-room doorway. 'I'm her boyfriend.'

Mim opened her mouth to speak and then thought better of it. On the phone she could hear Sam Burke half whistling, half humming the theme from *Star Wars*.

Chapter 15

'Would you mind if I called you back, Sam?' said Mim and hung up without waiting for a reply. She felt much in need of a coffee or possibly something stronger.

Babe sashayed in through the open front door, tail up, taking the time to weave himself in and out of Reuben's long slim legs before heading off into the kitchen. Reuben held onto the door with one hand resting well up the side so that he created an arch under which Linda – having said her goodbyes and her thank yous, and carrying a little shiny pink pvc jacket in the crook of her elbow – vanished out into the night with barely a backward glance towards Liam.

As soon as the door was shut Mim rounded on her son. 'Did you know she was going out with him?' She tried hard to keep any anger out of her tone, after all her beef, if she had one, was with Reuben certainly not Liam.

He reddened. 'Well, yeh, sort of.'

'What do you mean, sort of? What did Linda tell him she was doing coming round here?' Part of Mim was afraid for Liam, after all Reuben wasn't some schoolboy rival but a grown man. Her brain refused point blank to consider any of the other permutations and possibilities.

'That we were doing a project, for school. Reuben wants her to get her GCSEs before they get engaged.'

'Oh, for God's sake, Liam,' Mim said in exasperation, quite unable to help herself. 'Engaged? Linda is a child for God's sake. What is she? Fifteen, sixteen?'

He reddened and shifted uncomfortably from foot to

foot. 'I know, I know, there's no need to shout. She's sixteen, and I've told her she's wasting her life if she settles for him. Linda's not stupid, she could do lots of things, but she seems to think that it's all right,' he mumbled looking down at the floor. 'Reuben is such a git. I can't bear to think that she's with someone like him.'

Mim neither.

'All right,' she said after a few moments. 'I don't know what to say to you other than for God's sake be careful. I don't think you know what you're getting into here.'

Liam headed towards the stairs and then turned back, 'Thanks Mum.'

Mim lifted her hands in a gesture of resignation. 'Don't thank me. I think you're an idiot to get involved although I do understand why you are. She's really nice. But Reuben isn't.'

Liam nodded.

After Friday's dinner party and Saturday's tea party, Sunday was blessedly quiet and totally uneventful. First thing on Monday morning Fisher left early to get to Radio Washland before the rush, and Mim wrote Liam a note saying that he had been off ill all week with a mysterious virus. Harriet was eager to get to school. Mim made herself a coffee, aware that she was waiting for something to happen, something to begin, to break out and take her world apart. Part of her hoped she wouldn't have to wait too long.

As the children were about to leave Reuben Harnwell's van pulled up alongside the house. Mim suppressed a shiver. For once, instead of knocking on the door as Mim anticipated he got on with washing the windows straight away. He whistled as he washed and wiped and squeegeed.

In the pottery Mim tried hard to settle down to work,

but waiting for Reuben to finish was torturous. Eventually, unable to bear it any longer, Mim hurried into the kitchen. She would have to find him and sort things out once and for all. Sod's law being what it is, as Mim threw open the back door Reuben stepped up to knock on it.

'Morning,' he said with a grin. 'That'll be four pounds. Just done the downstairs this time, upstairs next week. Same time, weather permitting. You know how it is.'

She nodded and automatically stepped back inside to get her purse. He followed her inside. He was so close that she could smell his aftershave and the subtle musk of fresh sweat beneath it – and for some reason today the smell of him made her angry. But angry was okay. It was better than desire and lust and the hungry need to touch him.

In the seconds it took to count out the money Mim realised that this was part of the change she had been anticipating. What was it she wanted to say to him that had seemed so important?

When Mim turned back all the things she felt about Reuben had ebbed away, the lust, the need, the kick in the bottom of her belly that took her breath away when she saw him, all those things were gone, including the anger and the confusion. So, when Reuben Harnwell took the money and smiled Mim didn't feel any need to return the gesture.

'See you next week,' she said calmly.

He nodded, the smile turning to something more wry. 'Right you are, Mrs Pilgrim.' Fingers closing tight around the coins. 'How are you today? Okay? You look tired.' He was looking for a way in under her defences.

She nodded. 'No, I'm fine, thanks.'

There was a hiatus, when neither of them moved and then Reuben said, 'About Linda.'

Mim looked up and stared at him with the eyes of a

woman who knows she is about to hear some grade-A bullshit.

Her knowing stopped up Reuben's words, so Mim took the opportunity to say a few of her own. 'She's your girlfriend, which is absolutely fine by me, but make sure you leave my son out of the equation. I'm another notch on your bedpost which is also fine by me. You and I are both adults and both knew what we were doing. What worries me is that Linda isn't an adult. She's probably far too young for you and most definitely far too good for you. But whatever ever else Linda is, she is entitled to a relationship built on trust and honesty, Reuben. She is way, way too young for a bastard like you to teach her that love is a cynical exercise in manipulation.'

For the briefest of instants it looked as if Reuben might be going to say something else and then thought better of it. He nodded and then he was gone. Out into the garden. Just like that.

When the door was closed Mim sighed, and made herself another coffee, or would have done if her hands hadn't shaken so much and she hadn't been crying so hard. Although what it was she was crying over or for or about was quite beyond her. And then the phone rang. It was Sam wanting to know why the hell she hadn't rung him back on Saturday.

Angela closed her eyes tight and let Alfredo take control of her body. The slapping and pulling on her well-oiled flesh was absolute bliss. The masseur adjusted the towels as he moved slowly up her body. Before leaving Eelpie's offices she had tapped the last few words of the last of the Fisher Pilgrim articles into an e-mail on her laptop and pressed Send so an instant later her stories, captions and pictures would be zapped back over to Mel's desk at the *Argos*. Besides devising and then dishing the dirt she'd also hacked out a couple of fillers for the TV what's on slot, what's happening and what's about to happen columns and arranged for Fisher to do a fashion feature for the magazine section that fronted up the *Argos*' weekly TV pages.

Angela smiled and breathed out hard as Alfredo began to work on her back. He had meow in spades. It was a real shame Alfredo wasn't into women. This felt so good and the oils, which he mixed to a prescription of his own devising, made her almost drunk with pleasure. She hoped that eventually Fisher might do the same.

All it needed was a modicum of hype about Fisher in the media, a campaign involving little bits of extra exposure, snippets floated into the ether to get the names of the main players out there in the public consciousness and then, when they had taken root, she would deliver a tactical whammy. Or possibly a whole series of whammies. Affairs, love rats, love triangles and a lot of free publicity was the main thrust of her plan. And, if she played it right, Fisher would be part of her pay-off, as long as she could keep him away from Yolande Burke.

Angela glanced surreptitiously at the clock on the wall of the treatment room. Fisher ought to be back home by now. She needed to prime him about her proposals for plugging the new show and wondered how Alfredo would feel about her using a mobile. The more she thought about talking to him the more important it became.

'Pass me my bag will you?'

Alfredo stopped mid-slap. 'Eh?'

'Bag,' she said, waving towards her briefcase. 'Can you pass me my bag?'

He did as he was asked but was not amused.

'You s'posed to let go, let me ease tension while you are here,' he said in an outrageous Eastern European accent.

Angela shrugged it off. It wouldn't take long and who was paying for the bloody massage for Christ's sake?

She was relieved when Fisher and not Mim answered and once he had said the first tentative hello, Angela sailed ahead not letting him get a word in.

'I just wanted to say thank you for a super weekend. I'm convinced we've found the right place, right people. And I absolutely adored Yolande, what an amazing woman.' (It was important not to make Fisher think that there was even the slightest inkling of rivalry between them.) 'She's perfect.'

Alfredo whipped off the towel and started kneading her buttocks. God, he was good when he was angry. Trying to suppress little noises of pleasure and pain, Angela continued, 'I need you to come down to the studio to get the ball rolling. I've got the team working up the format even as we speak. We're sorting out schedules, arranged for Jimmy to go up to Ganymede. What we need to work on is a little cameo piece about the new show for Thursday's programme. Bit of background, little bit of a teaser to set the tongues wagging, get some feedback from the target demographic. How about if you came down Wednesday and stayed over?'

'Well,' Fisher began, but Angela knew by the tone that he wasn't going to put up much of a fight. 'I'll need to check –'

Angela suspected he was going to add, 'with Mim' but thought better of it. 'But take that as a yes,' he said after the briefest of pauses, 'and I'll call you back to confirm asap. Can you sort out a hotel?'

'Certainly,' Angela said, fingers crossed. 'See you here, bright and early Wednesday. We've got lots of things to talk about.'

Alfredo was still kneading her glutes like there was no tomorrow. Maybe she should piss him off more often.

She rang Yolande next.

'I wondered if you could come down to London for a meeting this week. I do appreciate that it's terribly short notice, but –' and here was the clincher – 'I've just spoken to Fisher, and he was absolutely desperate that I should ring you straight away. He was certain you'd want to be in at the ground floor with this. We need to talk about Ganymede, the content of the show and obviously your input. We'd like to send our outside broadcast team down to do a recce as soon as possible. I know Fisher respects your judgement and well – I respect his.' Angela's tone dropped from sales pitch aggressive down to almost deferential. It was a first-class piece of bullshit. Angela held her breath and waited for it to explode in her face.

There was a heavy silence and then Yolande said slowly, 'Fisher is so sensitive to this kind of thing. All right. When? What time?'

Angela grinned just as Alfredo grabbed hold of a great pillow of flesh and squeezed hard. God, she loved this job.

At Denham High School Harriet was making her way to English. As she was about to climb the stairs she heard footsteps hurrying along behind her and wasn't altogether surprised when Rob Grey caught hold of her arm.

'Harriet? Wait up a minute.'

Harriet swung round, after all hadn't she imagined this moment a thousand times?

'Yes?'

Rob grinned, which wrinkled up the lines around his eyes. Harriet shivered. In countless fantasies now was the moment he leaned forward and kissed her, although she doubted he would risk it in front of the rest of her class.

'I was wondering if you could baby-sit for us on Saturday evening – from say seven-thirty 'til about midnight?'

Damn

'This Saturday?'

Rob nodded.

'I should think so, but I'll have to check –' she was going to say with her mum but thought better of it.

'Sure. Not a problem.' Rob pulled a slip of paper out of his top pocket and handed it to her. 'This is my home telephone number, maybe you could ring me later and let me know one way or the other? Okay?'

'Yeh, sure,' said Harriet, as casually as she could manage.

Standing beside her Kate made a peculiar, strangled, throwing up noise.

'Your tennis is coming on a treat,' said Peter. He and Liam were walking back from the courts. 'I told you I knew the cure.'

Liam laughed. 'Some cure.'

The girls, deep in conversation, had wandered a little ahead.

'So, how far did you get with the lovely Linda then?' asked Peter in an undertone.

Liam looked at him and then laughed as if the answer ought to be obvious. 'Come off it.' Peter pulled a face, which persuaded Liam to continue, 'All the way, mate,' he said with a grin. 'And then some.'

Peter's eyes widened and his mouth opened a fraction wider than might be considered cool. 'Christ. You are joking. I thought the whole Linda Bremner thing was an urban myth.'

'So, what? You set me up then?' he said and then Liam had a revelation. 'What about you?' He nodded towards the retreating girls. He and Fiona had won today in straight sets.

Peter reddened and looked uncomfortable. 'You know, bit of messing around, but not all the way – at least, not yet. It's just a matter of time though.'

Liam squared his shoulders and grinned. It seemed that his mentor was at least a step behind him.

'Got a fag, have you?' Liam said.

'Yeh, sure,' said Peter, fishing one out of his bag. They stopped by the net shed to light up. 'So what was it like, then?'

Liam grinned. 'Are you serious? Bloody brilliant.'

Peter was hanging on his every word, leaning forward to catch whatever was coming next but Liam just smiled enigmatically and took a long, long drag.

It came as no surprise to Mim when Fisher hurried into the pottery after a flurry of phone calls to tell her that he planned to go down to London on Wednesday morning and stay overnight.

So this was it then, their lives together slowly unpeeling. As she had suspected not an ending but a gradual fading away.

'I'm just nipping over to Yolande's. She rang to see if I'd come over and discuss a few things with her. I'm not sure what time I'll be home.'

Mim nodded and started to tell him that it was okay, that staying away overnight was fine, that as he was going to Ganymede she'd put his supper in the fridge, when she heard the door close behind her.

Fisher sat in Yolande Burke's elegant cream drawing room and wondered why it was that their house didn't look like Ganymede. Mim just hadn't got the same touch, the same eye for detail, which was odd, as she was quite artistic.

He'd definitely have to have a word with her. Obviously there were one or two little DIY jobs that needed finishing off about the house. Once the new programme got going they'd have to entertain more, bound to, went with the territory. The sitting room definitely needed a lick of emulsion; maybe he'd be able to find time to make a start on it over the weekend, although Mim ought to put a little more effort into it.

Yolande handed Fisher a glass of iced tea and settled herself back amongst a billow of cushions on the sofa.

'As I was saying, I've always been a very complex creature and obviously Sam isn't. Don't misunderstand me, he's a wonderful man. It's not that I don't love him but in some ways I feel that we've outgrown each other. I am a woman who needs stimulation on many levels.' She leant forward and held his gaze to emphasise the point. 'The Swami feeds me spiritually, Jack physically and Sam, well Sam used to challenge me intellectually but these days –' she paused as though her silence should be explanation enough. 'I've worked hard to get to where I am, I don't want to give it up. Is that so wrong?'

Fisher shook his head and took a sip of tea, not altogether sure what his role was here. Normally clients were racked with grief or guilt or had something they wanted to shed or share or come to terms with but it seemed to him that all Yolande really wanted was an audience. She certainly wasn't seeking his approval. They had covered the same ground at least a dozen times in the last twenty-four hours. How she had built Sam's career from nothing, how much she had given up for him, how she loved him but how he was no longer enough and how much she felt for Jack Tully, although, obviously, she would only let herself see him as a diversion.

'He's beautiful and dangerous,' she murmured.

God, Yolande was boring. Rich but boring.

Fisher pursed his lips and steepled his fingers wondering, as Yolande began once again about her troubled childhood, exactly how he was going to get the subject round to the matter of money or perhaps it might be better if he just sent her an invoice for his fee. Ninety pounds an hour plus travelling sounded reasonable. At the practice he charged thirty but this was special and anyway he ought to be paid extra for house calls.

Yolande already knew that Monday was his radio broadcast and that he'd been in the studio all morning, because he'd told her. Twice. Fisher was tired and after a while even multiplying things by ninety ceased to give him any pleasure. He had told her three times now that he'd had a long day but she was oblivious. He had been at Ganymede for the best part of three hours and there was still no sign of a respite.

After speaking to Angela, Yolande had rung him and begged him to come over, saying that she was in the most terrible turmoil.

He still had no idea what it was. Sitting looking at her now, although there had been much pacing and wringing of hands when he first arrived, it was obvious that she was choreographing the whole show. Finally Yolande rounded on him.

'What do you think I should talk about for the programme? I know that Angela wants to discuss it all on Wednesday but I would value your opinion before we have the meeting.'

Fisher was about to speak but it appeared, at least in Yolande's mind, to be a rhetorical question.

'I did consider adultery but Sam would be devastated if he ever found out about Jack –' there was a moment's pause '– and the others. And what good would that do anyone anyway, other than open up all sorts of old wounds? Coping with childlessness? What about that? Or we could

255

talk about the Swami and the various charitable and educational projects that he is involved in but people always get the wrong idea about him, just because he has eight wives. People don't understand, it's a cultural thing.'

Fisher took another mouthful of tea and wished for all the world that Mim was there with him. If Angela hadn't been so certain that Ganymede would make a great backdrop and the Burkes an ideal first couple, he would have made his excuses and left. As it was, Yolande finally let him go at half-past ten, by which time he could barely see straight.

The following morning, not long after the children had left for school, Sam showed up at Mim's house. He was dressed in oversized shorts and a grubby khaki T-shirt and looked extremely dejected. He perched himself on the stool in Mim's workshop, looking like a bad-tempered eagle squashed onto a perch designed for a budgie.

'That photographer bloke was at the house again yesterday. He was up a tree this time, in one of the cornfields that butts up to the back of the house. There was no way he could pretend he was lost, but by the time I got to him he had gone, scarpered. I've tried to talk to Yolande about it but she doesn't seem interested, said she was in some sort of healing crisis.'

Sam pulled a piece of clay off the ball on the bench and began shaping it between his fingers. 'It's not right, something is going on. Yolande told me that Eelpie have organised for some guy to come down and discuss filming. Then a publicist rang up just before I left. I wondered if this bloke worked for them but surely to God if he did he wouldn't spend half the morning up a fucking tree. Would he? I can't cope with this, and then to cap it all the bloody phone calls come into the shed. I mean, how did they get hold of that number for Christ's sake? I can't stand it. It's like I've got no place to go, no say in what's happening. I'm being hounded. That's why I wanted to move to the country in the first place, you know. It used to be my dream, buy a big old-fashioned country house, long drive, rolling fields. Big gates.' He screwed up his nose. 'I can't be doing with this publicity. I can't relax. I feel as if I'm under surveillance like a lab rat.'

'But surely you're used to this sort of thing. You've had publicity before, for your books – your books are famous – and didn't you do a film too?'

Sam frowned. It made him look like an axe murderer.

'Yeh, but it isn't the same. Writing – or at least my kind of writing – is a private, insular sort of thing. People leave me alone to do it. I couldn't do it otherwise. There's just me and a cast of thousands conjured up by my overactive imagination. I've done signings, readings, the odd interview here and there, bit of TV. BBC 2 asked me onto a review programme to read a few pages of the thing that won the Booker, but nothing like this. And anyway all that was on my terms. They didn't come to my house and pester me. It feels like there's no place for me to hide. And the other thing is that with the book stuff Yolande has always taken care of it, sorted it all out for me.'

'And isn't she now?'

Sam pulled a face. 'No, I think she's being suckered in. She's not in control, that devious little bitch from Eelpie telly is.' His eyes narrowed. 'Her and your husband.'

Strangely enough it took Mim a few seconds to work out who Sam meant. 'Fisher?' she said, with genuine surprise. 'Are you sure?'

He nodded. 'He was there all afternoon yesterday talking to Yolande and before that she was holed up with Jack Tully in the office sorting out the bloody knot garden. It's got to the point where I need to book an appointment to see her.'

'But she rang and asked Fisher to come over. He didn't invite himself.'

Sam didn't look convinced. 'What is this programme going to be about exactly?'

Mim shrugged, trying to remember some of the things Fisher had told her. There wasn't very much.

'They're going to do some sort of problem page phone-in. Find a topic and then build a programme round it, starting off with someone famous who's got personal problems.' It didn't come out anywhere near as diplomatically as Mim intended.

Sam's expression hardened. 'Personal problems?'

Mim nodded non-committally. 'Well yes, that's what Fisher does for a living. He's a counsellor. But this is just a pilot, Sam, a practice run, it might not even get shown. And to be honest I would have thought they could have found someone more popular –'

Mim winced. Sam frowned.

She waved the words away. 'You know that isn't what I meant, what I mean is more populaist, someone with the common touch, a soap star or a pop star or a footballer or something. You know. Tabloid fodder. You're more of a broadsheet man.'

Sam pressed the clay into a thin wavy sheet between his bear-like paws. 'So, this is sort of a dry run, is it?'

'Uh-huh.'

'What sort of personal problems do you think they mean?'

Mim shrugged, 'I don't know, Fisher doesn't really talk to me these days,' and then said, quickly trying to deflect him, 'While you're here I wanted to ask you about the sculpture for the woods . . .'

'So people won't necessarily know anything about this programme then, even if it is made?'

Mim shook her head. 'I shouldn't think so. I mean

not yet. It's a new idea. And to be honest I wouldn't have thought Fisher would have been of much interest to anybody, really.'

Mim's mum rang up at lunch time to tell her there was a bit about Fisher in the *Daily Mail*. A woman rang straight after to book him for a fashion shoot for the *Argos*, and then when Mim nipped down to the post office to get a carton of milk, Doreen handed Mim the local paper, folded to page three, where there was half a page about a new TV series with Fisher Pilgrim as the host. The first programme to be filmed locally it said. At Ganymede Hall. There were big headlines and a picture of Fisher looking relaxed on the couch at the TV studio in his trademark denim shirt.

'Fancy,' Doreen said, standing by the cold cabinet checking the sell-by date on the Kraft cheese slices. 'It must be lovely for you, your Frank finally arriving. I did wonder whether we ought to order some more postcards in. I mean, there's bound to be a lot of interest, people coming into the village for a little look-see. Fancy your Frank of all people putting Maglington on the map.'

Yes, just fancy.

Mim bought the newspaper and the carton of milk that she'd gone in for and headed home, beginning to understand exactly what Sam meant about there being no place to hide.

But at least the kids were okay.

In the dark fetid shadows of the pavilion Linda grinned and didn't resist as Liam began to unbutton her shirt. 'I didn't think you'd come after the trouble you had with your mum about bunking off,' she murmured, pressing her lips into his neck.

'No, she's fine, but I haven't got very long.' He shivered

259

as his fingertips brushed the soft downy flesh of her breasts, pushed up and forward like some sort of glorious erotic offering in a black lacy bra. He groaned and pressed his face into her cleavage, desperate to breathe in the smell of her body.

'Seems like a really nice woman your mum,' Linda was saying. She was warm and wriggled about as he caressed her. God, this was so wonderful Liam almost wanted to cry with the sheer unadulterated pleasure of it. She helped him to undo her skirt and slide it down over rounded hips, chattering away like a busy little cricket as he did so. Underneath she was wearing tiny black frilly knickers that matched her bra.

Liam swallowed hard.

He'd got two private study periods and was meant to be working on *Othello*, considering the themes of jealousy and double dealing. Momentarily a vision of Reuben Harnwell scuttled through his mind like the black rain dogs of a summer storm and then he felt Linda's hand slide down into his groin. She giggled at what she found and moved closer. Bugger *Othello*. Liam had other things on his mind.

Across the playing field in room G3 Harriet was in a geography class or at least her body was. Her mind was curled up in somewhere warm and quiet and sensual with Rob Grey. Her mind was also as naked as the day that it was born, and those details of the male anatomy generally and Rob Grey's in particular, that she wasn't all together certain about, were discreetly hidden under a cream silk sheet. She could almost feel his lips on hers and the heat of his body as he cuddled her close.

'So, Miss Pilgrim, would you like to tell the class what you know about glacial deposition?'

Oh God, not again. Harriet reddened furiously as the

voice of Mr Gault dragged her sharply back into the here and now. Fortunately it was another revision lesson and Harriet had read her notes and learnt it first time around and certainly had no intention of letting a man with tufts of hair like shaving brushes protruding from each ear make her feel bad or inadequate.

This love stuff was troublesome.

She took a minute to compose herself and then said, 'It's the material that the glacier picks up as it moves and then leaves behinds as it melts and recedes.'

Gault grimaced. 'Oh, very good, Miss Pilgrim,' he said, in a voice dripping with sarcasm. 'Very good indeed. Can you just make sure that your attention stays with us for the rest of the lesson?'

Harriet nodded. Ten minutes to the bell, how hard could it be? In her imagination Rob stroked her cheek and she was lost.

Fisher spent most of Tuesday working in his study, with a brief trip into King's Lynn to visit the hairdresser, although as he sat in the queue waiting for his usual man to give him a bit of a trim, Fisher wondered if it might not be a better idea to wait until the fashion shoot.

Fashion shoot. He grinned to himself as he took his place in the swivel chair and the man shrouded him in a wrap and a strange rubber round-the-neck-over-the-shoulder thing that was meant to stop the hair going down the back of his neck.

'And how are we today, then, sir?' said the hairdresser, comb poised about his crown.

'Very well indeed,' said Fisher and meant it.

'And what do you fancy then? Same as usual or something a little special?'

Fisher shook his head. 'Bit of a trim, nothing too drastic?'

'Right you are, then,' said the man. 'Got to keep our public happy haven't we.' He winked at Fisher as if they were bosom buddies. 'I'll just give it a bit of spray, easier to work on when it's wet. My missus always watches you, you know.'

Fisher straightened his shoulders. Recognised in the barbers, they'd be asking him for his autograph next.

'So, what are you up to then? Your life as exciting as everyone thinks?' asked the hairdresser with a grin.

Fisher shrugged in an effort to appear modest. 'No, not really. Just a job at the end of the day, isn't it? We all need to put the bread on the table.'

The man nodded. 'S'pose you're right. Not bought a Roller or anything yet then?'

They laughed as if sharing some huge joke. Fisher let the idea develop for a few minutes as the man snipped and lifted and fiddled. No, he wouldn't buy a Roller he'd get a Mercedes. And then Fisher's attention drifted back to his reflection and he wondered again if he might have been better waiting to have the magazine stylist give him the once over.

Shirts, the woman from the magazine had said. A kind of tongue-in-cheek contrast piece, subverting his usual homely accessible denim look. The woman had laughed conspiratorially. 'Although to be honest I love the way you look, Fisher. It's just that publicity thought it would be really nice to do you a makeover. But don't worry,' she added hastily, 'we won't do anything drastic. We've done all sorts of other famous people.'

Other famous people, the words were music to his ears.

'That's all right then,' he'd said with a grin, pulling his diary closer. It felt as if this had been the kind of thing he had been waiting for all his life.

Chapter 16

Over all it was a slow news week, no nation ruled by a raging despot had invaded another or at least if they had it was in somewhere unfashionable. Nobody had resigned from the cabinet under a billowing black cloud of humiliation and nobody famous had done anything really shocking – or at least if they had they hadn't been caught. Yet.

On Wednesday morning Yolande drove over to pick Fisher up and then drove down to Eelpie's offices in her classic metallic bronze Jaguar. She'd talked non-stop all the way and drove far too fast. Fisher arrived with a throbbing headache and a sensation that at any minute his ears might start to bleed. And the meeting was not going exactly as Fisher had anticipated either.

Since they had last spoken Angela had decided they ought to go with childlessness and the effect it had on relationships. She called it infertility and Fisher couldn't help noticing that there was a real edge to her voice, almost an accusation when she spoke to Yolande. He didn't like the way things were going at all.

'Sam won't talk about it,' said Yolande emphatically.

They were sitting in Eelpie's conference suite. It was mid-afternoon. The sun was slowly heating the room's occupants to a simmer, and even double-glazing couldn't muffle the low rumble of passing traffic.

Angela smiled. 'So much the better. It'll add a real sense of poignancy. Lonely man in the mist, walking through his country estate all alone with his thoughts.

It would be a nice image over the opening titles. Do you think we can get Sam to say he won't talk about it on camera? I mean what is it? Too painful, too frustrating?'

One of the creative team scribbled notes down on a clipboard.

Yolande paled to the colour of clotted cream. 'I don't believe you. These are our lives that you're talking about. How can you be so bloody insensitive?'

Angela's expression didn't flicker. 'Practice. I understand what makes good television. The nearer the bone the sweeter the meat. And let's face it Yolande, the deal you've got on the table, we need to get some really good TV out of this.'

Yolande bristled. 'My fee is going to charity.'

'Your fee is going to some dodgy little foreign guy facing deportation.'

Yolande's expression hardened to tungsten.

'Harani Joshe is a living saint, a visionary.'

Angela looked as if she might be about to let rip and then thought better of it. 'Whatever his nibs is, if it wasn't *sub judice* we'd go after him, and the whole cult thing, but Sven says we've got to leave that sort of heavyweight investigative stuff to the big boys. Which in my opinion is a great pity.'

The meeting was not the easiest Fisher had ever been to. The two women seemed to take every remark personally and Yolande got incredibly upset when Angela started to talk about whether she had any sense of failure about not having a family.

When the discussion got heated or tearful Fisher sat back and nodded. He'd practised the expression and the exact angle of his head in front of the mirror for weeks until it was second nature – and it certainly seemed to have the desired effect, deflecting any need for him to comment, particularly if he pursed his lips at the same time and leant forward very slightly.

So far, everyone was agreed on the basic format for the programme. He would listen and Yolande, prompted by one or two short questions, would talk as they walked around the estate at Ganymede. Rambling in both senses of the word was fine, apparently. They'd cut it together later, a natural conversational style between counsellor and client was what Angela was after. There would be an invited audience waiting for them back at the house, probably in the conservatory but possibly in the cream drawing room. Besides the general public, Angela planned to slip in a few invited experts both allopathic and holistic and intercut the studio discussion with phone-in segments. The whole thing was shaping up very nicely.

Angela did ruminate aloud whether they could perhaps work in a gardening slot to break the open forum mould. Jack Tully was an extremely photogenic piece of kit. Angela made a point of getting his phone number; maybe they could include a little cookery too. It would be a great way to tap into the whole family experience and Angela could see how the framework could be adapted to various other famous personalities. Those without gardens could choose a favourite place, so for example they might talk about drug addiction and then go on to look at Cheddar Gorge or Blackpool Tower. *On the Road to Recovery with Fisher Pilgrim* was a possible title being mooted.

'The location thing is a great selling point, it adds a little twist to an old format,' continued Angela, cracking open another bottle of Evian. 'It might mean being away two or three days at a time,' she said directing a smile towards Fisher.

He nodded, as the occasion demanded.

'Right,' said Angela picking up a sheaf of papers and tapping them back into shape. 'I think that's just about it then. Thank you for coming –' she got up and shook Yolande's hand. 'Nicole will show you out. I'll pass the draft contracts on to our guys and we'll talk soon. Oh, and someone will be in touch to confirm the dates that we'd like to come up and do the recce.'

Yolande nodded. 'I'll look forward to hearing from you.' She turned her attention to Fisher. 'Am I right in thinking that you are staying in town tonight? Are you in a hotel? I thought that perhaps we could go for something to eat and talk?'

It had been a long and tiring day, the idea of listening to Yolande drone on any longer was almost more than Fisher could bear and so he was relieved when Angela stepped into the breech. 'I'm afraid Fisher and I have still got a lot of important ground to go over.'

Edged out, Yolande's smile iced over.

As soon as she had left, Angela started collecting her things together. 'Home,' she said.

Fisher frowned. 'But what about the important ground we've got to go over?'

'We can talk about it later over supper and a bottle of wine. There's a really good Thai place just round the corner from my house –'

He would have preferred to have discussed whatever it was over a pot of tea and a shepherd's pie but didn't like to say so, and he was a bit disappointed that the company couldn't run to a night in a hotel. He loved big fluffy white towels, bathrobes and room service. Angela smiled when he mentioned the hotel on the way down to the foyer.

'You'll be sick to death of them once we get this show on the road. We'll be away at least two nights a week. Besides this way we can talk and I've got lots of fluffy white towels.'

Mollified, Fisher followed her out to the car park.

Angela had a nice little house in a side street off the

Fulham Palace Road, within walking distance of Eelpie's offices although she'd brought the 4×4, for his luggage presumably, which was a nice thought.

Angela jogged up the steps to the front door. She eased off her shoes in the hall and showed him round, where the loo was, the spare room, that sort of thing. It was nice in a plain way, not cosy – stripped boards and cream furniture, a few plants dotted about the place.

Fisher tried to disguise a yawn, the combination of Yolande's company, the heat in the conference room and the extended meeting had exhausted him.

'Tired are you?' Angela said, handing him a gin and tonic.

He nodded.

'Why don't you go and have shower and a little lie down. It's early yet. Go and grab forty winks. We can eat later. It won't be a problem, I've got several calls to make.'

Gratefully Fisher nodded. Angela seemed a lot gentler when she wasn't at work.

He showered, letting the hot water ease the kinks out of his spine and then, still wrapped in a big white fluffy towel, settled down on the futon in the spare room and pulled the duvet up over his tired body. It seemed that while he was in the bathroom Angela had been up and pulled the blind, which was nice.

In the distance he could hear traffic, sirens and horns punctuating the dull city rumble. How people managed to live with all the noise was the one of the last rational thoughts Fisher had before sleep claimed him. The other was that he was hungry and that he hoped he didn't sleep for too long, but then again surely Angela would wake him if he did?

It was very dark when Fisher opened his eyes again. For a moment he had no idea where he was and panicked. Something had disturbed him although, he wasn't altogether sure what it was, and then he realised as consciousness came bubbling back into his brain like a cistern filling that there was something on his thigh. At first he thought it was the towel and then with a growing sense of horror he realised that it was a hand. A warm soft hand that was eager to explore.

The owner of the hand groaned with delight at what it found. Fisher gasped. It appeared as if his body had woken up some time before he had.

'Oh Fisher,' Angela sighed, moving closer. At least he knew who it was now and where he was, which gave him a momentary sense of relief, and then he felt Angela's knee and thigh slide over his thighs and before he knew quite what was happening she was on top of him. She was naked and warm and smelt of something flowery and exotic. As he struggled to find the light on the bedside table her breasts brushed his chest and this time it was him that groaned.

'Oh Fisher, I've waited so long for this,' Angela said, catching hold of his manhood and unrolling a condom over it with a deftness that would have taken his breath away had he got any breath left. She handled his cock as if it was a badly behaved hamster.

What could he do? What could he say? He was hardly in any position to fight her off. She wriggled closer and closer until it felt as if her body might just swallow him whole. Outside in the real world he could hear the wail of a siren and closed his eyes. He would have thought of England except that he didn't really have the time.

Meanwhile, at Maglington, the phone was ringing. Mim picked up the receiver and said hello.

'Hi, this is Rob Grey, is that Harriet's mum?'

'Yes,' said Mim. It was early Wednesday evening and she was enjoying the peace and quiet of an evening without

Fisher or the prospect of him. She and the children planned to nip into Denham to pick up a Chinese takeaway for supper. Knowing that the whole day was her own Mim had got an enormous amount of work done, she'd glazed the garden tiles, finally finished the bee bowls, and done some work on the mythological figures for Ganymede. If she made them small enough they could go into the craft shop alongside the mermaids. So far Mim had made a nymph and a dryad and, when the phone had rung, had been considering how exactly to make the satyr without it turning out to be Reuben Harnwell.

'I hope you don't mind my ringing but I wanted to make sure you didn't mind Harriet coming over to baby-sit on Saturday. She did say she'd check with you but my wife thought it might be better if we spoke. I'll make sure she gets a lift home.'

'That's very kind. Harriet hasn't sat for anyone before, but she is a very sensible girl and I'm not far away if she needs me.'

'Great. Our little boy Patrick will most probably be in bed by the time Harriet gets here. And even if he isn't, he's no trouble.'

Mim smiled when she hung up. It had been a nice day. She'd worked in the pottery until the kids came home from school. Babe had found a place in amongst the towels Mim used for the pottery, curled up in a puddle of sunshine on the workbench and purred and slept his way through the whole day. Liam had spoken to Linda on the phone, all that seemed okay and now Harriet had got herself a little job, and Fisher? Mim paused to look at her reflection in the hall mirror. She hoped with all her heart that Fisher would get exactly what he deserved.

And for herself Mim wished that it would soon begin, that she would finally have the time and the emotional space to do some of the things she'd always dreamed of. Without Fisher things would be different but not impossible. Maybe she could finally go to art school or do a degree. Today those dreams that had been hibernating at the back of her mind for years and years uncurled and stretched a little, no longer just pale fading possibilities. Odd how amongst the ashes there was so much hope.

'Mum?' Liam's voice broke into her thoughts. 'What time are we going to get the Chinese? I'm absolutely famished.'

Angela got up and ordered an Indian takeaway. Fisher had no idea what time it was, somewhere down the line, along with everything else, he had lost all track of time. As soon as Angela was gone Fisher got up, scurried across the landing and locked himself in the bathroom. He sat in the bottom of the shower tray for the best part of half an hour letting the water explode all around him, monsoon like, washing away the smell of Angela's perfume and shutting out almost everything except the wet and the roar of his thoughts.

He was outraged and angry and very, very shocked. He'd told Angela at least a dozen times since they'd met that he was married. Happily married. Good God, Angela had even met Mim and the children. He would have stayed in the shower a lot longer if the water hadn't finally gone cold and Angela hadn't banged so hard on the door.

The curry gave him indigestion.

He was too tired and perturbed to resist Angela's suggestion that they had an early night. Like a condemned man he followed her upstairs into the master bedroom and lay down amongst the explosion of lace cushions to await his fate. He didn't have to wait long.

At Maglington Liam went to bed with his arm wrapped around a pillow dreaming that he was snuggled up in bed with Linda Bremner. They'd arranged to meet up in the free period he'd got before lunch on Thursday.

Harriet dreamt of Rob Grey.

Yolande told Sam that after the day she had had in London she needed time alone to cleanse her aura. Sam didn't need to be told twice, he knew the score and ambled back out to his shed, watched a badger cross the clearing in the moonlight, and finally fell asleep on the sofa.

Jack Tully knew exactly what it was that Yolande needed to clear her chakras but at least had the decency to wait until the lights had gone out in the shed before going upstairs to take it to her.

In Hammersmith Fisher spent a lot of time trying to work out how the canopy above Angela's bed was fixed to the ceiling, Angela knew but wasn't telling.

And Mim, who took a pot of tea and a book to bed, slept like a baby. She slept diagonally across the mattress, wrapped in the duvet, in fact it was such a nice experience that when the alarm went off at seven she did consider getting the children off to school and going back to bed.

Angela and Fisher arrived nice and early at the studio to record the segment trailing his new show. Angela went off to her office as soon as they got in, Fisher went into make-up and settled himself down in one of the chairs.

The girl who always did him ran her fingers through his hair. 'You look a bit puffy this morning, Fisher,' she said. 'Rough night?'

Fisher groaned. Was it that obvious?

Meanwhile, after checking her messages, Angela settled herself into the control room with a cafe latte and an almond croissant.

The thing about sex is that it improves with time, that's what all the books said. New relationships, new bodies learning about each other always took a little time to get in sync. Surely that was part of the fun. Fun? Angela sniffed and tore the croissant into pieces. After all, the man had been married for – well, for ever, really. It was probably a once a week chore with the lights off thing for them, if they did it at all.

God, it would have been a miracle if he and Angela had got it together satisfactorily the first time. A miracle. Angela's mind paused in its defensive monologue while she took a big swig of coffee. All right, so it hadn't been the greatest night of her life. Of the nights she could remember, obviously, but if nothing else it had broken the ice.

Below, on the studio floor, Fisher wandered across the set, a little boy lost, and she felt an odd flutter in her chest. One of the technicians helped to get his mike and earpiece sorted out.

Angela flicked a switch and said, 'Okay, Fisher, get settled. I'll have them bring up the autocue; you know how this goes. Nice and slow. Eyes front, watch for the red light. We'll read through it once and then we'll record. I'd like to be ready in five, people.'

As the floor manager counted him in, Fisher looked up towards the control box as if waiting for Angela to give him a sign. He looked pale and so very alone out there on the sofa. The flutter in her chest got worse and worse and for a terrible moment Angela was almost overwhelmed by a great wave of compassion. It was a first. Angela wondered if it was love or a heart attack.

Fisher arrived home late on Thursday evening. Even Mim thought he looked exhausted.

Friday was quiet.

On Saturday Yolande rang Fisher demanding to know why she hadn't heard from him since their meeting in London and how it was she had got an invoice from him. He decided it would be better if he drove over to Ganymede to explain and placate her.

At seven Mim drove Harriet over to Rob Grey's cottage and just before she left Liam suggested he bike to the village to get him and Mim fish and chips. While Mim was gone Liam took the opportunity to ring and meet up with Linda in the cemetery. Liam wondered, as he shinned over the wall, whether he was too young to commit adultery.

Linda was waiting by one of the big tombs, framed by dappled sunlight.

'Hi,' he said hurrying across the grass. 'I haven't got long.'

'It's all right,' she said, slipping her arm through his. 'I need to talk to you.'

Liam nodded and settled down on the grass beside her. She grinned. 'How long have we got?'

Liam laughed. 'Half an hour?'

She leaned across and kissed him. 'Plenty of time to talk in a minute then?' she said before pouncing on him.

He kissed her back, hard. 'If you say so.'

'I can't. You know,' she said, waving her hands and blushing a little.

Liam nodded in a man of the world sort of way. He understood all about woman stuff. 'No problem,' he said, just about managing to keep the disappointment out of his voice.

It was such a nice evening that Mim ate her supper out in the garden with a book and a long fizzy drink. Liam ate his in front of the TV. Mim put Fisher's fish and chips in the microwave for when he got home.

He hadn't told her very much about his night away, or his meeting, in fact he had barely spoken to her at all since he got back and was quite unable to meet her eye when she asked him how things had gone with Angela. Mim was pleased that he'd gone to see Yolande, although she would be hard pressed to explain exactly why.

At Church Cottages, Harriet was getting the guided tour.

'And this is our son, Patrick. Patrick, this is Harriet.' A tiny boy with a mop of sun-kissed golden and honey-coloured curls, dressed in Winnie-the-Pooh pyjamas giggled and clung to Rob like a monkey, burying his head in his father's shoulder.

Harriet laughed and said, 'Hello, Patrick. I'm going to look after you tonight.'

He giggled again and said, 'Story? I need the bears and the porridge, and the train.'

Harriet smiled. Patrick Grey was a beautiful, beautiful child and for a minute stole the limelight even from his father.

'Come on rascal, up we go.' Rob indicated that Harriet should follow him upstairs. 'My wife is just finishing getting ready, she shouldn't be much longer. Paddy likes a story but don't let him play you up.' Rob slid his son into bed and pulled the duvet up over him. 'If you'd like to read to him for about ten minutes, once we've gone; then it's light out. He can have some music on, there's a tape recorder on the windowsill. He'll tell you what he wants.'

Harriet nodded and took hold of the hand that Paddy offered; he smelt of soap and baby powder and made everything inside Harriet go warm and soft with a kind of affection and joy that she didn't know she had.

Paddy leaned against her.

'I think you've scored a hit there. Help yourself to anything you want downstairs, Nina has bought in a pile of goodies, crisps and soft drinks and stuff. And we won't be late back.'

*   *   *

Nina Grey appeared from the landing and smiled, holding out a hand. 'Hi, you must be Harriet, Rob's told me all about you.' Harriet felt herself redden and tried hard to blot out the fact that Nina Grey was quite obviously a really nice person. She was dressed in a full-length emerald green velvet dress which had a medieval look to it. Her hair was swept up in a knot of soft curls, she was wearing long dangly silver earrings and like Paddy she was very beautiful, and try as she might Harriet couldn't avoid the truth; pretty didn't always mean nice, except in this case it quite obviously did.

And then Rob winked at Harriet. 'Come on, I'll show you the rest of the house and where everything is. Nina's parents bought it as a holiday cottage about twenty years ago – weird that we've ended up living here. We used to come down for weekends . . .' And as he extended a hand all thoughts about Nina Grey were pushed to the back of Harriet's mind.

When the light began to fade and Mim went back into the house she was not altogether surprised to find Sam and Liam curled up side by side on the sofa, the remains of a plate of chips between them, playing some manic beat-em-up on the PlayStation.

'Evening,' said Sam, not taking his eyes off the screen. 'Your old man is over at my place talking to my wife again.'

Mim nodded. 'I know. Yolande rang earlier. Fancy a coffee?'

'If you're making one.'

Liam looked at her appealingly. 'Can I talk to you a minute?'

'Sure love, do you want to come into the kitchen while I make a drink?'

Sam groaned theatrically. 'Don't leave me now, *mon*

brave. I've nearly kicked his sorry arse. You ever tried this, Mim?' He lifted the handset.

Liam snorted and Mim laughed, while Sam tried very hard to stop his player – a large well-oiled green man dressed in a loincloth and earring – from getting beaten to a pulp by physically moving the joy-pad violently to the left.

'Bugger, this is bloody tricky,' he said, sticking his tongue out as an aid to concentration. Mim grinned, thinking how easy he was to have around.

'Ah, ah, ah,' Sam squealed, as a purple demon with glowing red eyes kicked his man in all sorts of cruel and devious ways.

'What did you want to talk to me about Liam?' she said. She was at the hall door.

Liam waved her words away. 'Don't worry. It'll wait,' and then turning his attention back to Sam, shrieked, 'No, go left, left. Jump, jump!'

Sam obliged.

Patrick Grey was sound asleep by just after eight. Harriet sat by the bed for a little while and watched him sleeping, all pink and golden, breathing oh-so softly. Midnight suddenly seemed an awfully long way away. What the hell was she going to do to fill the long slow hours between now and then?

Rob and Nina's house was small but crammed to the roof with all sorts of weird and wonderful things that looked as if they had been accumulated over years. There were ostrich feathers tucked into bowler hats and bowls full of china eggs, tarnished gilt mirrors, a chaise longue on the landing with a stuffed cat curled up on it, stuffed owls, screens draped with fringed shawls. Dotted here and there amongst this amazing collection of possessions were equally mundane things that had got lost in the crowd; a tea plate with dried-up crusts curled on it, a pair of nail clippers and a packet of drawing pins lay amongst a table full of bric-a-brac.

Downstairs the kitchen was littered with the remains of the family's last meal. Harriet wondered if she was expected to wash up and then decided – looking at the green mould in the top of a saucepan soaking on the windowsill – that she wasn't.

On a tray on one of the kitchen units were the things evidently meant for her. There were crisps and a can of coke and half a dozen fun-size Mars Bars in a little blue bowl, on top was a Post-it note stuck to a tube of Pringles that read: 'Thank you for taking care of Paddy. Milk is in the fridge if you want tea or coffee. Help yourself to whatever you want.'

If only.

Harriet put the kettle on.

Tucked under a magnet on the front of the fridge was a photo of Rob. He was leaning back in an armchair, sunlight picking out his profile. He was suntanned and gorgeous and was looking out of the picture with undisguised interest. Harriet felt an odd sensation in her chest and slipped the picture out for a closer look. She wasn't brave enough to steal it, however tempting. After a few minutes she headed back upstairs, telling herself that she was going to check on Paddy, but what Harriet truly wanted was a glimpse into their lives – into his life. The idea made her nervous but what had she got to lose? Rob and Nina weren't due back until midnight. She had the best part of four hours.

Up on the landing the door to their bedroom was very slightly ajar, a wedge of light from their bedside lamp just framed by the gap, visible through the acute angle. Harriet hesitated for a long while out there on the landing, listening to Patrick's soft rhythmic breathing coming from the nursery and then very gently she pushed the door open.

Rob and Nina's bedroom was as extraordinary as the rest of the house. The bed was hung with heavy tapestry drapes, caught back with gold cords. Every surface seemed to be covered in mirrors and bowls and perfume bottles. A huge bamboo birdcage hung from one corner of the ceiling above an ornate dressing table strung with Christmas tree lights. Behind that was a green screen over which was thrown various items of clothing – not all of which looked as if Rob or Nina had ever worn them. Hats hung from nails on the wall, tricorn and berets, boaters and bowlers. On the ottoman at the foot of the bed was a long silky black wrap and a navy towelling robe. On a set of shelves were dozens and dozens of pairs of shoes and in amongst it all the bed was unmade, a white duvet, under a thin claret throw, rolled back to reveal equally white sheets and pillows all crumpled and mussed and hollowed out by sleeping bodies.

Rob Grey's sleeping body.

Very slowly Harriet picked her way across the room, every sense, every molecule of her, breathing in the intimate details of Rob's life. The air was heavy with the smell of him. On the dressing table were bottles of aftershave and perfume, hairbrushes, make-up, deodorant, make-up brushes.

It didn't matter that most of what Harriet was seeing was about Nina; somehow Harriet felt as if knowing all these things, seeing all these things, brought her closer to the middle of Rob. Carefully, Harriet sat down at the dressing table and picked up a hairbrush, turning it in her fingers before very slowly pulling it through her hair, imagining as she did that somewhere behind her in the soft lamplight Rob was waiting.

It was a compelling fantasy. Harriet swallowed hard as

her pulse quickened. This was stupid, this was dangerous, it was also wonderful. Let's pretend like a kid would do, playing with the grown-ups' things and then Harriet looked down at the make-up and the bottles. There were pretty tins and a great wealth of things that littered the top of the dressing table and the tallboy and the chest of drawers under the window. For God's sake, the woman had left what looked like her entire wardrobe scattered around the room. Who would ever know, who would ever guess if Harriet played for a little bit more, who would worry if she tried on a few of Nina's things?

On the floor by the ottoman was a pale, silvery, blue silk something. Very carefully Harriet extricated it from the muddle of clothes and held it up to show her reflection in the chevalier mirror. It was an evening dress set with tiny rhinestones and she could get it on. It might even fit.

Looking around in case anyone was watching, Harriet slipped off her jeans and T-shirt and quickly pulled the dress on over her head. Nina Grey was slim too. It didn't matter that the bodice was a bit big and the skirt a bit long. Harriet pushed up her hair and with one of the ornate silver clips from the dressing table secured it into an untidy knot, just like Nina's, adding earrings, perfume and a slash of bright pink lipstick.

It was an interesting transformation. Harriet stared back at her reflection. It would have been a lie, and she knew it, to say that she had been miraculously transformed into the woman that Rob was married to, but she did look wonderful, older, sophisticated, even though her heart was thumping like a piston engine in her chest and every nerve ending was stretched transparent in case she was discovered.

Even so, one act spawned another. Over the next hour Harriet tried on Nina's shirts and shoes, skirts, dresses and a feather boa that was draped over the green screen. Inventing the rules as she went along Harriet stuck firmly to the things that were lying around the bedroom, not bold enough to venture into the drawers or wardrobes.

Hanging over the back of a chair were the clothes Rob had been wearing at school on Friday, jeans, an emerald green cord jacket, cream linen shirt, creased at the elbows and body. The shirt must be destined for the laundry. Standing alongside the chair was a battered leather briefcase. It was as if he had just slipped them off and gone for a shower, as if he would be back at any second.

Dressed in Nina's pink silk chemise and silver high heels Harriet picked up the shirt and pressed it to her face, breathing deeply, letting the smell of Rob's body fill every sense.

The effect was so potent and so deeply disturbing that her eyes filled up with tears, and some part of her, beyond the tenderness and the sheer need, was suddenly furious with jealously. It was all she could do not to clear the dressing table of all Nina's possessions with a single swoop and rip the dress she was wearing to shreds.

Harriet stared into the mirror, terrified by the intensity of the things she was feeling. Backing away, Harriet moved very carefully, distancing herself from Nina's precious trinkets and pots, just in case she accidentally knocked something over, knowing instinctively that one act of destruction might set off a chain reaction. Still with one eye on the mirror, Harriet wondered if love and desire always felt like this. Was it always this unforgiving? This intense? As she understood it more would it get easier and more controllable? Was this like the first torrential flood of something that cleared the path for whatever it was that came behind? Harriet couldn't imagine her mum having ever felt this for her dad. When it calmed down would the same feelings run through her veins without such terrible, terrible pain?

Big wet tears rolled down Harriet's face cutting a channel through Nina's make-up. It hurt to breathe knowing that Rob loved someone else or at least if not loved them then was with them. There had to be some way to let him know, some way she could make him understand how she felt about him. And then Harriet had an idea.

Before her courage failed Harriet got changed – checking that things looked much as she had found them – washed her face, went downstairs, and took an A4 pad out of the bag she had brought with her. On a clean page Harriet began a letter telling him exactly how she felt, '*Dear Rob . . .*' and when she was done Harriet very carefully folded the letter up and slipped it into a diary in the briefcase upstairs.

It was such a relief to have finally found a place to say the things she felt, Harriet felt almost euphoric. She checked on Patrick, who was still sound asleep, and then settled back on the sofa to watch TV.

At around quarter to twelve the sound of a car pulling up woke Harriet out of a doze. She got to her feet, slightly disorientated and looked out of the window. Rob and Nina were making their way up the path holding hands, and under the soft gold arc of the outside light Rob pulled Nina close and kissed her with such an intense mixture of desire and tenderness that it made Harriet's heart skip a beat.

'So, how did it go?' said Nina as she came in, slipping off her coat and dropping it over the newel post at the bottom of the stairs.

'Fine,' Harriet began. 'Patrick went to asleep really quickly, and he hasn't woken up at all since then. I've checked on him a couple of times.'

'You didn't eat much,' said Rob's voice from the kitchen. 'Do you want a coffee before we run you home?'

Harriet hesitated.

Nina winked. 'Don't worry, if you want to stay a little while he won't grill you about why you haven't handed in your homework. Or are you all in? Do you want to go home straightaway?'

Harriet wasn't certain that she wanted to sit with the two of them together. 'I'd like to go home, really.'

Nina nodded. 'Rob?'

Harriet shivered. The idea of being with him alone in the sports car tonight was almost more than she could bear. She wondered if he would be able to smell Nina's perfume on her. She started to collect her things together, careful not to catch Nina's eye in case by some terrible alchemy she would guess.

'Rob?' Nina said again

He came through. 'What love?'

'What did you do with the car keys?'

He laughed. 'You were the one who drove home, check your pockets.'

Nina patted her coat. 'God, I'd lose my head if it wasn't screwed on. Are you ready then, Harriet?'

'Sorry?' This wasn't how it was supposed to go. Nina wasn't supposed to drive her home

'Oh my God,' Nina giggled, 'I've forgotten to pay you, sorry.'

Across the room Rob pulled a ten-pound note out of his pocket and handed it to his wife. 'All right, love?' he asked patting Nina on the bum. 'Next time I'll drive –'

Nina giggled again, 'And it'll be my turn to make a complete tit of myself on a bottle of house red.'

Rob pulled a face at the two of them.

Once they were in the car Nina flicked on the lights and said, 'You know, it's really nice for us to find someone reliable to baby-sit for Paddy. Would you be happy to come and sit for us again?'

'Yes,' Harriet said. 'Sure.' And next time it would be Rob who drove her home.

As they pulled out onto the main road, Nina said, 'Rob told me about you and he's right.'

Harriet reddened. 'I'm sorry.'

'He told me that you were really lovely – all bright and bubbly . . .'

Harriet's heart quickened.

'. . . And you look so much like Kelly. It's unbelievable.'

'I'm sorry, I'm not with you.'

Nina laughed. 'Of course not. Sorry. Kelly is Rob's baby sister. He's always had a real soft spot for her. We saw a lot of her when she was your age.'

Harriet felt the world shift away from under her. 'What?'

Oblivious to the landmine she had just detonated, Nina Grey continued, 'He told me the first day he met you how much you reminded him of his precious baby. She used to baby-sit for us when we lived in London. She's at art school now – the Slade – and all very grown up these days. We sometimes get the odd note from her. Now, whereabouts exactly do you live?'

Note. Note. Harriet froze. The note she had written and left in Rob's briefcase. Harriet felt a great fist reach into her chest, seize hold of her heart and squeeze it so hard that she was certain that she was about to die.

Chapter 17

The phone went at seven the next morning. It rang and rang until Mim – who had tried pretending it was part of a dream – couldn't ignore it any more, and rolled out of bed. Beside her, Fisher slept through the noise, head thrown back, mouth open, snoring like a buzz saw.

'Have you seen the papers?' said a voice at the far end of the line. No introduction, no hello, nothing. Mim blinked, by rights she felt it ought to have been Sam Burke but this was a female voice.

'Who is this please?'

'It's me, Doreen from the post office.'

Mim shook her head to clear it. 'It's Sunday morning, Doreen. It's, it's –' Mim screwed up her eyes trying to focus on the clock just visible through the open kitchen door. 'It's barely seven o'clock. I was asleep in bed,' she said, wondering why she was bothering to control the annoyance in her voice.

'So you haven't see the Sunday papers yet then?'

'No.'

'I think you ought to. Sunday *Argos*. Couple of pages in –'

'Why, what's in it?'

Doreen made a peculiar throaty little sound and then said, 'I think you need to see it for yourself. My Jack and me said that fame can be a terrible thing – I thought that you ought to be warned.'

Mim's brain, which up until now had been trying to

stay wedged in the no-man's-land between waking and sleeping, snapped to. 'Warned. Warned about what?'

'Fisher, you, them up at the hall, to be honest I think you need to see the paper for yourself,' she said carefully.

'Can you save me one? I'll pop in and collect it later.'

'Don't worry, I'll get the boy to drop you one off.'

It was all a bit abstract.

Mim looked at the receiver after Doreen had hung up and wondered if perhaps she had dreamed the conversation. She was back upstairs in no more than half a dozen strides, snuggled down into bed and pulled the duvet over her shoulders, and then the phone rang again. It was Mim's mother this time. She was a lot more forthcoming.

'Would you like to tell me what on earth is going on?'

'I don't know what you mean, Mum.' This was torturous.

'Haven't you seen the papers? My neighbour just rang, got me out of bed.'

'Me too.'

'I was hoping that you were going to tell me.' Her mother coughed to clear her throat and what sounded like residual embarrassment and then began to speak very slowly. It took Mim's mind a few seconds to register that she was reading.

'"The Writer, the Philanthropist, the TV shrink and his wife".'

Mim started to protest, but now she'd found her voice Mim's mother continued reading, '"Bad boy Booker prize winner Sam Burke and TV's new heart-throb counsellor, Fisher Pilgrim, pictured here with the programme's sexy blonde producer, Angela Fuller, in a tangled love –"'

Mim cut her short. 'I already know about Fisher, Mum. I just didn't know what to do next –'

There was a tiny razor sharp silence at the far end of the phone and then her mother began again, '". . . While

Fisher is busy with svelte power junkie, Angela, wife Mim was pictured this week in the arms of the star of the first episode of Eelpie's new programme, novelist and scriptwriter, Sam Burke. In this tangled web of sexual high jinx –"'

'What? Oh, for God's sake, you have got to be joking,' Mim snapped in horror, feeling cold fingers track down her spine.

'I wish I was. They've got the pictures and everything, Miriam,' said her mother in that, I'm not stupid, don't lie to me voice she had used lots of times before. 'I don't care what Frank gets up to, you know how I feel about him, but I'm very concerned about you and what all this is doing to Harriet and Liam. I mean, I had got no idea. It says here . . .'

Mim struggled to grab a breath and before her mother could read any more said, 'Look, I'll call you back later, Mum, when I've had a chance to look at the papers and sort things out.'

'But I'm concerned.'

'I know, but please believe me none of this is as bad as it sounds or looks. I promise –' and with that Mim hung up.

The instant Mim put the phone down it rang again. For two rings she thought about answering it, guessed that it would probably only be more of the same, unplugged it, pulled a coat off the rack to cover her nightie, slipped on a pair of shoes, grabbed the car keys and headed off down to the post office.

'I said I'd drop you one off later,' said Doreen as Mim hurried into the shop. 'And I think I'd better warn you that I've had two blokes in the shop asking where you live. Well, not you but Fisher and the Burkes –'

Mim pushed a handful of change across the counter. 'What sort of men?'

'Reporters I think. I was a bit circumspect, you know – not too forthcoming.'

Mim thanked her and then hurried home. The village seemed as quiet as ever for an early summer Sunday morning. There were a few cars about, the odd local walking the dog, hardly mob rule. Maybe Doreen had been wrong.

Mim didn't look inside the paper until she was safely back in the kitchen. It never occurred to her to wake Fisher, instead she made a pot of tea and settled down at the table with her glasses and a tin of digestives. Her mother had always been a worrier but everything would be fine, just fine.

Mim opened the newspaper. Perhaps it wouldn't be fine. The story was on pages four and five. Actually there was very little story and a lot of pictures by the look of things. There was a grainy shot of her at the back door giving Sam Burke a hug. It was hardly a sexual embrace, just one friend to another, in fact Mim couldn't actually remember having cuddled Sam at all but apparently she must have. Here it was in barely focused grey and white. Alongside it were a series of smaller frames showing the two of them in animated conversation on her back doorstep. It took a little while for Mim to work out exactly where it was the photos had been taken from. It was such an odd angle and then she realised with a growing sense of indignation that the photographer must have been at the bottom of their garden to have taken the shots.

Alongside those of her and Sam were three pictures of Angela with Fisher – one at a window of what Mim guessed was the hotel in King's Lynn, one of Fisher carrying luggage out to the Jeep and the final one was of the embrace Mim had seen in the car park. Looking at them, she knew now without a doubt that the whole thing had been staged. They had been set up. Her, Fisher,

Sam. It was a bear trap. No one could have anticipated those comings and goings by accident.

But worse, much worse than anything of her or Fisher was a photo in the bottom right-hand corner of a half-naked couple on a lounger quite obviously not just cuddling. It was of Jack Tully and Yolande out on the terrace at Ganymede Hall. Underneath it the caption read 'And while the cat's away the mouse, philanthropist and born again hippie princess, Yolande Burke is sunbedding the hired help.'

Mim's first thought was that she would have to let Sam know and then seconds later that she ought to tell Fisher. Maybe it had been Sam who was trying to ring earlier? Wondering if he had already had the papers delivered – was he the sort of man who would read the *Argos*? – Mim went into the hall, plugged in the phone and dialled his number in the shed. She wasn't altogether surprised to find that it was engaged.

Just then there was a knock on the front door. Mim would have opened it but some odd sense of foreboding made her hesitate. The knocking grew more insistent and then the phone rang. Instinctively she unplugged it again, went into the sitting room to peer through the net curtains to see who was knocking.

Out on the pavement were half a dozen people, none of whom she recognised. Someone knocked again, much harder this time. Mim hurried into the hall, turned the key in the lock, slipped the bolt across and was about to try ringing Sam again when Fisher appeared at the top of the stairs. He was dressed in a bathrobe, open down the front, under which were a pale torso, long spidery legs and a pair of well-worn pea-green boxer shorts.

He yawned, scratched his balls and then said, 'Would you like to tell me what the hell is going on? It's like trying to sleep in the middle of a bloody military coup.'

Whoever it was knocked again and again.

'And who is that at this time of the morning?'

'Reporters. At least I'm assuming they're reporters. I'm going to go and lock the back door, and then I think we should ring the police and get them moved on.'

Fisher frowned. 'Reporters? What on earth are you talking about?'

'Your exploits with Angela are all over the Sunday *Argos* this morning.'

He grinned. 'Really? Maybe we should nip out and get a few copies before they sell out. What is it about? The new show?'

Mim felt something inside her ice over. 'No, not exactly, Fisher. I've already been down to the post office and got a copy. I don't think you'll want to keep any of these for posterity.'

Fisher's frown returned. Mim couldn't bear to watch the thoughts hatching on his unshaven face and hurried into the kitchen.

She guessed by the clanking and gurgling from the pipes that Fisher had retired to the bathroom, presumably showering and getting dressed before facing his public. Not, she noted, coming down to help her deal with the man banging frantically on the door. Apparently he needed to be primped and preened even before finding out what the situation was that he was dealing with. Mim was way beyond angry into something stellar and all consuming.

Meanwhile, out on the front doorstep the reporters hammered on. The only good thing, Mim thought as she locked the back door and put the kettle on, was that because the letter box fitted so badly Fisher had eventually nailed it shut. Even so, a male voice called for the occupants to open up and come out and talk. While

289

she was waiting for the water to boil Mim nipped upstairs and warned the children.

By the time Fisher reappeared the reporters had made it round to the back door too and Mim had rung the police.

Sitting at the kitchen table, resplendent in cream chinos and one of his new denim shirts, Fisher read the story all the way through. Twice. He didn't say anything.

Angela – up at the barn in the Cotswolds for the weekend – spread the pages of the *Argos* out over the futon and read the headlines one more time. It was far better coverage than she had could have possibly hoped for, far better. Thank God for the dearth of news. This ought to stick the ratings for the pilot through the roof, although her immediate instinct was that the story had probably peaked a little too early. They would need to get the show off the ground before the buzz died. Maybe if she could find a way to get a bit more mileage – if they could get Sam Burke to do something outrageous or even . . . her phone rang again. It had been ringing constantly since around eight, she was using the machine to screen the calls. She had expected that Fisher might call or maybe even Yolande, but this one was from Sven, just two words: 'Good Girl.'

Angela smiled and poured herself another glass of Buck's Fizz. Mel had rung from the *Argos* the night before to tell her the story was definitely going to press, although not what it was exactly, but she'd had a good feeling about it and stopped at the off-licence for a bottle of Krug. Jimmy had put the oranges through the juicer.

Jimmy, the nice muscly little blond boy from the outside broadcast unit, rolled over onto his belly and took the glass she offered him.

'So, you got something going with this Fisher bloke

then?' Jamie said, dipping a finger into the champagne and idly outlining her nipple.

Angela nodded.

He might not be the brightest star in the firmament but he knew exactly the things that a woman's body needed and appeared very happy to give her all of them, regularly, and with a real flair for invention and deviation. He also had the longest tongue she had ever seen.

Angela ran her fingers through his thick cropped bleached-blond hair. 'Uh-huh, but nothing that need worry you, darling,' she said. 'Fisher's my baby.'

Jimmy grinned and pulled her down towards him, doing that masterful, me Tarzan, you Jane thing, catching hold of the hair at the back of her head and kissing her hard, something that Angela loved so very much. His lips tasted of oranges.

'Mim? Mim? It's me. Are you in there? You've got to let me in. Mim? Mim?' It wasn't the thumping on the door that made her jump, so much as Sam's voice. Mim had been holed up in the kitchen since the first volley of phone calls and door knockings. The police had arrived fairly quickly after she'd rung them and they had persuaded the reporters to move back onto the pavement.

Fisher had sent word via one of the constables that he would be out at half-past ten to make a statement, and had been in the study ever since preparing what he was going to say. Mim thought he was an idiot, it would be like sticking his hand into a piranha tank but she didn't feel obligated to say so in case one sentence led to another and another and all those things she had been wanting to say to Fisher for years might come tumbling out, she wouldn't be able to stop.

Harriet said she didn't feel very well and hadn't emerged from her room since Mim had taken her up a cup of tea, and Liam was still busy upstairs on the PlayStation. So, in all other respects it was a fairly normal Sunday.

'Mim, Mim, please let me in.' Sam's voice was growing more frantic.

Mim peered out around the net curtains to check that he wasn't some sort of trap and then undid the locks and pulled him inside.

'Sam, what the hell are you doing here? And how did you get through that mob.' Being so very, very angry with Fisher, Mim couldn't quite reconcile how pleased she was to see Sam and stood for a few seconds eyes full of tears holding onto his great paws.

'Took a leaf out of old matey's book,' he said nodding grimly towards the newspaper still spread out on the table. 'I came down the lane and got in over the back wall.'

Mim swallowed hard. 'I'm so sorry Sam.'

He sniffed. 'I suppose part of me had known about the two of them for a long while. I just didn't want to admit it, but there's no getting away from it now, is there?' A plump glittering tear rolled down his big rugged face, its appearance made all the more poignant by his letting it fall unchecked onto his chest. 'I came over to ask if you and the kids wanted to come and stay with me at Ganymede until all this shit blows over.'

Mim pulled a face, stunned that a relative stranger should step into the breech to save her from the wolves. 'Why?'

He laughed. 'What do you mean, why? I would have thought it was obvious. Where the hell is Fisher?'

Mim reddened. 'In the study writing his statement.'

Sam looked heavenwards. 'Come to Ganymede with me. I can close the gates and I've just been in touch with a security company who can guarantee to keep those bastards out of the grounds and off our backs until this whole thing blows over.'

Mim considered for a few seconds. 'Won't it make things worse? Feed the flames?'

Sam shrugged. 'How much worse can it get?'

'What about Yolande, where is she?' The idea of Ganymede with Yolande in it had to be far worse than anything Mim might encounter at home.

Sam's expression was impenetrable. 'The Swami called her away to London this morning, apparently. She left about a couple of hours ago. He sent a car for her – big black job, chauffeur, the whole nine yards.' He paused. 'Or maybe she just rang for one herself. Who can tell?'

Mim couldn't bring herself to ask after Jack Tully. It seemed as if he might have ended up claiming Yolande by default. Sam appeared to be ahead of her. 'And Jack's gone too. Apparently Yolande told him he was sacked first thing this morning. Fired. On the spot. Told him to get out. Just like that. Poor bastard. I almost felt sorry for him. She told him he'd got a week to arrange for his things to be collected from the cottage.'

Mim felt her colour drain. 'Are you serious?'

Sam nodded. 'Oh yes, you don't know her like I do, don't be fooled. Yolande is a born survivor, nothing sticks. See all this –' he pointed at the tabloid pages. 'As far as she's concerned all this is Jack's fault, nothing to do with her at all. I'm under no illusions about Yolande. She always wants to be seen as the good one. She told me this morning that this thing with Jack was all innocent. It was almost as if she could hardly be bothered to talk about it – and then when it was obvious that the story wouldn't wash, she said that Jack had seduced her. Tricked her. Got her drunk when they were at some festival or other and then blackmailed her into continuing the affair with him.'

Mim stared at him. 'That's ridiculous.'

Sam shrugged. 'Oh yes, but above everything else

293

Yolande wants to save her hide. And it worked once before a few years ago, when I really deserved to be called a bad boy. I caught this guy with her in our house one afternoon. I punched him out. Broke three bones in my hand and would probably have gone to court if Yolande hadn't paid him off.'

'And this time?'

Sam pulled out a chair, sat down and with a wry smile said, 'I'm nearly fifty, Mim, to be honest these days my bark is a lot worse than my bite. Jack Tully could most probably wipe the floor with me. And anyway we'd both know the truth. They're two of a kind him and her. He's too shallow to fight to defend her and I don't believe a word she said. Bit of an impasse, really.'

'Will you have her back?'

Sam shrugged. 'Will she come back? Maybe. I dunno, things have been rocky between us for a long while now. I thought maybe it would come right, and I've had her back before. Mind you I've never had it waved under my nose like this. Smarts a bit. We'll see.' He sounded sad and tired and at the same time horribly resigned to his fate.

Mim handed him a cup of tea just as Fisher walked in.

'Morning,' Fisher said briskly. In one hand he was clutching a clipboard on which was typed half a page of close script. 'I wondered if you'd listen to my state-ment before I go out there. Just a quick read through, help me to relax, get it straight exactly what I want to say.'

Mim shook her head. 'Please Fisher, not now.'

He glared at her. 'But I need to get this sorted out. Set the record straight. I need to have my say.'

Mim squared her shoulders, suddenly furious. 'What about, Fisher? The affair you've been having with Angela or cashing in on Sam and Yolande?'

Fisher's expression hardened. 'Don't be so ridiculous.

294

I'm not cashing in on them at all. Besides this is very important.'

'No, it's not. What is important is that your little friend Angela has sold us all down the river.'

Fisher snorted. 'Don't be stupid.'

Mim squared her shoulders. She wanted to hit him so much that it was almost unbearable. 'I'm many things Fisher but stupid is not one of them. Who else could it have been if it wasn't your precious Angela?'

'Anyone. Anyone at all. And everyone knows that there's no such thing as bad publicity.'

Mim stared at him in horror, but before she could collect her thoughts to come up with a reply, Liam wandered in. He was wearing a T-shirt and pair of Bermuda shorts, which he had quite obviously slept in, and was apparently oblivious to everything else that was going on in the room and that the house was being besieged by reporters. He lifted a hand in greeting to Sam and then said, 'Mum, do you think I can I have a word with you?'

Mim nodded. 'Sure, love.'

She was relieved to follow him into the hall. 'What is it? Do you want to talk about what's going on outside?'

He shook his head and pulled the door to. 'No, no it's about Linda.'

'Okay, that's fine. What about Linda?'

'She's pregnant.'

Mim heard and then felt an odd rushing sound in her ears. 'Pregnant. Oh no, Liam are you sure?' The words sounded as if they were coming from a very long way off.

He nodded. 'Yeh, positive. She told me last night. I met her when I was going to pick up the chips. She did one of those tests. Yesterday. I think she's going to go to the doctor's tomorrow morning, and then once she's been she's going to tell her mum.'

For some reason that was quite beyond Mim, Liam looked totally unperturbed by the news, but then again he was only a kid, he had no idea of the implications, whereas Mim saw all kinds of possibilities, tableaux and outcomes and not one of them had happy ever after as a title.

Behind them the kitchen door swung open and Fisher, running his fingers back through his hair, checked his reflection, once, twice, in the hall mirror, unlocked the front door and stepped outside into an explosion of flashbulbs.

Quickly Mim thrust Liam into the sitting room and kicked the door shut behind Fisher. They needed to talk. She was about to follow Liam when Harriet said, 'Mum?' She was standing at the top of the stairs, white as a sheet, eyes red from either sleeplessness or tears.

'What it is love?' said Mim with a horrible sense of foreboding.

'I really need to talk to you,' she said in a thick, emotion-soaked voice.

Slowly Mim climbed the stairs and listened on the landing as Harriet, between sobs, told her all about Rob Grey.

'I love him, Mum,' she sobbed. 'I really do. I can't help it.'

Mim put her arm round her. 'I know love, I know.'

'What am I going to do?'

'Don't worry, we'll sort it out.' It might not have been the most original thing to say but it was all Mim had left in her armoury.

From outside they could hear the baying of the hounds as they ripped Fisher to shreds. Mim went back downstairs and opened the kitchen door. 'Sam, when can we go to Ganymede?'

He looked up from his mug. 'Now, if you like. I've got my car parked in the lane.'

Mim nodded. 'I'll go and tell the children.'

Was it right to call a prospective father a child?

The front door slammed shut and Fisher came in red faced and quite obviously annoyed. 'The bastards,' he said, out of breath and raw with indignation. 'They wouldn't let me get a word in edgeways. I need a coffee.' He looked expectantly at Mim. 'Can you make me a coffee?'

Mim sighed. 'Did you get to read your statement?'

'Oh yes.'

'Well, in that case I'd like you to hear mine.'

Fisher looked confused, 'What do you mean, your statement? You're not thinking of going out there are you? They'll tear you to shreds, and besides what could you tell them anyway, Mim, you don't know anything?'

Mim stared at him up. Until that moment she hadn't been sure what she was going to say but now it all seemed crystal clear. 'I'm leaving, with Sam.'

Fisher's jaw dropped. 'What? Why? When?'

'Now.' Mim looked at Sam for confirmation that it was all right and he nodded, although his expression suggested that he was almost as bemused as Fisher by the turn of events.

'So, is this all true then, this story?' Fisher said, his eyes narrowing, as he picked up the *Argos*. He couldn't quite keep the derision out of his voice. Was it that Fisher thought that she was so safe, so plain that no one else might ever want her?

Mim shook her head. 'No, no, I've never had any sort of relationship with Sam beyond friendship but I think you ought to know Fisher that Liam's girlfriend is pregnant. Harriet has sent some sort of steamy love letter to her drama teacher, and I slept with the window cleaner. Twice. Now if you'll excuse me I'm going to go upstairs and pack a few things.'

There was a big silence. Fisher didn't move and then he said, 'How could you?'

Mim paused mid-stride. 'What?'

Mim knew it was a seminal moment, and for an instant held her breath wondering if Fisher would somehow pull it all back from the brink, leap tall buildings at a single bound. Rescue them all.

'How could you do this now?' he grumbled. 'This is my big break; my career is just about to take off. I've got an image to think about – an image I've been building, a little plot on God's own acre. How could you do this kind of thing now? It'll totally ruin my reputation. All the work we've put in at the studio – wasted.' Indignation and fury and the sheer unfairness of it all contorted his whole face.

Mim was stunned.

'I'm sorry?' she said, meaning 'pardon, what did you say?', but the point was completely lost on Fisher.

'Sorry? Sorry, sorry doesn't go halfway to covering it, Mim. You know how much this opportunity means to me, I can't believe you let this happen.'

'Let this happen?' she repeated. Now she was angry. Now she was murderous. Mim felt a terrible fury rising in her belly, pressing up the back of her throat as hot and destructive as molten lava.

'You know how important this is.'

'What?' she roared.

Fisher flinched.

'This is important, more important, how come you can't see that Fisher? We are important. You are a complete and utter bastard – self-centred, self-righteous, lazy.' Mim shook her head, while inside she could feel the words clamouring for attention, fighting to get out, desperate after all these years to be said, to be heard.

'You are totally and utterly unbelievable, Liam and Harriet's lives are in chaos, they're totally in the shit;

they need our help and all you're worried about is what it will do to your precious fucking reputation. I can't believe that that's your first priority, I really can't, Fisher. What sort of man are you? How could you be so fucking short-sighted. This is your family we're talking about.' It was all she could do to keep her hands off him. 'You make me sick. Sick.'

Fisher took a step back, realising he had just woken a sleeping giant. 'Maybe we should talk about this,' he said, extending a hand, trying out a professional smile. 'When we've all calmed down. Round the table, family conference.'

Mim lunged at him, fists raised, wondering what it felt like to hit someone really hard.

Before she had chance to find out Sam caught hold of her arm. He certainly wasn't holding her back but it was enough to take the wind out of Mim's sails. She swung round to confront him. 'What?' she shouted.

Sam was completely unfazed. 'While you punch the little bastard out I'll go and tell the kids to pack a few things, shall I?'

Mim let out the red hot breath she'd been holding and allowing her shoulders to drop, shook her head and laughed. It was a laugh of relief and comprehension. 'No, it's all right, Sam, stay where you are. I'll do it. He isn't worth the effort.'

'My car is over the back wall when you're ready.'

Mim nodded. 'We won't be long, what we haven't got I'll collect another time.' She turned back to Fisher, who was cowering. 'Oh for Christ's sake, Fisher, pull yourself together. I can't stand any more of this.'

Pale and puzzled, Fisher stood in the middle of the kitchen framed by a patch of damp on the wall behind him. It seemed a very fitting way to remember him.

*   *   *

Angela was relieved when Fisher finally rang her at the barn.

'How's it going?' she said. 'Are the press guys still there? We shook the tree pretty hard. But don't worry, we're bang on course, Fisher. We couldn't buy this sort of first-rate major press coverage. They mentioned the new programme three times in the story. Three times and we're bound to get some sort of follow-up.'

There was an odd little sob at the far end of the line.

'Do you want me to send someone down there, Fisher? I can get one of the PR girls to come down and –'

'Mim's left me,' said Fisher.

'Oh my God, Fisher I'm so sorry,' said Angela, struggling to keep the sound of jubilation out of her voice. 'What can I say?'

Fisher sounded inconsolable. 'The things is, Angela, I don't know quite know how to tell you this, but I think you ought to know, just in case. It's a job to know where to start really, first of all my son, Liam – you met him at the Burkes'? He's been going out with this girl from school. Well Mim's just told me she's pregnant, not Mim, the girl –'

Angela settled back and picked up her notepad. There is nothing so endearing to the public as a wounded hero, a man who has struggled and fought his way back from the edge of destruction against harrowing odds, complete but scarred. Angela smiled and as Fisher's story unfolded made sure that she made all the right noises in all the right places. Her instincts had seldom let her down – she'd known when she first met Fisher that she was onto a winner.

'What the hell am I going to do?' sobbed Fisher. 'I mean the window cleaner, for God's sake, I ask you. He can't be more than twenty-five, if he's that, it's disgusting.'

Angela ran a finger slowly along Jimmy's spine – oh yes, but so much fun. Her opinion of Mim had already gone up considerably. 'Don't worry Fisher, I don't want you to think you're on your own. We're a family at Eelpie TV; we'll see this thing through together. I promise.'

'Oh, Angela. You've got no idea how grateful I am. God, I was so worried.'

As soon as he hung up Angela rang Mel at the *Argos*. This was just the little boost they needed to keep the ball up in the air for a little longer. Infidelity, teenage pregnancy, crushes on teachers, the whole Lolita factor – the very stuff of the day-time chat show.

When she'd finished Angela poked Jimmy. 'How about we go out for lunch?'

He was naked except for one of her sarongs tied around his waist.

'How about we stay in and I cook? Open another bottle of bubbly.'

'I've got nothing in the fridge.'

Jimmy grinned and pulled her closer. 'I'm not that hungry.'

'Mum, Mum I really need to talk to you.'

Sam had settled Mim and the children on the first floor – between them they had two bedrooms, a dressing room, where Liam had volunteered to camp out, a small sitting room and a bathroom. They had been unpacking. Mim felt as if they were refugees who'd escaped from a sinking ship with not much more than they stood up in. At least she had remembered to bring the school uniforms. Everything they had with them seemed to be dwarfed by the sheer scale of Ganymede.

Harriet had gone off with Sam to see about some food, leaving Mim and Liam sorting the beds out.

'It'll be all right love. I want you to know that I do understand, Liam.'

Liam threw the pile of sheets down onto the bed. 'Mum, stop it. You don't understand at all. It's about Linda.'

Mim wondered how long it would be before the sound of Linda's name didn't make her feel uneasy.

'Liam, once she's had a test we can arrange to go over and see her mum, obviously. We all need to talk this through. Have you discussed any of this with Linda?' Mim was trying hard to find the right things to say and not let any regret slip into her tone. It wasn't easy.

To her surprise Liam grabbed hold of her arm. 'Stop it, Mum, please.'

'Stop it?'

'Yes, you're jumping the gun. She is pregnant, but it's not my baby.'

Mim stared at him. 'What do you mean, not your baby?'

To her surprise Liam laughed. 'Do you want me to draw you a picture? I mean that it's not my baby, it's Reuben's. You know Reuben Harnwell, the window cleaner?'

For a moment Mim's heart stopped beating, then she tried very hard to quash the hysterical laughter that threatened.

'Oh my God,' she whispered. 'Reuben Harnwell's?'

Liam nodded. 'Uh-huh.'

'Are you sure? I mean how can you be sure?'

'I've only been going out with her a couple of weeks and she reckons she's at least two months gone if not three and anyway, we used condoms. I'm not totally stupid.'

'Condoms?'

'Yeh. I got them out of the machine at the Swan.'

Mim could have kissed him.

Chapter 18

It was hard not to pace, hard not feel as if they were trapped and abandoned and lost inside Ganymede. Even Sam's attempts to play mein host couldn't dispel the feeling. As soon as she could Mim rang Rob and Nina Grey. Although she didn't want to set this particular ball in motion at least it gave her a sense of direction and realistically the sooner she spoke to Rob Grey the sooner it would be over.

A woman answered.

'Is that Nina Grey? I wondered if I could speak to Rob please? This is Mim Pilgrim here, Harriet's mum.'

Harriet was sitting on the bottom of the bed, with her fingers in her ears.

'Hi,' said Rob Grey a moment or two later. He sounded relaxed and warm and instantly Mim understood why Harriet felt she could talk to him. Maybe this wasn't going to be so hard after all.

'Hi, I wondered if it would be possible to nip over and see you some time today?'

'Sure. By the way, Paddy adored Harriet. Not any problems I hope, I mean I was going to ring and thank her for doing such a good job. Except – well the thing is . . .'

Mim preempted him. 'You've seen the story in the *Argos* this morning?'

She could almost hear Rob searching around for something appropriate and tactful to say.

'It's fine, really,' she said to take the pressure off. 'I took the phone off the hook this morning so even if you had

303

rung we wouldn't have known. But I would still like to see you if at all possible. This isn't about baby-sitting.'

'Sure? When? It's just that Nina and I were about to go out – if it's something to do with the play maybe I can catch up with Harriet in school tomorrow?'

Mim felt something tighten in her chest, as if she could sense the tick-tick-tick of Harriet's note counting down the seconds to its discovery in Rob's briefcase. Every instinct told her that it needed diffusing now.

'No, no, it's not about the play or school. It won't take more than ten minutes.'

As Mim spoke it occurred to her that she hadn't got the car and as the realisation flooded through her, Rob Grey was agreeing. 'Okay – what shall we say. Half an hour then?'

Mim struggled to gather her thoughts. 'The thing is –' She saw Harriet's expression register a great flurry of horror. Mim held up a hand to reassure her, guessing that Harriet thought she might be going tell him there and then.

'I've just realised that I'm car-less at the moment.' How stupid did she sound? Mim felt hot, no solution presenting itself.

But Rob was a more amicable soul than she had antici- pated. 'We could come over to your house if you like? It's on the way.'

'Actually I'm not at home at the moment,' Mim said, the discomfort level rising with every second. 'I'm staying at Ganymede with Sam Burke, although, not with Sam – not in the way the *Argos* implied.' Rob didn't need to know any of this, why did she feel the need to explain?

'The thing is there were so many reporters outside our house, Sam suggested that the children and I came over here –' Mim knew she was rambling and gabbling and tried very hard to make her mouth close. It was a real uphill struggle, and in her own mind everything she said sounded like a confirmation of what the papers had already implied.

Harriet's increasingly unhappy expression was the thing that helped her apply the brakes. Mim stopped abruptly and then said in a far less hysterical tone. 'It is important that I see you today, though, I wouldn't have asked you otherwise and it really isn't something that I want to discuss over the phone.'

There was a pause, where she sensed Rob Grey deliberating and then he said, 'Okay, well in that case how about if we come up to see you anyway? Ganymede is that big estate place up behind the primary school, right?'

'Yes, just follow the lane down to the gatehouse and turn right. If you come to the front door. I'll meet you there.'

'Okay, we'll be there, say half a hour?'

She could have kissed him.

In the kitchen, Fisher settled himself down at the kitchen table, opened a bottle of wine and made a cheese and pickle sandwich. It had been a long and difficult day. He was put out that Angela hadn't offered to come down and support him in his hour of need. Proposing to send a girl from Eelpie's PR department was all very well but not really the kind of support he expected. Or perhaps Angela was still cross with him. Thursday's programme had been a little tense after the events of the night before. After all, a man of his age could hardly be expected to manage it three times in an evening, particularly on a chicken curry and two pashawari naan. He'd done his best.

Fisher sniffed and poured himself another glass of wine. It hadn't been a bad performance given the impromptu nature of the event. He looked down at the photos in the *Argos*, how the papers had found out about it was beyond him. God, maybe it was because he was finally truly famous after all. Maybe the people in the hotel had put two and two together before the event and rung in. Fisher preened himself a little. Fancy, after all this time, him, Fisher Pilgrim, famous. No longer local celebrity but national celebrity, maybe he'd open another bottle.

The thought and his jubilation settled. He still had no idea what Mim thought she was up to and glanced at the clock wondering what time she planned to get back from Ganymede. She'd been very overwrought. He could understand her wanting to be out of the house with the reporters about. Fisher felt a little claustrophobic himself. He'd locked and bolted all the doors from the inside so Mim would have to knock when she got home, and for some reason that gave him a really good feeling. His instinct told him that she had been exaggerating about Liam and Harriet, probably about Reuben too. He paused and took another sip of wine. Definitely about Reuben. The whole thing was obviously meant to upset him. She would calm down, come home and have to ask him to let her in.

Right on cue there was a knock on the back door. With a triumphant smile Fisher got to his feet. He swayed a little, seemed like the wine had gone straight to his head.

Mim hung around on the gravel outside Ganymede Hall waiting for Rob and Nina Grey to show up, shifting uncertainly from foot to foot. She needed to find a way to talk to Rob on his own. Somewhere in the bowels of the house Sam and the kids were supposed to be playing on the computer although she wondered whether Harriet might be tempted to come outside and join her.

Watching the shadows lengthen and listening to the noises of the pheasants in the park and the peacock mewling a reply, Mim settled in under the lee of the front door. She had already planned her opening comments to Rob, turning them backwards and forwards in her mind to see how they looked in the light.

One of the security guards stood a few feet away on the gravel framed by an ancient yew tree. He looked conspicuously inconspicuous. He had very shiny shoes and a walkie-talkie clipped to the lapel of his jacket.

'Penny for them?'

Mim jumped and swung round, wondering how it was that someone as large and apparently clumsy as Sam Burke could move so quietly.

'Didn't mean to frighten you. I was wondering where you were. Are you okay?'

She nodded. 'I've arranged to meet Rob Grey here – one of Harriet's teachers. I hope you don't mind. Didn't Harriet say anything?'

Sam stuck his hands in his pockets. 'About the love letter?'

Mim was genuinely shocked. 'She told you?'

'Eventually.' He gestured towards the guard. 'Did you warn the heavy mob that this guy is on his way?'

Mim nodded.

'In that case when they arrive I'll take Mrs Woman round the house and give you a chance to talk to Heart-Throb Rob if you like.'

She stared at him and laughed. 'You know, you're really good.'

'I try. Harriet's completely gutted. Makes you wonder if this guy led her on.'

Mim shook her head. 'I don't know, what I do know is that we've got to get it sorted out.' As she spoke a snappy little sports car rolled up onto the gravel. To Mim's surprise the car only had one occupant, Rob Grey.

He lifted a hand in greeting as he uncurled from the cockpit, and as he did Mim could see exactly why Harriet was attracted to him. Rob Grey was rangy with a kind of boyish self-assuredness, tall, good-looking and there was no getting past the fact that he was very sexy.

Seeing the two of them looking back at the car, he said casually, 'Hi, you must be Mim?' He held out his hand, 'And –'

'Sam Burke,' said Sam showing remarkable social skill for a man who normally grunted.

'I've already dropped Nina and Paddy off; neither of them is very good at waiting about. It must be a bit of a strain for you what with the –' he nodded back towards the gate, 'you know, the press and everything.' Mim nodded, while Rob continued, 'They're still outside the gates up there. Now, how can I help you?'

Mim took a deep breath. 'It's about Harriet.'

'She's a bright girl. Pleasure to teach. One of the best in her drama set – good kid.'

Mim nodded. 'The thing is I'm afraid she is also a very naïve one. There is no easy way to say this. She has got the most awful crush you – and if we don't put a stop to it now, it's going to cause everyone problems.'

'Ah.' He stuffed his hands into the pocket of his jeans.

'While she was at your house baby-sitting last night she left you a note – in the side pocket of your briefcase, in your diary as far as I know. In your bedroom . . .'

Mim suspected from Rob's cocksure expression that he was used to being in this place, centre stage, adored and pursued. It made her want to slap him.

'Okay, right –' he said in an undertone. 'Unfortunately it's Nina's briefcase not mine – but I'll go home and get the note now before there is any more damage done. Thank you for telling me.'

Mim acknowledged his thanks and then continued. 'The note isn't the only problem here, is it? Although I'm hoping she's learnt her lesson, what about Harriet?'

Rob shrugged. 'I've got no idea. She's your daughter. It's hardly my fault she's got a crush. I didn't realise I could be considered responsible for her emotional life.'

His indifference stunned her.

'But more than once you've given her lift home, asked her to baby-sit, invited her to audition for a role in the school play –'

His expression hardened. 'It's hardly an invitation to pursue me though, is it? All I've ever done is be friendly towards Harriet. If you're implying that I encouraged her in any way –'

Mim stared at him. Surely to God he had to realise that was exactly what he had done. A man in his position ought to know better, weren't there rules about this kind of thing? Mim took a breath. Allowing him the benefit of the doubt might be more fruitful than pointing an accusing finger, however much her instincts told her that he knew exactly what he was doing.

'I was just hoping that we could come to some agreement. Maybe work out some sort of strategy. I've already talked to Harriet – but she is only a kid despite appearances. What I suppose I'm asking you, Rob, is not to lead her on, however well meant your actions are, she is interpreting your friendship as interest. Do I really have to spell it out?'

He shook his head as if in exasperation then lifted his hand and walked back towards the Spitfire, implying that the matter was closed.

To Mim's surprise, from beside her Sam said, 'A guy in your position should be aware that what you did – however innocent – encouraged Harriet to think you wanted her. You ought to be more careful, kids of her age are incredibly vulnerable, and impressionable. Puberty is such a bastard. All those hormones raging, surely you remember.'

Although hardly the most profound or original statement anyone had ever made, Mim was deeply touched by his concern and the kind of heated sincerity with which Sam spoke.

Rob Grey shrugged.

It was the most infuriating and astonishing gesture. A dismissal negating everything Mim had just said and everything she was afraid of – and with a horrible sense of certainty Mim knew that this wasn't the first time Rob Grey had found himself in this position.

She turned and caught a glimpse of Harriet's face pressed up against one of the downstairs windows. Harriet might have behaved foolishly but she deserved better than this.

'Does this sort to thing happen to you often?'

Mim's voice stopped Rob Grey in his tracks. 'Sorry?'

'Girls falling at you feet. Teenagers chasing after you?'

That shrug again. It was the strangest of gestures, and what did it mean? What did it answer?

'You know what girls are like,' he said in a very even, almost warm voice. 'It doesn't take very much.'

Mim stared. 'What do you mean?' she said slowly with a growing sense of unease.

'I'm friendly to them. I'm friendly to everyone. I don't lead any of them on. I'm – what am I? I'm *sorry* if your daughter misinterpreted any of my actions.' The apology would have been fine had Mim thought for one moment that he meant it.

'I think,' Mim said, 'that it would be better if I went in to see Harriet's head of year about this.'

For a fraction of a second Mim glimpsed a crack, a tear in the carefully controlled façade. One of the reasons she had wanted to talk to Rob informally was that she guessed that even the rumour of impropriety about a teacher could ruin them. She had no desire for that at all if – as she thought earlier – Harriet just had a crush, but the more she saw of Rob Grey the more Mim was convinced that there was the possibility of something darker and far more sinister lurking behind his principal boy good looks.

Rob lifted his hands in resignation. 'You do what you think is right, Mrs Pilgrim,' he said. There was an edge to his voice that hadn't been there before. 'What's happened, eh? If we get right down to it? Nothing really, except some little girl's got her knickers in a twist about a teacher – it happens every day. All the time. It's what girls do. And can you really blame her? Look at what's going on in the rest of your daughter's life at the moment – no wonder she's so vulnerable. Christ. I think you ought to look closer to home before you start pointing any fingers in my direction.'

There was a pause as the implications of what Rob Grey said hit home. It came from so far out of left field that Mim couldn't think of anything to say, but Rob could. 'Her old man's knocking off his boss, her mum's screwing around with some local celebrity while his wife is shagging the hired help. I mean, what's that about for God's sake? It's hardly surprising Harriet's so bloody screwed up –'

Mim saw something move – a flash – in the corner of her eye and then realised it was Sam leaping forward and grabbing Rob by the lapels of his ultra-trendy jacket. She was a fraction of a second behind him and seized Sam's arm as he was about to punch Rob.

Rob's colour dropped away like mercury in a thermometer.

Sam growled. 'You fucking bastard – just how many times have you done this before, eh? Eh?'

Rob straightened his clothing. 'I'll pretend that I didn't hear that or that you assaulted me.'

As he reached the car he looked back at Mim. 'You do what you think best, but at the moment I wouldn't throw any stones if I were you.'

Mim stared at Rob Grey as the Spitfire drew away and realised that she was shaking with a mixture of shock and pure unadulterated fury.

Fisher poured the last of the second bottle of wine into his tumbler.

'Are you sure I can't top you up? I can always open another bottle?' he said to Ms Coldwell, who was sitting opposite him. Apparently she worked for some magazine, the woman's something or other. Anyway she had brought the cat back because she was worried that he might get run over in the mêlée. Seemed she had finally got to grips with the whole cat issue, and then she'd asked if while she was there could she use the loo – said it was all right for the men, they could just nip round into the bushes any time nature called. Not that she would be able to. Obviously. It was an alder, hazel and elderberry problem she felt they might need to talk about when he was a little better.

'Nice place you've got here,' Ms Coldwell said, coming back a few minutes later. 'Or it will be once the builders get finished. I can really see the potential. Such a mess the builders make, dust everywhere, all upstairs even in rooms with the doors closed. Lived here long, have you?'

He noticed that she had covered the kitchen chair with a bin bag.

This conversation had to have been going on for at least an hour now although Fisher was gradually losing any sense of time. He had been feeling sorry for himself and much put upon, and so was glad of the company. He offered her a coffee and she seemed touched and said unfortunately she only drank organic decaffeinated, and then all of a sudden he'd found himself telling Ms Coldwell all about Angela and Mim and Reuben and Sam and Liam and Harriet – well, all of it really. And despite it being a terrible breach of the whole counsellor/client ethos she had nodded and opened another bottle of wine which he had expected to share but she told him she'd just have the one glass because she was on tablets, which was fair enough. And then she'd found him the brandy in the pantry – because she said after all it was a medicinal thing and Fisher was in shock. Then she'd asked him about counselling and his new TV programme and the radio show and how interesting it all must be, and how it was he had got into it in the first place and before he knew it Fisher was telling Ms Coldwell his whole life story.

It was great to have someone to talk to and then he'd laughed, said she ought to do his job, she was a great listener. And Ms Coldwell had nodded and smiled and just before Fisher passed out he'd said yes of course she could use his phone.

Mim found it impossible to sleep. After Rob Grey left, Sam had taken her inside and made her and Harriet tea. Supper had been beans on toast in the kitchen; they'd found the kids some Coca-Cola, while he and Mim had shared a bottle of Syrrah. They'd watched videos and eaten ice-cream in the playroom, trying hard to ease up and push all the other things to the outside edge for a while.

They'd talked too, talked about all sorts of things, and then Mim had yawned, feeling the weight of the day closing in on her. Desperately, almost more than anything in the world, she wanted sleep to close over her and take her away, let her mind stop boiling and bubbling and turning things over and over until she was sick of the thoughts gnawing away at her.

The kids didn't fight to stay up either and so by eleven everyone had gone to bed.

The room was dark, the bed comfortable and warm and yet Mim's body refused to sleep, refused to let go, despite

313

every molecule complaining of exhaustion and praying for some sort of relief.

Somewhere close by she could hear Liam snuffling out the same sounds she had heard since he was a tiny baby. In the little bedroom next to hers Harriet had slipped between the sheets, switched off the light and when Mim had gone to check on her after she had finished in the bathroom was sound asleep too.

Maybe they felt safe now, maybe having passed on their pains and their fears to her it was safe to let go and let the night carry them away; whatever it was it eluded Mim.

Finally, at around half-past one, Mim pulled on her dressing gown and headed downstairs. Waiting for sleep to come and listening to the children was sweet torture. Maybe it would be better to admit defeat and go and make a cup of coffee. As she got down into the hall a voice from the darkness said, 'Can't you sleep?'

Mim gasped as Sam emerged from the shadows.

'No,' she snapped. 'I always wander around in the wee small hours. I was thinking of getting myself some chains and seeing if I couldn't pick up a lamp from somewhere. That's three times today you've frightened the bloody life out of me,' she said, her nervousness making her sound annoyed.

He grinned. 'Sorry, I was just doing the rounds and heard someone coming downstairs, thought I'd check to make sure it wasn't one of the kids wandering about. Do you need anything?'

To her surprise Mim felt her eyes fill up with tears. 'That's a bloody stupid question, Sam. I could do with a hug and a big mug of coffee, but most of all I want this stupid bloody nonsense to stop,' she said, voice trembling with emotion.

And then he moved nearer and had his arms around her, holding her so close and so tight that it seemed that the world ended with his chest, and the warmth of his arms around her and the soft pounding of his heart up against her cheek.

She was about to pull away and protest, say something jokey or dismissive, when she realised that this was just what she'd asked for and, more than that, was exactly what she needed.

Mim stood there in the dark, safe in Sam's arms for the best part of ten minutes, letting the tears ebb away, letting the tension ease in her belly. Here, at that moment, she felt like a child, experiencing an odd sense of uncomplicated trust, as if nothing could touch her. It was remarkable and like nothing she had felt since she was seven or eight.

Finally, Sam said, 'So, do you want the coffee now? I've got some brandy as well if you'd like.'

She nodded and wiped her eyes with the sleeve of her dressing gown.

'Thank God for that,' he groaned theatrically. 'You're standing on my toe.'

It had to be a lie. Mim glanced down and then stepped back.

Smiling, Sam extended a hand. 'Come on. Coffee?'

Mim nodded and for an instant she saw something more than kindness in his expression and was suddenly nervous all over again. Life was complicated enough as it was. Mim looked down, blushing furiously.

'What?' he said gently. He hadn't moved and was still holding out his hand.

'You know,' she said. 'You went all misty-eyed on me. We can't do this, Sam. We're both in bits emotionally, wrecked. I'm afraid if I reach out to you now it will be for all the wrong reasons. I want comfort, but I'm afraid that this will do us both a lot more harm than good.'

Sam shrugged. 'You worry too much. And anyway I wasn't offering you a lifetime commitment, what I actually had in mind was a cup of Nescafé, a nip of brandy and maybe half a packet of Jaffa Cakes.'

Mim frowned.

'All right, all right,' Sam said, holding up his hands in a gesture of resignation. 'Maybe more than that, maybe a lot more than that and it isn't just because Yolande's gone, we were both beginning to feel this before the whole thing blew up in our faces.'

Mim paused a moment to weigh up if the words were true or not and discovered that she couldn't and shook her head. 'Please Sam, we're standing far too close to the explosion to see clearly what's happening.' Even so she took hold of his hand and was grateful for the warmth.

'So, in that case we'll stick to Nescafé and Jaffa Cakes then?' he said.

Mim nodded and hand in hand like Babes in the Wood they headed down towards the kitchen.

'Mim? Is that you?' Fisher snapped.

It was early the next morning. She and Sam had gone to bed at around three. Separately.

On the periphery of her vision, Sam Burke – dressed in the same clothes as he had been wearing the night before – hovered around waiting for her. It had been him that had dragged her out of bed to say that Fisher was on the phone and that once they had spoken he intended to unplug it.

Mim was surprised to hear Fisher on the far end of the line.

'What it is?'

'We need to talk. Have you seen the papers this morning?'

'Hardly. It's barely seven. I've only just got up. I haven't even got the children up yet.'

'You're not thinking of sending them to school, are you?' said Fisher. For the first time in years he sounded really anxious. Mim wondered if by some terrible trick of the light she could have misjudged him after all.

'Of course I am. Why? Fisher, what on earth is the matter?'

'I'd come over,' he said, 'but the bloody reporters are crawling all over everywhere again this morning. I've already called the police. I'm going to go to the radio station in a few minutes.'

'You could come here first.'

Fisher coughed. 'I don't think it's a very good idea. We've got a leak.'

'What do you mean? You know where the stopcock is,' and then she stopped as realisation dawned. 'A leak?'

'I did wonder if someone bugged the house.'

Mim shook her head. 'For God's sake, don't be so ridiculous. And who would want to?'

'It's just, just –'

'What is it, Fisher?'

'The papers know all about Liam and Harriet.'

Mim felt the breath being sucked out of her chest. 'What?' she hissed. 'How could they, nobody knew but you and me –'

'It's all over the front page of the *Argos* this morning.'

'But it makes no sense. How could anyone know, Fisher, how –' and then Mim stopped and mentally counted off the people on her fingers. Herself, Fisher, Liam and Harriet and now Sam. None of them had talked to anyone except . . . Mim felt an icy dark fury rising inside her. 'Fisher, did you ring Angela yesterday?'

'Of course I did, to let her know what was happening,' said Fisher defensively, 'for God's sake, she of all people had to know what was going on.'

'Uh-huh and what exactly did you tell her, Fisher?'

Mim's question was followed by a big uncomfortable silence and then Fisher snapped, 'Oh that's ridiculous, she wouldn't have. I mean, she was implicated – she, she . . .'

'Got a lot of free publicity for her company, you and the new show.'

'That's absolute rubbish,' snapped Fisher. 'Angela wouldn't, she's not like that, not like that at all. And she's, she's – she's very fond of me.'

Mim would have laughed if it wasn't so disastrous; amongst many other things she heard the certainty in his voice waiver, but any sense of triumph was soured by the realisation that between them Fisher and Angela had seeded a storm.

'You and I need to talk,' Fisher said again.

Mim shook her head. 'You astound me, Fisher. Why should I want to talk to you? So that you can feed your mistress another story and finish us off completely. I don't think so, Fisher. It's over. I've had enough.'

'Don't be ridiculous, you're overreacting,' he growled, but it was too late. Mim heard the last syllable as she slammed the phone down.

'And?' said Sam, handing her a mug of tea.

Mim shook her head. 'We need to get hold of today's papers.'

'Okay.'

And then Mim started to shake, not altogether sure what to do with the great wall of emotion that clamoured for attention.

'The kids' stories are in the press this morning. Fisher told Angela and – and what the hell am I going to do now? That bastard, how could he do this to us?'

Sam sighed and put his arms around her. 'Don't worry, we'll sort it out.'

Mim sighed. It might not be true but it was exactly what she wanted to hear.

*   *   *

318

Angela took the papers in for Sven's perusal; she'd managed to engineer a nice spin on the *Argos* coverage, Fisher Pilgrim the wounded hero, the perfect man to deal with the nation's pain. Some of the other tabloids were less sympathetic, but there were enough column inches to ensure that Fisher's name was on the lips of the nation.

Sven nodded. 'Good girl. How does this affect the first show? Can we still go with the Burke story?'

Angela smiled. 'Yolande rang in about an hour ago desperate to tell her side of the whole thing. It'll be perfect, and of course we're still hoping that Sam Burke might punch someone.'

Sven scanned the headlines. Teenage pregnancy, the possibility of underage sex, adultery. 'Great, how soon can we get this thing off the ground?'

'Soon as you give the go ahead.'

Sven took swig of Evian. 'Get on the phone and see when Yolande can come in. Do you think there's any chance we could get the rest of the family?'

'Oh please tell me this isn't true, Rob. Not again,' Nina Grey said. It was breakfast time. She didn't sound angry just sad and resigned.

'I didn't do anything, I swear. On my life I swear I never touched her, Nina.'

Nina's expression hardened. 'I want you out of here by tonight.'

'But I'm telling you the truth. I didn't do anything –'

'Yeh yeh, like that other kid in the last theatre project or that little blonde on tour – at least they were overage, Rob. You make me sick. I want you gone. Out of my life.'

'Nina, please, listen to me.'

She shook her head, closing herself off to him. From upstairs came the sound of Paddy crying. 'I've got to go and see to him.'

Rob Grey crumpled the *Argos* into a ball and threw it across the room, and as he did wondered, among a hundred other thoughts, who in God's name could have told the press.

Reuben Harnwell thought it was funny that anyone could think that little runt Liam Pilgrim had knocked anyone up. Linda's mum had rung him on the mobile just after eight and said she wasn't going to go into work, wanted him to come round so's they could all talk. Not a bad looker, Linda's mum.

'I think I might be pregnant, Reuben,' Linda had said Sunday night, down the pub, all tears and big eyes. Maybe it wasn't such a bad thing. Maybe it was time he settled down and Linda wasn't so bad, not really. He let the thought run through his mind. Fancy him getting caught after all this time. Ah well. Nice kid, nice little body, not too bright, she certainly wouldn't cramp his style.

He turned the key in the ignition. Without Mim he'd have a space Monday morning. There was that blonde just moved into the big house on the crescent She'd looked a little lonely last time he'd been there, maybe he'd drop by and see how she was.

Chapter 19

While Sam went downstairs to get a drink, Mim slid the TV remote control from under the pillow and flicked through the channels. There were adverts, cookery, some girl dressed in primary colours on a children's programme counting to ten with monkeys on sticks, a heated discussion on PMT. Back and forth Mim trawled. Downstairs from somewhere in the bowels of Ganymede, she could hear Sam whistling.

Through the windows the summer sun ricocheted off the trees, giving the morning a breathtaking clarity. Mim, for the first time in years, felt settled and happy. In love even. How very strange.

On the TV the adverts faded into jaunty TV titles, and as they did, a familiar face peered out from the bright blue sofa of a morning chat show.

Mim turned the sound up a little.

On the screen a bright-eyed young woman in a loud suit waved in welcome towards a good-looking man beside her on the sofa. His face had a certain lived-in quality. He was still wearing his trademark faded denim shirt, cream chinos, and looked as safe and liberal as he always had. His hair was slightly too long.

'And this morning,' said the presenter, 'our resident expert, Fisher Pilgrim, is here on the couch with us, talking about the rigours of family life. Fisher, let's face it, it's been a rough couple of months for you and your family. Details of your private life have been splashed all over the tabloids. It seems as if there is no part of your home life that hasn't made it onto our breakfast tables . . .'

The camera held him in an artfully composed close-up. Fisher smiled and nodded, there was a kind of puppyish charm about him, without a hint of arrogance or smugness. 'You can say that again. It's been really hard for all of us. I suppose at times like this we feel we need to find lessons from the things that happen. Life is never easy, never without complications. My wife and I have had to struggle so hard to hang on in there and to get through this whole process. It's been incredibly tough, I can't tell you. And the kids, well –' He looked as if there was a real chance he might be about to cry.

Mim looked on in amazement as Fisher then began to wax lyrical about the support he'd given his family, the pain and his sorrow, and of course his contrition, all of which, as far as Mim knew, were completely fictitious.

That the kids were okay, chipped and battered but not broken, was no thanks to Fisher. It had been Sam who'd gone to the school with her to talk about Rob Grey and had stood by Harriet and Liam while the record slowly began to straighten itself out.

But then again, from the way Fisher's eyes were fixed on a single spot, Mim suspected that Fisher was probably reading from the autocue, although God alone knows who had written the script. Even so, he came across as a real survivor, damaged, battle scarred and world weary but still unbowed. It was the performance of a lifetime.

Oh, how Fisher had suffered, he knew all about how terrible the stresses of real life could be and could so easily empathise with viewers and their problems. It didn't take him long to plug his new mid-morning dial-in-for-advice slot. Three mornings a week, ten till eleven; it seemed that Fisher Pilgrim would be there for you.

Mim shook her head in complete disbelief and fingered

the mute button, silencing her soon to be ex-husband's inane pop psychology, at around the same time Sam reappeared at the bedroom door bearing a tray of tea and what looked remarkably like a pile of bacon sandwiches. He was naked expect for a navy-blue striped chef's apron and looked like some strange cooking satyr, a mass of unruly dark hair framing his strong features.

Mim laughed. He was such a nice man, easy to talk to, good to be with, and at the same time it struck her that Sam really was quite beautiful in a quirky way. She couldn't imagine anyone else she knew cooking bacon naked.

To begin with Mim had worried that it was a mistake to get involved with Sam so soon, or perhaps even at all, afraid that they had been thrown together like survivors of a terrible storm. But with each passing day she worried less and less, and when it came down to it, what the hell? Did it matter how they got together? There were no secrets between them, maybe this was the chance they both needed to heal. She liked to be with him, he was gentle and warm and pleased to have her in his life and his bed and even though it might not be for ever it felt good, and the kids adored him. And in her own way so did Mim. Maybe it wasn't a fairytale ending but it was comfortable and safe and easy to live with.

He stood the tray on the bedside table and helped arrange the pillows behind her.

He had suggested that she set up a pottery and workshop in the sheds in the walled garden. Sam had arranged for her and the cat and all the children's things to be moved to Ganymede, although he pointed out again and again – in case Mim felt trapped – that there was no pressure for her to stay once she had sorted things out, not if she didn't want to. He gave everything he had with an open palm. She had already decided that the first things she was going to make, once the pottery was up and running, were

323

the figures for the clearing outside his office. A thank you, a gift that could in no way express the gratitude she felt for his compassion.

The last thing Mim saw, as Sam clambered back into bed, was Fisher mouthing his lines like a guppy gasping for breath, a benign smile fixed on his open boyish face, his new bridge work looking unnaturally white under the studio lights, and on the sofa beside him Yolande dabbing her eyes with a tissue. She looked immaculate in her grief.

'Do we really want to watch this?' said Sam pulling up a ruck of pillows behind him.

'No, not really.'

'In that case switch it off,' he said, 'and let's eat these while they're hot.'

And she did.

'And we're away in three, two and one –' said the floor manager.

'Great show everyone. That went really well,' said Angela over the mike from the control box, giving Fisher the thumbs-up. He grinned, off-camera now, and slipped the earpiece out.

'Nice response on the phone-in too.'

Fisher beamed and ran his fingers through his endearingly floppy fringe before shrugging modestly. Even now he was still a little unsure of himself and waited for one of the crew to come over and disentangle him from the microphone pinned to his shirt.

Angela teetered across the studio on her impossibly high heels, cradling the clipboard that shared her life. She was smiling, Angela was always smiling, although Fisher had recently come to realise that this did not necessarily mean that she was happy.

'Right,' she said flatly to no one in particular and

beckoned to Fisher. 'Are we still going out to lunch today?'

Fisher grinned, 'Er, yes. Yes, unless you want to cook when we get home.'

Angela didn't bother to reply, instead she ticked something on her board. 'I'll book a table at Constantine's. One-fifteen. I'll see you there.' She turned away and then quickly back, beading him with her dark Mediterranean eyes, and pointed her pen at the centre of his chest. 'And change that bloody shirt will you, I'm getting sick to death of it.'

Fisher was surprised, he thought she liked his shirts.

Lunch went reasonably well.

Angela chose and ordered the wine, but he was okay about that, he didn't need the secret boys'-club handshake with the sommelier to confirm that he was a real man. He would have ordered something a little less meaty, but then who was quibbling, after all the company was paying.

Angela's smile cooled as their waiter cleared away the first course. 'You know, Fisher, I've been thinking a lot about you recently. I'm beginning to wonder how much mileage there is in this whole wounded hero thing. Sven is a little concerned. A halo doesn't have to drop very far to become a noose. We're going to be watching the ratings on the new show very closely.'

But Fisher's mind was elsewhere; the woman on the table next to him smiled surreptitiously in his direction and then waved. His climb up the ladder to mid-morning magazine TV had been quite odd really. Fate, karma. Some might even call it destiny.

Across the table Angela called for the bill and handed it to him.